BEYOND FAME and FORTUNE

Afsaneh M. Varzaly

Copyright © 2021 by Afsaneh M. Varzaly.

All rights reserved. This book is protected by copyright. No part of this book may be reproduced or transmitted in any form or by any means, including as photocopies or scanned-in or other electronic copies, or utilized by any information storage and retrieval system without written permission from the copyright owner.

Printed in the United States of America.

Cover design by 100Covers.com
Interior Design by FormattedBooks.com

Prologue

≈≫≪≈

It was a pleasant sunny day in early October, not too uncommon for springtime in Adelaide, Australia. An immaculately polished silver Rolls-Royce limousine rolled into the beautiful grounds of a stately restaurant. It came to a gentle stop in front of a moderately grand, Victorian style manor. This was where John Bradcliffe, the powerful and highly regarded business magnate, was meeting his old Oxford friends for their once-a-month luncheon.

His chauffer quickly opened the door for him. He stepped out, and mid-phone conversation, entered the restaurant. Immediately recognizing him, the manager deferentially ushered him to the table where his friends were awaiting his arrival.

As he drew near, he overheard them saying, "John isn't going to like…"

He quickly ended his phone call. "Good afternoon," said John as he sat down. Then with a suspicious look, and a slightly curious smile, "What is it that I'm not going to like?" he questioned.

After a short pause, "You were not supposed to hear that," offered Professor Rishi Vavek, the head of the Electronics Engineering Department of the prestigious Lightsbridge University. "Now that you have, you might like to know," he went on hesitantly, "that your arch-competitor, Conrad Frost's company, Adeltec has been snapping up large numbers of our graduates."

"I have zero interest to know that," replied John coolly.

"Aren't you concerned about what he's up to?"

John appeared calm and collected. "Not in the least," he responded.

Surprised, Rishi said, "You're taking this quite well."

"That's because, following our recent challenges, we are reporting a return to profitability this quarter for the Bradcliffe Corporation," replied John with a hint of pride in his voice. Then with a focused and positive expression on his face, he continued, "There are far greater things for me to think about than Conrad's machinations."

His friends, suitably impressed, congratulated him warmly.

Following lunch, while savoring the robust flavor of his macchiato, something in the conversation caught John's attention. When he heard Rishi boast about the work of his research team, headed by one of the most ingenious and brilliant minds he had ever seen, the luncheon suddenly transformed from a social gathering to a stimulating business meeting.

John being mildly interested, enquired about this 'brilliant mind'.

"His name is Dr. Declan Harris," said Rishi. He then added, "His PhD research has led to a major breakthrough in the field of computer technology."

That piqued John's interest. "What is this cutting-edge technology?" he asked.

Rishi, with a definite sense of excitement, went on and said, "As a result of Declan's research, the design of an optical computer is within reach." He explained how such a development would revolutionize the computer industry by performing operations up to 100 times faster than current computer technology would allow.

John became so intrigued that as busy as he was, he cancelled his next meeting and accepted his friend's invitation to his office to continue their discussion after lunch.

By the time he got back to his office, John's head was racing. It had been his lifelong ambition to be involved in the high-tech electronics industry. Now, more than ever, with his company operating in the black, he had the desire to pursue this goal and establish a global presence in this highly competitive industry.

Was this his 'golden ticket' to enter the electronics arena? John wondered to himself. Could the Bradcliffe Corporation be the first company to produce commercially viable optical computers? To not only compete against the giants of the industry, but to establish his company as a major player. The thought of such a possibility captivated him. Yet, his mind immediately turned to the question of the risks and costs associated with such a monumental undertaking.

It was then that he decided to engage the services of Bartley & Howard, the internationally renowned Boston consulting firm. Their unique specialization in the electronics industry made them the ideal choice to assess the commercial feasibility of this new technology. With a healthy retainer in place, they agreed to give his work top priority. In just six weeks they would deliver their comprehensive risk benefit analysis of the optical computer concept, along with their recommendations.

What will be the outcome? Will there be a glimmer of a new hope, a new direction for John and his company at the end of these six weeks?

Chapter 1

A decision had to be made. John Bradcliffe, having received the Bartley & Howard report was faced with a most significant and difficult decision. Even though he excelled at making decisions, and good ones at that, this time it was different. It would mean a drastic departure from the mainstream business of the $14.9 billion Bradcliffe Corporation Ltd., the largest privately held corporation in Australia.

Can I afford to take this step? thought John. He was the firm's managing director and board chairman, sitting comfortably in his executive office high atop one of the newest and most modern of the Bradcliffe buildings in the Adelaide central business district. The smell of fresh paint and the scent of the new wooden and leather furniture still lingered in his office. It was an impressive office with its marble columns and display of rare sculptures and carefully selected relics. It would overwhelm anyone with its sense of power, that is, anyone who was of sufficient caliber and status to see it.

John, the third generation of Bradcliffes to run the family-controlled business, had proven to be the most ambitious and the most successful of the dynasty. He was the quintessence of strength and power in the corporate arena of Australia. At 5'10" with a medium build, sandy hair and piercing deep brown eyes, he had a stately stature and commanded everyone's respect.

Deep in thought he got up from behind his desk and walked over to the ceiling-to-floor glass windows surrounding his office. He took a long look at the picturesque, rolling Adelaide hills to his right and the deep blue waters of the Gulf of St. Vincent to his left. His thoughts seemed to follow the gulf all the way to the Southern Ocean and beyond. There was a strong sense of belief in him that the world and all it had to offer, were simply for his taking. Yet, he could not help but wonder about the risks associated with the ambitious vision he had for his corporation.

With only minutes left to go before having to make and announce his decision, he walked back to his desk. He pressed his personal secretary's intercom button and with a sense of urgency said, "Tracy, would you bring me the Bartley & Howard report?"

Momentarily there was a knock on the door. "Come in," said John firmly.

Tracy opened the door, promptly walked over to John's desk, and with a pleasant smile handed him the report. "Will there be anything else Mr. Bradcliffe?" she asked accommodatingly.

"No thanks. Just make sure I am not disturbed," replied John appearing preoccupied. "And let me know when it's time for my meeting." He did not want to keep track of time with so much on his mind.

"Certainly, sir. I will let you know," agreed Tracy politely and walked out.

He had previously gone over the facts and figures, but still he felt the urge to look through the report one more time. He leaned back into his chair, and he took a deep breath while shuffling through the pages of the report. What weighed heavily on his mind was not facts and figures, but rather his personal ambition. It had been growing within him ever since he could remember and had emerged more strongly during his university days.

Following the completion of his economic studies at Oxford University, like his father before him, he joined the Bradcliffe Corporation. He worked under the guidance of his father for 16 years in various capacities before he achieved the position of number two man in the company. When his father suddenly passed away because of a heart attack five years ago, John was ready to take over at the age of 40. However, the times were hard, and Australia was in economic recession. The giant Bradcliffe Corporation was nearly insolvent with record losses. As a result, John had to focus on saving the company and could not pursue his ambition. In fact, if it were not for his brash strategies, his quick thinking, and his unparalleled negotiating abilities the company would not exist today. His tireless efforts finally paid off. The company was now operating in the black for the first time in years. In fact, during the first half of the current financial year ending in December the company was expected to show a marginal profit of $50 million. To enter into a new venture at a time when the company was not quite yet financially sound and strong would mean risking all that he had accomplished at the Bradcliffe Corporation up to now.

The Bradcliffe Corporation Ltd., founded in 1865 as a gold mining concern had continually grown and expanded. Now the company was greatly diversified and involved with almost every sector of the economy including consumer goods, rural and primary industries as well as its base mining business. This range of business activity was impressive, but not satisfying for John. Now more than ever he felt the need to establish a global presence in the high-tech electronics industry.

The report confirmed John's thinking that while the business potential is immense, it would come at great cost. The venture would involve product development, manufacturing, and a full-scale commercialization program that could easily cost hundreds of millions of dollars if accomplished on the scale of his ambitions. It was the cost factor and the competitive nature of the high-tech electronics business that made his decision slightly more difficult. If the new venture became successful, he could then realize his lifelong dream and the Bradcliffe Corporation would become a key global computer company. The downside was that he would be risking the loss of hundreds of millions of dollars, which could potentially force the company back into the near insolvency status that it was in not so long ago. That would engender further cutbacks, the selling off of more divisions, and increased worker layoffs. None of these were acceptable to John. On the other hand, he also very much recognized that the long-term success of the Bradcliffe Corporation would require innovation and the taking of calculated risks. With all these thoughts in his mind, he finalized his decision.

Just at that moment his secretary buzzed to remind him that his meeting was to begin in a few minutes. It was a special meeting that he had called with five of his senior executives. They represented the cream of his staff, and he was about to test their mettle.

There was an uneasy silence on this mid-November Thursday morning in the conference room, and the tension could be felt in the air. In the five years that John had been in control there had never been such a hastily called meeting with such a shroud of secrecy. There was no agenda, and as the time grew closer his select group of five became anxious and uncomfortable about the reason behind this meeting. The economy was in recession, but the Bradcliffe Corporation had been performing relatively well. Was there a crisis of which they were unaware? Why only these five of the management staff? It was the uncertainty that injected the air with apprehension and doubt. Suddenly the group of highly competent and usually confident men and women were without a reference point to grasp onto to put them at ease.

They all knew that John was demanding and a perfectionist to a fault. Nothing ever seemed to meet his impeccable standards. They all had a certain fear of him almost as a student to his professor, and likewise they held him in deep respect. His sometimes outrageous demands overwhelmed them, but he had driven the company to new heights. And, he had rewarded their efforts generously. The tension continued to mount.

The door of the conference room swung open as the clock struck 8:00am and in walked the powerful John Bradcliffe. They all rose immediately and remained standing as he walked to the table. With his usual serious look, he gazed at his five executives for a moment. "Good morning," said John as he motioned them to sit down. "Good morning Mr. Bradcliffe," they responded feeling somewhat relieved sensing the calm in his voice and stature.

While still standing at the head of the table, John began to speak. "The future is about dreams, about the courage to dream the seemingly impossible, about creating new opportunities, to dare to go beyond the limits and set new boundaries, and to have the conviction to make it all happen so as to leave behind a legacy of new dreams, a better life for our children and a better world for humanity." He paused for a moment and then continued on, "It is not about living in your comfort zone. It is not about punching numbers on the balance sheet to show a profit. The future is about having faith to make better and greater things happen in life."

He passed around a copy of the report to each of them as he continued with a definite sense of enthusiasm and excitement in his otherwise reserved tone of voice. "We are about to set a new course in the unchartered world of the future, and this is how we are going to do it." He pointed to the report. "We are about to enter the world of high-tech electronics by designing and producing the first commercial optical computer." He paused again for a moment to observe their reaction. As he had anticipated they appeared almost horrified, that is with the exception of Allan Kelly, a 46-year-old who was the youngest of his executive team. He had brown hair and hazel eyes. His exuberance came across in his way of thinking, his management style, and the non-traditional designer business suits he wore. He particularly liked to take on new and difficult challenges. John looked at Bill Dutton, his chief financial officer (CFO) and said as he sat down, "Bill, I would like you to read aloud the executive summary."

Bill, with a slim build and mostly white hair was the eldest of the team. Following John's instruction, he took out his rimless glasses from his pocket, put them on, and very carefully read the summary while the others listened. He then began to quickly leaf through the report until he found the financials.

He stopped. Appearing rather disturbed and no longer able to contain himself, he said, "Mr. Bradcliffe, this is financial suicide!"

"Nonsense! You're just too conservative Bill," interrupted Allan, who could see the huge potential of this new direction. "This is exactly what we need at the Bradcliffe Corporation."

John, amused by their reactions, interjected, "Bill has a valid point as commitment to this will require more funds than we currently have. However, that is the downside. On the upside our corporation stands to reap enormous financial gain and to become one of the leaders in the industry. No doubt we must exercise reasonable caution and much wisdom in order to achieve our goal. For that reason, Bill, you will be personally and intimately involved in the financial management of this project. Your first task will be to apply for a $12 million industry innovation grant under Canberra's new Commonwealth Research Scheme. Here is the grant application and all the supporting documentation. The closing date is tomorrow, and the board meets in three weeks to make a decision. This is exactly what we need to fund and kick-start our development work."

"Isn't Malcolm Packard, the chair of the grant board, a personal friend of yours? Perhaps that will help," said Bill.

This question fell like a wet blanket over the room. John appeared distracted and withdrawn. He was suddenly reminded of the incident that had occurred the last time he attended a function at Malcolm's house. He wondered if that incident would be detrimental to him. Most importantly he did not want anyone to think that his knowing Malcolm would have any bearing on the potential success of his grant application. He then in a firm and almost demanding tone of voice replied, "Let's make this perfectly clear. The basis for our success in getting this grant will solely depend on the resulting benefit in terms of job creation, our abilities to perform and make it a success, and our professionalism. Nothing else!" He then continued, "I would like for all of you to read this report carefully to clearly understand this venture and your responsibilities. As you will see there is also a cover memo where I have outlined your responsibilities and have assigned the overall project management to Allan."

Allan was so overwhelmed to be chosen for this position that he almost fell off his chair. "I won't let you down Mr. Bradcliffe," said Allan eagerly.

"I know that Allan, and I'm counting on it," replied John. "Your first task is to liaise closely with Professor Rishi Vavek and Dr. Declan Harris to secure their commitment, and with their input, to make a final selection of the research and development team." John continued, "Allan, I would also like for you to arrange for Declan to come over to my office for a final interview two weeks from tomorrow as I will be back in Adelaide by that Friday." After a short pause he said, "At least there will be one bright point that day." He then continued with a firm and positive tone of voice, "During the morning you meet with Declan. Then you bring him to my office at noon."

John rose from his chair, which prompted everyone to stand up. As he looked at his executive team with a definite sense of power, he assertively said, "Let's make it happen!" He then exited the conference room leaving his executives in awe and wonder of the project upon which they were about to embark.

Chapter 2

During the two weeks that John was away things were quite hectic for his top five executives. They each had to deal with the added responsibility of the new computer venture, above and beyond their already heavy workload. Even though stressful and frantic at times, it was a welcome challenge for them all, except for Bill. Being constantly worried about financing the venture, he initially did not embrace the idea. These two weeks however, helped him to come to terms with the new project, that is until the morning of John's return to Adelaide. While reading through the Friday edition of the Australian News, something caught his attention. Suddenly his worries that he had finally put to rest began to resurface.

Bill quickly made his way to the office of Richard Addison. He was the executive in charge of sales and marketing. At 6' 2" he had dark brown hair and brown eyes and dressed for the part. His multinational background gave him a deep sense of appreciation and understanding for different cultures. He was a people person with marketing skills second to none.

"Richard! Have you seen today's article in the Business Section of the Australian News?" asked Bill with a concerned look on his face.

"Do you know what I would like to see?" replied Richard in an uptight tone of voice. "I would like to see us do away with Friday mornings altogether, especially the first Friday in December. There is always some kind of crisis related to the Christmas shopping season." Becoming even more tense, he went on, "I got to the office at 7:00am. You would think that that's early enough, but apparently not," he said in a sarcastic tone. "Mr. Bradcliffe was already here, and so were these problems with distributors, suppliers and so on that needed to be resolved. Otherwise, it could have meant the loss of millions of dollars in revenues which we couldn't afford, especially with the new venture we're getting involved in. Anyway, that's how my morning got started, and things just got worse from there. And then **you** ask me if I've read the paper!" As if he could not wait to get everything off his chest he continued, "Now it's almost noon and I've already been to Mr. Bradcliffe's office twice today. I was pleasantly surprised to find him quite tolerant. I mean, on a day like today, with so many things happening I thought he would have given me the tenth degree. but he didn't. Instead, he handled a couple of the problems himself. I think that's because Declan Harris is here for his interview. And that's taking him a step closer to his computer venture…"

Bill interrupted him at this point. "He's not going to be tolerant after he sees this article on how progressive our chief competitor, Adeltec Industries is."

Richard, with a worried look on his face, took the tablet and read the headline—**Adeltec Industries Leading The Way Into The Burgeoning Market of Computer and Communications Technologies**. "No, definitely not! He's not going to like this at all," exclaimed Richard as he glanced at the article.

"I suggest that you show Mr. Bradcliffe this article," offered Bill.

"He might have already seen it," said Richard.

"He may not have seen it on a day like today. So, you better go see him now. I mean right now, before Allan takes Declan to his office. The article states that Adeltec Industries is the first in leading Australia into this global market by developing new technology. He might want to discuss the ramifications of this development with Allan and Declan," reasoned Bill.

"I guess you're right. Let's see. That gives me about two minutes to get there," replied Richard, quickly disappearing down the plush, long corridor with a flustered look on his face. He rushed up the wide-open staircase, which curved around a serene softly flowing waterfall, briskly walked over to Tracy's desk and asked to see John.

"Sir. Mr. Addison is here to see you. He says that it's urgent," announced Tracy, on his intercom.

"All right. Send him in," replied John.

"Sir, have you seen this article in the Australian News about Adeltec?" asked Richard in a worried tone of voice.

"Yes, I have," replied John. "I'm not concerned. It's not who starts first, but rather who commercializes first. What we're about to do will blow them all away."

Richard nodded, and feeling somewhat relieved, left John Bradcliffe's office. After the door shut behind him, he exhaled in a long and deliberate manner, his tension and anxiety had been removed by John's unanticipated response. As he looked up he found that Allan and Declan had arrived for

Declan's interview. After a brief exchange of greetings, Allan walked over to Tracy's desk and said, "Good morning Tracy. Dr. Declan Harris is here for his twelve o'clock meeting with Mr. Bradcliffe."

"Mr. Bradcliffe is on the telephone right now," said Tracy. "Please have a seat."

"All right then. I'll leave Dr. Harris here, as Mr. Bradcliffe wanted to see him privately at first. When it's time for me to join the meeting, just give me a buzz," said Allan. Then as he headed towards the elevator, he turned to Declan and remarked, "By the way, everything looks good. I'll be seeing you in a little while."

Declan had brown colored eyes and wavy brown hair which partly covered his forehead and ears. Having completed his PhD at the young age of 23, he never seemed to have time or interest to pay attention to his appearance. His tie was slightly off center and almost matched his shirt and suit, looking as if he had borrowed it for the interview. He came across as a pleasant and accommodating person as he thanked Allan. Happy to wait for his interview he sat down. Suddenly he appeared uneasy and fidgety as the reality of where he was and who he was about to see hit and overwhelmed him. When he looked around, he was even more taken by the whole dynamic atmosphere in which he was engulfed. He could see in the distance how John Bradcliffe's staff were all hard at work. He could feel the excitement of working for a big corporation, the thrill of conducting leading-edge technology research in a results-oriented environment. Thinking back, it seemed that he had spent his whole life studying, reading, and learning. Now here was the answer to all his hard work, the opportunity of a lifetime to work for such a prestigious firm under one of the most well known and respected executives of the century.

"Mr. Bradcliffe is finished with his phone call," said Tracy pleasantly. "I will announce you now." She then turned around and picked up the receiver. But before she had a chance to make the announcement, her attention was suddenly drawn to Mr. Bradcliffe's private elevator that had just arrived on the floor. As she watched intently, while still holding the receiver in her hand, the elevator doors opened. To Declan's amazement she had become so enraptured by the young man who had just exited the elevator that she totally forgot the announcement she was about to make.

He was wearing a perfectly fitted $10,000 dark grey Italian cut bespoke suit. As a result of his presence things had suddenly become quieter. He stopped in front of Tracy's desk and took a long look around. It was as though he found everything to his satisfaction. After all, he was the center of attention. Then without any hesitation he took the receiver out of Tracy's hand and put it back in its cradle.

"Hold all of Mr. Bradcliffe's calls," he said in his usual arrogant tone of voice. "He," pointing to Declan without looking at him, "can sit and wait until I'm finished." Then very confidently, without knocking, he just opened the door and walked into John Bradcliffe's office.

Declan could not believe his own eyes. He seemed awed by who he had just seen. *Could it really be who I think it is*, Declan thought to himself. Then he walked over to Tracy who still seemed to be up in the clouds and asked her, "Is that really **the** Aden Bradcliffe?"

"Of course. Who else?" replied Tracy still mystified by Aden's presence.

Declan walked back to the armchair he was sitting in and made himself comfortable in it again. He found his thoughts drifting back to when he was about 15 years old. That was the first time he had come to know of Aden Bradcliffe. He remembered how he used to love to read, especially at that age. He was a high school student and a very good one at that, but he was not good at sports, nor did he feel comfortable in social situations. Therefore, whenever he was not studying to pass the time, he used to read almost anything and everything. That was how he came across the article about Aden Bradcliffe in the high society section of one of his mother's magazines called The Australian Woman. He began to smile as he recalled how it was mentioned in the article that Aden had put glue on his teacher's chair and how she had ended up walking back to the office with the chair stuck to her clothes. This was just one of the many unorthodox things Aden had done by the time he was twelve years old. Because he was a Bradcliffe he had always gotten away with having done all of those things. Declan could still remember how he enjoyed reading that article and how impressed he was with Aden. In fact, he was so impressed that ever since then he found himself looking for articles about him. Aden was everything Declan wished he could be, to be bold, to do things out of the ordinary, to step out of bounds. These were all common place for Aden. But realizing that he could never be like Aden, Declan used to pretend and imagine doing all those things to satisfy his desire to be different.

Having seen Aden today, eight years after reading his first article, Declan who was a definite success in his own right, still found himself admiring Aden. Feeling a little envious of Aden's great looks, confidence, and moreover that he was the most popular man in Australia, he thought to himself, *Aden must be the luckiest guy in the world.*

Chapter 3

Aden Bradcliffe was all that, and more. He had a strong, toned, and athletic build standing 6'1," with light brown hair which was always fashionably styled, and greenish-blue colored eyes. He had an extremely high self image. As such, he dressed immaculately, only in the latest designer fashions unrivalled by anyone in the whole country. At the age of twenty he had such a powerful presence that commanded attention regardless of where he went. He was always cool and in control. Nothing ever seemed to excite or overwhelm him. Being extraordinarily strong willed he did whatever pleased him. People, friends or otherwise, were irrelevant to him. All that mattered was that he got what he wanted and that they did what he wished. Therefore, contrary to Declan's perception, to have gotten whatever he wanted, Aden had no reason to feel lucky or appreciate all that he had.

John knew without looking up that it was Aden who had just entered his office, as he was the only person who would dare walk in without being announced. "Couldn't it wait, Aden? You have picked the worst time to come calling," said John in a firm voice while still busily looking through some of the pages in front of him as though trying to beat time. Aden quite confidently walked over to his father's desk and sat on the corner of it quite carefully so as not to wrinkle his suit. This suit, like all of his other suits, was uniquely designed and tailored for him. It had his monogram 'AB' sewn on the right sleeve of his jacket near the buttons which matched those on the cuffs of his shirt. His sophisticated citrus cologne, polished platinum cufflinks, diamond encrusted white gold Rolex presidential watch, 100% silk Italian tie and handmade Italian shoes gave just the right final touches. He looked as though he had just walked out of a top-level meeting with the highest paid executives on Wall Street.

"Good morning to you too...Father."

"I am too busy for social amenities Aden." Then reluctantly he said, "Well, whatever it is, let's get it over with, and quickly."

Aden put his hand into his inside pocket, took out some papers and threw them on the desk in front of his father. The more John looked at the papers, the more his patience grew thin. By the time he got to the last page he had just about had it. He was visibly upset!

"This time you have gone too far Aden. This is a bill for $1,000,000 for another fancy sports car and some repair work! What do you need another car for when you already have seven?"

"Correction father, had six," replied Aden in his usual cool conceited kind of a voice. "That is until this morning when I got delivery of my special edition Zonda."

"What is a Zonda?"

"Zonda is one of the finest supercars. It has a 7 liter 550 Hp, V12 Mercedes Benz AMG engine that will go from 0—60 mph in 3 seconds, and a top speed of over 200 mph. But it's more than just another car Dad. They give you tailor-made luggage to match the interior and your personal pair of Italian driving shoes made by the Pope's own personal cobbler."

"I don't care that you are given a pair of driving shoes. All I want to know is what happened to the other seventh one?" asked his father.

"I crashed my Bimmer the other night," said Aden matter-of-factly.

"No doubt on one of your usual wild nights and having had too much to drink." With a disgusted look on his face John continued, "Couldn't you wait until it was repaired?"

"No! A repaired car is not for me. I will **not** drive anything but a new car," replied Aden emphatically.

"Let's see. If I can remember correctly, that should leave you with a Porsche, Lamborghini, Lotus, Corvette, Mercedes, and your latest addition Enzo Ferrari, none of which are ordinary cars by any stretch of the imagination. So then, what's wrong with just having six expensive cars?" asked John out of frustration.

"Plenty, dear old Dad. Aden Bradcliffe will not be seen driving the same car twice in a week. I must have one car for each day of the week. After all, we Bradcliffes have an image to uphold."

"This is just too much Aden. Just last week I paid $250,000 for some of your other bills, $65,000 of which was for your clothes. Do you realize that you have spent over half a million dollars in the past two months? This has got to stop." By this time John sounded rather angry, and almost explosive.

Aden on the other hand, not having been affected at all by his father's anger or comments still maintained his cool. He then casually got off his father's desk and made himself comfortable on the arm of one of the large chairs in front of the desk. As he put one foot on the coffee table next to him, he looked at his father and in his arrogant way said, "My dear father, it never seemed to bother you all of those years while I was growing up to spend money to buy me the most expensive toys and clothes as though a payoff to keep me out of your way. And you still spent more to get the so-called proper British and American nannies so that you wouldn't have to spend time with me, and instead could drown yourself in your work and your precious Bradcliffe Corporation. Why should it bother you now? I'm just a little older, and therefore have more expensive toys and clothes. Except now, I do the choosing myself, and all you do is the paying. In return, I'll stay out of your way." Aden stopped for a short moment. Then with a smirk on his face he continued. "Well, somebody has got to enjoy all of the money you've made. Since you're too busy working so hard, I'll enjoy spending it for both of us father," he said in a facetious tone as he carefully studied his father's reaction.

In the heat of the moment John could not help but think about how both he and his father had worked so extremely hard. So much so that the name Bradcliffe had become synonymous with high achievement. It pained him to no end to think that his own son had done nothing with his life since graduating from high school three years ago. *What do I have to do to shake him out of his slumber?* John wondered to himself. No longer willing to hold back he lashed out and said, "Aden, you are a disgrace to the Bradcliffe family."

Aden, with yet another one of his conceited looks on his face said to his father, "I don't know what you're talking about. Just last week I was chosen as the most eligible bachelor in Australia by two of the top women's magazines."

"In the same article it was mentioned that you had no compassion at all," said John. "Does that add to your eligibility?"

"A mere complement," replied Aden casually.

John was becoming more upset and more frustrated with Aden as the conversation progressed. As he shook his head, he looked him straight in the eye with an angry glare and said, "You being the most eligible bachelor and your womanizing ways are only additional embarrassments to our family, so much so that I dislike going anywhere with you. Whether it be a high society social event or a family dinner party there are always a group of women, young or old, single or married waiting for your highness to notice them and grant them an audience. You're not even nice to them. You're inconsiderate, rude, and treat them like dirt. And yet they can't wait to be chosen by you as the 'lucky' one to get your attention. That's absolutely absurd!"

"Why father? It's the highlight of their lives to say that they have been with Aden Bradcliffe. Don't underestimate that."

"You make it sound as though you're doing them a favor."

"Of course, I'm doing them a favor, and they know it too. But for me, they must be special, so I can find them worthy of it."

John could not believe this conversation, and he was not going to take it anymore. "It's bad enough that I have to put up with your womanizing ways in social situations, but to put up with it at home is even worse. I just can't stand this constant flow of girls in and out of our house as well as the constant stream of telephone calls. I didn't think that I would ever say this to you, but I am so fed up that I actually can't wait for you to move to your…whatever you call it."

"My bachelor pad," said Aden helpfully.

"You mean your pleasure pad," replied his father. "Anyway, just to be clear I don't want to know where it is, how it is going to look, or anything about it. I'm sure that no matter what it is, I'll find it distasteful. So, you keep it to yourself and let me keep the happy thought that before long you'll move there and take your entourage of girls with you. Then once more I'll be able to have peace and decency in my own home."

John was now faced with making a decision about the cost of Aden's house. *I can't just give him any amount of money he wants*, he reflected deeply. *How will he ever learn to value anything he has?* With that thinking in mind, and before Aden had a chance to respond, he continued, "One more thing, I'm putting a ceiling of $15 million on the cost of your so-called bachelor pad."

"That's impossible. There's no way that I can have it built the way that I want for less than $18 million. There's just no way."

His father thought for a minute and then said, "Do you realize that I could buy a couple of businesses or an office building with that much money? I'll only go up to $16 million. Take it or leave it."

In reality he could have had it built for $15 million since his father had already paid for the land, but he always liked to make things difficult. So, with a 'poor me' type of a look Aden said, "All right, I'll take it."

John, having gotten all of this off of his chest and having set a cost limit for Aden's new house, felt somewhat relieved, but not pleased, especially about what he had to tell him next. "Mrs. Malcolm Packard, Sharon, has called me every day this week since you haven't been returning her calls, to make sure that you will be attending her 30th birthday party tomorrow night. So, would I be correct to assume that you'll be going?"

"I wouldn't want to disappoint her," said Aden with a grin on his face. "I guess I'll put in an appearance."

"Then I want you to go with me so that I can keep an eye on you and your activities. Of course, if I had my way you wouldn't be going at all, especially given your abhorrent behavior last time at Malcolm's 50th birthday party in September."

"What was wrong with my behavior?" asked Aden conceitedly.

"Don't be coy with me Aden. I mean, how could you do such a thing? Going to bed with Sharon in their own bedroom right in the middle of her husband's birthday party?"

"Oh, yeah. She wasn't bad at all. Made it worthwhile going to that boring party."

"How could you sink so low Aden? You are nothing but a moral degenerate!"

"Now hold it right there. Just because I enjoy myself by doing what I please, where and when I please, doesn't make me a degenerate person. In fact, I'm no worse than any of your friends with so called high moral standards. The only difference is that I don't hide anything, and I don't pretend to be something else like so many of your hypocritical friends with endless affairs. So don't you go calling me names," said Aden defiantly.

"No matter what it's called, I just do **not** want anything like that to happen this time. Do I make myself clear Aden?"

"Well dear father, clear or not, you don't have to worry about it. It just so happens that the novelty wears off after the first time. So, I have no intentions of breaking my tradition and missing out on new opportunities. But why all of a sudden do you have such an interest in what happens there tomorrow night?"

"I suppose I might as well tell you, not that I expect you to understand, but if you know, it can't hurt. Malcolm Packard resides on the chair of an important committee which will be reviewing and deciding next Friday whether the Bradcliffe Corporation should receive a government grant. The grant bears great political clout. Therefore, there are great implications for us to get it versus some other firm such as Adeltec Industries."

"I see. So, you need me to secure the vote for you?"

"No, not at all! Our work stands on its own merit. I just don't want you to jeopardize our chances of getting it."

"I'll see how I feel tomorrow night."

"No! That's not an acceptable answer. Aden, I want a commitment from you that you'll behave and that you won't get carried away with your drinking and womanizing. All I'm asking is that you control yourself during the short time that you plan to be there. That's not asking too much, is it?"

Aden stood up and put his left hand in the pocket of his trousers as he looked out toward the ocean. His thoughts seemed to be far away. It was as though he was trying his best not to feel hurt by his father's total lack of concern for him. Then he looked at his father and said, "Your problem is that all you have ever cared about has been the Bradcliffe Corporation and the Bradcliffe name, and nothing else. You could be the most successful executive in the world, but you'll never be happy and content with your life because your life has been reduced to nothing but business deals and ventures. No matter what, you'll always find another business deal to worry about. So, if it isn't this grant, it will be something else. And now you want a commitment from me…Well, you're not going to get it. Because you see, dear father, I don't care about the Bradcliffe Corporation or your business deals."

"Why do you always have to be so difficult Aden? Why couldn't you have been more like, well, like…Declan Harris?"

Aden having maintained his cool arrogance all along suddenly felt a surge of anger rush over him. His ego was shattered. One thing that he could not handle was having his father compare him to others to show him how they were better than him. One could sense the anger in his voice when he said, "Who? Do you mean Mr. Polyester out there, the 'nerdy' looking guy?"

"The 'nerdy' looking guy, as you put it, who is only three years older than you, has just completed his PhD and has graduated at the top of his class. His research work has provided a breakthrough in the computer field. At the age of 23 he has such an impressive resume of accomplishments, research work and publications that I am about to offer him a job with one of the highest salaries ever given to a new graduate in the country. I'm going to offer Mr. Polyester, as you called him, $300,000. Now there is nothing nerdy about that, is it?"

Aden, who had found this rather amusing said, "$300,000 isn't bad. I think that I could live on that…per week."

"No! That's not per week."

"Oh well, it would be difficult, but I suppose that I could possibly manage to stretch it over a month."

"No, Aden. That's a yearly salary, and an excellent one at that."

"Well, thank you dad."

"Thank you for what?"

"Thank you for making up my mind not to ever want to go to university to study."

"Don't make me laugh, Aden! There isn't a single university anywhere that would let you in, not with your grades and IQ. That is, unless I buy you one, just like I bought every grade for you all the way from kindergarten through high school. To this day I still don't know whether you really graduated from high school. But not this time, you are going to have to learn it the hard way because I do **not** intend to buy any university degree for you."

Aden's personal pride was badly hurt by his father's comments about his intelligence. Whether true or not he felt that there was no reason for his father to say any of those things. That made him furious. He could not even bring himself to look at his father. He walked angrily to the door and before opening it he said, "That suits me just fine because I have no intention of ever going to university."

He then stormed out of his father's office without saying goodbye, slammed the door behind him as hard as he could, and walked straight into his father's private elevator. He walked so fast that he almost knocked down Declan who had been waiting so anxiously outside the door in the hopes of meeting him. Declan realized that he would have to hope for another opportunity to meet Aden, his idol, as he watched the elevator doors close.

Chapter 4

It had been several minutes since Aden's abrupt departure. John still did not want to be disturbed. To keep his mind off his argument with Aden he unsuccessfully tried to look at the article on Adeltec. He glanced at the headline and began reading down the page. Nothing seemed to be registering in his mind. His thoughts kept drifting back to Aden and the fiery conversation that they had. He was thinking how he would have preferred it not to have been that way, but it was almost impossible to have a calm and normal conversation with Aden. He had always been difficult and argumentative.

As John leaned back in his hand stitched leather chair, he felt disheartened by Aden's attitude. He had given him all there was to have, yet he was perplexed by his son's lack of appreciation for what he had done for him. He wondered what more he could possibly want. He acknowledged that he spent nearly all of his time at work, but without that, Aden could not have all the things that he now has. Although John came from a very wealthy family, he never had any of the things that Aden had been given, not to mention that he was never allowed to speak back to his father. He was expected to say 'Yes Sir!' and he did. His father would have disowned him had he ever spoken to him the way that Aden speaks.

He failed to realize that perhaps he should have spent more time with Aden. Instead, he thought that maybe he was not tough enough, or perhaps he should have tried to control and direct his actions more. Since he had far too many responsibilities and obligations, he could not do any of that. It was the price he had to pay for his success. He hoped that someday Aden would understand that it was not easy to be successful, to prove yourself, and to show that you could outperform your father as he had done. All these thoughts were going through his mind as though trying to convince himself that he was in the right and that there was not much that could be done to change the situation. For now, he had far too much work to take care of and had to get on with his busy schedule.

As always, so conveniently his work took precedence over his family. The thought of accepting and loving Aden for who he was, rather than rejecting him for what he was not never occurred to him, not for an instant. His focus quickly changed as he instructed Tracy to send in Declan and to have Allan join them in fifteen minutes.

Declan, who had been waiting anxiously with mounting anticipation nervously walked into John's grand office. He had a great deal of respect for John Bradcliffe and felt a sense of gratitude for having been given the opportunity of a personal interview with a man of his status. "Good afternoon," said Declan as he tentatively shook hands with John, trying hard not to expose his sweaty palm.

John, having met Declan for brief moments during several meetings with his friend, Professor Vavek, held some preconceived ideas about him. He believed that he was an intellectual and a knowledgeable young man, although a bit shy. As their conversation progressed his initial feeling was confirmed. Almost surprisingly, he found it rather easy to talk to Declan. After covering some of the normal introductory topics of most interviews, John looked Declan straight in the eye and said, "Let me get to the crux of the matter."

"Yes sir," said Declan beginning to feel less nervous and more comfortable.

"I only believe in doing your best and being the best in whatever you do. I never settle for, or accept being, second best. It has got to be the best or nothing at all. Therefore, I will only decide to embark onto a new venture when I feel certain that the Bradcliffe Corporation can be at the forefront and that my staff will do their best to ensure the achievement of the leadership position in that industry. Nothing short of that will be acceptable. And I do mean nothing," he said emphatically.

John stopped for a moment, reflecting further about what to say next. He then continued, "My vision is for the Bradcliffe Corporation to enter the electronics industry and within two to three years to become a major player in that field by producing the first commercial optical computers. That is to be achieved by you and the special research and development (R&D) team, to advance your breakthrough research to the commercialization phase, to patent the new technology and then for us to enter the world market on a scale never before seen." He paused as he glanced across the desk to see Declan's reaction. To his satisfaction Declan appeared positive. He was nodding his head indicating how he welcomed the challenge. As he went on, John was no longer thinking about the article or Adeltec Industries. "And about the special R&D team, I expect that you have an appropriate course of action in mind."

"Yes sir, Mr. Kelly, and I, after consulting with Professor Vavek, have come up with a brilliant start-up team," replied Declan confidently.

"You and Mr. Kelly have done well as I knew that you would," said John as he continued on, "I designate you as the team leader and as such you will report directly to Mr. Kelly."

"Sir, I am honored. However, I would like to think of myself as the coordinator of the group as every member of the team is equally capable and equally accomplished."

"Is modesty a trait of a scientist?" asked John. "Well, you don't have to be. We are all aware of your accomplishments."

"A person can be considered a scientist only after having made worthy contributions to humanity. To make such contributions he must do extensive research, and in doing so he can't help but to recognize how insignificant his work is in the large scheme of life and the vastness of the universe. Therefore, he who is not humble at the onset, will only find himself feeling foolish for his lack of humility at the beginning," replied Declan.

Declan's answer put a smile on John's face thinking how he wished, as impossible as it seemed, that Aden could have such an intellect. He nodded his head in an approving manner and said, "I like a man with integrity. All right, you may be the group coordinator." He then extended his hand to Declan. He stood up with a great sense of pride and shook John's hand firmly this time. It was a done deal.

As they shook hands John said, "It's good to have you on board. You're an asset to the Bradcliffe Corporation's new venture, a man with the right ideals for a new beginning."

Declan was so pleased that he was almost speechless. All that he could manage to contribute was, "Thank you, sir. Thank you very much." Then with a sense of determination and excitement in his voice he said, "We will make it happen."

At that moment Tracy called to say that Allan had arrived to see him as per his instructions.

"Perfect timing. Send him right in," said John. In his usual decisive and quick minded style, he did not waste a second and began interrogating Allan as he walked through the doorway, "I trust that everything is in order for hiring the rest of the team. When will they be starting? You know that I want this project in motion yesterday."

Having anticipated his boss's wishes, as a senior executive working for John Bradcliffe must, he was able to assertively reply, "All of the necessary arrangements are being made as we speak. The target date is mid January for the rest of the team to start work. During the interim Declan and I will be working with our legal staff to initiate the first round of patents based upon Declan and Professor Vavek's research work to date."

"I look forward to reviewing the progress of the team," said John firmly.

Allan and Declan both left the meeting with a feeling of optimism and were anxious to get started.

Chapter 5

~~~~

Filled with rage and anger, Aden quickly got into his silver Zonda. Nothing seemed to matter, not even the new prize of his collection. As a result of the argument and confrontation he had had with his father, he could no longer feel the thrill and excitement of owning such an extraordinary car. He felt furious and wondered why his father could not accept him for who he is. As he backed out of his parking space he nearly crashed into the car on the opposite side of the aisle. *Why does he always have to tell me how everybody else, including that polyester nerd, is doing better than I am? Just because I don't go to a university? Who needs that anyway?* thought Aden driving away with such acceleration that his tires were spinning and squealing all over the basement garage as he left the Bradcliffe building. He was so upset that he did not care whether he crashed or not.

Aden was far too independent and rebellious to give in to his father's ways. Yet on the other hand, more than ever before he wished that he could have his father's unconditional love and acceptance. Encounters like the one that he just had with his father made him doubt that he would ever have his father's approval. All these thoughts left him feeling even more frustrated and disillusioned with his life. He was so deep in thought that he found himself turning onto the private road lined with beautiful gum trees leading to the magnificent Bradcliffe estate without remembering how he had gotten there. As he approached the paved driveway the two large heavy black iron gates swung open barely in time as his car roared through, down the long drive, and around the fountain where he came to a screeching halt in front of the mansion.

The Bradcliffe estate was located in the eastern Adelaide hills with a breathtaking panoramic view of the city. Aden's grandfather had built the mansion and left the entire estate to his only heir, John, who implemented a program of extensive renovations and expansions to the original structure. Through his discriminating and immaculate taste the old mansion was transformed into a work of art. It now stood out as a magnificent centerpiece in the midst of one hundred acres of woodlands which he had finely landscaped. The gardens immediately surrounding the mansion were beautifully manicured in the style similar to the gardens of Versailles.

The mansion was elegantly furnished with European furniture, hand made Persian carpets, and a rare family collection of fine paintings including the works of Renoir, Bonnard, and others. Each was exquisitely placed to complement the open and spacious architecture of the mansion. All had served to create surroundings filled with beauty and elegance which were all too often taken for granted. This left an atmosphere lacking in warmth and happiness. As Aden and his father were too busy being discontent with each other and life in general, they never enjoyed all that they had.

"Sounds like Aden is home," remarked Brian Forbes, who had been waiting for him in the spacious foyer of the mansion, where beautiful silk tapestries and the wide colonial style staircase created a grand decor reminiscent of the *Gone With the Wind* era. Brian was Aden's best friend. They had been friends since their first year of high school. He was about 5'11" and had chestnut brown hair and azure blue eyes. He looked quite handsome and was well built, as he trained with Aden whenever he could. However, his looks and fitness could not compete with Aden, and he knew it. No one could be compared to Aden Bradcliffe.

"Yes sir, it certainly does," agreed Randall with a nod. He was Aden's personal English born and bred valet who had been with the Bradcliffe family since before Aden was born. He had a slender face and build and often held a military-like stance indicative of his unwavering attentiveness. He was always proper, extremely kind, and one of the most loyal and trusted of the staff working for the Bradcliffe family.

"But it doesn't sound as though Master Aden is in a good mood," added Randall thoughtfully.

"That's ridiculous. How could he not be in a good mood? He loves fast, expensive cars, and he just got a new one."

But Randall could tell from the way Aden stopped the car to the way he slammed the car door that he was not to be toyed with. He also knew that when Aden was not in a good mood he did not have the patience to wait for the door to open. Hurriedly he made his way to the front door and managed to open the door just in time for Aden to enter.

"Good afternoon Master Aden," said Randall warmly.

As anticipated by Randall and to Brian's surprise Aden seemed upset. He did not even say hello to Brian, nor did he reply to Randall. He just took off his tie, unfastened the top two buttons of his shirt, walked across the foyer, and fell back into an armchair next to Brian.

"Well, tell me all about your new car. I've been waiting all day to see it," said Brian excitedly.

"There's nothing to tell. I mean, what's there to talk about a car? If you've seen one sports car, you've seen them all," replied Aden with a distant look on his face. Unlike Brian, he was anything but excited.

"Park it in the garage for me," said Aden as he threw the keys to Randall.

Randall's jaw dropped. "Me sir?" he asked in surprise. "You want me to park your brand new sports car?" he further questioned in amazement. Nobody was ever allowed to as much as touch, let alone drive Aden's sports cars.

"That's what I said," replied Aden abruptly with a chilling glare. "Why are you standing there and questioning me? Just do what you're told to do."

"Yes, Master Aden," said Randall as he quickly walked to the door to accommodate Aden's wishes.

Brian waited for Randall to leave. Then he looked at Aden who still seemed distant and said, "Don't you think you were a little rough on Randall?"

"Don't you start with me. I talk how I want to whoever I want," said Aden in his usual irascible way.

Brian having been Aden's best friend for so long knew him well. He quickly figured out what might be wrong. "You had another fight with your old man. He doesn't approve of your new car does he?"

"He doesn't approve of anything I do," said Aden discontentedly. "You're lucky. Your father thinks the world of you and approves of everything you do."

"Don't let that fool you," Brian was quick to respond. "My father is like that for one reason and that's because I've always done exactly what he has ever wanted me to do, no questions asked, simple as that."

"Come now. It can't be as simple as that. Look, you were always good at school. You worked hard and were able to get into med school. Even now, as difficult and demanding as medicine is, you're doing fine. So tell me, who wouldn't be proud of that?"

"Did it ever occur to you that I would have been happier doing something other than medicine?" asked Brian.

"No, of course not. I couldn't imagine you doing anything else. I mean with your father being such a successful surgeon and having built one of the best medical clinics in Adelaide, with you having always been such a good student, and being so close to your father, it seemed the right choice for you."

"Don't you see, that's exactly the point. Since my father was a doctor, it was always assumed and expected that I would also become a doctor. I never had a choice. I was expected to be good at school, so I was. I was expected to study medicine, so I did. Do you know what it's like to feel that you have no choice or control over your life?" But before Aden could respond, Brian quickly answered his own question. "No, I don't suppose that you would. You have always done whatever you've wanted to do and liked to do. So, let me tell you how it feels, you never feel content with your life, and often you feel frustrated."

"I didn't know you felt that way. Why didn't you ever say something?" asked Aden, rather surprised to learn that he was not the only one discontented with his life.

"There was really nothing to say," said Brian. "You see, unlike your father, my father wasn't from a long line of aristocrats. My grandfather was a simple farmer, who had a small farm outside of Adelaide. He worked very hard, but all the hard work got him was a bad back and a small farmhouse. My father had promised himself that he was going to change all of that. He was determined to make a better life for himself and his family. And he did. He has never let us forget what he's done for us, and that we should take advantage of all the opportunities that he's provided for us." Brian stopped for a moment. Deep down he appreciated what his father had done, "That's why I had to do what I did. But I felt that it was a small price to pay to make my father happy." Then in an attempt to change the serious mood of the conversation, Brian forced a smile and said, "Look on the bright side. How else could you have met such a great guy like me?"

Aden still seeming rather distant, turned, looked at his friend and said, "At least you have a goal, a purpose, a direction in your life…I have none."

"But you have something that is quite rare and admirable, and that's your great strength of character. I wish I could be more like you, but I'm not and probably never will be. You have the courage to do what you want, and not what's expected of you. Honestly, who does that?" asked Brian trying to get

Aden to look at things more positively. "So, you don't have a goal now, but you will. And when you do there will be nothing stopping you." To make him feel better he thought that he would humor him. "I'm not just saying this to cheer you up. I'm saying it because I believe it. I'd be crazy to say it to someone whose ego is matched only by his bank account."

That brought a smile to Aden's face. "You're alright…for a farm boy," said Aden with a tone of conceit.

"Enough philosophizing," said Brian. He was glad to see Aden returning to his normal, arrogant self. "We have the weekend ahead of us. Just think of the wild time we'll have tomorrow night going to Ice Bar, then to Pulse, and whatever follows."

"Not this Saturday night."

"Why not? Don't tell me you're thinking of going to that boring birthday party at Packard's tomorrow night?"

"What if I am?" asked Aden defensively.

"I don't understand why you'd want to go there when I have all these hot girls lined up for tomorrow night."

"Girls are always lined up. I have my reasons."

"Do your reasons have anything to do with a certain Mrs. Packard?" asked Brian sarcastically.

"What if they do?"

"Well, you'll just get yourself in more trouble with your father."

"But it's my father who wants me to go to Sharon's birthday," replied Aden.

Brian started to laugh but seeing the serious look on Aden's face he stopped and said, "I don't think I heard you right mate. It sounded like you said that your father wants you to go. That's like asking the wolf to watch over the sheep."

"Stop clowning around," said Aden with his voice shaded in disgust. "Yes, he does. And that's because Sharon made him promise that I'd be at the party."

"Aahh! Now I see."

"No, you don't. I'm only going to appease my father, and I'll have nothing to do with Sharon," said Aden adamantly.

"Sure! And you expect me to believe that? Especially the way she's always all over you," remarked Brian.

"I don't really care whether you believe me or not. I'm just telling you the way it is."

"This I've got to see. Actually, that boring party is beginning to sound more and more interesting," said Brian. "If nothing else, at least I'll get to ride in your new car."

"No, you won't. My father wants me to go with him. I guess that I'll do it his way," said Aden reluctantly. "But you should drive so we'll have a car when we want to leave. I don't intend to stay there all night, only until I've taken care of what needs to be done."

"Alright! Now you're talking." said Brian with a content smile. "Maybe tomorrow night won't be a total loss after all."

Chapter 6

The silence was deafening inside the silver Bradcliffe Rolls Royce limousine en route to Packard's residence as father and son rode in the back of their elegant and luxurious family car. The two of them could never find anything common or non-contentious to talk about. Their conversations always seemed to result in big arguments. This night neither one was about to chance another argument, not even a trivial comment about the weather could be heard.

As they were approaching the house John broke the awkward silence in a final attempt to ensure Aden's proper behavior at the party. He carefully, choosing his words with a concerned look, said, "Am I correct to assume that you will…?"

Aden abruptly interrupted his father, "You don't have to worry. I know what I need to do."

John could not take comfort with Aden's response, but saw no choice. The Bradcliffe Rolls Royce had already arrived at the Packard's front entrance and Edmund, the family chauffeur had just opened the car door. He turned, looked at Aden with his piercing eyes, and said, "I certainly hope so." He then stepped out of the limousine with Aden following behind.

The party was already in full swing when they entered. The Packards were well known for their extravagant parties. Only those who met the 'standards' of the exclusive Adelaide Club were invited. This party was no exception. It was a grand affair in their usual high society style held in their exclusive mansion ballroom. The entertainment area was quite large and spacious, spanning most of the first floor. There were people everywhere, quite fashionably dressed as if to outdo one another. The sound of the band playing at the other end of the ballroom could be heard. Jugglers, balloon artists, and magicians could be seen all around the room entertaining the guests and creating a special jovial birthday party atmosphere.

Sharon, the beautiful and charming hostess was wearing an exquisite Armani evening gown. Her perfume filled the air as she received the guests at the entrance of the ballroom. She was visibly pleased to see Aden. Her proper and rather fake smile suddenly changed to an excited look of happiness as the newly arrived guests approached the grandly decorated ballroom. John shook hands with Sharon and wished her a happy birthday. Then Aden in his usual cool and aloof manner followed. He also shook hands with her but did not say a word.

Sharon, expecting a warmer greeting from Aden said, "What? Not even a kiss for the Birthday Girl?"

Aden looked at his father who was intently watching him. Still maintaining his aloofness, he gave Sharon a peck on the cheek to appease her wishes. It was not exactly what she had in mind, but she considered it an icebreaker that she would pursue later. John felt somewhat relieved, at least for the moment.

As the two Bradcliffes walked in, they found themselves quickly becoming the center of attention. Aden, whose mannerisms always provoked attention, was enjoying it all. John on the other hand did not care for the attention. So, in an attempt to change the situation and amidst greeting the various guests, he looked at Sharon and said, "So. Where is that lucky husband of yours?"

"Malcolm is around somewhere. I'll get him," said Sharon as she walked away to find him.

Brian had been anxiously awaiting Aden's arrival and was happy to see him. He quickly made his way to him and said, "I've got to talk to you mate."

"Ok, what's up?"

"Not here. Let's go somewhere a little less crowded."

Aden did not see any reason to stay with his father. He excused himself and walked away with Brian.

John, who could see Sharon returning with Malcolm from the opposite side of the room, thought to himself that the timing was perfect.

"What's so important that it can't wait?" asked Aden.

"I met these two hot girls after I got here."

"So what? What's the big deal about meeting two girls? There's a house full of them," said Aden, completely disinterested.

"Wait 'til you at least hear what I have to say. These two are good friends and one of them is Elise Morgan," said Brian with enthusiasm.

"The only Elise Morgan that I know is a little kid," replied Aden.

"Not anymore. She's all grown up and gorgeous and is dying to see you. So, how about it?" asked Brian eagerly.

Aden thought for a moment and said, "Anything to liven up this boring party. But she'd better be what you say, otherwise forget it. I'm not interested in wasting my time."

"Don't you think that I know that by now?"

"I guess," said Aden as he looked around. "There. At last I see the bar, my favorite spot. I'll go and get a drink before I choke on all of the small social talk around here."

While Aden was ordering his drink, Brian went to get the girls. Elise was thrilled to be seeing Aden Bradcliffe, the most eligible bachelor in Australia.

Aden had his drink in his hand and was leaning against the bar when Brian walked over with the girls following closely behind. He introduced them to Aden. "This one on my left is Kim and on my right is Elise."

Aden, maintaining his typical cool arrogance, showed no reaction at all. He took a sip of his drink as he looked Elise over, up and down, checking to see if she met his exacting standards before he would bother even talking to her. Elise with light brown hair and blue eyes was a refreshingly young and beautiful girl. So, Aden in his usual cocky style and without any concern for the girl, thought that she would fit in well with his plans for the evening as he said, "Last time I remember seeing you, you were a tomboy with short hair, fighting with boys."

"I was thirteen then. Now I'm seventeen, and I don't fight with boys anymore," said Elise. She then moved real close to Aden, leaned over him as she spoke very softly in his ear saying, "And for you Aden I'm anything you want me to be."

Aden looked at her and said, "Seventeen, you say?"

"Only on the outside. But, more like twenty on the inside. Would you like to find out? I guarantee you won't be disappointed," said Elise with a lustful look in her eyes.

This was all too common for Aden. There was never any challenge. No personal involvement, all too easy. Then, without any reaction Aden finished his drink, looked at Brian and said, "Let's go somewhere with a little more privacy."

"The study," Brian suggested, "that's somewhere quiet and private. I don't believe anyone is going to be reading books tonight."

John was content to see that Aden had left Sharon alone. Sharon on the other hand, was getting impatient. She really wanted to be with Aden, and already the party was half over and she had not seen him at all.

Sharon kept thinking about him. *Where could Aden be? I've got to find him…but where?* All of a sudden, her eyes lit up and she became ecstatic when she saw Brian slipping into the study with several drinks in hand. *Of course, the study.* She then very discretely made her way to the study and walked in. She became furiously jealous to see Aden kissing another woman. She slammed the door shut and walked over to the sofa where Aden and Elise were now uncomfortably reclining. "How could you do this to me Aden?" asked Sharon, feeling hurt and upset.

Aden very casually unwrapped himself from Elise and looked at Sharon without uttering a word. It did not seem that he was the least bit bothered by the noisy interruption. It was as though he had been expecting it. He then turned to Elise and said, "Go out and wait for me."

"But Aden I really want to stay with you…please," said Elise in a pleading whisper.

"Don't question me. Just do what I tell you," said Aden with a flash of anger.

"Yes, Aden," said Elise as she got up very quickly while pulling down and rearranging her dress. Brian, realizing the delicacy of the situation, quickly ushered the girls out of the room.

Sharon was glad to finally be alone with Aden. She threw herself at him, put her arms around him, and began kissing him as though possessed.

Aden very calmly pulled her arms away from him and said, "Not tonight."

"Why not? I can't wait anymore. I need you," said Sharon as she continued her attempts to kiss and seduce him.

"It's your husband. That's why," said Aden, not responding to her passionate affections.

"Don't worry about him. I can take care of him anytime," said Sharon almost breathlessly.

"Not this time. He seems to be in charge of some sort of grant that my father wants for his company. If he gets upset tonight, he may not support that grant for my father, and I can't let that happen."

"I keep telling you not to worry about him. He'll do whatever I tell him. If it's the grant that you want for your father, then I promise you will have it. Now let's not have that spoil our evening," said Sharon as she slowly moved her slinky body against Aden.

Aden very calmly and casually got up and said, "That's not good enough. First, you deliver, and then I'll consider what you want." He buttoned his jacket as he walked toward the door and said, "Friday is the day." He then opened the door and walked out. Brian and the girls were waiting for him. "I have had enough of this party. It's time to go and live it up," said Aden. He saw his father standing near the study talking with a couple of his business associates. He walked to his father and told him that everything was under control and that he was leaving. Hearing that phrase and seeing Sharon walk out of the study shortly after Aden left him particularly worried, but there was not much that he could say except, "We will talk about this later, at home."

John tried waiting up for Aden that night to no avail. It was very late, and Aden showed no signs of appearing anytime soon. He then decided to retire for the night and deal with Aden the next day.

Early Sunday morning, John went to play a round of golf. However, he found it rather unenjoyable, because of his preoccupation with thoughts of Aden. For the entire time he was not able to get him off of his mind. *What could he possibly have "under control"?* It was almost noon when he had finished showering and changing, and still there was no sign of Aden.

Enough is enough. I'm not going to wait another minute, he thought to himself as he walked into Aden's bedroom without warning.

The curtains were still drawn closed, and the room was dark. He threw open the curtains and then walked over to the bed to wake up Aden. He tried pulling the sheet off, but could not. So, he tried again, but this time much harder as he angrily said, "No you don't Aden!" No sooner than having said this, the sheet came off.

To his great surprise, it was not Aden, but instead it was Elise wearing Aden's shirt, hiding under the covers. She very quickly said, "Please Mr. Bradcliffe, don't tell my father about this. He thinks that I was sleeping over at my girlfriend's house last night."

John, in addition to being angry, was now in a state of shock. He did not know what to say. "Please Mr. Bradcliffe," pleaded Elise who was by now both concerned and embarrassed.

"I suppose I won't say anything," responded John with a bit of strain in his voice.

Aden had just finished showering and had not had a chance to completely dry himself when he heard the voices in his bedroom. He put on his bathrobe and quickly walked back to his bedroom.

John could not contain his anger any longer, erupted at Aden and said, "You have some explaining to do, serious explaining!"

"I'm not the one who has rudely barged into the room," said Aden abruptly.

"I can see that we are not going to settle this right now. So, I'll be waiting for you downstairs," said John as he stormed out of the room.

That really irritated Aden to no end, but he restrained himself from saying anything to his father in front of Elise.

Elise was still on a high from having spent a night with the man of her dreams, walked over to Aden, put her arms around him and said, "That was the best night of my life Aden."

Aden never reacted to such displays of emotion towards him, not even on a good day. Now, after that brief confrontation with his father, he certainly was not in the mood to respond to Elise's emotional show of affection. He just removed her arms from him and walked away towards his dressing room.

She did not care that he was being mean to her. All that she could think of was seeing him again. "When will I see you again Aden? Last night was such a special night for me."

"Any night with me is."

"But you don't understand. I love you. I love you very much," said Elise as she moved closer to Aden.

"All I did was sleep with you for one night, and here you are talking all this nonsense about love. You girls are all the same," said Aden callously.

"But I'm different from all of the other girls. I really do need to see you." She appeared upset. Desperately wanting to see him again, she said, "I'll just do anything for you, if you let me see you again."

"Do I look like someone who needs to have anything done for me?"

"I know you don't. But please let me see you again," insisted Elise.

Aden was becoming more frustrated by the minute with this kind of hassle. To end this conversation he said, "Put your name in any space in my date book." He then began dressing.

Aden was in a rush as he was to meet Brian on the tennis courts in 10 minutes. The courts were just part of an extensive sports complex that Aden's father had added to the Bradcliffe estate which included an indoor and outdoor swimming pool, spa, sauna, and exercise rooms, just to mention a few. This was where Aden spent a lot of his time, that is when he was not womanizing or partying. At a very young age Aden had found that sports were a good way to help him deal with his troubles and a good way to vent his frustrations.

The more troubled or frustrated he was, the faster he ran, the harder he hit, the more he exercised. As a result, he grew to really enjoy sports. His love of sports and the use of the best coaches that money could buy, made him an all-round athlete.

In a matter of a few minutes Aden had finished getting ready. On his way out he grabbed his tennis racket and said a cool and quick goodbye to Elise. As he was walking down the stairs, he saw Randall down in the foyer. He knew that he was waiting to remind him that his father wanted to see him. Before Randall could say a word, Aden said, "Ok, where is he?"

"Your father is waiting for you in the sunroom, Master Aden."

Aden could never be bothered with social amenities. So, without saying anything to Randall he quickly went to the sunroom and walked in.

The sunroom was a delightful and bright room with all of the windows facing the southern rolling green, grassy gardens of the estate. The room was filled with indoor plants and bouquets of freshly cut flowers to complement the color and the décor of the room. As cheerful as the sunroom was, it could do very little to improve Aden's dark mood.

His father was so filled with anger that he wasted no time in dealing with his son. As soon as Aden entered the room, he yelled at him, "How could you do this Aden?!"

"Do what?" asked Aden with clearly a puzzled look on his face.

"Don't pretend that you don't know what I'm talking about. I'm talking about Elise. I know her, and I know her family. She is just a child. How could you take advantage of her innocence?" said Aden's father impatiently.

"She wasn't an innocent child as you would like to think. She wanted me to sleep with her. She practically begged me to do so," said Aden in his defense.

As true as this may have been, it did very little to help his situation with his father, who by now was even more furious having heard his response.

"You stop that Aden!" said John rising to his feet. "You should be ashamed of yourself. Yet you have no remorse about what you do. At the rate that you are going I won't be able to look anybody in the face anymore. As much as I wish it were not the case, you are a Bradcliffe. As a member of this family, you must act with dignity and decency. We Bradcliffes, because of our social and financial standing, have a certain responsibility to the people and our society."

"I don't need any lectures on how a Bradcliffe should be," said Aden defiantly. "I have seen them all, and I wouldn't want to be any one of them. I especially don't need any sermons from you on responsibility." He was angry and rebellious.

"You need more than that after what you did at the Packard's last night."

Aden, almost hurt quickly cut in and said, "After what I did? I did exactly what you wanted me to do. I went to the boring party. I didn't touch Sharon. And I even got you your grant that you were so worried about. What more can you want?"

"And what exactly do you mean by saying that you got me the grant?" asked John with noticeable concern in his voice.

"Sharon was very unhappy that I hadn't paid enough attention to her. I simply told her that I wasn't going to have anything to do with her until after she got you the grant. She'd do anything for me."

Aden's father virtually hit the ceiling, "How dare you do such a thing?!" He was so upset that he was now shouting at Aden, "I told you that I had the best research and development plan put together. It was a thorough and well-thought grant proposal. All that I needed was for you not to interfere and ruin my chances of getting it honestly. Now you have done worse than that. You have disgraced me! I'm telling you. You have disgraced me for the last time! I can think of no punishment fitting for what you have done."

"Don't you talk about punishing me as though you have had nothing to do with any of this. You are as guilty as I am. You stand here and talk about responsibility to people. What about family responsibility? Or are you too busy to even consider the thought of responsibility to your son?"

Just then there was a knock at the door. John, too angry to see Aden's point of view, yelled out, "Who is it?!"

"It is I sir," responded Randall meekly. "May I come in?"

"Alright, come in," said John with a slightly calmer tone of voice.

"Sorry to disturb you sir, but your luncheon guests have arrived. I thought that perhaps I should let you know," said Randall politely.

"Inform my guests that I will be with them shortly," said John. Then he looked at Aden and said, "We will continue this after lunch. No, that won't work either. I'll be leaving for Melbourne then. I suppose that I'll have to deal with this after I return."

"That is, if you can find the time," said Aden sarcastically.

"I don't need snide remarks from you. What I need is for you to stay out of trouble until I get back, which should be this Thursday. Now that is not very long, is it? I mean I have used up all of my influence to get you out of trouble so many times that I have lost count. So, will you stay out of trouble at least until I come back?" asked John firmly.

"I guess you'll find out when you get back," replied Aden mischievously. "Now I've got a tennis match to play, and I see that you have your snobbish friends to attend to," said Aden as he walked out of the room. He did not even bother saying hello to any of his father's friends who were busy talking in the foyer. He just diverted to one of the side doors exiting to the tennis courts and slipped out.

John did not even stop for one moment to think about what Aden had said or consider for once not allowing his work and social life to take precedence over his son. He momentarily entered the foyer, greeted and welcomed his guests in his usual charming manner as if nothing had happened between him and Aden.

While John was busy being a gracious host, Aden spent the afternoon having a rigorous workout, the kind he usually had to help him keep in shape and to vent his frustrations. After his tennis match with Brian, lifting weights, and an intense marshal arts training session with his private coach, he was feeling a bit better and ready to join Brian who was relaxing in the spa. "I like the way you Bradcliffes live, private swimming pools, private tennis courts, private coaches, private everything, and with your monograms on everything. This is the life, partying, relaxing, and then partying some more. You gotta love it! Let's do this again tomorrow afternoon. I'll be finished with my classes at 3:00pm," said Brian with a complacent look on his face.

"Not tomorrow. Have you forgotten that the foundation work on my house is starting tomorrow? I must go to make sure that everything is done the way that I want."

"Only for a second, it's the effect of all this pampering in the lap of luxury," Brian replied defensively. Then he excitedly continued, "Now I have something to really look forward to for tomorrow. Tell me, have you met your new neighbors yet? How are they going to be with the wild parties and loud music?"

"No, I haven't met any of them, and I'm not concerned how they will react," replied Aden. "All I can tell you is that somehow they have found out that I'll be their new neighbor and already some of the girls have started passing their phone numbers to my builder to give to me."

"Have you called any of them?"

"No, I can't be bothered. I already have enough dates for the next couple of months," replied Aden with total lack of interest.

"With those kinds of neighbors, now I'm even more interested in seeing it. So where is this new neighborhood of yours?" asked Brian curiously.

"You have to wait until tomorrow. I want it to be a surprise. I'll pick you up shortly after 3 from uni."

Chapter 7

It was Monday afternoon. Aden and Brian were on their way to Aden's new house on this beautiful, warm summer day typical of December weather in Adelaide. Music was playing loudly and there was a sense of excitement inside Aden's sleek red Enzo Ferrari. Unlike his other cars that had been transformed into a one-of-a-kind with all of his personal touches and additions, this Enzo was one of only 349 manufactured. With so few of them and made to such a high standard Ferrari only offered them to a select few. Aden, being a Bradcliffe, was approached by Ferrari to be an owner of their most prestigious model.

"So where is this house of yours," asked Brian anxiously.

"You'll see it in a few minutes," said Aden. He then turned onto the palm lined Ocean Drive leading to the waterfront.

"This is even better than I had thought. I've got to hand it to you, it's a great area. Just think of all of the beach parties we can have," said Brian excitedly.

"You can have parties anywhere. I chose this area because I just find the water so calming…" Brian interrupted and said, "Certainly calming considering that it is clear on the other side of the city from your father's mansion."

The peace and quiet of the neighborhood were broken by the roaring 12-cylinder engine of Aden's Ferrari echoing down the street as he came to a stop in front of a rather large, vacant block of land with a magnificent panoramic view of the ultramarine blue ocean facing southwest down the Gulf of St Vincent.

"Look at the size of this land," Brian exclaimed as he slid out of the leather bucket seat. "Are you building a hotel here?"

"It had to be large to fit all of the things I wanted," said Aden as he handed the floor plan to Brian. "Here, take a look at this while I go to talk with my builder. It will show you everything."

Brian took the plan and began to curiously look over it. After becoming amazed with the sheer size of it, he only grew more impressed with the details he saw such as indoor and outdoor swimming pools with waterfalls, a tennis court, a seven-car garage, a separate and detached living quarters for Aden's personal valet, and a massive main structure. However, it was the extensive entertainment area that particularly caught his attention which included a large ballroom for parties and a state-of-the-art light and sound system.

Aden walked to the site where excavations had been done according to the plan in preparation for the pouring of the foundation. The six workmen busily placing and securing the steel wire mesh in the trenches stopped momentarily to say hello to him. The builder quickly came over to greet him, give him a run down of what had been done, and seek his approval.

Brian was so engrossed in the plan that he did not even notice Aden's neighbor until she was practically standing next to him. "Hello! My name is Betty. I live in the house across the street. And you are…?" "Brian." "A relative?" asked Betty somewhat amused at catching him off guard. "Oh, no. But a very close friend."

"It certainly is very nice to meet a friend of Mr. Bradcliffe." Then as if she could not wait to talk to someone, she continued, "I can tell you we are happy to have such a prominent neighbor. I bet that the prices of homes here have already gone up. In fact, Brian, I can tell you anything you want to know about all of the neighbors here, that is, except the one that lives in the white villa next door to Mr. Bradcliffe. All I can tell you about her is that she is very attractive because I have only seen her driving by in her car. I don't know why she keeps so much to herself. Why do you think she does?" It was a rhetorical question to which, of course, Brian had no answer. He just shrugged his shoulders. "Perhaps you and your friend can find out," she continued, "I mean who wouldn't warm up and open up to Aden Bradcliffe?" Brian smiled. How could he disagree? Then without a moment to waste she started rattling off things about the various neighbors.

Brian was not at all interested in any of the local gossip but did not know how to get away until he heard Aden call him. That provided the perfect excuse he needed to end the uncomfortable 'conversation'. He quickly excused himself and walked over to where Aden was standing.

"Who is that homely looking woman, and why are you talking to her?"

"Her name is Betty, one of your neighbors from across the street. She was just telling me about everyone in the neighborhood. For example, did you know…?" Aden quickly interrupted, "I am not interested. And I don't want her nosing around here. So just get rid of her before others start to come."

He had no sooner completed his comment when Aden noticed Betty making her way toward them with a big smile on her face, "I wanted to welcome you to our neighborhood and to say that if there is anything that you need, just let me know."

"Thanks," replied Aden in a disinterested tone of voice.

"I really do mean it. I would be more than happy to help," said Betty accommodatingly.

"Ok," said Aden as his gaze turned elsewhere anxiously wishing to end the conversation. "Now if you excuse us, a few things need to be taken care of."

The two friends were finally by themselves. "So, what do you think Brian?" asked Aden.

"It is magnificent! The view, the beach, the house, everything is just perfect for a single's lifestyle. But don't you forget it, I'm going to be there helping you to enjoy it all."

"Don't get too excited yet. It probably will take about a year before it's done." Aden then finished talking to the builder and started walking to his car.

"You're not leaving now, are you?" asked Brian who was not quite ready to go.

"Yes. I'm finished for now," said Aden eager to get going.

"What about your next-door neighbor, the one in the white villa that even Betty doesn't know anything about? Don't you want to find out who she is?" said Brian who was himself curious to find out about her.

"No, I am not interested in meeting another homely looking one," said Aden a bit annoyed by the suggestion.

"But she is supposed to be very attractive."

"Just the same," said Aden, now waiting by his car, "still not interested. There are attractive women everywhere."

"But she sounds intriguing, and I just love watching women lose themselves over meeting you," said Brian with just a devilish hint of eagerness.

"As if you haven't seen enough of that."

Brian did not want to pass up the opportunity. "Come on. Let's go brighten up her day and have a little fun." At Brian's insistence Aden reluctantly relented and agreed to go over with him. They walked through a black rod iron gate into a formal garden setting courtyard to an elegant front door inlayed with beautiful leadlight and knocked.

"Somebody is at the door Mommy. Should I get it?" asked Timothy.

"No, Timothy. We're running late. I'll get the door while you and Natalie run upstairs and get changed for your swimming lessons. It's probably another salesman. I'll get rid of him," said Christina to her seven-year-old son.

Not knowing what to expect when the door opened, Aden and Brian were pleasantly pleased to see such an attractive woman. Christina was, in fact, a stunning 26-year-old woman of slender build. Her long brown hair hung as though to frame her naturally beautiful face with high cheek bones, radiant complexion, dazzling almond shaped brown eyes, and perfectly shaped full lips. She was stylish in appearance even in her casual outfit which perfectly fit her 5'7" height like a model on a catwalk.

Aden was standing directly in front of the door looking aloof as he greeted her with a very cool "Hello." Brian standing beside Aden with a smile and in a much more friendly disposition said, "Hello. How are you today?"

With a vibrant smile Christina replied, "I'm fine. Thank you." But being pressed for time and wanting to save them from the trouble of going through their sales pitch, she quickly continued on, "I'm sorry. I don't really need anything today. Perhaps some other time but thank you for coming." She then closed the door as she said goodbye.

Aden and Brian were astonished not only to be thought of as salesmen, but to have the door slammed in their faces. "That did not just happen," said Aden more shocked than upset.

Both of them were quite confused about the whole ordeal. "I don't really know what just happened. I'll knock again to find out," said Brian trying to compose himself.

Brian knocked again. Christina was halfway up the stairs when she heard the knock. *Some salesmen sure are persistent,* she thought to herself as she went back down to get the door.

"I'll handle it this time," said Aden. When Christina opened the door he said, "We are not salesmen. In fact, I'm going to be your new next-door neighbor. This is my friend Brian Forbes, and my name is Aden…" But before he finished saying his name, Christina was distracted by giggling coming from the top of the stairs and did not even hear his last name. She turned around and saw Timothy and Natalie in their underwear about to come down. "Excuse me for a moment please," said Christina politely as she closed the door again. She then gave the children a stern look and said, "Where do you think you are going? You know that you can't come and say hello to people when you are not dressed. Now, quickly go back to your rooms and get ready."

Aden glared at Brian. Then as he shook his head, he looked away and facetiously remarked, "Brighten up her day, you said. Watch her lose herself over meeting me, you said…I knew I should have left you in the car." Then with a strained voice he continued, "That's the last time I'll ever listen to you."

Christina, feeling embarrassed about closing the door again, opened it and said, "I'm sorry. I'm really not in the habit of closing doors on people."

"You're an American!" said Aden sounding surprised.

"Yes. I get that a lot. And you are our new neighbor. Welcome to the neighborhood. You're going to like it here. It's very nice and quiet." Realizing that she was running late, she tried to end the conversation. "Well, it was nice meeting you both. I'm sure I'll be seeing you again."

Aden on the other hand, felt as a matter of pride that he had to be the one to end the conversation. He continued on in his usual, arrogant style, "You have a lot of stained glass work in your house. I wanted to look at them to get some ideas." He was thinking that naturally she would invite him in, but yet again to his surprise, that was not the case.

"I really am sorry. I'm running very late. Why don't you come by tomorrow? I'll be glad to show them to you then," said Christina whose only interest at this time was to get her children to their swimming lessons.

That was the final blow to Aden's ego. "No, I'm busy tomorrow," he said without a moment's hesitation.

"That's all right. Whenever you have time will be fine," said Christina kindly.

"Whenever," said Aden very coolly. "We must go now." He then walked away as he said, "Goodbye."

No woman had ever responded to him like that. Brian on the other hand, got such a kick out of it that he was having a hard time keeping himself from laughing out loud. But he did manage it long enough to say, "It was a pleasure meeting you, and we'll be seeing you soon."

Aden was livid, and it showed in the way he drove off. He gave Brian a death look as he said, "You and your bright ideas! 'Let's make her day'," he said in a mocking tone. "I don't ever want to hear another one of your ideas. And wipe that stupid smile off your face!"

"I don't know what you're so mad about. I thought that she was rather nice and quite beautiful."

"She was either emotionally dead or mentally disturbed," said Aden still seething.

"I don't know what you're talking about. I quite liked her even though she isn't the usual ravishing and flashy kind that hangs around you all of the time, and I think that she liked me too," said Brian, quite enjoying how bothered Aden was by this encounter, something that he had not seen in him before.

"In your dreams! Anyway, I was the one that she invited back," said Aden. "She obviously was playing hard-to-get. I bet she can't wait for me to go back so that she can throw herself at me."

"You're probably right. Why should she be any different?" said Brian. "Anyway, what about tonight?"

"I don't feel like doing much tonight," said Aden.

"Me neither. Let's go over to your house, order in some pizza, watch a couple of movies, and just lay back and see how much we can drink."

"That's the smartest thing you've said all day," responded Aden sarcastically as they continued the long drive back to the Bradcliffe estate. Behind them the sun was slowly descending to the horizon with hues of amber and rouge beginning to appear across the coastal city skyline.

Chapter 8

It was late Tuesday morning. Aden had just woken up and was feeling lousy. It was not an uncommon feeling for him as that was how he felt most days after a heavy night of drinking. So, every morning while still in bed he would let Jane, the housekeeper, know that he was up and whether or not he required anything. As demanding as Aden was, Jane always knew that she was to drop anything that she was doing and attend to Aden's needs right away.

"Good morning Master Aden. May I come in?" asked Jane as she caringly knocked softly on the door. Her nurturing disposition was evident on her face as she always appeared calm and pleasant. She had a medium build and a light complexion. She always dressed immaculately and neatly tied back her chestnut brown hair.

Aden forced out a couple of words to allow Jane to come in. She walked in and put down the small, elegant silver tray with a glass of water and two aspirins on the table next to his bed. "Would you like me to open the curtains for you Master Aden? It's such a beautiful morning."

"The only thing beautiful about it is that it's almost over," said Aden as he swallowed the aspirins. "Go ahead and open the curtains. Sooner or later, I'll have to subject my body to the shock of the sunlight. Might as well get it over with!"

"Master Aden, I have the breakfast table set on the terrace for you. You must come, have a big breakfast and enjoy this lovely day," said Jane as she opened the curtains.

"I'm not really hungry. Just a cup of strong hot coffee will do for me."

By the time he finished showering and getting dressed, the aspirins had started to take effect. He was feeling better as he sat at the breakfast table enjoying his cup of coffee. The gardens immediately below the terrace looked like a tapestry of color made up of row upon row of yellow and orange roses, marigolds, and carefully trimmed, low green hedges, all surrounding a round crystal clear water pond in the middle.

As he gazed at the gardens and the beautiful rolling green fields beyond, his thoughts seemed to be drifting away. He found himself thinking about yesterday and the woman he had met, or sort of met as he did not even get her name.

He was so deep in thought that he did not hear Brian walking onto the terrace until he said, "I don't believe it, you're already up. I mean the way I feel I wouldn't have gotten up if it weren't for the fact that I had to run errands for my mom. Anyway, I thought that I was coming here to get you out of bed."

"To avoid that is enough incentive to get anyone out of bed early," said Aden facetiously.

"I don't know whether to be insulted or not. But it's good to see you're in a good mood. I know, your old man is still in Melbourne, isn't he?"

"That's why things are peaceful around here," said Aden, appearing relaxed.

"Are you two ever going to get along?"

"I doubt it. I'm sure you didn't come here to discuss that," replied Aden annoyed at the thought of it.

"Actually, I came to see if you would like to go with me to take care of a couple of things for my parents' party tonight."

"Can I offer you a cup of coffee and some Danish pastries Mr Brian?" asked Jane pleasantly.

"Yes please, they look delicious," said Brian as he chose a couple of them. "So, what about it Aden?"

"Sorry Brian. I have a few things to do myself," said Aden as he took another sip of his steaming coffee.

"I bet that it has something to do with that house of yours, doesn't it?" asked Brian.

"Yes, it does."

"I suppose I would be out there all of the time if I was having such a place built for myself," said Brian understandingly. "Ok. So, I'll see you tonight, and don't forget…7 o'clock."

"Don't worry. I'll be there."

After Brian left, Aden remained on the terrace for a while. There really was not anything pressing to be done for his house. Yet he felt a certain urge to go back. To go back to see her, to find out her name, or perhaps to prove to himself that she was no different from anybody else he had ever met. So he drove out there, walked over to the white villa next door, and knocked.

A minute later the door opened. She was a little surprised to see him there. "Oh! Hello…," she stopped to think for a moment. Then she looked at him with a smile and said, "Aden, right?"

"Yes, that's right."

She came across as a kind and gentle person as she said, "Come in. You have come to look at the leadlight windows?"

"Yes, I have," replied Aden feeling relieved that she did not make mention of him saying that he was going to be busy that day. "By the way I didn't get your name yesterday," he said as he entered the house.

"My name is Christina, Christina Ashton," she replied as she closed the door. Aden felt welcomed both by the invitation and also the look of her house. The entry foyer connected to a broad hallway that extended all the way to the terrace overlooking the ocean. On one side of the foyer there was an open curved staircase going up to the second floor. On the other side there was a corridor connecting to the yard and play area for the children which adjoined Aden's property. The hallway separated the formal living and dining room from the kitchen and the family room. All of the rooms had a light and airy feel to them as they faced the ocean, with the exception of the study that faced the front courtyard and was located behind the formal entertainment area. The use of well-placed lead lights throughout the house, along with color coordinated throw rugs, decorative pillows, and scented candles added color and fragrance while creating a warm and comfortable feel to the family room in contrast to the more elegant setting of the formal area.

"Why don't you take your time and look around?" she said hospitably. "I've got to go upstairs and take care of something."

"Is that where the bedrooms are?" asked Aden.

"Well, yes they are," said Christina thinking that it was an odd question to ask, but without thinking much about it, she went upstairs, leaving him behind to look around.

"Bedrooms upstairs, take my time, how unoriginal," Aden thought to himself. After a minute he started to walk up the stairs thinking, "I might as well get it done and over with."

As he got near the first bedroom, he heard Christina say, "Come and give me a big hug and a kiss."

"How predictable. No challenge at all. This is far too easy," thought Aden feeling rather disappointed. He started to unbutton his shirt. When he walked into the room, he was absolutely surprised with what he saw. There was Christina kneeling down on the floor hugging and kissing her little girl. Since her back was turned towards the door she did not see or notice Aden walk into the room.

"Who is that strange man Mommy?" asked the little girl.

Christina was startled with the thought of having a strange man in her room. She quickly turned around and was relieved to see that it was Aden. She laughed and said, "That's no strange man. That's Aden, and he is going to be our new neighbor."

Aden tried very hard not to show his surprise, but he was still rather puzzled when he looked at Christina and said, "What is that?"

"This is my daughter, Natalie," said Christina warmly.

Natalie was an adorable little girl who looked very much like her mother. She had big brown eyes, thick curly eye lashes, and shoulder length brown hair with a slight natural wave. "Hi," she said in a cute soft toned voice. She then turned to her mom and asked, "Can I go and play in my room now?"

"Sure sweetheart, go ahead," said Christina affectionately patting her on the head.

Aden who was still a bit baffled said, "Is she always like…that? Kissing and…hugging?" It was almost as if it was alien for him to see such love and affection.

"Yes, she is so sweet. She's such a joy to have around," replied Christina with a vibrant smile.

"Is she always home with you?" asked Aden curiously.

"Unfortunately, not anymore. Now that she's five she goes to school every day. Today she wasn't feeling very well. So, I had her stay home. But tomorrow it's back to school for her." As she walked out of the bedroom she said, "Let's go downstairs. I'll give you a tour of the house so you can see all of the stained-glass windows and doors and the quality of work that has gone into them."

"They certainly are very beautifully designed," said Aden still trying to come to terms with how things had turned out differently that he had anticipated. "Who was the designer?" he asked while thinking to himself that she was unlike anyone he had ever known.

"A very good local company. If you like I can give you their name and telephone number," said Christina.

"Yes, I'd like that."

Christina walked over to the cabinet to get the information for Aden. While quietly waiting he could not take his eyes off of her. She was tastefully dressed in a pair of Lauren jeans and a matching light blue Lauren T-shirt. He could not help but notice her shapely figure, her slender waistline and her beautiful silky and straight long brown hair draped over her shoulders. He was so involved in looking at her that he had almost forgotten what he was waiting for until Christina handed him a note and said, "Here's the name and telephone number."

"The telephone number…?" said Aden as he took the note from Christina trying not to show that it was not what he had been thinking about. "Oh yes, the telephone number." Then he looked at Christina with a smile, which was uncharacteristic of him and said, "Thank you for your help."

Christina smiled back at him and said, "You and your family must be very excited about your new house."

"It's only my father and I. I don't have any brothers or sisters, and my mother passed away a long time ago."

"I'm terribly sorry," said Christina in a truly sincere manner.

"That's all right. I never knew my mother. She died when I was very young."

"That must have been very difficult for your father to raise you single-handedly."

"Not really. In fact, I'd say it was quite easy for him since I was raised by a long line of British and American nannies."

"That explains why you don't have an Australian accent," said Christina. "But anyway…," she continued on always trying to put things in a positive perspective, "I'm sure you and your father are very excited about having a new house built for you."

"Actually, this is going to be my bachelor house," said Aden arrogantly, thinking how this would impress Christina.

"Oh, no!" was Christina's candid and automatic response much to his dismay.

"And what do you mean by that?" asked Aden sounding rather irritated by Christina's reaction.

"Well, I mean…, I mean this is a family, residential area with…children," said Christina trying very hard not to hurt his feelings.

"So, you think that I'm too 'wild' for this neighborhood," said Aden rather impatiently.

"I'm sorry," said Christina. "I was only thinking of the children. I didn't mean to offend you."

Aden so appreciated her sincerity and concern for his feelings that he could not feel upset about her response. He just smiled, letting her know that he understood.

Just then Natalie ran into the open and spacious family room where Christina and Aden were standing and talking and said, "Mommy is it time to pick up Timothy from school now?"

Christina looked at the clock, saw that it was 3:00pm and said, "Yes, it is."

"Who is Timothy?" asked Aden interested to know.

"He's my son, and he's seven years old," answered Christina.

"How many children do you have?" asked Aden finding all this unexpected.

"Just the two, even though at times it feels more like twenty," laughed Christina as she replied. She then put her arms around Natalie and said, "They are really wonderful children." She continued on and said, "Anyway I hope you'll find this lead light company suitable, and you'll be able to find the right designs for your house."

"I appreciate your help Christina," said Aden courteously. He then began to walk toward the front door, and as he was walking, he said, "I'll let you know how it works out."

"If you need any more information, just ask. We finished building this house a year ago. In the process I learned a lot about having a house built. So, if I can be of any help, just let me know," said Christina with warmth and sincerity.

Aden could not get his mind off of her while driving back to the estate. When he returned home it was time for his daily workout. Nearly everyday he spent around two hours to keep in shape and strong. That afternoon he found it very difficult to maintain his concentration. He especially had the hardest time during his self defense workout. Normally it was a way to vent out his anger. At times he was even too aggressive for his trainer, but that afternoon there was no aggression in him at all. He was intrigued by Christina and the encounter he had with her earlier in the afternoon. It was not at all what he had expected. He kept wondering how she seemed to be different from all of the other women that he had met, or was she really?

Aden was still preoccupied with all those thoughts when he arrived at Brian's house that evening. It was a spacious heritage house surrounded by a rather large yard that had been renovated by the Forbes family while still maintaining its original charm and character. The stately house had polished timber floors, high ceilings, ornate floral cornices, crystal chandeliers, and cream painted doors and windows contrasting with the mushroom-colored walls. It was furnished with fine leather chairs and sofas, solid oaken tables and rare antique lamps and furniture throughout. The spacious lounge and formal dining rooms together made for a large entertainment area which would comfortably accommodate about 100 guests. In the background a pianist was softly playing a medley of classical tunes, adding just the right touch of elegance to the party ambiance.

He was fashionably late, stylishly dressed and exuberantly arrogant, all the right ingredients for a high society party. Everyone was dressed in the latest fashions, talking and trying to catch up with all the current gossip. One of the hot topics of the night was, of course, Aden's ocean front bachelor house which only made him more of a center of attention. As a result, he barely had enough time to greet the Forbes and Brian before he found himself surrounded by essentially all the girls at the party, trying desperately to capture his attention and anxiously trying to find out more about his house.

Being the center of attention was a way of life for Aden, but that night he found he had no interest in it. He felt that he wanted to be left alone. After a while he stopped talking, excused himself, and to everyone's surprise, walked away. Brian quickly excused himself too and went after him.

"What's the matter Aden?"

"Nothing is the matter. I got tired of all the small talk. I just came out to get some fresh air, and I don't want to be quizzed about it."

"It's just that I have never seen you walk away like that, I mean, from so many good-looking girls who were only trying to impress you," said Brian with a puzzled look on his face.

"I do what I feel like, and I don't intend to explain myself," said Aden sounding rather irritated.

"Mate, I'm your closest friend," said Brian sensing that something might be wrong. "I only wanted to help you out."

"Nothing is wrong. And I don't need any help."

"Alright. I'll take your word for it," said Brian not wanting to upset Aden. "Anyway, I thought you'd be happy seeing how everybody is so interested and excited about your new house."

"That is, except her."

"Who?" asked Brian in surprise. "Who could possibly not be excited? I don't believe that. Show her to me," said Brian, looking around to see who she might be.

"She isn't here. It's Christina," said Aden reluctantly.

Brian guessed immediately who Christina might be. "So, that's her name. Well, what do you expect? You said it yourself yesterday, that she is emotionally dead, or something like that."

Aden knew then that what he had said was not true and got a chuckle out of having said it. He thought about it for a minute. Then he looked at Brian and said, "You're right. What does it matter what she thinks? All that matters is that we are going to have a great time there."

"Now you're talking!" said Brian as the two friends went back inside to join the party.

Chapter 9

"Hello Sean," said Christina as she gave him a kiss. "Did you have a good day at work?"

"The usual, it was hectic. A couple of unexpected problems which fortunately got resolved by the end of the day, a couple of meetings with prospective clients, and the list goes on," said Sean. His work was the main focus of his life. As a result, he often seemed preoccupied and came across as rather unfriendly, although if he chose, he could be quite charming. He was six feet tall, had light brown eyes and wavy blond hair that he kept short and combed back for a more professional look.

"Timothy! Daddy is home," said Natalie as the two of them ran excitedly to greet their father.

"Hi Timothy. How was school today?" asked Sean.

"It was good. I played basketball with my friends during recess and lunch break and that was fun!" Timothy with hazel eyes and light brown hair, resembled his father. He had a caring disposition more like Christina and took his role as a big brother seriously.

"And hello Natalie. What about you? Did you have a good day at home with your Mommy?"

"Yes, it was great fun. Guess what Daddy? There was this strange man in Mommy's bedroom, and I got to meet him. I liked him. He's very nice," said Natalie as she ran outside to play with Timothy.

Sean looked at Christina and said, "What is this about a strange man in your bedroom?"

"That was no strange man," said Christina as she laughed. "His name is Aden, and he is going to be our new neighbor. He had come over to look at our stained-glass windows and to find out where they were made."

"That's fine," said Sean without any trace of concern in his voice.

"No! It really isn't fine," said Christina. "You see he's a bachelor and I don't like the idea of having a bachelor living next door to us. This is going to be his bachelor house, not an ordinary family home."

"Anything on four prime blocks of land can hardly be called an ordinary home," said Sean. Then with a hint of envy he continued, "He sounds like a very lucky guy."

"Sean, I'm concerned about the children. I mean what if he has wild parties all of the time with all sorts of girls going in and out of his house? That is not something I'd want our children to see or to be exposed to," said Christina sternly.

"Come on Christina! You can't be protective of the children so much. They have to learn to live in the real world."

"You just don't care enough about our children," replied Christina, feeing a little disappointed by Sean's response.

"I do care, but I think differently than you do. Anyway, I don't want to get into that now. All I want is to have dinner early. I have a board meeting first thing tomorrow morning. So I have to work on my management report tonight to get it ready for the meeting," said Sean as he walked away.

The family had dinner early that night. The children ate quickly hoping to play with their father. "Daddy! Since we've finished our dinner early tonight, can you come out and play with us?" asked Timothy. "Please Daddy, please," also begged Natalie.

"Not tonight, I'm just too busy," answered Sean.

"But Daddy, last night you said you would play with us tonight."

"I said, not tonight," said Sean growing impatient. "No matter how much I do for you, you two always want more. I'm tired of you two asking more of me all of the time."

Christina, seeing the hurt look on the children's faces quickly went to the rescue and said, "You two always play so nicely with each other. Why don't you go out and play some more? Daddy has a lot of work to do for a very important meeting tomorrow morning. Perhaps he can play with you some other time. But now we must let him do his work."

"All right Mommy."

"Thank you for being so understanding," said Christina as she gave them both a kiss before they ran out to play. When she turned around Sean was also gone.

Later in the evening after the children had gone to sleep, Christina went to the study to talk to Sean. "I know you are busy and probably still have a lot more work to do, but I needed to talk to you about the children."

"What about the children? They seem quite fine to me. Besides I'm tired of having you talk to me about the children every time I turn around. Can't it wait until tomorrow?"

"No, it can't wait. I'm sure that you'll have something else to do then too. You always do. Anyway, what I have to say won't take very long." Christina then continued on as Sean reluctantly listened. "They are both such good children. All they want and need is for you to spend a little more time with them. It doesn't have to be very long. It could even be 5 or 10 minutes that would make them very happy, and it will still leave you plenty of time to do what you have to do. That is not asking a lot."

"That's easy for you to say since you're not under all of the pressure that I am. And it's never 5 or 10 minutes. That's not enough for them. It always ends up being longer than I can afford to spend," said Sean angrily.

"Even if you can't spend any time with them, you can at least be nice about it so you wouldn't hurt their feelings," said Christina appealing to his sense of compassion, "Perhaps you could be more like the way that I am when I talk to them."

"You be the way that you want to be, and I'll be the way I am. I have worked very hard to give you what you wanted, your dream home, your BMW, designer clothes for you and the children, all kinds of money for their classes and their toys. I have given you all that so that you would be happy and leave me alone to do what I want to do. Now stop hassling me and let me finish my report," said Sean. He then turned towards his desk and continued on with his work. He had said what he wanted and did not care to pursue the conversation further.

Christina felt a sense of despair as she walked out of the study. All she had wanted was for him to be kinder toward the children which she thought was not an unreasonable request. Instead, she got more angry arguments from him and not even the slightest willingness for him to consider her point of view. She felt such emptiness inside wondering how she could ever get him to understand her and that there were more important things in life than expensive homes and cars. They are nice to have, but they do not bring you happiness. Nor can they be a substitute for tender loving moments you can spend with each other or the kindness that you can show each other. After all, the way that you treat each other is the true basis for happiness. Even with all these thoughts going through her mind, Christina was able to manage to stay positive. As she started going up the stairs, she thought to herself that some day soon perhaps when Sean had less work and less stress that he would understand. Then he would be kinder and more willing to spend more time with the children.

Chapter 10

"Good morning Randall. Isn't it a beautiful Wednesday morning?" said Brian cheerfully. "I know it's early for Aden but seeing how nice it is and how much he likes sailing I thought I'd come over to get him to go sailing."

"Good morning, Sir," replied Randall, welcoming Brian with his courteous demeanor. "You probably won't believe this, but Master Aden isn't here. He was up early today. He made a few phone calls and left the mansion half an hour ago."

"What?! Before 11:00…in the morning?" exclaimed Brian with a shocked look on his face. "You're right. I don't believe it. Did he say where he was going or when he was coming back?" he asked in amazement.

"He said that he was going to be at the building site and that he should return by 3:30 this afternoon."

"Of course, his bachelor house again. Now I understand. Well, have him give me a call when he gets back."

Aden had not wasted any time. He had called the stained-glass company and made an appointment for 11:00 that morning. He was very anxious to find out what they had. After spending an hour looking at and discussing the various designs, he had gotten several books and brochures and was now on his way to his house.

On the way he thought about Christina. Once he got there he parked in front of his property. He grabbed the books and without looking at the work being done on his new house, he went directly to Christina's house. He was glad when she answered the door and was pleased to see her. As usual she looked very attractive in her casual clothes. Everyday she would wear a different outfit, and this time she was wearing a pair of light grey jeans and a white Polo T-shirt. She had her hair tied back which only accentuated her beautiful eyes more.

"Hello Christina. I had a chance to look into and stop by the company that you recommended," said Aden very casually. He then continued as if naturally she would be interested to know, "They gave me these books and brochures on stained glass designs."

"Hello Aden," replied Christina. Because of her kindly nature she invited him in despite her unhappiness about the bachelor house being built next door, "Come in please. Let's go to the family room."

The beauty of the family room was only enhanced by the use of a warm color scheme of antique pink, musk and copper which lent itself to creating not only a cheerful, but also a serene atmosphere. The L-shaped modular beige leather sofa with its matching chairs, cushions and throw rug provided a feeling of comfort. The beautiful flower arrangements of pale and dark roses with long green fern leaves on the coffee table and light pink carnations with baby's breath on the dining table made the room very welcoming. The large and wide glass windows extending down to within a foot of the floor and a set of French doors leading onto the terrace on the ocean side added to the openness of the room. On the side wall there was a fireplace. Above it was a well-placed stained-glass window depicting branches of pale pink and white magnolia flowers with darker pink buds surrounded by green leaves. The colors appeared vividly as the sun shone through the stained-glass window and softly brightened up the room.

"I thought you might have some recommendations about their designs," said Aden as he put the books down on the table.

Christina smiled and said, "That is such a personal thing. I wouldn't want to be responsible for a design that later you may find you don't like."

"On the other hand, if you don't help or make some suggestions, I might choose something too wild that you may not want right next door to you."

Aden's clever response made her smile and agree to help. "Alright, you've got me convinced. But before we get started perhaps, I can get you something to drink. What would you like?"

"Johnny Walker Black please."

"I meant more like a soft drink," said Christina as she was reaching for the glasses.

"Alright then, I'll have a light beer."

Christina laughed and said, "No, I mean a non-alcoholic drink."

Aden shrugged his shoulders and said, "You got me there. I don't usually have non-alcoholic drinks."

"Then why don't you have a tall glass of cool apple juice for something refreshing?"

"I guess that would be fine," said Aden with a puzzled look on his face. "Don't tell me that you don't have any alcoholic drinks."

"No, I don't," said Christina.

"Never?" asked Aden in surprise.

"Never. It doesn't make sense to drink something that is harmful to my body and makes me lose control of my mind and my actions."

"Come on. Everybody drinks," said Aden finding her response rather strange. Unable to relate to it he then asked, "How can you have fun without drinking?"

"That is some kind of fun that you can't even remember the next day," responded Christina frankly. "Tell me. How many times have you gotten up the next morning feeling lousy and not remembering what you did the night before? Not to mention that every time you drink it damages your liver, brain, and other cells in your body. So what fun is there in losing control and harming your body?"

Aden did not really know what to say at first for he had never considered those points before. Nobody had ever talked to or questioned him like that. Since she seemed to make sense and was sincere about it, he did not feel threatened or offended by it. After he thought about it for a minute all that he could say was, "I just drink socially."

"The problem with social drinking is that one drink can lead to another, and another, and before long you lose count and lose control," Christina pointed out. "I think that a better question is why do you need to drink at all? Can't you socialize without drinking? Is it that drinking helps you to do things that you normally don't have the courage to do, or is it that you are concerned that you won't be accepted by your friends unless you drink?"

"That is not the case at all." He appeared disturbed at the mere suggestion of such an idea. "It is just the opposite. I do what I want, and it's everybody else who wants to be my friend and be accepted by me," said Aden assertively.

"Then why not try going one night without drinking the next time you go out with your friends?" Christina challenged him.

"That's crazy," replied Aden.

"No, it isn't crazy. It's difficult."

"What's difficult about it?"

"It's difficult not to give in to social pressures. In fact, it is not giving in which determines how tough you are, and not how much you can drink."

"And you don't think I can spend one evening with my friends without drinking?" asked Aden, beginning to get over his initial surprise.

"I don't know," answered Christina thoughtfully.

"Well, I know! If I decide to, I can do anything," said Aden very conceitedly.

"Well, if you do, you'll be doing your body a service and giving yourself a chance to see what happens when someone else around you gets drunk and loses control. That will give you something to really think about," said Christina with a smile, as she finished pouring two glasses of apple juice. "Come on; let's sit down at the table."

Before she had a chance to take the glasses, Aden reached for them and said, "Allow me," in a gentlemanly manner. Then he waited for her to go to the table in the meals area of the family room before taking the glasses over. Looking out of the large window beside the table the view was magnificent with clear blue skies, shimmering deep blue water, sea gulls flying by, and a white sandy beach. It was all such a perfect background for the way he was feeling. As he sat across the table from Christina, he was thinking how wonderful it was to be there with her. He found himself enraptured by her, a feeling that he had never felt before. It was all intriguing to him. Even though he had only known her for two days he felt close to her and enjoyed being with and talking to her. He was fascinated by how unlike other women she was, not throwing herself at him or being obsequious of his every whim. It was as if she could see beyond the way he looked and his exorbitant designer clothes. This was something he had not experienced before. As a result, he did not even mind having his way of thinking and ideas challenged. In fact, he rather liked it. Aden's thoughts were interrupted as Christina looked at him with a smile and kiddingly said, "Well, aren't you going to try your drink? Don't worry, it won't kill you."

Aden smiled as he picked up his glass and took a sip. He swallowed it slowly as if he were expecting to choke on it and said, "How can anyone drink this stuff?" When he saw the surprised look on Christina's face, he laughed and said, "Actually, it's not that bad. I suppose that I could get used to it."

Christina laughed as she took a sip of her drink. She then looked at him and said, "Tell me Aden. What do you do?"

"What do I do with what?" asked Aden, honestly confused by the question. Conversations had always centered around who he was. What he did had never mattered before.

"I mean with your life. What do you do everyday?"

"Everyday I work out for a couple of hours, play sports, and then spend the rest of my time on dates and going to parties, clubs, restaurants, and things like that," said Aden proudly.

Contrary to his thinking Christina was not impressed. She smiled and said, "I was just wondering if you were doing any kind of studies."

"Studies?" asked Aden, still not understanding the purpose of this conversation.

"I guess that you would be too old for high school."

"Yes. Of course," Aden interjected defensively. "I finished high school three years ago."

"Then you are attending university?" asked Christina.

"No," said Aden.

"Are you working then?" she persisted.

"Of course not. I'm a Bradcliffe" retorted Aden proudly as he sat up even straighter and taller as he awaited her response. He was sure that now she would give him the respect that he deserved.

Not being familiar with Australian high society, Christina asked in her sincere and candid way, "What's a Bradcliffe?"

"That's my family name. The Bradcliffes are one of the oldest and wealthiest families in Australia," said Aden almost sounding snobbish about it, while feeling deflated from her less than revering response. Everyone knew of the Bradcliffes, he thought.

"I see," said Christina. "But what does that have anything to do with not working?"

"That has everything to do with it. My father was the only heir to my grandfather's fortune, who was by the way, the richest of the Bradcliffes. As a result, now my father runs and owns a major part of one of the largest and most diversified corporations in Australia," boasted Aden, still trying to gain her admiration.

"Your father obviously sounds very accomplished and successful. That's wonderful, but what does that have to do with you?"

Aden was somewhat taken aback with Christina's questions. They were things that he had never really thought about before. He quickly pulled his thoughts together and said, "It has to do with me because when I'm finished having fun, I can just take over from my father and run the family business."

"And how do you expect to do that without any background or business knowledge, university education, or experience?"

"That's easy. I'll just delegate everything to my executives. My father always says he has many qualified executives. They should be able to help me," said Aden as he leaned back in his chair thinking that it was a pretty good response.

Christina knew better. She knew that Aden had to be made aware of the cold reality of the situation, that it is not easy to take on such a huge responsibility. She hated to be so direct with him but saw no choice if she were to help him. "But how can you delegate responsibility when you don't know anything about running a corporation? For instance, do you even know what a balance sheet is or the difference between that and a profit and loss statement? Without such basic knowledge you wouldn't even know where the corporation stands, let alone what direction to take." She paused for a moment; Aden had gone quiet. She did not mean to discourage him, but rather guide him in the right direction. "And those executives would soon lose respect for you. But on the other hand, if you were educated, you would be able to confidently enter any decision-making process and offer new ideas and solutions based upon your pool of knowledge. Soon you'd gain their respect for being competent, not simply because you are a Bradcliffe."

Deep down Aden had not really considered, nor thought it possible for him to ever run the Bradcliffe Corporation based on his relationship with his father. Yet, he found himself somewhat drawn to the idea. With a questioning look on his face he gazed at the ocean and then turned to Christina and said, "They would do that? I mean, they would come to respect me, if I were educated and knowledgeable?"

"Yes, that's right. As Francis Bacon said in the sixteenth century 'Knowledge is power.' So, with knowledge and hard work you can achieve anything."

For the first time in his life Aden could begin to see a direction, and how a lack of any goal or purpose was what had made him frustrated with his life. Perhaps going to university was what he needed to make his life meaningful and challenging. But how could he? Remembering his father's comment that he could never be accepted into a university, he felt uneasy and anxious about it, but still maintaining his cool style he asked, "How do you get into a university?"

Christina's face brightened in pleasure upon hearing his question as she replied, "I'm not very familiar with the university system here in Australia, but from what I know, entry to university is based on your year 12 results. So, how were your results?"

"I don't know."

"How could you not know?"

Aden hated to admit it but saw no choice. "I vaguely remember taking those exams, but I couldn't tell you what exams I took or how I did. I guess too much drinking and too many wild nights."

"But shouldn't you have received the results in the mail?" asked Christina who was only trying to be helpful and not judgmental.

"Well, I don't remember receiving anything like that," said Aden with a concerned look on his face.

"Maybe it's somewhere at home, and you just need to look for it."

"Even if I could find it, what would be the point if they aren't high enough? Then what will I do?"

"You shouldn't be negative about it. Anyway, it all depends on what you want to study."

"What would be best for me to study if I were to run the Bradcliffe Corporation?"

"I would say business administration or a combination of business and law," said Christina. "In fact, if that's what you are interested in, you might want to look at a few issues of something like Business Week magazine to get a feel about what is happening in the business and corporate world. How does that sound to you?"

"That sounds alright," said Aden with guarded enthusiasm.

"Great! I'll get you a couple of recent issues from the study." Being so involved with talking neither of them had noticed the time. When Christina went to get the magazines, she was surprised to see what time it was. "Oh! It's past 2:30!"

Aden was also amazed how quickly time had passed by. "And now it's time for you to pick up your children from school. Isn't it?"

"Yes. It is," said Christina as she busily looked for the magazines. "Sean must have put all those magazines somewhere else. I'll have to look for them later and give them to you next time you come by."

Aden liked the idea. This way he did not need an excuse to come back. "There's no rush. That'll be fine."

Christina then noticed the books about stained glass windows. "Oh, I'm sorry that we didn't get to look at those books today."

"That's alright. I know you're in a hurry. There's still plenty of time before I have to make any final decisions."

"Are you sure?"

"Yes, I am," said Aden as he gave her a long look thinking how he wished he did not have to leave her. But it was time. "Thanks for the drink."

"You're welcome," replied Christina with a smile.

After he left Christina, he could not get over the conversation he had had with her, or her genuine interest in helping him. He felt a sense of guarded optimism and enthusiasm towards his life which was quite uncommon for him. With so many new thoughts and ideas racing through his mind he got into his car and drove back to the mansion.

Chapter 11

Christina was feeling good that she had been able to show Aden a new way of thinking and a new attitude towards life. Later that evening when Sean arrived home from work, she was still in a good mood and it showed. She had a smile on her face; her eyes looked brighter; and there was a sense of energy in her voice.

"You seem to be in a good mood this evening Christina."

"That's because of a conversation I had with Aden today."

"Why? Did you get him to stop moving in next door?" asked Sean jokingly.

"I'm serious Sean," said Christina earnestly.

"Then what happened between last night when you were so concerned and upset and now?"

"You know that I always have believed that there is a reason beyond our understanding for the way that things happen in life. Here is Aden who seems to be from a very wealthy family…"

Sean interrupted in his sarcastic way, "That doesn't require any analytical thinking considering what he's having built. Even a blind man could see that his father is very rich. But what does that have anything to do with what we were talking about?"

"His father, just like so many rich and successful fathers, has no time for Aden. Nor has he spent any time with him in the past. Just look how you are too busy to play with the children."

"Can't you even once talk about something without commenting about me? Here you are talking about Aden. What does it have to do with me?"

Christina did not intend to criticize him, "I was only trying to point out how often parents come up with rationales to use their busy lives as justification for why they can't spend time with their children," she clarified. "They overlook the fact that more than anything else in the world children need to have their parents to spend time with them, to give them love, and to guide them in the right direction." She then continued on enthusiastically, "In the case of Aden, since his mother died when he was very young, he seems not to have anybody to give him any of that. He tries not to show it, but I believe even at his age he needs someone to guide him or at least challenge his ideas and show him that there are better alternatives to his way of thinking."

"Not again Christina, you and your ideas on fate and destiny," said Sean facetiously. "So, you think that somehow fate has brought this person next door so that you can guide him in the right direction? You know what I think? I think that it's ridiculous."

But Christina was genuine about it. "I feel that I can help him. I can perhaps show him how to accomplish things and make positive contributions in life."

Sean did not share Christina's point of view, "What makes you think that he needs any help at all? He's so rich and seems to have everything he could possibly want. So, what is there for you to show him?"

"Don't you see?" explained Christina, "his family's wealth has nothing to do with him or his sense of achievement. He hasn't even done anything since he finished high school three years ago. So, I talked to him about going to the university. I pointed out to him the value of getting a higher education. Seeing his reaction and his positive response made me realize that perhaps it was what he needed, and that made me feel good."

"He doesn't need a university education. His father can get him any job that he wants. His father can probably even buy him any university that he wants."

"All you talk about is what his father can do. But what about him and his personal growth and aspirations?"

"Actually, I don't really care. I don't even care to continue this conversation. I just don't see any point in you trying to help a rich arrogant kid. If he needs help, let his father get him counselors, advisors, shrinks, or whatever," said Sean becoming a bit annoyed at the whole conversation.

"What about caring for and helping people? Helping just for the sake of helping and without getting paid or having ulterior motives?" asked Christina sincerely.

"All I know is that I have already spent more time discussing this topic than I want to. I also know that you'll just be wasting your time. But it's your time. You can do whatever you want with it as long as you leave me out of it so that I can do what really needs to be done, which is to end this pointless conversation and get started on my work."

Before Christina had a chance to say anything more, the children who had been playing together outside came in to talk with their father.

"Daddy! Daddy! Can you come and play with us now?" asked Natalie and Timothy.

"No. I can't. I have a lot of work to do tonight."

"But that was what you said last night," said Timothy sounding rather disappointed.

"Perhaps next week. I should have less work to do then."

"This Friday is our last day of school," Timothy said excitedly. "Maybe this weekend we can go to a park and have a picnic? We haven't done that for a while. It will be a lot of fun."

"Yes Daddy, it will be a lot of fun. Can we go? Please?" asked Natalie jumping up and down delighted with the thought.

Having had the conversation with Christina on how some fathers get too involved with their work and do not spend enough time with their children and seeing the look on her face as well as the faces of the children, Sean knew that he had no choice but to agree. "Not this weekend," he said, "I have a conference to attend. Maybe we can do something this Monday. No, better make that Tuesday."

The children were excited which made Christina happy too. "Awesome," said Timothy. "We can't wait," cried Natalie as they went outside to play.

Chapter 12

For the first time in his life, Aden found himself questioning his actions as a result of his conversation with Christina earlier. He began to wonder, *Could I really be wasting my life by not having any goals or direction? Should I be doing something other than what I have been doing?* After all, he had everything he wanted, or did he?

Questions such as these were going through his mind as he sat on the terrace overlooking the peaceful and beautiful gardens below and the open grassy area beyond. It was a perfect setting for him to think. The more he thought, the more he was coming to the realization that he wanted more out of life. Now he wanted to make a difference in the world, and to be remembered for something other than being the son of wealthy John Bradcliffe. But how…?

"I'm terribly sorry Master Aden," said Randall apologetically with phone in hand. "I know that you didn't want to be disturbed, but Master Brian is insisting that it is most important for him to speak with you."

"Everything is always important for Brian." Aden paused for a moment thinking that it was going to take longer to resolve these issues, agreed to talk to him. He then took the phone. "What's up Brian? What's so important that couldn't wait until tonight?"

"I just wanted to let you know that everything is set for tonight."

"Ok," said Aden very casually.

"Is that all that you're going to say? Considering that you have a date with Melanie, the newest fashion model in Australia, and how she is smokin' hot! Any of this ringing bells?"

Aden was still preoccupied, that even the thought of going out with yet another sex symbol could not pique his interest. "Every girl that I take out is hot. So what?"

"Haven't you heard what happened last week when Melanie went out with your cousin James…?"

Aden abruptly interrupted. "That idiot James!? And if you think I'm going to take her out after having gone out with him, then think again."

"Where have you been mate? It's all over Adelaide. She only went out with him to find out more about you, and evidently all night long she only talked about you. James is still seething about it, and Melanie can't wait to see you tonight. Does that interest you?"

"Just enough not to cancel the date."

Having known Aden for as long as he had, Brian knew that there was no use in trying to change his mindset, even though Aden's lack of interest made no sense to him. He figured that once the evening got started, they would all have a great time. "I have arranged for two limos to pick everybody up. So, what time would you like to be picked up?"

"No need for that. I'm driving tonight" replied Aden.

"That's too risky Aden. You really shouldn't drive."

"I don't need to be told what to do. I'll see you around 8."

That was just too egocentric, even for Aden, thought Brian. *The past couple of days he has been acting differently. I wonder what's up with him? Maybe I'll find out tonight.*

When Aden arrived at the restaurant, everybody was already there waiting for him. As always he was fashionably late. Brian immediately introduced Melanie to him. She was so captured by him that she could hardly speak. Aden, showing no particular interest in her nor in any small talk just quickly said hello to her and everybody else before walking over to the reception desk. When the manager saw Aden, he obsequiously made his way to the desk to greet him personally. "Good evening Mr Bradcliffe. It is a pleasure to have you and your friends here tonight. I have arranged for you to be taken care of. So how is that busy father of yours?"

"He's fine. What table do you have ready for us?" asked Aden as he casually looked down at the reservation book. Suddenly, something next to the book caught his attention. It was a Business Week magazine.

"As always we have our best table prepared for you."

Aden's thoughts were only focused on the magazine and he was oblivious to what the manager was saying. He just looked at him and asked, "How much?"

"How much for the table?" asked the manager completely confused by his question.

"No. Not the table…the magazine next to your reservation book."

"Oh, the Business Week magazine," said the manager with a sigh of relief. He picked up the magazine and courteously handed it to Aden. "Please, you may have it with our compliments."

Aden accepted his offer gladly, and with a content look on his face said, "Thanks. We are ready to be seated."

At the table Melanie was extremely friendly and bubbly toward Aden. But he was more interested in the magazine than her, so much so that he was beginning to get annoyed by her. The situation was saved by the waitress, who recognizing Aden, gave him a big smile as she asked for everyone's drink order.

When it was Aden's turn, as if it were an automatic response for him, he said, "Black Label on the…" He stopped in the middle of his order. He suddenly remembered Christina's challenge. He thought about it for a minute and to everyone's surprise he said. "Mineral water, please."

"And Black Label on the side?"

"No. Just mineral water will do," said Aden firmly.

Hearing Aden's response, suddenly an uneasy silence overcame all of his friends seated at the table. After all Aden had always been the heaviest drinker among them. Brian broke the silence. "Aden, why don't you ride back in the limo with us?"

"No, I want to drive myself tonight," replied Aden, who was actually enjoying his friends' reaction. As if there was nothing unusual, he continued on with the small talk and the jokes, and everybody got back into the swing of the evening. As the night went on everybody continued on with the drinking and revelry. Aden could see them getting drunk and found himself having less and less interest in wanting to be there. With all those thoughts about life and the future on his mind, he tried a few times to have a meaningful conversation with Melanie but could not. It got to the point that he just could not take another minute of sitting there. To maintain his cool, he thought that it was best to go out for a few minutes.

Brian quickly went after him. "What's up Aden?"

"Nothing. I just wanted to get some fresh air."

"You don't fool me with that answer. I know you too well there's something bothering you. Just tell me."

"Ok I just don't like talking to air-heads. Every time I said something to her, it echoed back."

"Since when do you care how intelligent a girl is? All you want to do is sleep with her."

"Don't tell me what I want!" replied Aden angrily, taking out his frustrations on Brian for not understanding him. Deep down he could not really blame him. It was all new to him, too.

"Sorry Aden. I was just trying to help you have a good time. It's just that recently you seem…well…you seem not to be having fun like you used to," said Brian hesitantly, not wanting to spark any more anger from his friend. He paused for a moment. Aden was still calm. So, in a final attempt to find out what was wrong he asked, "Is your old man back in town? Is he giving you some grief?"

"No. My father's coming back tomorrow. I'm not in any kind of trouble, and I have fun the way that I choose to," retorted Aden emphatically.

Brian realized that it was best to drop the subject since he was not getting anywhere and seemed to be upsetting Aden even more. "Why don't we forget about all this? Let's go back inside and have some fun."

Aden took a quick look at his friends at the table. A strange feeling came over him. For the first time in his life, he felt that he had no interest in being part of that. He looked at Brian and said, "I don't think so. I'll take care of the check and leave."

Brian could not believe it. "You can't be serious. It's not even 10 o'clock yet."

"I'm dead serious."

In a desperate attempt to keep Aden from leaving, Brian said, "If you want someone intellectual, just say so. You don't have to leave. There are lots of girls who are intelligent. Just name one and she'll be running after you. They all do!"

Aden chuckled at Brian's simplistic view. "I actually do have a couple of things that I must take care of. Catch you later," said Aden as he walked back inside. Brian stood out there for a minute in a state of disbelief, and then he followed Aden inside mumbling to himself, "I wish it wasn't so impossible to change his mind."

Aden briskly walked to the table to get his magazine and to say a quick goodbye to everyone. Naturally, all of his friends were shocked. They all wanted to know why he was leaving, and whether there was something wrong. They knew that it would not be the same without him. Aden in his usual aloof style just simply replied that he had to take care of something important. He looked at Melanie and said, "Brian will look after you." Then without any delay he walked to the front desk, took care of the check, and left.

It was a beautiful, warm summer night. The stars suddenly appeared even more brilliant against the dark clear sky. With a sense of gratification, he got into his Lamborghini supercar and drove off. After all he had just done what he told Christina that he could do. He had always done things that were different, but nothing like this and nothing that felt so good. He felt in control which made him realize more fully that it was exactly what he needed to do with his life, to take charge, to make something of himself, so that he could make a difference to his family and society. These thoughts of having goals and purpose in life were actually exhilarating to him far more than anything that he had experienced in the past.

Aden's mind was so preoccupied with all these thoughts that he did not notice the flashing police lights and the police officers signaling him to pull over, until he was nearly past them.

"I've just hit the Jack Pot!" said the officer-in-charge to his partner. "It's a pot-of-gold with the license plate 'AB'. This is going to get me that promotion that I have been wanting. Do you know how long I've been waiting for this moment? Now I finally got him!"

Aden slammed on his brakes as quickly as he could. His car came to a sudden stop.

"This is better than I thought," said the officer thinking that Aden must really be drunk to have stopped in that manner. He was quite haughty as he walked to the car, Breathalyzer in hand. "Good evening Mr Aden Bradcliffe. Isn't this a great evening?"

"I certainly wasn't expecting such a warm and personal reception. I didn't realize that I was that well known among police officers," said Aden in a cool and controlling kind of voice.

"And you are going to become even more well known before this night is over," said the officer with a 'gotcha' kind of smile on his face. "Let's see how you test out." When it was time, the officer confidently took the instrument away to record the reading. Aden, knowing what the outcome would be, just sat back, relaxed, and patiently waited to see the officer's reaction. As he looked at the instrument, his jaw literally dropped. His smug smile quickly disappeared. As if he had just seen a ghost, he looked shocked. "What?! No alcohol. That's impossible! This must be broken," he exclaimed as he shook the instrument in disbelief. He cracked a smile to cover up his shocked reaction and said, "You just stay here. I'll be right back."

The officer very quickly walked over to his patrol car and grabbed another instrument. "Let's try it again, and no funny business this time."

Aden very calmly blew into the Breathalyzer again. The officer got the same shocked look again, except this time he was too furious to force a smile. "I'll be right back." He asked his partner for his instrument. "Why? Is he so drunk that he broke yours?" he replied jokingly. But when he saw how serious his friend was, he said, "All right, I'll test him with my instrument." They walked over to Aden's car. "Would you please blow into this Breathalyzer?" After reading the result, both officers stood there staring at the instrument in disbelief.

"I hate to break up the party officers. I know that it's been fun, but if you don't have any more instruments for me to test, I'll be off."

Both officers nodded their heads.

"Thank you. And by the way, it is a great evening," said Aden with a smile as he drove away.

Aden could not believe how wonderful it felt experiencing this new sense of freedom, the freedom to drive anytime and anywhere, simply by not drinking. As he turned up the volume on his sound system, he really could feel how great the evening was.

Chapter 13

"It sure is peaceful and quiet with Mr. Bradcliffe away and Master Aden out for the evening," said Jane, sipping her tea as she sat comfortably in the spacious staff sitting room which was located next to the kitchen.

"When they are both home, they sure make up for it. You know, I've been with this family for as long as I can remember, and nothing would please me more than seeing this father and son patch things up…become friends," sighed Randall, as he picked up his cup and made himself comfortable in his armchair. "But for now, I do agree with you. I might as well enjoy all this serenity and silence while it lasts."

Suddenly, the peace and quiet was broken by sounds coming from the foyer of the mansion. They both looked at each other in surprise. "Who could that be? It can't be Master Aden?" wondered Randall as he carefully checked the time on his pocket watch. "It's only 10 o'clock. Perhaps…he forgot something." He paused. Then with a worried look on his face he said, "You don't suppose he is in some sort of trouble? That would explain why he has been acting differently these past couple of days. I'd better go and find out." As he approached the family room, he saw Aden sitting and reading. "Good evening Master Aden."

"Ah! You are still up Randall. Shouldn't you be asleep?" asked Aden as he quickly closed the magazine and casually put it down beside him so Randall could not see it.

"It's only 10 o'clock sir. Excuse me for asking, but isn't this too early for you to be back? Is everything alright?"

"Absolutely," replied Aden calmly.

Aden's calm demeanor was so unusual and unexpected for Randall that he could not think of anything else to say. So, he started to walk away. Then he realized that he had forgotten to tell Aden about his messages. "Sir, would you like to see your messages? There is a pile of them."

"No, thanks."

"Is there anything that I can do or get for you, sir?" asked Randall in his accommodating manner.

"I'm going to go up to my room now. Just see to it that I am not disturbed."

"Of course, sir."

"Then I'll see you in the morning. One more thing, ask Jane to have my breakfast ready at 7:30."

Randall courteously agreed to take care of Aden's request. He then returned to the sitting room. He appeared concerned and baffled as he looked at Jane and said, "There is definitely something wrong. Master Aden is home to stay, does not want to be disturbed, wants breakfast at 7:30, and is reading! I'm really worried about him."

"Thank goodness Mr Bradcliffe is returning home tomorrow. He can sort out whatever trouble Master Aden is in before it gets too out of hand," replied Jane.

Once in his room Aden was content. All he wanted to do was to read his magazine so that he would have some intelligent topics to talk about with Christina. He stayed up and read the entire magazine. He found himself enjoying it all, even though there was a lot that he did not quite understand. He thought it best to get some rest since he wanted to get up early the next morning.

His mind was racing with thoughts of Christina, what he had read, how he liked being intellectually stimulated, and his new attitude towards life. After a couple hours of tossing and turning, he gave up.

He sat up in his bed thinking about how badly he wanted to be able to get into a university. He got out of bed even though it was only 5 o'clock in the morning. He had to find his year 12 results. He looked everywhere, inside every drawer, box, and cabinet in his room. By the time he got through, his room looked like it had been hit by a tornado. Yet, the results were nowhere to be found. Now he was even more determined to find them. As he sat back in the midst of the huge mess in his room, he thought of checking with his old school, but he had to wait for the offices to open.

So, he did his workout, showered and was ready by 7:30 for his breakfast. He was a man on a mission.

Neither Randall nor Jane could believe their eyes. After breakfast Aden called his old school, but unfortunately, they did not have his test results. They referred him to the State Education Department.

There was no time to waste. He decided to go down to the department right away. The staff there could not be more helpful. They either recognized him from his pictures in the newspapers and magazines, or naturally liked him because of his good looks. Before long they had worked out that the person that he needed to see was Kate. Since she was away for the day at a workshop, her supervisor offered to have Kate call him first thing tomorrow morning. Aden did not want her calling his home, so he left his cell phone number for her to call him directly.

After he left the department, an unsettling feeling came over him with the thought of having to wait for another day to find out his results. *What if I hadn't successfully completed them or the results were not high enough,* Aden wondered. He had never been one to doubt himself, but it seemed never having had his father's approval had an effect on him, making him question himself. But he was too close to the end now, he thought. So, he decided to put all feelings of doubt out of his mind for the moment.

As he got into his car, the only thought on his mind was driving to his house. There was a strong desire within him to see Christina. He had been looking forward to seeing her since yesterday afternoon. As he got closer to his house, he found himself feeling a bit anxious at the thought of seeing her, a feeling that he had never before experienced. He wanted to understand what was causing him to feel the way he did.

Chapter 14

After he parked and got out of his car he was met and greeted by the building supervisor. Aden answered his questions while checking the construction progress. When he found it to be satisfactory, he turned off his cell phone and went over to see Christina. Even though he had only known Christina for four days, he felt so close to her that he was comfortable talking to her about anything.

"Good morning Christina," said Aden warmly as he walked in.

"You mean good afternoon, since it's past noon," said Christina with a welcoming smile.

"So, it is. That goes to show how busy I've been all morning," said Aden as he made himself comfortable on the sofa in the family room. "I tried to find my test results, but it will have to be tomorrow. The person in charge of records at the Education Department is out of the office today." He paused for a moment and then continued, "After our conversation yesterday I began to think and decided to consider going to university and doing something more with my life." Then emphatically he said, "I want to make a difference."

Christina sat down across the coffee table from Aden. Her smile showed how pleased she was to hear that. As she looked at Aden, she sensed that there was something more on his mind, and she was right.

Aden, a little less sure of himself, continued, "What if I didn't pass all of the tests, or my results aren't high enough? What if my father was right in saying that I could never get into a university?"

"With such high goals in mind," replied Christina in a reassuring manner, "this is no time to have doubts about yourself."

"My father never believed in me…"

Christina interrupted him, "In life you must believe in yourself, and through that, others will come to believe in you." Then in her naturally supportive and positive perspective she continued, "Everybody is unique. You have your own spiritual strengths and abilities, and that is what makes you unique and capable of achieving things that others cannot. That's why it doesn't matter whether others believe in you or what your results are. Using your own abilities and through determination and perseverance you will be able to reach your goals, no matter how unattainable they may seem."

Aden appreciated her positive and caring response. He found himself uplifted and ready to face anything, no more doubts. Finally, with a smile, he looked at Christina and said, "You know, I won our bet."

"I'm not quite sure what bet you're talking about?"

"You didn't think that I could go out with my friends and not drink."

"I didn't make such a bet. I was just saying…," she stopped. The impact of what Aden had said just hit her. "You really didn't drink?" asked Christina as her big brown eyes lit up as if she had just heard the best news of her life.

"No, I didn't. And, it felt good."

"Well, that calls for a celebration, and I know just the thing for that, a glass of apple juice."

While Christina was getting the drinks, Aden walked to the window. He was feeling content and happy to be there. As he looked at the magnificent view of the shimmering ocean and sail boats slowly drifting across, he wondered what these emotions were that he was feeling. Just then he heard a love song being played in the background. While still looking out the window he said, "I don't get it, why all this preoccupation with love?"

Christina walking back to the family room, lightheartedly replied, "I take it that you don't approve of it."

"I can't really approve or disapprove of it, when I don't really know what it is."

Christina was somewhat surprised with his response. She wasn't being judgmental, but to clarify it she asked, "You really don't know?"

"No," replied Aden. It was the first time in his life that he was experiencing such feelings that were growing stronger every day. To work out what they were, he turned around and looked at Christina and said, "Perhaps you can tell me what you think it is."

Christina was not expecting such a question and found herself lost for words. "That is probably one of the hardest topics to talk about. Throughout the ages there has been so much said and written about it, and yet, it still remains elusive. I don't see what I could possibly add to all that."

"Your thoughts," said Aden. "Do you think love is what they show in the movies and on television, that you are in love one day and out-of-love the next? Or do you think love is what every girl I have taken out has told me at one time or another, without knowing anything about me?"

Christina was not one to share her personal thoughts, but when she saw how it might help Aden, she agreed. She handed him his glass of apple juice. "Let's go sit down as I think about it." A minute or so later she figured out what to say.

"Love is the most powerful force in the universe," said Christina as she looked at him with her dazzling eyes. "It is what fulfills our lives." Then with her gentle voice she continued, "Love is a rainbow of many beautiful emotions growing stronger and deeper until true love is reached. Not everyone experiences true love for it depends upon the intensity and purity of feelings. It can begin with merely a simple attraction. You will know when you are in love as suddenly everything in life is more beautiful. You feel a new sense of energy. All you want and desire is to be with her and to get to know her, and you accept her and everything about her without question. When you are together, hours seem like minutes, but when you are apart minutes seem like hours. If your love grows deeper, you will feel the compassionate love where her joy is your joy, and her sorrow is your sorrow. Then comes the unselfish love where you put her happiness before yours. If your love grows deeper still, to the point where your souls merge into one, then you will have found true love. It lasts for an eternity, and it is pure ecstasy when you are together." Christina paused, smiled and said, "I probably said more than you wanted to hear. Did it somehow answer your question?"

Aden was captivated by Christina. He had enjoyed listening to her and learning about her ideas. His deep thoughts were broken by Christina's question, to which he replied, "Yes, it did clarify a lot of things."

Christina was pleased. She then thought of how else to help him, "In fact, you need to be careful," she said caringly.

"I'm not quite sure what you mean by that."

"Many girls would say or do anything they can think of to get you to marry them. But, you need to make sure that the one that you fall in love with and choose to marry is someone who really loves you, for who you are inside, and not for what you own and what family you are from."

Aden had never experienced such a genuine display of concern for him and his future by anyone. "Thanks, but I believe it'll be a long while before I'll have to worry about that," he said matter-of-factly, since the only one he had ever had real feelings toward was Christina.

Having made her point, Christina thought that perhaps it was a good time to move onto another topic. "How is the work on your house coming along?"

"Pretty good. They're almost finished with the foundation work. In fact, I must go and check a few things since tomorrow they will begin pouring the concrete for the foundation." Aden would have liked to stay and continue talking with Christina, but it was time to go.

After he was done, with so much on his mind, he felt a need to go somewhere where he could think without being disturbed. He drove to the top of Mount Lofty, one of his favorite lookout points where out in the distance the panoramic view of the city could be seen. It was all quiet and peaceful as if it were an oil painting on canvas, with toy sized skyscrapers all nestled inside the square mile of parklands and miniature sized houses and buildings beyond separated by match sized streets and avenues extending to the powder blue ocean.

As he leaned against his car looking at the picturesque view below, he found himself, as Christina had said, with a new sense of energy, strength, and determination to go after what he wanted. The more he thought about it, the more clear it became. In his personal life he simply wanted to be with Christina. It did not matter that he could not have her. All that he wanted was to see her and to talk with her. To achieve his professional goals, he wanted to first get into the university. He wondered what he would do if his grades were not high enough. He decided that he would do anything, even repeat year 12, as undesirable as that would be.

To have come to these clear pathways made him feel good. He was not about to overanalyze the distant future, nor was he going to let the uncertainties surrounding his decisions stop him from achieving his goals.

Chapter 15

It was six in the evening when John Bradcliffe arrived back. He was greeted by Edmund, the family chauffeur, who was waiting for him by the limousine just outside of the domestic terminal at the Adelaide International Airport. He immediately took his bag and opened the door for him. "Welcome back. I trust you had a good trip sir."

"Yes thanks, very hectic as always. I'm looking forward to a couple hours of quiet time at home before my next meeting this evening," said John as he got into the limousine. The ride from the airport usually provided him additional time to get more work done. By the time they were near the mansion he had completed reviewing the financial reports and the proposal submitted by one of his suppliers that were to be discussed during his evening meeting. He decided to stop, relax, and enjoy the remaining few minutes of the drive. His peaceful ride ended abruptly when he saw a group of girls waiting outside the mansion walls as the gates opened to allow entry of his limousine.

By the time the limousine reached the main entrance doors of the Bradcliffe mansion, Randall and Jane had made their way to greet and welcome him. "Good evening sir. Welcome home." They were happy and relieved to have him back.

John was anything but happy. "I'll tell you if it's a good evening after I talk with Aden. Get him right away. I want to see him now," said John with a firm and demanding tone of voice as he walked briskly into the mansion.

"I'm sorry sir, but Master Aden isn't home now," replied Randall as he and Jane followed closely behind him.

"That figures. He's never around when he needs to be. Then would you kindly tell me why in the world he has all of these girls waiting outside of the gates? It's bad enough that he has girls inside the mansion, but now, outside too? That's unacceptable. I'm not going to let him turn this mansion into a circus."

"Yes sir, I realize that," agreed Randall, "but it was Master Aden's strict orders not to let the girls in the mansion. He doesn't want to see any of them."

"What? For a moment I thought that you just said Aden doesn't want to see any girls?"

"That is correct sir. He doesn't want to see them or any of their messages."

"Why messages? What happened to his cell phone?" asked John trying to make sense of what he was hearing.

"Well sir, evidently Master Aden has been turning off his phone and not answering messages at all during the past few days."

"That's impossible. He is constantly on his cell phone. I don't understand. What has he been doing?"

"I'm not quite sure sir. All that I know is that he hasn't been with Brian since he has been calling daily looking for him. Also, he has been getting up and leaving the mansion rather early," replied Randall.

"How early do you mean? Before noon?" asked John with his eyes opened wide and eyebrows raised in obvious amazement.

"No sir, I mean before 8. It was even earlier this morning."

Jane could no longer contain herself and interjected, "That is not all sir. This morning Master Aden left his room in a big mess with everything thrown out of drawers and cabinets as if he was looking for something."

By this time John's disbelief had turned into concern mixed with anger. "I really thought I could leave him for a few days without him getting into trouble, but obviously I was wrong. Now I won't even get to talk to him to find out what trouble he is in until late tonight."

"Actually, Master Aden has been coming home early. So, you may not have to wait…," Randall stopped. He thought that he may have heard Aden's car. He was right.

A minute later Aden walked in. Empowered by the decisions he had made earlier, he appeared in a good mood. Quickly it became obvious to him that such a feeling was not shared by anyone else at the mansion as he was confronted by his father's unfriendly glare and Randall and Jane's concerned looks.

"Hello Dad. You 're back early," said Aden, still maintaining his positive posture.

"Hello Aden. Yes, I finished earlier than I had anticipated. So, I caught the earlier flight back."

"Will you be having dinner before your meeting sir?" asked Randall.

"Yes, I will be."

"And what about you Master Aden, will you be having dinner at home?"

"Yes, Randall."

"Very well, Jane and I will have dinner ready shortly." They then left the father and son to talk.

"Tell me Aden, are all of the restaurants closed tonight?"

"It's nice to be having dinner with you, too, Dad," Aden remarked sarcastically.

"Just because for once you decided to have dinner at home, you want me to be overjoyed?"

"No, I just want to feel welcomed."

"Let's cut to the chase Aden. Tell me what trouble you're in. I'll get my checkbook, buy your way out of it, and then things will be back to normal until you get in trouble again."

"I'm not in any trouble!" Aden was outraged. For the first time in his life he had not done anything wrong. In fact, the opposite was true. He had thought that this should please his father. Instead, he was upset with him, as usual.

"Then how do you explain not wanting to see these girls, not wanting to talk with them, and having your cell phone switched off?" asked John, demanding to know.

"My phone hasn't been off much," said Aden as he took his phone to show his father in his defense. "Ah, I forgot to turn it back on."

Just then Randall walked in. "Sorry for interrupting, but someone called Kate is insisting that she needs to talk with you. She has been trying to call you, but your phone has been off. She said that it is very important and that if I tell you her name and something about…test results, you would definitely want to talk with her. So, what would you like me to do?"

This was very awkward for Aden. That was the last thing that he wanted his father to hear. Now it would almost be impossible for his father to believe that he was really not in any kind of trouble. With Randall waiting, and his father looking on wondering what this was all about, he did not see any way out of it. "Alright, I'll take the call."

As anxious as he was to find out about his test results, Aden knew that he had to be discrete and brief. He did not think that his father would understand. "Hi Kate."

"Hello Aden. I'm sure glad that I was able to get hold of you. Listen, I was just calling about your test results, and…" She got cut off by Aden who was determined to keep it short.

"That's really good. I'll come by first thing in the morning. See you then." Aden hung up and casually handed the phone back to Randall. "Thanks. When is dinner? I'm starved."

"The main course will be ready in ten minutes," said Randall as he attentively took the phone, "but if you would like sir, I can serve the soup immediately."

John and Aden, without saying another word to each other, walked over to the large and elegant dining room and sat down. Then John suspiciously looking at Aden, took the linen napkin, carefully unfolded it, placed it on his lap, and said, "Who is Kate, and what is this all about?"

"I don't know her personally. I know of her, but I haven't met her yet. So, I can't tell you much about her," said Aden, truthfully.

"You expect me to believe that? A girl that you haven't met calls and says it is important for her to talk to you, and you immediately take the call, when all week you have refused to talk to any of your friends. So, I ask you again, what kind of trouble are you in? Have you gotten her pregnant and that is what these test results are about? Is she using that to get you to do what she wants, and is that why you have stopped seeing all of these girls? Tell me so that I can help you," said John in complete frustration.

"No, it's none of that."

"What is it then?" asked John now with an extremely worried look on his face. "Is it drugs?"

"No, I would never do drugs," replied Aden firmly.

"Then, what is it?" asked John sternly.

Silence filled the dining room. Aden was thinking and wondering what to tell his father. Not knowing his test results, he did not feel comfortable telling his father the truth. On the other hand, he did not want his father to continue being upset with him over these crazy speculations. In the end he thought it best to perhaps tell him of his intentions. "I have decided to go to the university, and I am trying to find out my year 12 test results so that I'll know what options I have."

To Aden's surprise, instead of this pleasing his father, he burst out laughing. After having had a good hearty laugh, he gave a piercing and angry look to Aden, and said, "What do you take me for that you think that you can sit there and tell me such nonsense, when we both know that you most likely didn't even graduate from high school? And just a week ago you stood in my office and told me that you would never consider going to a university. Well, it's not going to work! You can't cover whatever it is you have done. At least you could have come up with a more intelligent excuse. But then again, how could you?"

Aden felt hurt and angry. He took the napkin off of his lap, threw it on the table, got up from his chair, and started to walk away. Randall, who had been busily and quietly preparing the main course plates, hurriedly said, "But Master Aden I am about to serve the main course. It's Chateaubriand, your favorite."

"No thanks. I've lost my appetite."

"We're still not finished," said John. "Where do you think you're going?"

"Away from here," said Aden as he walked out.

Randall served the main course for John. "Thanks Randall. With or without his help I'll get to the bottom of this." He then attempted to eat in his usual calm and collected manner as if nothing had happened. But not this time. Even with his controlled temperament he could not pretend that nothing was bothering him. After a few minutes he motioned to Randall to take away his plate.

"Sir, didn't you like your dinner?"

"The dinner was fine. The problem is with Aden. I just don't know how to get through to him." He thought for a moment. "I know. I'll hire a private detective tomorrow. No, I am far too busy tomorrow, and…Monday as well. I'll take care of it some time next week, before my trip to Europe." As usual, his work took precedent over everything else in his life.

"That is a very good idea, sir," replied Randall.

John remained alone at the head of the 30-seat dining table. A large grandfather clock ticked in the background. He began to look through the documents he had brought to the table. It was as if the confrontation between him and Aden had taken place in the distant past. There was no longer any trace of concern on his face, nor any thought about Aden. His focus was now on his meeting and how he could prepare for it.

Chapter 16

Minutes and hours could not go fast enough for Aden. He did everything he could to keep his mind off the time, his test results and his father's comments. After the confrontation with his father, he went out with Brian and his other friends. He stayed out late, got up early, and did a longer workout than usual, until it was finally time for him to see Kate. He was at a point where he just wanted to know, even if it was not what he wanted to hear.

Kate was expecting him. She gave him a warm welcome and immediately got to the point. "I must apologize; I don't know how this could have happened that you didn't get your results. I'm surprised, weren't you invited to the Governor's Mansion?"

"Yes, a couple months ago my father and I were invited to some function."

"No, I'm talking about the time when you graduated?"

"So, you mean I graduated?" asked Aden in surprise.

"Of course! With results like these you not only graduated, you were among the top 20 students in the state. That is why you should have been invited to the special ceremony at the Governor's Mansion."

Aden was totally puzzled. "Do you know who I am?" asked Aden thinking maybe she had mistaken him for someone else.

"Of course, who doesn't? Especially after the last issue of Women's Weekly," replied Kate with a smile. "Here are your results; you can see for yourself that you got four perfect scores of 20 and one almost perfect score of 19."

Aden carefully looked at his results. There was no mistake; it had his name, correct date, and other relevant information. "This is great," said Aden without showing much emotion. Inside he felt both shocked and thrilled. When he left it was as if he was walking on air. He could not wait to tell Christina; he drove there in record time. When Christina opened the door, he thought to have a little fun with her. He put a somber look upon his face as he handed his results to Christina, "Can you believe these results?"

Seeing the look on Aden's face Christina became concerned, and without delay she started to look at them as they walked to the family room. Aden was happy to sit back and enjoy watching Christina figure out what his results meant. Before long she figured it out. "I see…a perfect score is 20." Looking pleasantly surprised with such excitement in her voice and a big smile on her face she said, "These are absolutely great results, and…you didn't say anything?!"

"It was fun to see your reaction."

"There was no need for you to worry, with results like these you can study anything you want."

"That's true. I can go to any university and study anything I want." Aden paused for a moment, "But there is something that puzzles me. I was assured that these are my results and there is no mistake, but I don't see how I could have gotten such scores. I never studied," he candidly admitted.

Christina started searching for answers. She felt at a time like this Aden should be happy, not troubled. Then a possible explanation came to her mind. To confirm her thinking she asked, "Were you a troublemaker at school?"

"Yeah, always," replied Aden, "but what does that have anything to do with my results?"

"I have an idea, I'll explain later. When did it start?"

"That's easy, from the time I started going to school."

"I bet you were always bored?"

"Extremely, I had to do something to make it bearable."

"Here is something else I want you to do." Christina pointed to a couple of business magazines on the coffee table. "I've put these together for you to take and read at home, but for now…," she grabbed one of the magazines, opened it to the index page with all the financial data, handed it to Aden and said, "I would like you to take your time and read this entire page."

Aden did so. It did not take him long. He then handed it back to Christina, "Well I didn't understand what it all meant, but I'm finished reading it."

"That is fine. Can you tell me what the Production Index was?" asked Christina.

"It was 196.4 for the latest month and 196.8 a month ago, with 3.9% change a year ago," replied Aden very casually.

Christina was amazed. She even checked the magazine to make sure he could not see through it. She then continued on asking him about all other various indicators and figures on the page. As she had suspected Aden answered everything correctly. "You can remember everything you read, can you also remember things you hear?"

"Yes," replied Aden.

Christina was in awe of his ability. "That is very impressive."

Aden could not see what all the fuss was about. "What is impressive about remembering things you read and hear? Doesn't everybody do that?"

"No, at least I don't know of anyone who can. That is a very unique talent to have. Your mind seems to go even beyond that, it also sorts out and applies information it recalls. That puts you in the category of genius," she stated matter-of-factly to Aden.

Aden choked on his drink when he heard the word genius. "Right," said Aden in a state of total disbelief.

"Obviously, your talent wasn't detected." She went on to explain how that could have happened, "There are usually two kinds of students who get into trouble, mentally challenged and gifted children. Unless someone is looking, it is easy to mistake gifted children for troublemakers who are poor performers. Gifted children learn everything quickly and then they are bored; grounds for causing trouble. It was easy for everyone to think that you were a troublemaker because you were a rich spoiled brat who was not bright. That got your father's attention, and got the school your father's generous donations, therefore there was no reason to change."

"That still doesn't explain my results."

"Actually, it does. All along you had learned everything your teachers had said and shown, so when it came to your exams all you probably did was write what came to your mind without knowing what it meant or whether it was correct."

Christina's explanation began to make sense to Aden as he recalled the events of his exams three years ago, how he never studied, partied every night, and was even hung-over when he went to his exams. But he did not care, for he was certain that he was going to fail. "You're right," he said to Christina. "During my exams I put down whatever came to my mind, with time to spare. I remember thinking that I must have failed everything so badly, that I put the entire incident out of my mind. And now you're telling me that I'm a…genius."

"Yes, you are," said Christina with a warm smile.

Aden no longer had that casual attitude. "I can't believe it, and if I can't believe it, how is anybody else going to, especially my father?"

"You don't need to tell or convince anyone; they will come to believe it when they see your achievements."

"You don't know my father, just last night he broke out laughing at the thought of me going to a university."

"Everything takes time. I'm sure a year from now he will be telling you how proud he is of you. By then you will have finished your first year of university, with top marks, of course." Christina then assured him, "You will soon see, after he learns about your achievements, there will be a change in his attitude toward you."

Aden was beginning to get over his shock and was starting to accept Christina's explanation. He even smiled for the first time when he asked, "What does all this mean?"

"It means that the sky's the limit for you. It is very impressive how you combine your photographic memory with problem solving. You did so well on your exams without even trying, now imagine what you can achieve by trying and applying yourself," replied Christina sounding thrilled.

"I guess I have a lot of thinking and decision making to do."

"Yes, you do."

After he left Christina's house his mind was racing. During his drive back, he was still trying to come to terms with all that had happened. He was thinking how he could never forget this week, especially this day, Friday the 9th of December. How so much had changed in his life because of Christina and how she had been such a positive influence in his life. To help him with his thinking he stopped by the university and got some information about the various programs and degrees being offered. By the time he returned to the Bradcliffe Estate, he was pretty much feeling on top of the world. He was eagerly looking forward to not only reading the university brochures and the magazines he had gotten from Christina, but also accessing more articles and information online.

As he was walking to his room, he was thinking that nothing, not even a confrontation with his father, was going to bother him. That is, nothing except what he saw in his room; Sharon was waiting for him. Anxious to see him she had come directly from work wearing her business suit. To make herself comfortable she had taken off her jacket and shoes. She was sitting on his bed, smiling, and ready to entice him. A week ago he might have welcomed that, but now it was just unacceptable. Because of his feelings for Christina, he had no interest to be with her or any other woman. Also, with his new priorities he simply wanted more out of life. He did not want to waste his time chasing frivolous things anymore.

"What are you doing here?" asked Aden curtly.

"That is no way to greet someone who is bringing you good news," replied Sharon in a very friendly manner.

"This is my room, and I do as I please," said Aden as he stormed out looking and yelling for Randall. He was upset that he had disobeyed him not only by letting Sharon in the mansion, but to his room without his permission. His father, who was just then coming up the stairs, stopped him and asked what was wrong.

"Randall, against my instructions, has let Sharon into my room, that's what's wrong."

"It wasn't Randall, it was me. Sharon said she had something she wanted to personally give you, so I let her into your room."

"I wish you hadn't, Dad," said Aden sounding a bit calmer. "I guess I'll go and take care of it myself."

"Wait Aden. I'm leaving for Sydney shortly, and I'll be back on Monday. I just wanted to make sure you have not forgotten about the Bradcliffe family Christmas party on Monday night. This year it is at my cousin Trudy's house, and you can't miss it like you did last year. I know it's boring to listen to a bunch of pretentious snobs bragging all night about their latest real estate acquisitions, latest cars and so on; and especially to Trudy bragging about James and his accomplishments. But it is one of the few times we get together as a family in a year, and I don't want to…," John was still continuing on with more reasons to convince Aden when he stopped his father and said, "That's Ok, I'll go, anyway I wouldn't mind seeing and talking to Aunt Nellie."

John was relieved with Aden's answer. "I hope your talking to Aunt Nellie isn't because it annoys James."

"I'm not like that at all. If I wanted to annoy someone, I'd be much more direct. I like talking to her because she's the only one who isn't a phony. Anyway, can I help it that I am her favorite Bradcliffe?"

"Well try not to rub it in or cut him down."

"Where's the fun in that?" seeing the stern look on his father's face Aden agreed. "Ok, I'll try."

"That's good. Just one more thing, make sure you're there before dinner is served."

Aden then went back to his room to clear things up with Sharon. He was direct and firm, "I would like you to leave now."

Sharon was shocked. "I don't understand, I did what you wanted and today your father got the grant. Doesn't that make you happy?" She then moved close to Aden, put her arms around him and said, "All I ask in return is for you to spend some time with me, I'll make it worth your while."

"I'm not interested," said Aden abruptly as he pulled her arms off from around him.

"Nobody has ever treated me this way. Men are always chasing after me and at work. I'm a financial manager so people jump when I want something. But you can treat me anyway you want as long as you let me stay."

Aden was about to tell her again to leave when 'financial manager' caught his attention.

"Are you really a financial manager?"

"Yes, one of the best."

"In that case you can stay," he said. "There is something that I want to talk about."

That was not what she wanted to hear, but she went along with it. Aden handed her a couple of the business magazines he had gotten from Christina and said, "Let's talk about these."

That was exactly what they did for a couple of hours. Aden then thanked her as he walked her to the door.

"It was my pleasure. Just too bad you didn't want more. But if you should change your mind, you know where to find me," said Sharon playfully as she left.

During the weekend in between his social commitments, Aden spent a lot of time reading, looking at various universities' websites, and thinking about his options. By Sunday evening, he had made his choice and had come up with a decision for his course of study. It felt good to know what he was going to do. He leaned comfortably back in the plush armchair in his room. There was a sense of strength in his eyes and a content smile on his face. Now he could not wait 'til morning to make it all happen.

Chapter 17

Aden was not about to wait for the university offices to open. Early Monday morning he called his father's old Oxford friend, Professor Sandra Klossen, head of the Business School of Lightsbridge University and asked if he could see her. It so happened that she was about to go to her office to take care of a few last-minute things before leaving on her end-of-the-year holidays. She told Aden to come by around 10 o'clock.

When Aden got to the university, Professor Klossen was waiting for him at her office. "Good morning Aden. Come in," she said amicably. "You have come at a perfect time. I was just about to take a break." She then got up from behind her desk, walked over to the front of her office where there was a table with four chairs around it. She shook hands with Aden and invited him to sit down at the table. "Tell me Aden, how is your father? Busy running his empire I suspect."

"Yes, he's fine and busy as always."

"That's good. So, what brings you here?"

"I might as well get right to the point. I have decided to go to the university," said Aden confidently as he handed his test results to Professor Klossen.

"That certainly is a commendable decision." Professor Klossen paused for a moment as she looked at them, "With impressive results like these, you can really attend any university that you want. John never told me that he had a genius at home."

"I am thinking of going to the University of Lightsbridge, initially anyway."

"If that is the case, perhaps I can convince you to come to my department."

"You could convince me if you were to offer me what I want."

"And what would that be?" asked Professor Klossen amused with Aden's pointed response.

"I plan to get a dual degree in Law and Business, which is a 5½ year program. What I want is simple, to be permitted to double up each year and finish my course of studies in 3 years instead," replied Aden assertively.

"That is a highly irregular request. That program is already a difficult and demanding program without adding this extra load, which would require taking a course and its prerequisite at the same time. I don't see how that could work."

"Easy. I can study the prerequisites prior to the start of the university every semester."

"Even so, those programs and the course structures have been in place for a long time and have been set up to best serve the needs of the students. Why change what is working?"

"I like a challenge," persisted Aden maintaining his positive posture. "Anyway, the university structure that you referred to, isn't that set up to expand the minds and not to slow down the progress and limit one's learning? Besides, the university doesn't have anything to lose. If I am successful, the university will become a showcase of progressive teaching, and if I'm not, I will have to repeat the courses which will bring more money to the university." Aden appearing quite in control even went as far as saying that not only would he not fail, but that he would get distinctions or better in all of his courses.

"That's a very compelling argument you have there," replied a very impressed Professor Klossen. "I like that, and I'm not saying that just because you're John's son. I've never heard a student ask for more work. In fact, just the opposite is true. Having said that, I believe that we can offer you what you want here at the Business Department, but I can't speak for the Law Department. Just leave that with me and I'll have a talk with them. Of course, with everyone going on holidays at this time of the year, I don't know when I'll be able to get a response. But as soon as I have an answer, I'll let you know."

That was exactly what Aden was hoping to hear. "Well, you have me half convinced." He then thanked her and shook her hand as he said, "I'll be anxiously waiting to hear back from you with the outcome of your talks with the Law Department."

"My pleasure Aden. You must come back when I have a bit more time so that I can tell you stories about your father when he and I were at Oxford."

Aden was content with how things had gone with Professor Klossen. In fact, it was even better than he had anticipated. There was only one person that he wanted to share that with, and that was Christina. He really wanted to see her and talk with her, but with schools being off he did not know how it would work out with her children. He decided that he was not going to let that stop him. He had to chance it and hope for the best.

When he got there, he could hear the children talking. He walked over. When the children saw him, they stopped talking. "Hello Natalie, do you remember me?"

"Yes, you are that strange man who is going to be our neighbor," said Natalie in a sweet voice as she looked on with her big brown eyes.

Aden got a chuckle out of how cute she was, wearing a light purple T-shirt with flower appliqués, three quarter length denim shorts, and a matching purple hair pin keeping her silky brown hair out of her face. He was quite taken by how much she looked like Christina. He promptly introduced himself, and not having seen Timothy before he said, "This must be your brother Timothy." Unlike Natalie, Timothy appeared to be unhappy.

"Yes, it is."

"Why the long face Timothy?" asked Aden.

Timothy was reluctant to talk. So, Natalie did the talking for him. "His friends are coming over to play basketball and he sucks at it," she said authoritatively.

"No, I don't!"

"Yes, you do. I could even beat you."

"No, you can't!"

Aden decided to go to the rescue, "I can help you play better."

"You can?" asked Timothy in a state of surprise. "Really?" he said as his eyes lit up.

"Yes, let's get started." Aden then picked up the ball, dribbled a few times, and threw it to Timothy. "Show me how you play."

Being good at all sports, it was easy for Aden to see what Timothy was struggling with and what pointers he needed to improve his game. He showed him how to hold the ball when taking a shot and how to improve his footwork when dribbling. To help him put it into practice he began playing a little one-on-one with him. Very quickly Timothy began to show some signs of improvement. He was now moving faster and beginning to score more baskets.

By the time his friends arrived he was feeling more confident and ready to play. With the help of Aden from the sideline, he was making shots he had never before made. As their game went on, more kids of all ages stopped by, including a few teenagers, who as they had done in the past, were ready to take over the game. This time Timothy was feeling too confident, especially with Aden there, to let that happen. He challenged them to a game. If Timothy and his team were victorious, then the teenagers would leave him and his friends alone for the rest of the summer. They laughed at Timothy saying, "Is that some kind of a joke? The three of us just won our divisional championship."

"Is it a deal?" asked Timothy boldly.

"Sure, why not kid?"

"My name is Timothy," he said assertively. Then he continued, "That will be myself, and my friends Mark and Aden." This was not at all what Aden had in mind. He was not even dressed for playing basketball. But seeing how it meant so much to Timothy, he agreed.

"This is going to be sweet, beating the little Timmy and Mr. GQ here all in one go." They may have known who Aden was, but they did not know what a competitive athlete he was. "First to 21," said Aden, giving them a look of, "in your dreams."

They had a shaky start as the teenage boys were all over Timothy and Mark, not allowing them to make a shot. Aden then changed the game plan and had them pass the ball to him. With his near flawless shooting, he scored two three-point shots in a row and turned things around. As an element of surprise, when all the boys were on him, he would pass the ball to Timothy or Mark, who were in the open to make the shot. It ended up being a close game which created a lot of excitement for the neighborhood kids that had come to watch the game. Aden used his defensive tactics against their point guard and prevented him from making shots. Then amidst all the cheering, Aden made the winning shot.

"We did it!" screamed Timothy giving a high-five to Aden and Mark.

Aden had instantly become the hero of the younger kids and at the same time had gained the respect of the older ones. They all gathered around him. "Not bad Aden! Perhaps you can show us how to make shots like those sometime," said the older boys. Aden was in the middle of saying "Sure," when Timothy jumped in and said, "No, he's **my** coach!" Everybody laughed.

Christina having heard all the noise and cheering, came out to find out what all the excitement was about. As soon as Aden saw her, his entire focus and attention went exclusively on her. The children turned around to see what Aden was looking at. They saw Christina, and excitedly ran to her. Timothy, with the help of his friends, started telling her what had happened. Seeing them so happy, made her happy too. "That's wonderful. All this excitement calls for ice cream and cold drinks for everyone. Timothy and Natalie, you two come in and help Mommy with serving."

"Why don't you let them play with their friends? I'll be happy to help you," said Aden.

The kids all came in to get their ice cream and drinks, and then ran out. Finally, when it was quiet inside Christina had a chance to thank Aden, "What you did was very nice," she said gratefully. "Thank you for that."

"Not necessary to thank me. Serving ice cream is really very easy," said Aden jokingly.

"Thank you for that, too. But I meant for playing basketball with Timothy."

Aden knew what Christina had meant, but he wanted to have fun with her and at the same time downplay what he had done. "No big thing. It was my pleasure," he said. "Anyway, I enjoyed getting to know Timothy and Natalie. Children just need help and attention, and I was happy to give it to them."

Christina was surprised with Aden's understanding of children's needs; something she wished Sean would understand and appreciate. "And how would you know what children need?"

"Never having my father around when I was growing up gives me all of the qualifications to know that."

Christina understood. "I agree," she said. "That's a problem. Too many parents always seem to be too busy to be with their children. The children are often neglected and suffer as a result. What children need are their parents to be there for them and spend time with them."

Just then Timothy and Natalie came back inside. "Mommy, the kids are going to the park at the end of the street to play cricket. Can we go with them please?"

"Alright, you can go, but only if you look after your sister. And Natalie, you must stay with Timothy. Ok?"

"Ok Mommy," they both said as they kissed her. They then thanked Aden, especially Timothy, and asked him to come back again before dashing after the other kids.

That made Aden smile. "They're such wonderful children, a credit to their mother. I never had a mother, but if I did, I would have liked her to have been like you."

That was the nicest thing anyone could have said to Christina. She very much appreciated Aden's complement, but since it was her nature to do something good for others, she felt compelled to change the conversation so she could be helping him. "Thank you, Aden. But let's go sit down and talk about what you have done to get into the university."

Aden of course had a lot to tell and share with Christina, which he gladly did.

"So, you want to complete a 5½ year program in just three years? That's extremely impressive. I believe it's good to set your goals high." Knowing his abilities, she then said, "And if there is anyone who can do it in three years, it would be you."

"I hope that they share your optimism in the Law School. I wish that I knew their response now."

"I'm sure that it will work out fine, but in the meantime, you should put it out of your mind."

"Maybe the boring family Christmas party that I have to go to this evening will help keep my mind off of it," said Aden sarcastically.

Christina smiled. Aden then casually looked at his watch and was surprised to see how late it was, which unfortunately meant that he had to leave so as not to be late for the party that evening.

Chapter 18

William Bradcliffe, John's father, had three brothers and one sister. He had always been closest to his sister Nellie. In fact, they had been each other's best friend when growing up, and they continued to be so until his passing. As a result, Nellie always considered John and Aden as her own son and grandson.

Among the brothers William was the one with business acumen, who through hard work and dedication had been able to expand the family-owned business into a major corporation. Over the years he had taken his brothers under his wing and given them, and some of their family members, various positions in the company.

After his passing some of them were envious of John and resented having him as the head of the corporation. However, seeing how John capably saved and made the corporation profitable after an unanticipated and disastrous market downturn, they had come to accept and respect him.

During this time, it was Nellie who had fully and firmly supported and backed John and kept the family together. She was strong and always spoke her mind. What was unique about her was her ability to read people. She usually knew immediately if she was going to like someone or not. It was as if she could see through to a person's heart. That was why, unlike the rest of the Bradcliffes, who thought of Aden as the bad boy of the family, she actually was very fond of him. She admired his strength of character, his unpretentious manner, and his open frankness. In many ways he reminded her of herself when she was young.

She of course loved her grandson James, son of Trudy. But she felt that, like his father, he lacked sincerity which was unacceptable to her. That was why she favored Aden over him. That was a sore point for James. Knowing that he could never compete with Aden's looks or popularity, he cut down Aden's intelligence any chance that he got. This evening's party was no exception; especially since the party was at their house which James felt gave him an advantage.

Trudy was pleased to have the party there so that she could show off her newly built house. It was an ultra-modern and spacious house with a very large entertainment area consisting of a living and dining room that opened to a formal courtyard which served as an extension for larger gatherings. This evening the living room was glittering with candles in gold candelabras, tea lights in gold and silver holders, and flowers in shimmering crystal vases. The outdoor area was enchanting with fairy lights and frosted tea light holders.

When Aden arrived at the party virtually the entire Bradcliffe family was there. About 30 of them were sitting in the living room and another 50 or so were in the outdoor area. All were wearing Armani, Gucci or Versace garments and were dripping with diamond jewelry, as to out-do and out-snob one another. But Aden was not to be outdone as he was stylishly dressed, wearing the latest Ralph Lauren Black Label suit and shirt. He quickly made his way around and said hello to everyone.

Aunt Nellie waited for Aden to finish and then asked him to come and sit down next to her on the sofa to James's dismay. "Finally, I have someone to talk to who isn't interested only in my money."

Aden smiled, "You're absolutely right Aunt Nellie, I'm only interested in your company," he said sincerely.

James, envious of Aden, his perfect manner, and how nice his grandmother was to him, could not hold back anymore, "You're such a suck-up, Aden."

Aden's intention was not to cut down James, but he felt that he had to say something to defend his sincerity. "Are you trying to say that no one can be nice to Aunt Nellie for the lovely person she is?"

That was too easy for Aden, which of course put James on-the-spot with his grandmother waiting for his answer. "Yes. No, I mean no…" Both Aunt Nellie and Aden burst out laughing.

His mother, Trudy, came to his rescue and stopped the conversation by getting everyone's attention. She had been waiting for everybody to come before making her big announcement. "Can I have your attention please? I have some wonderful news to share with you. My brilliant son, James has completed his year twelve exams with one perfect score, and high overall marks to study business at the Lightsbridge University." Everyone clapped.

"Thank you all. I guess that there is finally someone smart enough in the Bradcliffe family to be following in Uncle John's footsteps and climbing the corporate ladder," said James proudly, half seriously and half jokingly. He then looked at Aden as he continued on, "Unlike Aden who doesn't know the meaning of either success or achievements. Who am I kidding? How could he know when his IQ is the same as my perfect score of 20?"

The elegant sitting room filled with silence. Aden looked at his father and then around the room. Everybody seemed to be waiting for his answer. He thought for a moment and saw no point or anything to be gained by continuing with this banter. He was no longer insecure about his intelligence, even though James's comment hurt his pride. He knew that there was not anything that he could say that would make a difference or change anyone's thinking. So, he made no reply.

John broke the silence. "Tell me James, how intelligent would someone be who gets a perfect score?"

That's my father all right, always praising and defending others, thought Aden feeling disappointed.

James had a smug look on his face, "Naturally, quite intelligent."

"What about someone who gets two perfect scores? Would you say also quite intelligent?"

James, not being quite sure where his uncle was going with that line of questioning, responded positively.

"Very well then, what would you say about someone who got four perfect scores of 20 and one 19?"

Aden was astounded. Those were his scores. *Could his father possibly be talking about him?* he wondered. *No, he couldn't be, there was no way for him to have known.*

James no longer had a smug look on his face, as he replied, "I would say very intelligent and very hard working."

"What would you call a person who got these scores without studying?" asked John as everyone intently listened.

James, thinking how no one could get scores like that without studying, considering how hard he himself had worked just to achieve one perfect score, without a hesitation said, "A genius."

"Good, then you just called Aden a genius because those were his results."

Suddenly, whispers of astonishment filled the room. "Wow, that's impressive." "Did he really?" or simply, "That's unbelievable," were what some said softly. James's jaw hit the floor. Aunt Nellie was pleased. Aden was stunned.

He did not know what to say. This was the first time in his entire life that his father had acknowledged him for something that he had achieved.

It was then announced that dinner was being served and everybody was invited to go to the dining room. The extra long solid mahogany table was elegantly decorated with beaded and embroidered silk table runners, solid crystal candleholders, and flower arrangements adorned with hand blown glass ornaments. Loose glitter and sequins on the table added to the festive atmosphere of the party.

Before going to the dining room various family members stopped to congratulate John and Aden. Soon everybody had left the room except for father and son. John looking at Aden in admiration said, "That was quite an accomplishment."

"Thank you, Dad. How did you find out?"

"I had a call from a very excited Sandra Klossen. I hadn't heard her that excited since she won the chess tournament at Oxford. She was going on about how she got their agreement, which of course I was completely oblivious about. So, I asked her. She then explained everything and told me about your plan." John then paused for a moment. "Aden…, I owe you an apology. I behaved poorly the other night when you were trying to talk to me about these things, and I didn't give you a chance. I'm sorry."

"I never thought that I would hear you say this," said Aden in total amazement. "Though I guess that I never made things easy for you."

"Well, I never thought that I would ever live long enough to hear you admit that," said John with a smile, a smile that said it all.

After 20 years John finally had come to accept and even admire his son. He had never stopped blaming Aden for the loss of his wife, who had passed away due to unforeseen complications while giving birth to him. As irrational as it was, his way of dealing with the situation was to push Aden away and immersed himself in his work. Now for the first time he was allowing himself to see the love that he had for his wife in Aden.

"So, they have agreed? That's great," said Aden sounding pleased.

"Yes, Sandra said that she had agreement from both departments to allow you to complete the program in three years as you had requested. You know that I am all for progress, but are you sure that you want to do that?"

"Yes, definitely. I feel that I have wasted the last three years of my life, and now I want to make up for it."

"There you are," Trudy interrupted. "You'd think that you two hadn't seen each other for years," she said as she walked into the room. "You must stop and come have some of this delicious dinner that my chef has prepared, before it gets cold."

Later that night after they had returned to the mansion from the party, Aden feeling quite content said goodnight to his father and was about to go to his room when his father asked him to wait. "Aden, as you know I'll be leaving for my annual holiday and ski trip to Europe. I thought…, it might be good if you could come with me. What do you say?"

Just when Aden thought that he had had his share of surprises for a lifetime, here he was shocked once more. "There were lots of times in the past that I wanted to go with you, but you never asked. Now that you have finally asked, I can't. I've promised Brian and my other friends that I would go with them to Sydney."

As disappointed as his father was, he understood and accepted Aden's decision, "I realize that it is very short notice, but why don't we make a date of it for next year?"

"Ok, you're on."

"Then, next year it is," said John as he embraced Aden for the first time that he could remember.

Chapter 19

Tuesday morning turned out to be a spectacular, picture perfect summer day with low humidity, a temperature of 87°F, and not a cloud in the sky. It was as if it were made to order for Brian's annual swimming party that would begin around 11am and continue long into the evening. Everybody always looked forward to it. There would be an all-day barbeque and an ice cream bar. There would also be games, swimming, water polo, and even beach volleyball in the sandy area of the back yard. This being their last get-together of the year before the holidays, made it particularly special.

This year Aden was indifferent about going to the party. Instead, he had a very strong urge to see Christina. There was so much that he wanted to tell her. Therefore, he decided to go to Christina's house first, before going to the party.

When he got there the children were upstairs playing, and Christina was busy preparing the picnic basket for their planned day at the park with Sean.

"Christina, you were absolutely right," said Aden as he walked in.

"Of course, I was. Was there any doubt?"

"Do I detect a trace of modesty there?"

They both felt comfortable enough with each other to have fun. Aden's response made her laugh, "What was I right about?"

"About my father," said Aden. He then proceeded to tell her everything that had happened at the family party the night before, with an occasional smile or two.

Christina felt very happy for him. Their conversation was interrupted by Timothy, "Mom, your phone is ringing. It's Dad."

"Sorry Aden," she said. Then she asked Timothy to answer the call.

A minute later they both ran into the family room, neither one was looking happy at all. They were surprised to see Aden there. They said hello to him and then quickly turned to Christina with Timothy doing most of the talking. "Mom, Dad is saying that he can't come. Can you please talk to him and make him come?"

"Alright, I'll see what I can do." Christina then again apologized to Aden, took her phone from Timothy, and went to the study to call Sean. But no matter how she tried, she could not convince him. Feeling disappointed she returned to the family room. "I'm sorry. Dad can't make it. Something very important has come up," she said while trying to think of a way to cheer them up, but to her surprise the children did not seem unhappy.

Timothy was sitting on one side of Aden, and Natalie was on the other, each had their arms wrapped around his arms looking happy. "Don't worry Mom. Everything is taken care of. Aden is going to come with us," said Timothy.

"Yes, it seems it's all settled," said Aden while looking at the children holding his arms.

"I couldn't possibly think of imposing on you like that. I'm sure that you would rather be with your friends doing a million other things."

"It's no imposition," said Aden thinking only if Christina knew how much more he would prefer going to the park with them rather than doing anything else. "I'm always with my friends, and I'll be seeing them later today. I'll just make a phone call, and then we can go when you're ready."

"Only if you promise not to let my children stop you from leaving when it's time for you to meet with your friends. They never want to leave, and they never get tired of playing." Aden agreed. Christina then took the children upstairs to help them to get ready.

Aden walked outside on the terrace and called Brian. "Hey Brian."

"Hi. If it isn't the man of the hour. I guess that congratulations are in order."

"For what?"

"For those results of yours."

"News travels fast around here."

"Are you kidding? Without you Aden, life would be boring. Nobody would have anything to talk about. You don't do things like everyone else. When you do something, it's always in a big way! By the way, I heard that you made James upset."

"That's not true. Anyway, it was my father who did all the talking."

"Does this mean that now we have to start calling you 'genius'?"

"Only if you want your lifespan shortened!" replied Aden resenting the mere suggestion of it.

"Good. You're still the same."

While talking he noticed through the glass that Christina and the children had returned and were ready to go. "Listen Brian, something has come up. Just wanted to let you know that I'll be a bit late for your party."

"Just try not to be too late. Everyone will be asking about you."

"Ok, I'll see you later."

Aden went back inside. The children were excited, "Can we do other things than just going to the park?"

"We can do anything that you want as long as your mom agrees," replied Aden in a caring way, quite uncharacteristic of him, until now.

Soon they were on their way. First, they went to the playground, and afterwards to the zoo. When it was time for lunch they went to the Botanic Park.

This picturesque and delightful park with its large open grassy areas was a perfect place for a picnic. Its tall, majestic sycamore and ficus trees with their wide imposing trunks soared high into the afternoon sky and provided just the right amount of shade with their long branches and leaves spreading out, wide like a paisley canopy, softening and diffusing the rays of the sun.

Throughout the morning the children had had a lot of fun with Aden, so much so that when he sat down for lunch, they both went and sat next to him. Christina got a kick out of how much they both liked Aden. She was touched by his caring ways toward Timothy and Natalie. This was something she could only attribute to his understanding of children's needs based on his own life. Because of her strong values, the possibility of Aden being romantically attracted to her would have never entered her mind. Yet, Aden was overwhelmed with his feelings toward her. As he looked at her and her beautiful smile against the background of soft, velvet-like green grass covered with patches of wildflowers, and the sweet, happy faces of the children clinging to him, he found himself overcome with such a feeling of happiness that he had never experienced, nor thought possible only a week ago.

"Aden, what are you doing over the holidays?" asked Timothy.

"My friends and I are flying to Sydney tomorrow. First, we'll sail around the east coast, then we'll come back to Sydney for the New Year's Eve fireworks display and parties, and then I'll stay on for a couple more weeks just relaxing."

"We're going to the Gold Coast," said Timothy excitedly. "Our plane will go through Sydney. We'll look for you, and we'll wave to you as we fly over."

Timothy and Natalie quickly finished eating and went off to play. "I've never seen them like this with anyone before," said Christina. "You are really wonderful with them."

"The feeling is mutual. Actually, I find it rather interesting how almost everyone I have ever known has either been too busy with their social life or with their careers, that instead of raising their children themselves, have had them raised by nannies or left them at childcare centers. After being with Timothy and Natalie for these two days, I realize how much fun and joy they would have missed."

Christina's face brightened up. "I couldn't agree more. With that thinking no doubt you'll make a great father someday."

Timothy and Natalie ran back to their mom asking her and Aden to come and play chasey with them. They agreed and all began to play. It was a lot of fun. Timothy had just become 'it' and started chasing his mom. As she was running away, she heard Natalie calling her. She stopped to respond to her, but Timothy was too close to her to stop in time. He ran into her which made her lose her balance. Aden who was standing near to her, reached out his arm behind her to stop her from falling. But as she fell, he lost his balance and fell down with her, only being able to break her fall.

While they were falling, he felt her in his arm, and suddenly everything around them, the images, the sounds began to fade away in what seemed like a slow-motion scene. All that he could see was Christina, her face, her eyes, her lips. It was as if they were in a world of their own where time appeared to have stopped, and there were only feelings of serenity, contentment, and love. He had never before experienced anything like that. For the short moment that they lay on the ground, he found himself wishing that it would never end. Soon it all changed as Christina looked at him and said, "You know what this means, don't you?" Her question brought him back, trying to reorient himself, wondering what she meant, he could only say, "No."

"It means revenge!" said Christina with a big smile as she sat up. Timothy and Natalie were laughing. "Come on Aden. You catch Timothy and I'll catch Natalie. Then we'll feed them to the ducks!"

Timothy and Natalie started to run away screaming. Soon Christina and Aden had caught them. They were all laughing. Unlike Christina and her children, it was not common for Aden to be laughing and having fun like that. In fact, very seldom was there ever a smile on Aden's emotionless face.

"No Mommy, you can't feed us to the ducks."

"And why not?"

"Because there aren't any ducks here," said Timothy.

"We'll just have to think of something else to do," said Aden. "I know. We'll make them eat ice cream!"

They then got some ice cream and continued to play and have fun throughout the rest of the afternoon until it was time to go. "We had so much fun with you Aden," they both said as they hugged him before saying goodbye.

"I hope that we didn't keep you too long from being with your friends." Christina then thanked and wished him a happy holiday. "Enjoy your trip and see you in the new year."

"It was my pleasure. You too enjoy your holidays," said Aden. He then waited by his car for Christina and the children to leave. As she drove off an empty feeling came over him.

When Aden got to the party, he did not have that harsh and unyielding attitude towards things. He felt good after having had an enjoyable day with Christina and her children. Outwardly he appeared the same to his friends. He only seemed distracted which they attributed to the new things happening in his life. In reality he was preoccupied with thoughts of Christina. Departing the next day to go sailing was exactly what he needed.

The vigorous work they did during the day sailing their 40-foot yacht on the open Pacific ocean was what kept his mind off of things. But at night as he stood on the deck feeling the fresh ocean breeze, watching the moon calmly dancing on the water and the waves gently rolling away, he would find his thoughts drifting away to Christina, the last day in the park, and that purely emotional and spiritual experience that he had had.

After a week of sailing, Aden and his friends returned to Sydney. There they stayed at his father's penthouse apartment right in the heart of Sydney, overlooking the magnificent view of Darling Harbour and the architectural masterpiece of the Sydney Opera House. It was a perfect place and location for enjoying the night life of the city.

Aden felt the need to find out if he could repeat the feeling that he had experienced in the park. But no matter which girl he was with, he could not experience it again. The more that he tried, the more disillusioned he became, and the more frustrated he felt not to be with the one person that he really cared for the most. It was something he came to accept as he treasured that experience within him.

Even though he was trying not to show it, his friends had noticed his frustration and his more than usual lack of interest in the girls pursuing him. They assumed that it was because of his newfound genius and the over ambitious study program that he wanted to undertake. The good friends that they were, they just were supportive of him. That suited Aden perfectly, as he had no intentions of ever explaining how he truly felt inside.

To cope with how slowly time appeared to be passing, he began to read business books and novels, something he had never before had any interest in doing. He even read such literary works as Shakespeare's *Romeo and Juliet* and Pasternak's *Doctor Zhivago*.

"Look at you, reading all these novels," said Brian in surprise, "as if you need to read any love stories with all these girls at your feet."

"Have you ever wondered about true love?" asked Aden appearing deep in thought. "Is it unattainable like in these novels where it only happens if you can't have the one you want?"

"Personally, I haven't given it much thought," replied Brian casually. "But I'm very simple. I'd be happy to just find someone that I like." He then paused and said, "I get it now. You're concerned that you won't find true love because you can have any girl you want. Is that it?"

Seeing how far from reality Brian was, Aden simply said, "Something like that."

"Don't worry. My father always says that love will find you."

Love had found Aden, but like those novels, it was with the one that he could not have. By the end of his trip Aden had come to the conclusion that instead of trying to analyze how it was ever going to work out, he would enjoy seeing and being with Christina whenever he could. As he looked out the window of his penthouse, enjoying the view one last time before departing for Adelaide, he found himself filled with a new sense of energy and eagerness. He felt quite optimistic that with building his house and then moving there, he would have plenty of opportunities to see her. In addition, by putting his full focus and attention on his studies, he felt that things should work out perfectly.

Chapter 20

It was mid-January when Aden returned from Sydney and was thrilled to be back. The thinking and the reading he had done while away had been good for him. In a way it had served as the final step toward becoming a new person. He indeed was a changed person. The people around him not only noticed it but liked the changes in him and had come to respect him more for it. His arrogance and anger had given way to him being caring and calm. He still had his dominant and powerful personality, if anything he was even more strong-minded than before. But now he knew what he wanted in life. He had a purpose and a goal, and he was determined and focused to achieve it.

The construction of his house had resumed following the holidays and things were progressing well. He was pleased that they had already started building the walls of the first floor.

He was particularly happy that he got to see Christina and the children almost every day, that was until early February when their summer holidays were over, and they went back to school. Then he saw them occasionally while he still continued to see Christina nearly daily. By now he no longer wanted his house to be built based on his ideas alone. He admired Christina's high sense of style and beauty and wanted to incorporate her ideas as well. Often, he would ask her questions about the house. Wanting to be helpful she was always glad to offer her thoughts and suggestions.

Aden was also quite busy reading and preparing himself for the start of the university at the end of February. Professor Klossen had provided him with a list of the books he needed to read or at least familiarize himself with, which took up a lot of his time.

Finally, the day that he had been so anxiously waiting for, the first day of university, arrived. On that day and during the first week he only had lectures to attend, which he enjoyed and found easy to follow. By the end of the week, the news of who he was and what he was trying to accomplish had spread, increasing his already high popularity even more. That did not matter to him at all. As far as he was concerned, he was there for only one reason and one reason only. It was to achieve his goal of getting his Business and Law degree in the record time of three years with top marks of distinction or better. Because of his new, caring personality he was friendly towards everyone, but that was as far as it got. No girl had any chance with him. He only had strong deep feelings for one person and saw and treated all the other girls merely as friends.

The tutorials started during the second week. One of his first tutorials was on economics and was being run by a rather demanding and accomplished tutor who was himself a post graduate student at the university. Recognizing and knowing who Aden was, he decided to put his mettle to the test, to find out what Aden was about and how capable he was. Halfway through the tutorial he picked Aden to answer a question. With the reading he had done and his photographic memory, it was easy for him to answer the question. However, Aden's response came across as a mere quotation from the book which gave his tutor the excuse that he needed. He came down hard on Aden, pressing for the analysis of his answer, which he was unable to provide. He did this a couple of times, and by the end of the tutorial Aden felt discouraged. He found himself doubting his abilities. The experience had left him feeling challenged and uncertain as how to accommodate what had happened, a feeling that he could not overcome, not even by the time he got to see Christina that afternoon.

Christina immediately sensed that something was bothering him. "What is wrong Aden?"

Aden knew if there was anyone who could understand him, it would be Christina. So he told her what had happened.

"Nothing worthwhile achieving is accomplished without difficulty and hardship. Having said that, you should never doubt yourself. With your abilities you can overcome anything," said Christina in her usual, compassionate manner.

"I don't see how? So, I can recall volumes of books, but what good is that, if I don't know what it all means?"

"Can you repeat the question that he asked you?" Aden did. "Can you also tell me your response?" Aden easily told her that. After thinking for a moment, she proceeded confidently to explain it all to him.

He was pleasantly surprised. It all made sense to him. Now he understood what his tutor was expecting to hear. "How did you know that? I think that you are the genius."

Christina laughed. "I know that because I studied Business Administration with a minor in Economics at Stanford University."

Aden was impressed. With a look of admiration and wanting to learn more about Christina, he asked, "What did you do after you finished your university?"

"I had Timothy and then two years later, Natalie. My plan was to go on to get my Master's degree, and then go to work. I met Sean in my junior year at Stanford. We fell in love and got married in the summer of that year before my senior year. We weren't planning on having children until much later. It's funny how so often in life things happen contrary to our well thought out plans, as I ended up having Timothy the following summer shortly after my graduation."

"Were you disappointed?"

"Not at all," said Christina without the least hesitation. "They each brought with them such joy and happiness. Certainly, pursuing one's education and career not only is necessary and challenging, but also highly commendable. However, I believe that it all pales in comparison to the challenge and value of raising your children. After all, the children are the promise and hope of our future. That is why I wanted to raise them myself." Her face was beaming with joy as she continued, "Besides, when I held them in my arms after they were born, I knew that I couldn't leave them."

"What about Sean? Was he disappointed?"

There was a pause. It was as though she was searching for the right response. "Sean dearly loves both of them," she replied.

Then to her own amazement she found herself feeling comfortable enough to be open with her thoughts. "I know he feels under pressure to provide for his family and to be successful. His old university friends are either unmarried, pursuing their careers and enjoying the single's life, or recently married with no children enjoying a two-income lifestyle. Perhaps at times it's hard for him not to think of them as more successful. But what is success?"

Not anticipating a response, she continued, "To me, it is in having those things that money can't buy."

Aden was intently listening to Christina. He was enjoying learning about her and getting to know her and her thoughts. Still wanting to find out more he asked, "Do you miss not using your business education?"

"I guess a little, but I plan to go back for my Master's degree when the children are older."

"Then teach me what you know."

"Excuse me?" said Christina caught off guard. It was not that she had not heard Aden. It was that his suggestion was so unexpected.

"Teach me all you know," repeated Aden in a confident, positive, and up-beat tone of voice. "That way you'll be helping me with my understanding and in the process, you'll be able to get back to what you have studied which is something you'll have to do before going back for your Master's degree."

"It has been quite a few years, seven years to be exact since I've looked at any of that. I don't know what good I would be, and you should have the best tutor possible."

"I would, if you accept."

Christina was flattered, but not convinced, "You don't need to be kind."

Aden meant what he said. "My tutor explained that question in the class, but it wasn't clear to me until you explained it. Your explanation was in depth and yet simple and easy to follow. In fact, I believe with your help I'll be able to **at least** get straight distinctions."

"That's like getting all Bs, isn't it?"

"Something like that."

"I don't know. I think that I'd better sign a disclaimer statement," said Christina kiddingly.

"It won't do you any good because I will personally hold you solely and entirely responsible, if I get anything less than a distinction average," replied Aden in the spirit of having fun.

"Ok, you're on. I accept the challenge!" said Christina with a smile and determined tone of voice. "Actually, that will be a lot of fun." She sounded excited and felt enthusiastic about it, consistent with her effervescent personality and zest for life.

Her response was more than he could have hoped. Everything had been going so well for Aden that he could not have imagined it getting any better. Yet, it just did. It was like a dream come true to have Christina as his personal tutor. No more coming up with excuses to see her. Now she would have to see him everyday during the week. Combining both year one and two, there would be a lot to cover.

If there could have ever been an ideal year, this year would have had to have been the one. John could not have been happier. He was feeling more proud of Aden with each passing day. With Aden spending all his evenings at home, he also had cut down his evening meetings so that he could be there for his son. The two of them got along well. They would always have dinner together unless John was out of town. Their dinners had been transformed to joyful times for them to catch up with each other's day with pleasant conversations. At times they would be laughing together about something amusing that had happened during the day and at other times they would be having intellectual or philosophical discussions. John particularly liked being able to talk to Aden about his new venture into the computer industry.

The entire staff at the Bradcliffe mansion felt happy. Aden was like a son to many of them. They could not be happier seeing how the father and son were getting along and how well things were going in Aden's life.

At work things could not be better for John. One of the most elite research teams had been put together by Rishi Vavek and Declan Harris. All the required research equipment and computer networks had been purchased and installed, offices and research labs set up, and the research project was successfully underway. At times, the development work seemed to be going slower than John would have liked, but he had come to accept it and looked forward to having the first prototype ready in about 12—18 months.

Sean was also happy with his work. In January he had gotten the promotion he had wanted, the vice president of marketing for the Australian branch of Chip Systems International. This new position, plus his ambition for the next level of promotion kept him quite busy and often away on business trips. Christina, as always, was very supportive of Sean and his commitment to advance his career. She never complained about his long working hours and went along with whatever Sean wanted.

As it turned out, his overly committed work schedule meshed well with Christina's heavy commitments. She was totally involved with the children, their schoolwork and after school activities, which of course was evident with their excellent performance levels in school. She also had reading to do to prepare and refresh her memory in her new role as tutor for Aden. She had dedicated several hours each day around Aden's university schedule for his tutoring sessions. She also had the housework to do as well. But she was happy because she was helping others.

Aden was very content with his newfound relationship with his father. He also quite liked the challenge of learning and having his mind expanded by his university experience and all the reading that it involved. But the happiest moments for him were the times that he got to spend with Christina each day.

The more time that they spent together, the more enraptured he became with her. What he found particularly attractive about her was her intelligence, charm, kindness, and especially her positive attitude towards life. She only saw solutions, never problems, and was always happy and pleasant to be around. Most of all he enjoyed the stimulating and intellectual talks they had on a wide range of topics such as management, economics, world affairs, and more. These were unlike any conversations that he had had before.

With Aden's thirst for knowledge, he read all that was required for his courses and more, such as research papers, magazines, and reference books. This tremendous amount of reading and his inherent intelligence made it possible for him to bring the more scientific and analytical perspective to their discussions. Christina on the other hand was able to bring the understanding and based on her personal beliefs, the ethical and moral perspectives not readily found in business journals, research papers and books. She believed the spiritual aspects to be equally important to the material ones regarding the prosperity and well being of mankind. Often their ideas would clash during their lively and thought-provoking talks resulting in much clearer and deeper understanding of the topic that they were discussing. Regardless of how different their thoughts were, their discussions would never turn into arguments, as they both had too much respect and interest in each other's ideas. In fact it was just the opposite. No matter how serious and intense their talks were, with Aden's sense of humor and Christina's cheerful character, they always had laughter and fun together.

As a result of his new passion for learning and Christina's help, he was now able to think critically and give an in-depth analysis of what he had read. With his enhanced understanding he no longer had any difficulty in any of his classes. In fact, he now challenged his professors and tutors. He could simply analyze and answer any questions put to him and turn it around and pose a much more profound question. After a few such instances, even his economics tutor came to respect him and accept that the allowance of the special program for Aden was quite justified.

Chapter 21

Days went by quickly for Aden, and before he knew it, March was over. Aden had just finished his first two lectures of the day when he found out that his next lecture, before his free time, had been canceled. *This is a perfect chance to spend more time with Christina and see her an hour earlier than usual,* thought Aden to himself. Without any delay he was in his car driving and before long he had arrived at her house. As usual he walked to the ocean front and walked across to Christina's house. Before him was a beautiful panorama of waves rushing onto the beach, sea gulls flying by, the sun glistening on the water and reflecting off the seashells like gold and silver nuggets imbedded in the sand. On this warm, sunny autumn day, she was sitting on the terrace underneath a rather large hexagonal shaped white umbrella amidst the pink, purple and white garden flowers. She seemed to be writing. The sea breeze was ever gently blowing, pushing her long brown hair over her shoulders.

A picture-perfect sight, fit for a postcard, which lifted his spirit high. With his eyes locked on her, he started to walk up the steps leading to the terrace. When she heard someone approaching, she looked up to find Aden there to her surprise. Christina smiled. He returned her smile, but still could not take his eyes off her, her dazzling eyes and vibrant smile.

She stopped writing, greeted him in her usual cheerful way and said "You're early! Are we cutting classes today?"

"No, our lecture got cancelled," replied Aden with a chuckle. "So, what are you doing?" he asked as he sat down.

"I'm writing a letter to my parents. My father is somewhat old fashioned, more so than my mother, and they still like to receive handwritten letters through the post and not typed or emailed. Even though I talk to them regularly, I also try writing to them every couple of weeks, and on special occasions

I send them cards and pictures of Timothy and Natalie, which they really enjoy receiving."

While listening to Christina, Aden noticed the envelope on the table. "Your parents live in Los Gatos, California?"

"Yes, they do."

"Do you miss California?"

"Of course, I like California, but what I miss is my parents, I'm very close to them, especially my mother."

"Tell me about where you lived," asked Aden sincerely wanting to learn more about Christina. Even though he had spent a lot of time with Christina over the past two months the focus had always been on his studies and there had never been a chance to talk about personal things.

"My parents live in a picturesque area. They have a beautiful cream color, two-story house. The front yard is landscaped with evergreen plants and shrubs. But my favorite part is the backyard which is quite large. It has a lawn area with a white gazebo in the middle and ornamental pear trees, purple flowering shrubs and white roses along its perimeter."

"White roses, whose favorite flower is that?"

"My mother's."

"What about you Christina, what is your favorite flower?" He was curious to know.

"Pink roses, especially those that are very pale pink. There is a certain innocence and timid feel about them that I like," replied Christina with a warm smile that matched her pure feelings inside. She then continued, "Beyond the lawn area is the part I really like, the rolling foothills, green in the winter and golden in the summer, with scattered scrub oak and gum trees, which give rise to a feeling of majesty and serenity."

"That sounds quite nice. Is this where you grew up? Is that why you liked those hills, because you used to go and play there?"

"No that's a long story and I wouldn't want to bore you with it," said the enigmatic Christina who very seldom talked about herself.

"That's ok, I don't have anything better to do," replied Aden jokingly. Deep down, more than anything he wanted to learn more about Christina. "I promise I'll try not to fall asleep."

"With that kind of promise how can I resist," said Christina laughingly. With the extra time, Christina felt more relaxed and even to her surprise she found herself willing to share with Aden what had happened. Perhaps it was because she looked at him the same as her own children and she would not mind sharing her thoughts with them. She put the top back on her pen, put it down on the table and in her charming way she began as Aden listened intently. "Actually, I was born in the Midwest and that's where I grew up and lived until I was about 14 when my father was offered a very good job opportunity in San Francisco Bay area. The caring and loving parents they both were and wanting so much to give their daughter the best, my father accepted the job offer. What they wanted was for me to go to one of the best universities and be close to them, by moving to California that would be possible. Ideally that was a good idea and looking back later it was a good decision. But at the time I hated the move. It meant leaving my best friends behind, some of whom I had been friends with since kindergarten and that wasn't easy. To make matters worse my father had to be at his new job by mid March which in the U.S. is near the end of the school year. Everybody loves to go to California, but I didn't. There I was in a new place missing my friends, in a new school, not fitting in and not being accepted by the Californian teenagers."

Christina paused. She was unsure how to continue. She looked at Aden. Over the past two months they had talked about many fascinating topics most of which were of great interest to him, but she had never seen him this absorbed in what she was saying. Seeing his intense interest, she hesitantly continued. "I found living there very hard to cope with. I even hated the hills behind my parents' house. Those trees, especially the gum trees appeared so messy and unkempt. Of course, later I came to like and appreciate their beauty. Not having made any friends, everyday, after school I would go home feeling lonely and depressed, a feeling that stayed with me through that summer. Seeing how happy and excited my parents were, especially for me to be in California, I didn't have the heart to say anything. To hide my feelings, I used to go to those hills and cry uncontrollably for a while. Those hills had become like a friend, I would take my troubles and sorrows there and leave them behind. The closer it got to the end of summer, the worse I felt. It meant going back to school and feeling rejected again. I thought I had been successful in keeping my feelings from my mother, but I was wrong. With ten days to go to the start of school, my mother came to me and in her loving and kind tone of voice said, "Christina, I know this move hasn't been easy for you, but just remember there are a lot of people in the world who have it a lot worse than you think you do." My mother's statement got me thinking. That day I walked along those hills, but I no longer had the urge to cry. I thought about how all that crying hadn't done me any good or changed anything in my life. Perhaps it was time to stop feeling sorry for myself."

She stopped as she looked down. It was as if she was taken back to that difficult period of her life, recalling the emotions that she had felt. Then she looked up, and with a bright and warm smile said, "I realized life is about our attitude towards it. It's not about what happens in life, because things are always going to happen. It's about how we handle the situation. It's up to us to look inside, find the inner strength that we all have, and use it to fight back and move forward. Not to be unhappy about what we don't have but be joyful for what we do have. It was time for me to accept what had happened and make the best of it."

Hearing Christina's thoughts gave Aden a much-needed new perspective toward life. "That's such an admirable attitude," he offered with a sense of appreciation.

There were traces of emotion in her voice as she continued on, "I decided that I had cried enough for the rest of my life. I made myself a promise not to cry ever again." Then with a soft smile she said, "You know I haven't cried since then except for the tears of joy when I had Timothy and later Natalie."

Christina had been upbeat all the while, but now it seemed that all this talk had stirred up strong emotions hidden within her. There was a sudden pause. She had a far away look on her face, appearing even vulnerable for an instant, before regaining her composure. She then smiled at Aden in an attempt to hide her deep emotions. She was wandering what it was about Aden that made her let go and lose control of her thoughts to the point of sharing such deep personal feelings that she never had shared with anyone before, not even her mother, not even Sean. Her smile disappeared, and she uncharacteristically appeared uneasy. She ran her slender fingers through her long hair, pushing it away from her face, giving herself time to gather her thoughts, but still she was not able to continue.

Grateful in her openness in sharing what seemed so close to her heart, Aden responded in a very caring voice, "That was very mature thinking for a 14-year-old." In praising her he wanted her to know how he was impressed by her and that she had no reason to feel uneasy about sharing her personal thoughts.

That response brought the smile back to her face. There was a sign of relief on her face as she replied, "Thanks. I guess it was."

To make her feel more comfortable, he continued, "Most people don't come to such an understanding even as adults. When I was 14 all I could think about was…well no need to get into that now." Christina could not help laughing. "But I would like to know what happened after that?" asked Aden.

"Well, the next day I asked my mother to take me shopping. She did and we had so much fun. I got a whole new wardrobe, a new hairstyle and a new look. With a touch of modesty, I can say I looked good, and I felt good. I was a new person with a new attitude. As a result, when I went back to school, I met a lot of new people, made a lot of friends, and guess what? I became one of the most popular girls at school," said Christina with a content smile on her face.

"I'm not surprised," said Aden, pleased to see her happy again.

"Anyway, I had fun going to school, but I also studied hard, extremely hard. My hard work paid off and I got into Stanford University. That was a dream come true for my parents and I, and the rest is history." A sense of calm came over her as she finished. She leaned back in her chair and said, "I told you it was a long story. I hope I didn't bore you."

Aden was quick to respond, "Not at all. It was quite uplifting. I was particularly impressed by how you shared with me something so personal, something that you hadn't shared with anyone before," said Aden matter-of-factly, sensing her vulnerability.

Christina was astonished with his sense of perception and made no reply. She thought it was best to move on. "I believe it is time for us to work on your courses. I'll get us some tea and coffee." Christina was beginning to feel in control once again as she picked up her letter and envelope.

"I can wait for you to finish your letter."

"No, that is alright, I'll do it later," replied Christina seemingly touched by his offer as well as his display of thoughtfulness throughout their conversation.

While waiting for Christina to return, Aden found himself elated. He felt closer to her than before, having learned something so personal about her. As he gazed at the endless deep blue ocean, he could not help but wonder about the effect Christina was having on him. He knew one thing for sure, that the more he learned about her, the deeper his feelings grew for her.

Chapter 22

Days and weeks of this perfect year were swiftly passing by. As the year drew closer to the end, the busier Aden's life became. The more hectic things got, the happier he became. It was not just because he enjoyed being busy and on-the-go all the time, which he did, but rather it was because it gave him more reasons to ask Christina for her help. The more she helped, which she did gladly because of her nurturing nature, the more time he was able to spend with her.

By mid-November he had finished taking all his exams, and the university was over for the year. This meant that he had just completed both his first and second years of university studies. Now all he had to do was to wait until early December to receive his results.

Aden did not mind the wait. He was having a great time with Christina taking care of all the final details that needed to be completed on his house. With his house scheduled to be completed by mid-February, and he and his father to be departing by mid-December on their five weeks European tour, it did not leave him with much time. All the final selections for the interior and the exterior of his house, as well as the choice of the décor and selection of all of the furniture had to be made during these four weeks. Without Christina's help, that might have been an impossible task, but with her help and input everything went smoothly, and he was able to take care of most things.

One evening early in December Aden had just returned home. It had been a hectic, but enjoyable day with Christina, followed by meeting Brian and some of his other friends. After greeting him, Randall brought him his mail. He anxiously looked at them and noticed that there was one envelope from the university. He immediately dropped all the other mail on the table and hurriedly opened this one. He glanced down the page as quickly as he could, to find to his satisfaction that he had gotten distinctions for all his subjects. "Yes, I did it!" exclaimed Aden excitedly.

That caught Randall's attention, "What did you do Master Aden?" curious to find out what it was that had made Aden so happy and excited.

"These are my university results, I got all distinctions."

"That's wonderful Master Aden," said Randall. He then excitedly called for Jane to come, who along with several of the other mansion staff including Debbie, John Bradcliffe's personal assistant, came running to find out what the excitement was all about. Aden had become very special to all of them, and in a way, they thought of him as their own son. They were all happy and enthusiastic to learn about his achievement.

"Where's Dad?"

"He should be home any minute," replied Randall.

This was not something that he wanted to share with his father over the phone. He wanted to personally show these results to him. While waiting for him to get home, he decided to call Brian, "Hey Brian. I just got my results. I got all distinctions."

"Congratulations! But was there ever any doubt?" replied Brian.

In the midst of all this excitement, Aden's father arrived home. "Thanks Brian…I see that my Dad's home now. I'll have to call you back later."

Without any delay Aden showed his results to his father, as all the staff looked on with big smiles and happy hearts. John looked at the results. He then looked at Aden with admiration, pulled him closer and gave him the most tender and loving hug of his life. "I am so proud of you Aden. You have made me the happiest father in the world," he said with his face beaming with joy. There was not a dry eye among the staff. Jane and Randall were particularly touched by such a display of loving emotions.

"Is that a tear I see in your eyes, Randall?" whispered Jane.

"No, it is my allergies," replied Randall softly, maintaining his reserved demeanor.

"Since when have you had allergies?"

"Since today, alright?"

While they were all talking, Brian together with his father, Ian Forbes, who lived nearby arrived at the mansion. Brian and his father, who was one of John's closest friends, were very happy for Aden. Both, along with all their friends, knew how important it was to Aden to achieve these results. They had come to congratulate him and to celebrate his accomplishment.

On the way Brian had taken the liberty of sharing the news with a few friends, who in turn had told a few others. It was not long before a number of them arrived to congratulate Aden. Shortly after that, Sandra Klossen, who knew about Aden's results also stopped by. With everyone there, the celebrations got started and continued with a lot of laughter, joking, and stories to share. There was even some reminiscing by John, Ian, and Sandra about their university days.

Aden's success, against the background of where he had started from, was quite significant. That had triggered a good feeling in everyone. They all felt part of it, almost as if they somehow had something to do with his success. As a result, it ended up being a very special and joyous night in an otherwise hectic world where there is no time to slow down. That night was different, everybody wanted to stay and socialize. There were no pretences. Everybody was happy to let go, relax and share their thoughts and life experiences. They all continued talking over dinner and celebrated into the late hours of the night. If it were not for the next day being a working day, they probably would have continued all night.

Later that night, after everyone had left and his father had gone to sleep, Aden had a chance to be alone and to do some thinking. He walked to the balcony in front of his room. As he looked at the night skyline of Adelaide, every light seemed to be shining just a bit more brightly that night. The traces of contentment were still lingering on his face, yet in his heart he had an aching, heavy and somehow hollow feeling…he was missing Christina. He wished that he could have seen her and shared it all with her. True, it was he who had accomplished what he had set out to do, but he owed it all to Christina. Her high vision and ideals, her continuous encouragement and ceaseless support had made it all possible. He could not help but smile when he thought of circumstances leading to and then meeting Christina nearly a year ago. Thinking about where he was in his life then, and where he had now come to, he wondered how he could ever thank her. Somehow, he knew that she would simply say, "Be the best you can be, academically, morally, ethically, and in every way." That's exactly what he has tried to be.

Morning could not come quick enough. When he finally got to show his results to Christina, she was ecstatic about it. She felt so happy and proud of him that she could hug him. "That is absolutely great! I knew you could do it."

Aden smiled. "You never stopped believing in me. I appreciate that and I know I couldn't have done it without you." He truly meant it as Christina had been a continuous source of inspiration, understanding and intellectual stimulation for him.

Christina was touched but did not require any words of appreciation. What she had done for Aden was based on her belief that we must help each other in the spirit of true giving, without any self interest or personal gain. Her modesty and her high regard for his abilities would not let her accept such high complements, "Not true! You did it with **your** hard work and dedication, and that is commendable."

"I'm not quite sure. Anybody can get results like these," retorted Aden.

"Sure, lots of people can do many things, but very few in fact do because very few have the conviction and the determination that is needed above and beyond their inherent talent. That is what you demonstrated in achieving your goals."

"Then I shouldn't have any problems getting all high distinctions. That is what I have decided to achieve next year," said Aden adamantly.

"That certainly is a very high goal considering that you will be doing both years three and four in a single year." Then with a big, approving smile she said, "If there is anybody who can do it, it's you."

"Glad to hear that. The way that I see it, you've just volunteered yourself for some hard and heavy tutoring for next year."

Christina laughed, "Then I think that you are going to be in big trouble," seeming not quite sure about her ability to tutor him.

"Are you saying that I can't do it?"

"No, not at all. Of course, you can do it…but not with my help. All your courses will be more advanced and more difficult."

"What happened to that spirit of 'Yes, I accept the challenge. It'll be fun' that you so boldly maintained at the beginning of this year? Look at the results. They speak for themselves," said Aden convincingly.

"Alright, I'll be happy to help in whichever way that I can," said Christina, committing to what was going to be a very significant challenge for her.

That was exactly what he wanted to hear. Now he had another year to look forward to being able to see her, perhaps even more often than last year now that he would be living next door to her and having more demanding course work. "And once again you will be held responsible," said Aden jokingly. He then continued on a more serious note, "talking about the past year, made me think of how certain you were about my father accepting me, and you were right. But, how did you know?"

"That was simple, having children myself I can understand how parents might feel and think."

"Now he can't praise me enough. Through it all I have also come to gain such respect for him, after all those years of rejecting him. Now I see what an amazing man he really is."

Christina was more than pleased to hear that. She was beaming with a smile. "That's exactly how you should feel towards your father."

"It's funny. Ever since I was a child I always wanted to go with my father on his European trip, but he never took me. Now with this new attitude towards me, he is even more excited about having me go with him than I am. He can't wait for us to go and for his friends to meet me." After having been so busy with his exams and his house, this was the first time that he had brought up his trip and his thoughts about it.

Christina was sensitive to his openness and shared her thoughts with him, "I believe that things in life somehow always work out the way that they are meant to be. Obviously, it was meant for you and your father to be close. It just took a while for it to happen."

"Do you know that this is the first time that we will be spending holidays together, ever since I can remember?"

"That's wonderful," said Christina feeling genuinely happy for him. "So, where in Europe will you be going?"

"We will be going to Germany, Austria, and England for New Year's Eve, and then off to Switzerland for skiing and relaxation. My father also wanted me to go to the US with him where he'll be having some high-powered meetings with some of the leading electronics companies there. But, I said no, I'll just go to Europe with him. Even five weeks in Europe seems a bit too long, especially with all that needs to be done here." In reality it was not that he did not want to be traveling with his father, for he did. It was that he did not want to be away from Christina. He was feeling mixed emotions, and he did not really know how to deal with them.

Christina sensed his hesitation, and in her usual style went to the rescue. "Aden, you need to relax and have some fun. You've earned it. You've worked so hard all year on your studies, and you have taken care of almost everything for your house with the exception of a few minor details that can easily be finished when you return. Now is the time for you to have your holidays with your father."

Aden could not really argue against what she was saying, even though he wished things were different. Christina, sensing that Aden was not quite convinced continued on, "Once you start traveling, you will see that even five weeks is not enough. I wish we could spend five weeks in California, but we can't. Sean has got a couple of very important projects due by the end of January. So, he cut our trip down to two weeks."

"I'm sorry to hear that," said Aden not just to be polite. He sincerely meant it. Over the year the intensity of his love for her had grown so much that he found himself overwhelmed by the feeling that he never wanted to see Christina disappointed or unhappy, and if he could, he would do anything, even lay down his life to make her happy.

While appreciating his sincerity, in her true character of only seeing the good in every situation, Christina replied, "That's alright, it doesn't matter how short it is, as long as we get to see my parents, Sean's family, and the children have fun; then I'll be happy. That's exactly what you need to do, forget about everything else, just go and have a good time."

Usually, all he ever needed was her warm smile and encouraging words to get him going. Not this time. Nothing short of seeing and being with Christina was going to stop him from missing her. Regardless of how he was feeling, he appreciated her kindness of wanting him to have a good time and tried to look at things in a more positive light, "You're right. Just being with my father should be all that matters." He then paused, thinking how his father had not said much about their trip, and said, "I think my father wants our trip to be more of a surprise for me. I guess that not knowing what to expect, makes the trip more adventuresome, like going to some far-off, distant jungles in South America looking for a two-headed giant creature."

Christina laughed. "Now you've got it, but hopefully Europe will be safer than looking for your two-headed creature."

"Hopefully. I will certainly let you know."

Chapter 23

It was mid-December and the day had finally arrived for Aden and his father to depart for Europe. After having boarded the plane and making themselves comfortable in their plush, first-class seats, Aden set his watch on a five-week countdown as the plane took off.

The first destination was Frankfurt where they were to attend a charity gala and visit some of Germany's beautiful countryside. There they were to meet some of John's high society friends, some of the richest in the European circle. Among them were also a number of notable high thinkers. Some he had known and been good friends with since his university days at Oxford. Others he had met over the years during his annual European trips.

The charity gala, a high society, black tie event, was first on their agenda after they arrived. This was where Aden would meet his father's friends for the first time. Aden had gone on this trip to keep his promise and make his father happy, but his heart still was not in it, not even by the time that they arrived at the gala.

This special event was held in one of the most elegant and exclusive halls in Frankfurt. It was exquisitely beautiful with its crystal chandeliers hanging from its lofty ceiling, magnificent life-sized oil paintings with gold ornate frames on every wall, flower arrangements, candles, and ice sculptures on the tables and scattered throughout.

As they were about to enter Aden was thinking to himself and wondering, *What am I doing here? I don't know anybody here, and I don't want to be here.* Feeling rebellious about the whole thing he acted aloof and standoffish, even for him, when introduced. He was hoping to be left alone and not have to engage in all the boring small talk. However, with aloofness being almost a requirement for acceptance at this type of function, his thinking actually backfired. It was no surprise that before long his aloof and cool behavior, along with his good looks and that Bradcliffe stately mannerism, made him the hit of the evening. He was being pulled into all kinds of conversations, with many people wanting to meet him or at least have him meet their daughters. That was something that he really was not interested in doing. His thoughts and heart were focused only on Christina.

The savior of the night for Aden was meeting his father's old friends, who in their true, typical form engaged him in rather stimulating and intellectual conversations as their way of 'testing the water'. Was he to be accepted into their circle, or dismissed as shallow as most of the young people, who in their opinion, were not sufficiently intellectual or serious minded? John had not told them anything about Aden. He wanted them to learn about him independently, and they did, to their surprise. They were impressed and amazed at his depth of understanding, breadth of knowledge and his remarkable ability to quote any fact or figure.

After spending the last year involved in intellectual talks and discussions with Christina, he was more than prepared for any conversation or philosophical question posed to him. In fact, it was a pleasant welcome for him. To the disappointment of the young people there, he ended up spending the entire night talking with his father's friends and enjoying it all. They were not only intellectual. They were also witty and knew how to have fun. By the end of the evening there had developed a mutual respect and admiration between Aden and John's friends. They were now earnestly looking forward to having Aden with them for the next few weeks. John, who had been on a high all evening from the overwhelming way that Aden had been received, could not have been more proud.

After that evening there was a change in Aden's attitude towards the trip. He seemed more relaxed and accepting. Even though he would not openly admit it, he was beginning to think that this might actually be an enjoyable trip. He liked his father's friends and the mind game that had evolved that evening, which continued throughout their trip. They were to come up with a challenge that Aden could not solve. But regardless of how they tried, they were unable to achieve this. They all had fun, and also a good laugh about it.

The days that followed were quite pleasant as they were chauffeured through the picturesque villages along the Rhine River, the old town of Rotenberg, the many castles, and other historical sights. It was then time for them to go to Vienna. It had been a week since they had left Australia, and Aden had not stopped thinking about Christina. As they were packing to depart for Vienna, he was thinking how Christina would also be preparing to depart for America with her family.

Christina was, in fact quite frantically finalizing all the last-minute details, when Sean came home and said that he was not able to go on the trip. His personal assistant, Mrs. Terreli, who was going to be completing the market research and finalizing the work on his presentations while he was away on the trip, had just come down with a highly contagious and extremely painful case of the shingles. This left him no choice but to stay and complete the work himself as this was for a critical project which could not be delayed. Naturally, Christina and the children were disappointed. But Sean did not see any reason for them to stay as he knew that he would be too busy working on this project to spend any time with them. Christina felt bad about leaving him home to work, but in the end she came to accept that it was the best option for everyone.

The next day Christina and the children departed for San Francisco and Sean, feeling quite concerned went to work. To his surprise Mrs. Terreli, out of her kindness, had arranged for her 21-year-old niece, Vicky, to come in to be of some assistance to him over the next two weeks while she was recuperating. She had finished high school with only one goal in life, to marry a rich man. She had light brown curly hair, was not very tall at 5' 5," had a medium busty build and wore tight clothes. She had a friendly personality and was very accommodating which made up for her lack of know how and experience.

Vicky was uninhibited and unscrupulous. She immediately saw in Sean the kind of man that she wanted to have; successful, ambitious, and his good looks were just icing on the cake. It did not matter to her that he was married, with only two weeks to go; she pulled all stops and started to work on him from day one. With no sense of modesty and hardly anybody at the office, the field was open for her. She turned on the charm and openly flirted with him. Anything that Sean wanted and more was done, including staying late every night. Even though for the most part he was focused on his work, he could not help but notice her coming-on to him. At first, he found it amusing, but after a few days he found it enjoyable. After all, it was hard to resist all the devoted attention that he was getting. It was the kind of attention that he felt he was missing in his marriage, with Christina always being too busy with the children.

When Vicky learned that Sean's wife was overseas, there was nothing stopping her. She invited him to her family's New Year's Eve party. At first Sean declined, but at her insistence and seeing that he did not have any other plans, in the end he agreed to go.

That was the opportunity she was not about to miss. She wore a low-cut halter dress intended to entice Sean. When he arrived, she was a most charming hostess introducing him to everyone, serving him food and drinks, waiting for the right moment and the right excuse to get him to her room. Under the guise of showing him some of the trophies she had won over the years, she succeeded.

Sean always thought that the grass was greener on the other side. As a result, he never fully appreciated the wonderful family life he had. He often thought that having gotten married when he did, and having children shortly thereafter, had tied him down too early in his life. He felt that he was missing all the excitement of the single's life. With many of his friends still unmarried and living it up, at least in his mind, he sometimes wished that he could have fun like them. Lacking the strength of character and the moral conviction that Christina so richly possessed, when Vicky invited him into her room, he accepted.

With complete disregard for her parents, she locked the door. Then in her conniving way she seduced Sean. Weak with desire for the thrill and excitement that he felt was missing in his life, he went along and did nothing to stop her. It was his ambitious personality of always wanting more, that lost him the battle of morality and fidelity that night.

After the heat of the passion subsided, he began to feel guilty for what he had done and how he had betrayed Christina's trust. He told Vicky that it was all a mistake and that it should, and could not happen again, and that they both had to completely forget what had happened that night. This was not at all what Vicky wanted to hear, but she went along with Sean's wishes to regain his trust.

During the following week prior to Christina's return from California and before the recovery of Vicky's Aunt, things with Vicky went back to a purely professional level to Sean's satisfaction. To the outside observer there was no indication that anything had happened between them.

Chapter 24

Vienna had much to offer for entertainment and sight seeing with concerts, the Vienna Boy's Choir, the Lipizzaner Stallions of the Spanish Riding School, the Schönbrunn Palace, and the Liechtenstein Museum. Also, there was a number of high society lunch and dinner parties, some of which were specifically organized to honor their visiting guests, John and Aden. Each one had been arranged with such extravagance and elegance as if the hosts were in competition to outdo each other. Such a hectic schedule left them with little time for themselves. This busy schedule continued in London. There they also attended an exclusive New Year's Eve ball where celebrations went on through the night.

At every one of these functions Aden got to meet many people, some were his father's old friends, but most were girls who wanted to get to know him, catch his attention, and capture his heart. The reputation of his great looks, cool arrogance, and intelligence, among other things, had spread like wildfire through Europe's high society community, making him a most highly sought out bachelor wherever he traveled. Having lost his heart and soul to Christina he had no interest in any of them. Their beauty, fortunes and social standing had no effect on him. For the most part they came across as shallow and superficial. He had been with girls and women like them ever since he was 17 years old, leading to meaningless sex, which now he found empty and distasteful. After meeting Christina his standard had changed to a much higher level. Now he wanted everything in a woman: beauty, intelligence, and strong sense of morality; all the things he had found in Christina. Nothing short of this was any longer acceptable to him. So very courteously he continually declined the many invitations that were offered to him for more personal get-togethers. He was relieved that his father respected his wishes and, even though at times he seemed disappointed, he did not try to influence or pressure him in any way to accept these invitations.

On the third day of January, with two and a half weeks left of their holidays, they departed for the Swiss Alps. Being a strong athlete and an accomplished skier, Aden was actually looking forward to this part of their trip for some challenging skiing.

The snow-covered Alps, soaring high into the sky were particularly magnificent at this time of the year. Their 6-star exclusive ski resort complex was situated in a wooded area of the Alps, surrounded by glaciers and peaks with breathtaking views of the mountains and valleys below. The resort was renowned for its excellence in service and beauty. Its chalet style architecture blended harmoniously with its mountain setting. Each chalet had been uniquely decorated in classical elegance, offering all the possible comforts and luxuries desired. The complex consisted of several interconnected main buildings housing gourmet restaurants, coffee shops, an indoor swimming pool with spa and sauna, clubs, boutiques, and specialty shops, just to mention a few of its amenities.

Shortly after their arrival and check-in, Aden, John, and his friends gathered in the elegant and spacious lobby with a high ceiling and mirrored marble floor. They sat by the large granite fireplace, talking, and enjoying the warmth of the fire. Soon it became apparent that they were waiting to meet some other friends who had arrived earlier, before going to their chalets. Aden learned that among them were a couple of royal guests; a Duchess Alanna and her late husband's niece, Princess Elexa. Duchess Alanna was a true friend and a trusted companion of Princess Elexa, who accompanied her during her travels.

As they waited, the mood of the lobby was rather mellow and subdued. With the arrival of the royal guests, the atmosphere changed and there was a sense of excitement. John and his friends got up and warmly welcomed Alanna and Elexa. They had not seen each other for a few months and were happy to be together again.

Duchess Alanna was in her early 40's and had a colorful and outgoing personality. She was very attractive and glamorous, with short perfectly styled blond hair and light brown eyes. She openly showed her affection towards John. After she greeted him with a kiss, she stayed in his arm with her arm behind him as she and Elexa went around to individually say hello to each of their other friends. Aden was surprised to see such an uncharacteristic open display of affection by his otherwise reserved father. Seeing his obvious attraction to Alanna, he realized that his father had more than simply skiing in mind. Then it was time for them to meet Aden, who up to this time had stayed in the background. John with his arm still around Alanna introduced her first, and then Princess Elexa who was accompanied by two of her minders.

Elexa was a beautiful and charming young princess with long chocolate brown hair and green eyes, who above and beyond her royal standing and duties knew how to enjoy life. It was her fun loving and bubbly personality that struck Aden. She was the first one he found easy and enjoyable to talk to of the many girls that he had met during this trip.

After they had been talking for a while, one of her minders came over to ask a question. When she answered he replied, "Thank you, your highness."

"Your highness? Is that what everybody calls you?" said Aden with a disapproving attitude.

"Well, that is part of royal social etiquette."

"I like Elexa. That's what I'll call you, and you can call me Aden."

Elexa laughed. "Whatever you want Aden." Then in a friendly tone of voice she said, "That's exactly what I had expected you would say."

"Why is that?" wondered Aden.

"Simply because of what I've heard about you."

"And what would that be?" asked Aden casually.

Before Elexa had a chance to reply, their conversation was interrupted by his father handing him the key to his chalet. He told him that his luggage had been taken there and he could go to his chalet whenever he liked. Aden then looked at the number on the key and asked where it was. "I'll show you where it is," interjected Elexa.

"Very well then, I'll see you at dinner," replied his father with an approving smile as he left together with Alanna.

A few minutes later Elexa, escorted by her minders walked Aden to his chalet. Once inside she dismissed her minders and made herself comfortable on the plush sofa by the fireplace, motioning for Aden to come and sit next to her. Aden simply ignored her and offered to walk her to her chalet.

Elexa laughed, "But I am in my chalet."

Aden assumed that there must be some mistake. "That's alright," he said. "I'll call the front desk and have it sorted out."

Elexa was surprised. "From your reputation I didn't think that you would react like this."

"I don't know what you've heard," Aden replied defensively, "but obviously it isn't correct." Although Aden's values and behavior had changed over the past year, it had not been reported in the media.

To defuse the situation Elexa said, "There are two separate bedrooms here. Only the living area is common." Liking what she saw in him she continued on, "This was my Aunt Alanna's and your father's idea. They thought that in this way we could get to know each other better."

This was unacceptable to Aden. Although his father meant well, he did not like something like this imposed on him without being consulted. He also did not want to have to explain why he would not be interested in entering into a relationship at this point in his life. Without saying anything, Aden just picked up the phone and proceeded to call when Elexa said, "There's someone else, isn't there?"

He cancelled the call. He had never been confronted like that before and was caught off guard, "Why would you say that?"

"Because no one has ever resisted me and that can be the only explanation," said Elexa with a conceited smile. "Besides, I am very good at reading people. So, tell me about her?"

"There's nothing to tell."

Elexa was amazed at the thought of such news, knowing how much Aden was in the spotlight and how much he was sought after everywhere he went. "Then I'm right," she said as she waited to see his reaction. When he made no reply, she knew that she was right. "There is someone that you love." Having been so quick in discovering Aden's deep secret, it was easy for her to figure out the rest as she continued, "Even your father doesn't know about her. Otherwise, he wouldn't have set us up like this. Seeing how you don't want to talk about it my guess is that you haven't told her either."

"I don't think this is going to work out, I'll just call and ask for another chalet," said Aden not wanting to discuss any of this with her or with anybody for that matter.

"You won't find anything for miles, everything here gets booked out months in advance."

"I can still try."

"Don't worry; your secret is safe with me. Actually, this could work out really well," she said in her friendly manner.

"How do you mean?" asked Aden.

"Usually, it is such a hassle for me to try to avoid the paparazzi that I can't enjoy myself. But now, with nothing between us, I don't have anything to hide, and who better than Aden Bradcliffe to be seen with in public?" Elexa expressed. Then with a smile she continued, "We can go anywhere, do anything, even pretend to be madly in love, and they can take all the pictures they want. We'll have a lot of fun and it won't matter what they print or what they say, because none of it will be true. We can have a good laugh about it all. So, what do you say Aden?"

Not wanting to disappoint his father and realizing that this had been his surprise for him, to be with Elexa, he agreed. "Alright, this way I'll be able to keep my father happy."

"And my aunt," she added positively.

Excited about all the fun they were going to have Elexa went up to him and gave him an affectionate hug. Then she walked into her bedroom.

Later that evening Aden and Elexa met up with his father, her aunt, and their other friends for dinner, and had a good time. Everyday after that they spent most of their time together skiing, dining, dancing, shopping, and much more. To keep up the appearance, Aden let her kiss him in public, but it was strictly a platonic relationship whenever they were in their chalet.

It was the end of the first week; Aden was lying down on his bed thinking about Christina and how she would be returning to Australia and wishing he could be there to see her. With these thoughts on his mind, he found it hard to fall asleep, so he got up and went to the living area. The curtains were open. As he looked out the window, he could see the dimly lit complex below. In a distance the snow-covered ridges and mountain peaks loomed against the dark night sky. It had just started snowing. It was majestically beautiful, peaceful, pure, and untouched, like his love and his feelings for Christina. It was late at night, not a breeze and not a soul around, a perfect setting for him to imagine being out there walking in the snow with Christina alongside of him. A smile came over his face. He was so lost in the moment and his thoughts that he did not hear Elexa walk into the room. Even when she put her arms around him, he did not take any notice of her. It was not until she began to kiss him that he snapped out of his thoughts.

He stepped back and stopped her.

She was confused, especially after what would have seemed to her that he was going along. "I don't understand, after having such a great time together over the past week. I thought that things were different between us. I thought that you now like me, don't you?" she asked looking hurt.

"I like you very much Elexa. You're beautiful, warm and lots of fun to be with," said Aden, "but I am in love with someone else." This was the first time he had openly admitted to his love for Christina. He felt he had to in order to be fair to Elexa.

"I can't believe this. I can have any guy in the world, and I have to fall for the one person I can't have," Elexa said with tears in her eyes.

Knowing how that feels, he sat her down on the sofa across from him, took her hands, looked into her eyes and said, "Don't think of it like that. Think of this as a very special and unique friendship, a friendship I have never had nor could imagine having with anybody else."

"But I want more than that."

To make her feel better he said, "You must then realize from my reputation that after I have been with someone once or twice, then I'll have nothing to do with them. Is that what you want? Or wouldn't you rather keep our friendship that will last forever without letting these physical things get in the way of us having a great time like you wanted?"

This was not exactly what she wanted to hear, but she had to admit what Aden was saying made sense. The fact was that she really enjoyed being with him and, not wanting to jeopardize that special relationship they had, she agreed. No longer appearing sad, she said, "Ok, we'll do it your way, but you must promise me that I'll be the first to know if things don't work out between you and her."

Aden gave her his promise, even though it was a possibility that he did not even want to consider or think about. Actually, he did not know what to think. All he knew was that he was the happiest when he was with Christina. There was something extremely special between them, unlike anything he had ever experienced; it was on a much higher level, beyond this physical world, beyond what mere words could express.

Being the gentleman that he was, he walked her to her bedroom and said, "You'd better get some rest. You'll need it for all the things we have planned for tomorrow."

Elexa feeling a little better, gave him a little goodnight kiss on his cheek, and said, "Thanks, Aden."

"Goodnight Elexa," said Aden looking forward to the next day.

Chapter 25

It was the night before Christina and the children were to return from California. Sean was busily taking care of some of his work ahead of time so that he would be able to have some spare time to spend with them. He had made some good progress when the doorbell rang. He was not expecting anyone. As he was walking to the front door, he wondered who it could be at such a late hour.

He was surprised to see Vicky there. "May I come in?" she asked in a businesslike manner while holding a number of files under her arm. "I've brought you the final part of the market research that you had asked for. I wanted to make sure that you got it since my aunt returns tomorrow, and I won't be coming to work anymore."

"Sure, come in. I'll take a look at it, but it will have to be quick. I still have a few things to take care of before Christina's return tomorrow."

"Perhaps I can help, that way you'll be able to get through them twice as fast."

After thinking about it for a moment he accepted her help. Then they spent the next two hours working on his project and tidying up the house. When it was all finished, she said, "It's pretty late. I think I'd better go now."

"Yes, it is rather late. I'll walk you to the door."

Halfway to the door, Vicky stopped, turned around, looked at Sean with the saddest face and said, "I can't pretend any more Sean. I love you. I need you," she then moved close to him, "I need to be with you, to be in your arms." She started to kiss him.

At first, he was not responding to her affections. "This isn't right. Christina is coming back tomorrow."

"Please Sean, just one last time." Having seduced him once before, she knew very well how to do it again. She continued to kiss him while whispering in his ear how she could make it worth his while. And she did. Before long, she had succeeded in seducing him and staying with him all through the night.

During that time, she had very cleverly managed to talk him into keeping her as his personal assistant and giving her aunt a different job. She enticed him by telling him how she could help him achieve his goals of moving up the ladder to better positions and higher salaries. And she was not far off from reality. In fact, she could through her persuasive and unscrupulous ways open doors and pathways for him that neither her aunt nor anybody else would be able to, and Sean knew it. She was as ambitious and ruthless as he was and would do anything for money and power.

"But I won't be able to see you outside of working hours," said Sean.

"I guess we'll have to have very long working hours, late into the night and sometimes on weekends," said Vicky with a diabolical smile.

"I have to think about Christina and the children," said Sean seeming to have second thoughts about it.

Vicky was quick to put that to rest. "What's there to think," she said. "She'll just continue living her little uneventful domestic life and take care of the children, while I'll make your wildest fantasies come true."

"Look, I can't do this to her."

"You aren't doing anything to her. She isn't going to know. This will be our own little secret. No one will know," said Vicky expertly manipulating and enticing him.

Sadly enough, Sean agreed to go along. His sense of morality and ethics was again tested, and once again he failed miserably. Over the years his ambition had grown and had changed him into a driven man consumed with passion and desire to the point of sacrificing his principles for his personal gain, with no regard for his family or the inevitable impact that his actions would have on them.

The next day Christina and the children returned after having had a wonderful time with Christina's parents and Sean's relatives who lived near San Francisco. As pleased as she was having seen her parents, she was equally feeling guilty for having left Sean for two weeks. She was happy to see him; an enthusiasm that she sensed was not shared by Sean. She naturally assumed it was because she had not stayed to support him. With her belief that marriage is an eternal bond, she had total trust in him, and the thought of infidelity would never enter her mind.

She was only glad to be back to make up for not having been there for Sean. Little did she know that the world she had left behind no longer existed. Unaware of how things had changed, she had returned with a new sense of energy. She was determined to be even more loving and supportive to make things less demanding for him at home so that it would be easier for him to cope with the stresses of work.

Sean gradually spent less and less time at home. His big projects being due later in January were all the justification that he needed to spend more and more time at the office, and with Vicky. A pattern that continued with Christina taking on more responsibilities at home doing things that had previously been done by Sean. This left her with less time to spend with Natalie and Timothy. Both were understanding and did their best to occupy themselves by playing with each other or with their friends.

A week had passed since they had returned. Natalie was passing time by browsing through her Mom's Women's Weekly magazine that had just arrived in the mail that day. Suddenly, she got all excited. "He's here! He's here! Look, he's here!" she yelled.

"Calm down Natalie. Who is where?" asked Timothy.

"Aden is in this magazine," she replied as she showed him the magazine. Timothy got excited too, seeing the two-page spread about Aden. There were pictures of him in restaurants, night clubs, on the ski slopes, and more. Timothy hurriedly read the captions to find out that the girl in those pictures with Aden was a princess. Not only were they thrilled to see his pictures in the magazine, but they also thought, *Wow! it was so cool that he was hanging out with a real princess.*

"That is what I want to be when I grow up, a princess," said Natalie in her cute voice, "and you can be a prince. I'll wear beautiful dresses, and then we'll go dancing." They started acting out the parts of being a princess and a prince. Just then, Christina was walking by when she heard them laughing and having fun. She walked into the room and asked what they were so happy about. They both excitedly showed her the magazine.

A big smile came over her face. She felt really happy for Aden. "A princess? Definitely less dangerous than the two-headed creature he was concerned about," she exclaimed without thinking that the children were listening.

"What do you mean Mommy?"

Christina laughed, "Nothing, really."

She thought how it was so fitting for Aden to be with a princess. As she looked at those pictures, for an instant of time feeling tired and overworked, she lost control of her thoughts. She found herself wishing that she had been the princess with Aden and wondering what it would have been like. No sooner than the thought crossed her mind, she stopped herself, knowing very well that she should not have made such a wish, not even in her private thoughts. It was as impossible as it was improper. She took herself back to her normal thoughts and to her work. She left the room leaving the children to continue with their fun.

Chapter 26

It was finally the end of those five hectic and eventful weeks. Aden said goodbye to his father who was departing for the USA, and anxiously waited for his flight to Australia. The countdown on his watch was nearly over now with only hours left until his return home. Soon it was time to board his flight to Sydney and then on to Adelaide. He arrived at Adelaide International Airport at 10:20pm Tuesday evening. Having been constantly busy and on-the-go during the past five weeks, he actually welcomed the idea of spending a quiet night at home by himself.

However, unaware of what had transpired back home, with pictures of him and Princess Elexa splashed across every magazine, newspaper and social media, his friends had different plans for him that night. It had been a while since they had been together. They all wanted to catch-up and more importantly, to find out about Aden's trip and Princess Elexa. Shortly after his arrival, Brian with some of their friends came over. Those who could not make it then, stopped by later and all stayed until late hours of the night. They were having too much fun to leave.

They were anxious to hear about the princess. In fact, they were more excited about her than he was. Aden's lack of enthusiasm was not entirely surprising to them. After all, that was the hallmark of his cool personality. Nothing overwhelmed him, that is, nothing except for his feelings for Christina.

Brian was the first to break the ice. "Come on Aden. Tell us about the princess," he asked excitedly as everyone listened eagerly.

"There's nothing to tell," replied Aden with an indifferent attitude, much to their dismay.

"What did I tell you guys? Didn't I say he's not going to want to talk about her," said Brian knowing his friend's personality as well as he knew his own. "He loses interest in a girl after being with her once or twice. This time he was with her for over two weeks, the longest he has ever been with a girl. No wonder he's lost interest and doesn't want to talk about it."

"At least tell us about the things that you did with her."

"You probably know more about it from the media than I could tell you."

"Aden you're killing all the fun, here we thought we were going to have some hot gossip to talk about."

"Then I suggest we talk about what you guys did over the summer. Brian, you go first."

"I know you're just trying to distract me," said Brian. "But I'll take it anyway."

That got them all started which suited him fine as he had no interest, nor could he think of anything he cared to talk about.

Next morning with only thoughts of Christina on his mind, Aden went to see her. It was a warm summer day. Natalie and Timothy were playing outside in their backyard when he got there. He found himself overcome by feelings of joy to see them, a feeling that was equally shared by the children. As soon as they saw him, they ran as quickly as they could toward him, with smiles on their faces they gave him the biggest hugs that they could, "We're so happy that you're back. We missed you so much."

He warmly hugged them back, "I missed you guys, too. It's really good to be back."

The two of them had always enjoyed being with and talking to Aden, and they could not wait to get started. "Guess what? We saw your pictures in the magazine, and you looked so handsome," said Natalie in her adorable way.

"When my Mom saw the picture of the princess, she said something about a two-headed creature. Why? Did you see any?" wondered Timothy.

Aden laughed at hearing Christina's response and felt content with her reaction. "No, I didn't," he said. Then he asked them about their trip, "Tell me, how was California?"

California was the magic word. It instantly got them both talking at the same time, telling him how great it was.

"Ok Natalie, you go first," said Timothy being the big brother and the more mature one.

With no hesitation Natalie started, "We had so much fun going everywhere, and look at what my Mom got me in San Francisco, this ring. Isn't it the prettiest ring in the world?" asked Natalie as she extended her little hand showing off her ring to Aden. It was in the shape of a flower with a small diamond in the middle of it. Aden looked at her flower ring and could not agree more. Natalie continued, "I like it so much that I am going to wear it all the time. See, it can be adjusted," pointing to the back of the ring. "I can wear it even when I am all grown up."

Seeing Christina's caring qualities in both of them brought a smile to his face. The way Natalie was clinging to his arm while talking, and Timothy holding on to his other arm while patiently waiting for his turn, was heart warming to him.

Then it was Timothy's turn. "Look at what I got in San Francisco, this cable car keychain," said Timothy as he handed it to Aden to inspect. "When I grow up, I want to get a sports car just like you and use this keychain for its keys."

"That's a good idea," said Aden as he handed the keychain back to Timothy. "So, tell me, what have you two been doing since you got back?"

"Not much. My Dad has been very busy with his big projects. So, he doesn't come home until very late. That leaves Mom with more work and less time for us," said Timothy, looking disappointed. "That's why we're bored," said Natalie.

"Well, we'll have to do something about that. Won't we?" said Aden wanting to bring back their smiles. And it did as they asked, "Do you really mean that?" "Of course, I do. You can say goodbye to being bored. In fact, I have an idea of what we can all do for fun today, which could also give your mom a break from all her work."

Their little faces lit up. "Can we go now? Can we?" they asked excitedly.

"Well, that depends on your mom."

"Come on! Let's go and ask her now!" they both yelled as they each took one of his hands, pulling him towards the house. It was not that he needed any tugging to encourage him to see Christina. They were just so anxious that they could not wait, not even for a second.

Aden, who could not be considered emotional by any stretch of the imagination, suddenly found himself experiencing a sense of exhilaration and nervousness just at the thought of seeing Christina. He could feel his heart racing as he walked into the house. The moment that he had been waiting for the last five weeks had finally arrived.

Christina was in the kitchen. As he laid his eyes on her a feeling of calmness came over him. He could not see her face. She was down on her knees doing some work under the kitchen sink. He felt this protective urge to help her. He could not bear to see her overworked like that. He had to find some way to make things easier for her. As he looked on wanting to stop her and offer his help, he heard the children call to their mom, "Mom! Look at what we brought!"

"Just a minute sweetheart. I just have to…loosen this."

Just then her hand slipped and hit the side panel. To stop the pain, she put her other hand over it, when to her surprise she heard, "Can I give you a hand with that?"

She turned quickly to unexpectedly find Aden standing there in the kitchen with the children. She immediately got up and with a big smile on her face said, "Hi Aden. You're back. So, how was your trip?"

He felt overjoyed to see her and mesmerized by her vibrant eyes, warm smile, and beautiful face. Even though she was dressed plainly in comfortable clothes, with her hair pulled back in a ponytail, to him she was more beautiful and more glamorous than all the girls that he had met and seen during the last five weeks. With his eyes still locked on her, he pulled his thoughts together and responded, "Hi Christina. My trip was quite good. It was great to be with my father. I liked getting to meet so many of his friends, and I was impressed by them and the intellectual conversations that I had with them. In each country we traveled to, we attended a number of functions as well as doing some sight seeing."

"What was your favorite part?" asked Christina.

"I would have to say Switzerland," replied Aden without hesitation.

Christina smiled. "Of course, that's quite understandable," she said, thinking that he would have liked it there because that was where he was with Princess Elexa.

Aden, suddenly realizing what she must be thinking, was quick to set the record straight. "Actually, unlike what you're thinking, I liked it there because of the magnificent views and the skiing that I got to do on the Alps." Remembering how there were times, especially after seeing children on the slopes, he had wished that Christina and her children were there, he continued, "You all would have liked it there. That's why I was thinking that we should go to the Ice Arena today for some indoor skiing and ice skating." After being away for five weeks, he did not want to wait any longer. He wanted to spend the whole day with Christina and the children, and to help them have a good time.

The children loved the idea. "That'll be a lot of fun. Can we go now? Please Mommy?" asked Natalie and Timothy in unison.

Christina responded hesitantly. She did not want to disappoint the children but saw no choice. "I can't. This sink is backed up, Daddy didn't have any time to fix it, and a couple of plumbers that I called couldn't come until tomorrow. I can't leave all this mess here. I'm going to see if I can do something about it myself. If not, I'll have to try to find someone who can come today and then wait for him to come. It just never ends…I hope you understand."

"What if I fix it for you? Will you then agree to go?" asked Aden confidently.

"You fix it? I don't see how you could possibly do that."

"That hurts," said Aden light-heartedly. "I didn't know that you had such a low opinion of my abilities."

Christina laughed, "Not your abilities…well only your plumbing abilities…growing up in a mansion hardly lends itself to acquiring plumbing skills."

"Normally that would be true, but you are forgetting one thing, and that is how I was always so bored when I was growing up. To keep from being bored, I had to create entertainment for myself," said Aden trying to be discrete with the children listening closely. "Let's just say that lots of things broke down around the mansion. While thinking what to do next I got to see how things got fixed, including backed up sinks…many times. With my memory I can still remember it all. I knew my genius would finally come in handy one day," said Aden jokingly. "So, how about it?"

"With an offer like that how can I say no?"

"Is that a yes, Mommy?" asked Timothy as Natalie looked on with her big brown eyes waiting for her answer.

"Yes, it is."

"Hurray! Let's go Mommy. Let's go help us get ready. We don't know where our winter clothes are."

"First let me see, if I can be of some help to Aden."

"Thanks Christina, but I'll be fine. It's better to help them get ready. The sooner that they're ready, the sooner we can go."

By the time they came back down, to their surprise Aden had finished. The in-sink disposal was working, and the drain was running, but unfortunately Aden's clothes had gotten slightly wet and dirty.

"Wow that was quick! I'm impressed. Have you considered a career in plumbing? Seriously, you don't know what a great help you've been." Christina could not thank him enough, "I'm sorry about your clothes."

"It doesn't matter. I'll just go home and get changed before going to the Ice Arena." He then looked at Natalie and Timothy who were ready and asked if they would like to go with him. "I'll get my housekeeper Jane to make you the thickest and tastiest milkshakes you've ever had, and afterwards I can show you around where I live."

"And we'll get to ride in one of your cool cars," said Timothy sounding thrilled.

Things kept getting better for the children. "But are you sure it's not too much trouble for you?" asked Christina.

"Yes, I'm sure. It'll be fun, and it'll give you a chance to get changed in peace and meet us at the Ice Arena whenever you're ready," said Aden with a caring smile.

Touched yet again by his kindness, Christina could only agree.

Soon Aden and the children arrived at the Bradcliffe mansion. They followed Aden in and were totally stunned by the sheer size and elegance of the mansion. Natalie, wide eyed at the sight of the chandeliers, elegant draperies, and the wide and long staircase, naively asked, "Is your father a king?"

"No silly! Australia doesn't have a king; it has a prime minister and a governor. We learnt about it at school. Is your father one of those?" asked Timothy.

Their questions made Aden laugh, "No he's just a wealthy man. Come on, let's get you two some milkshakes," said Aden as he called Jane.

Jane came over right away. She was pleasantly surprised to see the children there as she inquired, "What can I do for you Master Aden?"

Aden introduced the children to Jane. "I would like you to make them a couple of your special milkshakes," he replied. Then as he smiled at the children he said, "And get them whatever else they want."

Soon the rest of the staff also learned that there were children visiting the mansion. It was not long before they all came to see them. The fact that there were so many staff only increased the children's amazement of their surrounds. It was also quite a novelty for the staff to have Timothy and Natalie there. After all, there had not been any children at the mansion since Aden was young. It was a welcomed change in their daily routine to have children around to talk to, to do things for, and to hear playing and laughing. With Natalie being so adorable, and Timothy so precocious, and both so well behaved, it was no wonder that they were so well liked by all the staff.

While Aden was getting changed, Jane and Randall took care of them, got them their milkshakes and whatever else that they wanted. Being so pleased to have them there, they just could not do enough for them. Before leaving, Aden gave them a quick tour which only impressed them even more, and if it were not for their plans to go to the Ice Arena, they would have liked to have stayed there all day long.

The children were so happy to see their mom at the Ice Arena. They had so much to tell her. While Aden was getting their skis and the few minutes before they got completely distracted by the whole atmosphere of the arena, they both, almost talking at the same time, told her all about the fun time they had with Aden.

Since Christina had always been the one to help others without expecting anything in return, she could not get over how helpful Aden had been all day. She was particularly touched by all that he had done for the children. It meant the world to her to see them happy. Still, there he was continuing to be caring by helping the children put on their skis. Then after they got on the snow, he started to give them instructions on how to ski and snowplow. She could not help but begin to see him in a new light. He was no longer that self-absorbed young boy lost in life, but rather a deeply caring young man who knew what he wants in life.

When the children were ready, they all went to the top of the slope and skied down. Aden with Timothy went first and then waited for Christina and Natalie to come down. Looking at her against the misty background of the slope lifted his spirit like he had never before experienced. There he stood, living what he had thought and dreamed so much about during the past few weeks, spending a whole day with Christina and the children. Every look, every glance of her was more breathtaking for him than the entire spectacular view of the Swiss Alps. He was back, and with her, feeling happy and content again.

Chapter 27

John, at the conclusion of his European visit, flew first class from Zurich to San Francisco. At the international terminal he was met by Allan Kelly, his executive in charge of the optical computer program, who had arrived a day earlier. He was waiting for him outside of Customs. He warmly greeted John and helped him with his luggage. He then directed him to their stretch limousine that John's office had arranged for his use in San Francisco. The limousine took them directly to the Fairmont Hotel where two suites had been booked for their stay.

Shortly after their arrival at the hotel, Allan brought John up to date with all the progress that had been made during the last five weeks. John then focused the discussion on determining where they currently were in their overall plan. Based on this review John finalized his thinking in terms of what to offer to the companies they were going to meet with during the next ten days.

John's status, based upon his family's long-standing position among the wealthy of the world and his personal achievements, had earned him the reputation of being one of the most accomplished executives of his time. In the US however, he was breaking new ground both in earning recognition for his accomplishments as well as entering into an entirely new industry, one which was comprised of well-established companies anchored as key players. As a minimum he was hoping to achieve two goals from these meetings. First, he wanted to be viewed by the key companies as a strong, credible player. Second, he wanted to ascertain how he could position his company in the existing industry structure to ensure his venture would have a high probability of success.

From his first meeting it was apparent that his reputation had preceded him. As a result, he was not only given the red-carpet treatment there, but also in all the other meetings that followed. His meetings with the medium sized but growing companies such as Gamma Corp and OptoCellular Technologies went well. They were with the key executives usually including both the Chief Executive Officer (CEO) and the Chief Technical Officer (CTO), who were cautiously interested in the processor that he was offering. His final meeting was with Digicomp Communications, the largest and most powerful of the dominant players in the industry. Even though he felt that he had to meet with them, he was unsure of the outcome. Would they potentially see him as a threat to their market dominance and therefore attempt to block his market entry? Or would they also be cautiously interested since his product was still in the early stages of development?

Digicomp was located in a building that had been specially designed and built for it in a unique, grand and modern architectural style, reflecting its successful image and its commitment to excellence. The meeting took place in their plush and spacious board room which was fitted out with the latest in audiovisual and communications equipment providing for power point presentations as well as interactive videoconferencing. The strategic and high priority nature of the meeting was evident by the executive level of the participants from Digicomp that included the CEO, CTO and CFO.

To John's pleasant surprise Digicomp's interest was not just casual curiosity, but rather a keen interest in the Bradcliffe Corporation processor as a strategic component in the company's future.

John first gave a quick overview and background of the Bradcliffe Corporation. He then described the history of the fundamental research and technical development of its revolutionary processor and how it had all begun as a research project at the Lightsbridge University. He further explained that the processor was a technical breakthrough in the industry, and how he saw it as a vehicle for his corporation's entry into the Computer Technology world. He continued to say that the research work had been taken up by his company and had been further advanced and expanded in order to develop a commercially viable product.

"Our initial product offering is very near," said John with certainty. He also advised them of the broad intellectual property protection program that had been embarked on to ensure total protection of the research worldwide. Patent filings were in the final stages in all Patent Treaty countries, and his company had both the resources and the will to ensure that they would not in any way be infringed.

"Our research team likes to think of it as our magic light processor," said John with a sense of pride, "or in short, **The Magic Light**, whereby using light instead of electrons, calculations are carried out at an exponential rate. In other words, as soon as you start the calculations, you will have the answer." As he looked at the Digicomp executives he noticed from their positive expressions on their faces that they all seemed familiar with what he was saying. With that observation he confidently continued, "The purpose of our trip is to identify a strategic partner with whom to work."

"I see that we are both men of vision," replied Mark Thomson, the CEO of Digicomp. "You wanting to enter this field, and I wanting to maintain leadership of it."

"At least for the time being," interrupted John, wanting to let Mark know that he intended to become one of the leaders himself.

"In this business, today is all you have. There are no guarantees about tomorrow. The best you can do is to increase the odds in your favor." Mark then paused seeming to want to give himself a moment to finalize his thoughts. "I don't like to beat around the bush that's how I've been able to succeed in this competitive and volatile industry. So, I'll get straight to the point." He had done his homework. Appreciating the cutting-edge value of John's proposed processor, he continued, "We're interested in your product, and I believe by working together we can improve the odds for both of us. We can offer you our engineers to work with your research team to develop a processor best suited to the needs and demands of the market of which we are extremely knowledgeable. The new product can then be sold through our worldwide market channels."

"And in return?" asked John.

"We will be looking to your company to work with us on an exclusive basis, and to develop a working prototype within eighteen months from now."

The ball was now in John's court. Would he accept their offer, or would he try to work with another company that did not require an exclusive arrangement? He needed time to think about it. And if he were to accept their offer, he would need to consult with Allan and the research team before actually committing to an eighteen months delivery date. Acknowledging Digicomp's offer and Mark's openness, John suggested that the meeting be adjourned and be resumed the next day. He told Mark that he would have his answer tomorrow, at least in principle.

Mark was accommodating. "Certainly," he replied. He understood that it was a question that John could not decide on the spot. To facilitate the process, he proposed for them to sign a memorandum of understanding (MOU) before ending the meeting.

After the MOU was drawn up and signed, Mark appeared content. He then, as a demonstration of Digicomp's commitment to work with Bradcliffe Corporation, said, "I will have our lawyers prepare a letter of intent by tomorrow, which can then be signed should your response be positive."

"That can be followed by a due diligence," said John thinking ahead.

"Once everything checks out, as I have no doubt it will, then our lawyers can prepare and mutually work out the formal agreement," said Mark setting in place the final step needed to carry forward and finalize their partnership negotiation.

John nodded his head in agreement. "That would be the appropriate process," he said.

Mark appeared satisfied. "In the meantime," he said, "we would be honored to have you as our dinner guests this evening." John accepted. They had an enjoyable time, and Digicomp spared no expense in entertaining their VIP guests.

By the next day Allan had the response from Declan indicating that he was confident that they would be able to have a working prototype ready within the eighteen months timeframe, and John made his decision to work with Digicomp on an exclusive basis. Normally, he would not have agreed, but to have access to the engineers as well as the market channels was more than he could have hoped. In fact, it was exactly what he needed at this initial stage to strongly enter the new market.

The tension in the room was palpable when the meeting resumed the next day. It seemed to have a perceptible drain on everyone there until John stated his position and accepted Digicomp's offer. The letter of intent was signed both by John for Bradcliffe Corporation and Mark on behalf of Digicomp Communications, marking a new and exciting partnership for the two companies. It also marked the beginning of a potentially disruptive technology that would soon impact the computer industry worldwide. Following that, the focus of the meeting changed from business to technical discussions dealing with issues relating to the processor itself, as well as its firmware and hardware compatibilities. John agreed to have the research team look into developing firmware that would bring the processor into conformance with Digicomp's strategic needs. Mark agreed to take the responsibility of bringing the necessary hardware companies into the fold. By the end of the meeting all the key strategic elements of the project had been identified and were in a coherent enough state to be passed onto the project and technical managers to begin this unprecedented collaborative project.

Following the departure of their VIP guests, Mark and his CTO returned to his plush office. Mark sunk into his fine, soft leather executive chair with the signed letter of intent in his hand. He finally seemed relaxed and relieved.

"I don't get it Mark. You would think that your job was on the line the way that you've been acting," said the CTO expecting his boss to lash out at him for having made such a statement, even though it was said half humorously. But to his surprise Mark remained silent, not even making an effort to deny it.

"How could that be?" asked the CTO in surprise. "I've been around long enough in this business to know that you're one of the most powerful and indispensable executives that Silicon Valley has ever seen."

"I wish things were that simple, but they aren't," replied Mark. "As you know Digicomp was acquired by ESE six months ago." He then continued, carefully choosing his words, "Their philosophy, generally speaking, is to maintain a low profile and not get involved with the daily operation of the companies in which they invest. When they took over Digicomp, true to their philosophy, they didn't make any changes in Digicomp's organizational structure. However, ESE's management gave me a directive to develop the next generation of processors which are generally anticipated to be based either on optics or quantum principles, and to achieve that within 18 months." With a pained look he said, "The race began, as you know, and ended abruptly when Bradcliffe Corporation, from out of the blue, filed for patents and took the wind out of our sails. That put me in a very tenuous position with ESE. As I was grappling with the idea of approaching Bradcliffe Corporation, they contacted Digicomp requesting this meeting. So, you can appreciate that this deal was a make it or break it proposition for Digicomp and especially for me."

"ESE's management should be very pleased with what you just accomplished today."

"I believe so," said Mark appearing content again. "They'll have what they wanted, except this way Bradcliffe Corporation will fund the development, and we will reap both the benefits and the profits. But between you and I, money is not the only thing that ESE is after; rather it's the world dominance of the industry. ESE wants to maintain their worldwide leadership and global power base through owning key technologies in communications and locking up strategic partners to broaden that power structure."

"That is very progressive and forward thinking."

"Personally, I don't think it's all that altruistic. ESE is very powerful and doesn't want its power eroded, and it will do anything and go to any length to maintain it," said Mark with a sinister tone. "As cold and calculating as I may be, ESE's management make me look like an angel of mercy." Then with a sigh of relief he said, "At least for the time being, I can say that with this deal in our hands, we will be in their good book."

Chapter 28

Early in February, shortly after John's return to Australia the final agreement was signed and sealed signaling the beginning of a promising and productive collaborative relationship between the two major corporations.

The research team was happy with the input that they were receiving from Digicomp's engineers and with the direct involvement of Allan in the process, the progress could not be better.

As content and satisfied as John was with the outcome of his trip to the US and the positive way in which things were shaping up with his electronics venture, he had an unsettling feeling that he could no longer ignore or conceal. Aden's house was near completion, which meant that soon he would be moving out of the mansion. Merely the thought of it was more than he could bear.

His love and respect for Aden had gradually grown over the past year. It had begun when he first learned of his year 12 results and his intention to go to university. Then watching him do so well through the year with his studies, and finish with such excellent marks had only enhanced his admiration of Aden. After spending five weeks together with him in Europe and seeing how well he was accepted and respected by his friends brought him even closer and made him more proud of his son than ever before. Having enjoyed all the time they had spent together every night over dinner and on weekends, he did not want that to end. More than anything he wanted Aden to continue living at the mansion.

With only one week to go to the end of February, John decided to tell Aden what he thought. They had just finished dinner when John told Jane to serve coffee and dessert in the family room, a comfortable and warmer room more conducive to personal conversations.

Aden could tell that there was something on his father's mind. Once in the family room he asked thoughtfully, "Dad, is something bothering you?"

John was appreciative of Aden's perceptiveness, and with a loving look on his face he responded, "When I look back, I realize that I treated you very unkindly. I remember a year ago I told you that I couldn't wait for you to move out…and I wanted to say that I am sorry for having said such a thing to you."

"Don't worry about it Dad, that was a long time ago. You shouldn't even give it a second thought. I don't."

John still appeared concerned and reflective as he replied, "No, I really shouldn't have said that. The truth is…that I don't want you to move out. There is more than enough room here in the mansion for the both of us." To add levity he said, "There is more than enough room here for ten families." He then looked directly at Aden and said, "I know I haven't said this before, but you're an important part of my life. Everyday I look forward to our dinners and conversations together. I wouldn't want that to change."

Aden was impressed and surprised by such an unprecedented expression of affection from his father. Suddenly, he found himself faced with a dilemma. If he were to move, he would be disappointing his father and, in a way, hurting his feelings. And if he were to stay, he would be giving up the opportunity of being near to Christina. Neither option was acceptable to him.

Deep in thought in search of a solution, he got up from the sofa and slowly walked around it. His father was looking on with a sense of hope in his eyes that Aden would agree not to leave. By the time he finished circling the sofa, he had it figured. He sat on the arm of the sofa across from his father and said, "I'm glad that you shared your thoughts with me because I would not want to do anything against your wishes, and I believe that I have the perfect solution." His father listened intently. "I'll spend weekdays at my house. The ocean has such a calming and peaceful effect on me making it the perfect place to study. I'll come here everyday for dinner. That way we'll be able to spend the evenings together as we do now. Afterwards, I'll go back to my house to continue with my studies. And weekends I'll spend here. How does that sound?"

John thought about it for a moment. He was impressed by Aden's quick mind in arriving at such a good solution so rapidly. "It sounds good to me," he replied satisfactorily. He then said, "But based on one condition, and that is for Randall to move there with you."

"You drive a hard bargain, but I accept." Both father and son were now content.

"So, when is the big move?"

"Next Monday is the turnover day as promised by my builder," replied Aden. "On the Friday, after dinner," he pleasantly offered, "I'll take you to my house to give you the grand tour. I want you to be the first person to see my completed and fully furnished house."

"I would like that very much," said John. Since he felt happy with being able to still see Aden every day, to be supportive he suggested, "Let's go out for dinner to your favorite restaurant to celebrate the completion of your house."

Aden liked the idea and agreed. "I just hope that everything will be delivered on time."

Throughout the week all the various furniture and appliances were delivered, setup, and installed. On Friday, the last remaining items such as some of his clothes and personal effects from the mansion were taken to his house. Aden spent every day of the week overseeing the move. By the end of Friday, all had been completed and everything was in its place. To Aden's satisfaction the final product was a showcase of fine architecture and design.

When the work was finally finished, it was almost time for dinner. Very quickly Aden showered, dressed, and was ready to go. Randall, however, was running late and Aden was unable to leave. He was supposed to be bringing the last of Aden's clothes and belongings. With things being so hectic during the move, it had slipped his mind to give Randall a set of house keys. Not wanting to be late for dinner with his father, he decided to go over to Christina's to ask if he could leave the extra set of keys with her for Randall to pick up when he arrived.

As Aden was knocking on her door, the thought suddenly crossed his mind that it could be awkward if Sean was home and answered the door since he had never seen nor met him. His concerns disappeared however, when Christina opened the door.

As always, the mere sight of her lifted his spirit. He pleasantly greeted her and proceeded to explain his predicament, but before he had a chance to finish, he was interrupted by Timothy running to his Mom and saying, "Daddy wants to see you right now." Christina apologized to Aden for the interruption and asked Timothy to tell his Daddy that she was talking with someone and that she would be there in a few minutes.

Sean had been coming home late every night, but that night he was home early to change his clothes before going out again. It was Vicky's birthday. He had planned a very special, romantic night for her and was in a rush to leave. Vicky had given him a necktie as a gift, and he wanted to wear it. Since he could not find it, he needed Christina to tell him where it was.

Christina, not aware of Sean's self-imposed sense of urgency and out of common courtesy, tried to quickly finish her conversation with Aden before going to see Sean. He had barely begun to talk when he heard Sean's harsh, angry and loud voice, "What?! What is she doing? Yapping away instead of doing something worthwhile..."

Aden was shocked to hear such an offensive tone of voice directed at Christina, who was by far the nicest person he had ever known. He backed away from the door and said, "I'm sorry. I've come at a bad time. It can wait."

Even though Christina felt hurt, she said, "No, that's alright," trying to cover-up her pain and to mend the situation.

Over the years Sean had become temperamental. Unfortunately, Christina's supportive attitude seemed to have the opposite effect on him, and now after having gotten involved with Vicky, he had become even more abrasive. Christina as a good wife silently tolerated it all, hoping that someday he would change. Certainly, it was not going to be tonight. His angry voice could be heard again preventing Aden from continuing. Christina turned around and when she saw Sean coming down the stairs, she said, "I'm sorry Sean. I was going to be coming up in a minute."

Aden was in a state of disbelief, wondering, *Why in the world she was apologizing when she had done nothing wrong. If anything, he should have been apologizing to her.*

"The whole world is going to wait because you are yapping away. It doesn't matter that I have an important meeting to go to," blasted Sean.

"You obviously found what you were looking for, and that's good," replied Christina meekly.

Her attempt to put it in a positive light had no effect on Sean as he impatiently continued, "No thanks to you! I work hard all day and you can't even do one thing for me when you sit around all day and do nothing, and...." He stopped in mid sentence. He just then noticed Aden. Suddenly he was this charming and friendly person as he walked towards Aden. He extended his hand and said, "Hi. I'm Sean, and you are...?"

By this time Aden was filled with rage. He literally wanted to strangle him for saying such unkind things to Christina, all of which he knew were unjustified and downright cruel. Without saying anything, in his cool and aloof manner, he reluctantly shook Sean's hand. "This is our new neighbor, Aden Bradcliffe," said Christina, hoping to break the tension. "Aden has just moved in today."

"This is a good neighborhood. You'll be happy here."

"No doubt," Aden replied in an unfriendly manner.

"I must be off now," said Sean to Christina. He then turned to Aden and told him that it was nice meeting him. He quickly said goodbye to the children and rushed off to see Vicky.

Aden was outraged by Sean's behavior and lack of care. The anger he felt toward Sean was only matched by the anger he felt towards himself for having said or done nothing to protect Christina. It had all happened too quickly and unexpectedly. The dignified and tolerant look on Christina's face calmed his anger and made him realize that she would just as soon not talk about it. Without any mention of it, he picked up where he had left off, and finished what he had begun telling her.

As always, Christina was happy to help.

Chapter 29

Aden met his father at the Grand for dinner, as they had previously agreed. As its name indicated it was a grand restaurant with elegant décor and place settings and comfortable fine leather chairs. All the tables either faced the large centrally located atrium with lush green shrubs and small trees or overlooked the beautiful outside gardens with flowering plants and running streams. What made the Grand so special and popular was its exquisite food, together with its warm friendly service and atmosphere.

Expecting him to be happy and excited with the big move, John was surprised to find Aden rather quiet and subdued. "What's wrong?" he asked, after unsuccessfully trying to engage him in conversation several times.

"Nothing," said Aden appearing distracted and distant.

"It has to be something," John insisted. "You haven't said much, and you've hardly touched your dinner. Is it the food? If you don't like it, you can order something else."

"No, it's alright. I'm just not hungry," said Aden as he put his dinner plate aside for it to be taken away.

"How much?" asked his father desperately wanting to help him out.

"How much what?" asked Aden confounded by his father's question.

"Money, of course. Whatever you want is yours. I understand that building a new house can cost more than originally planned."

"This has nothing to do with my house, and not everything is about money, Dad."

This must be serious, if it has nothing to do with money, he thought to himself. Having believed that wealth and riches can solve any problem, John became worried. What he had not considered was that many problems require spiritual solutions. Aden's response made him suddenly realize that this was such an instance.

The protective father that he was, he could not bear to see Aden troubled. He had to remedy that. He was quite well known and respected for his negotiating skills. He was also known for his problem-solving skills as he could easily see through complex issues and logically break them down into simplified ones that could more easily be addressed and solved. In fact, Aden was very similar to his father in this regard. But in this particular case he was far too emotionally involved, and it was impeding his ability to see a way out.

John, with all of his wealth and power had assumed that his son's life would be trouble free. He had never imagined until this moment that he would need to use his skills to assist his son. Yet, that seemed to be his best option. Therefore, with a kind and calm voice he asked, "Tell me Aden, what's bothering you?"

"I'm not sure that you would understand."

"After all that we've been through, don't you think that I deserve a chance to be the judge of that myself?" asked John, earnestly wanting to help.

His father's reply got him thinking. After what seemed to be a rather long pause, Aden agreed. "Today I saw something that was disconcerting to me… upsetting."

"What was it that you saw?"

"Well,…I saw someone being abusive and cruel towards a very nice person that I know."

"Was it justified?"

"No, it was not justified," replied Aden defensively. "And that's beside the point Dad," he continued assertively. "No one has the right to do that. We should all treat each other with dignity and respect."

"You're absolutely right, but unfortunately things like that do happen," said John. While thinking that Aden's reaction was commendable, he became a bit concerned at Aden's seeming inability to cope with what he considered to be such a minor issue. "That's why you can't let something like that," he continued encouragingly, "as disappointing as it may be, get you down."

As a result of this incident, however, Aden for the first time was experiencing intense emotions of compassion, helplessness, and also guilt. These emotions were new to him, and he did not know how to handle them. "Yes, I can," he retorted, "because I personally feel responsible for what happened." He then continued, "I believe that my being there is what triggered it, and I just can't accept that."

"You're being too hard on yourself."

"I don't think so Dad," replied Aden with a deep sense of remorse. "A year ago, my thoughts began to expand beyond myself. For the first time in my life, I came to realize and accept the belief that our highest aspirations in life should be that of being of benefit to others and of service to humanity. That's why I decided to go to the university, learn as much as I can, and use my education to make a real difference in the world."

"I wasn't aware of that, son. Your thoughts are very high minded, and I am truly impressed," said John, feeling very proud of Aden's thinking.

"That's the problem," said Aden solemnly. "High ideals only mean something if they are realized in action. When it came down to it, I did nothing." What made it more difficult for him to handle was the fact that it involved Christina. She was the one person that he would do anything for, even sacrifice himself for her sake and her happiness. "I can't stop blaming myself," he continued, "knowing that I was the cause of another person's sadness and pain."

"Aden," said John kindly, wanting him to get through this, "you may have been there when it happened, but you were not the cause of it."

"I know what happened Dad," said Aden still blaming himself.

"True, but your being there did not alter that person's personality."

"What are you trying to say?"

"People don't suddenly become abusive. That person is obviously an abusive person and would have been that way whether you were there or not. By being there, you got to see it. You did not cause it."

"What kind of person would do such a thing?" asked Aden rhetorically. Before his father had a chance to respond, he answered his own question, "Someone devoid of values. Someone morally corrupt."

"That's why you can't be so hard on yourself."

"Still, I feel I should have done something to stop this person."

"I don't know whether you could have done something or not. All we can do in life is learn from our experiences and move on." John reflectively continued, "The point is that we all make mistakes. That's so we grow, improve, and do better next time."

Aden could not fault his father's logic. Even though, deep down he still felt bad for what had happened, he saw no point dwelling on it. This was something that he would have to sort out later.

Appearing calm again, Aden said, "You know what the problem is Dad?" John with a questioning look listened, "You are just too rational." John chuckled as Aden continued, "Thanks for listening Dad." Back to his collected self he even had fun with his dad, "I really didn't think you had it in you."

Nothing could have pleased John more than having been able to help him. "Well, that just hurts."

"You're just getting soft in your old age!"

The tension was gone and both father and son were joking and having fun together.

"After having had such a big meal," continued John kiddingly, "how about topping it off with some coffee?"

"I have a better idea. Let's have that coffee at my house where the taste is exquisite, the temperature perfect, and the ambiance is out of this world," suggested Aden with a chuckle.

"That's a good idea," said John as he motioned for his check.

Not having seen or wanting to know anything about Aden's house, he was both impressed and astounded at what he saw. Unlike what he had imagined, it was a dignified house with a grand style. Its understated elegance was balanced with warmth and comfort. The beauty and airiness of its design was evident from the entrance and carried through the rest of the house. A set of beveled glass double doors with side panels and fan light above opened to a wide granite floor entry. On the two far sides of the foyer were diverging staircases coming together on a high landing leading to the second floor. Stepping down from the semi-elliptical shaped entry there was a rather spacious sitting area with an open view of the ocean. The sitting area extended all the way to the terrace and provided an elegant access to the various sections of the floor. The designer furniture in a range of soft leather as well as fine upholstered sofas and chairs, glass and metal coffee and end tables, hardwood dining tables and desks added to the stately character of the house. The use of both modern and classic artwork throughout the house provided for the ultimate expression of strength and style.

Following the grand tour of the house, with Randall having gone back to the mansion, Aden prepared the coffee and suggested for them to have it in the family room. It was a spacious room like the rest of the house, overlooking the beautifully landscaped and well-lit ocean side terrace gardens.

John's face was beaming with pride and joy. He made himself comfortable in the armchair. He then had a sip of his coffee, "Not bad Aden. This has the bitterness yet with the full-bodied flavor that I like in my coffee."

"Glad you like it."

He took another sip before continuing. "Now it's my turn to say that I didn't think you had it in you."

"It is only coffee Dad. I know with all of the butlers and house keepers, I never made it, but it's quite simple."

"I guess what I'm trying to say…, at the risk of sounding sentimental," expressed John, "is that I'm very proud of you, of what you've done here, and of what you've become. I already had such a high opinion of you for successfully completing two years of university in one, and I felt that I couldn't ask for more. Yet, earlier tonight I found myself feeling even more proud as I learned what a caring person you've become and with such high ideals." After a pause he continued, "Not knowing what to expect, I was dreading the thought of finding a 'pleasure palace' here. Instead, I see this. If it were any more dignified, I would think that I was in the Vatican," he said laughingly. He then smiled and said, "Don't you let any of this go to your head!"

Aden chuckled and sarcastically said, "Too late, Dad."

In reality his father had nothing to be concerned about. Aden in the process of wanting to help others and being of benefit to mankind, had gradually become more humble and down-to-earth, a quality that would endear him even more to his father. What had started to be a rocky evening ended up being very enjoyable and brought them even closer to each other than they were before. They continued talking a while longer before returning to the mansion.

Later that night when Aden was alone in his room, his thoughts drifted back to earlier that evening. Even after considering what his father had said, he still could not stop, nor reconcile in his heart feeling responsible for what had happened. It was not until Monday, after finding Christina cheerful as always, that he was able to let go of those negative thoughts.

After that day, very seldom did he ever think about that painful night that he first met Sean. All that mattered to him was for Christina to be happy, and as long as she was cheerful and had that vibrant smile on her face, he was content. Now, with living next door to her, he was in a perpetual state of joy. Seeing her had become so much easier. Everyday he looked forward to being with and talking to her, especially about his studies. As always, the high-level intellectual discussions that he had with her were the highlights of his day.

His university workload, as a result of combining years three and four, had not only increased in comparison to the work that he had experienced the year before, but had become even more demanding. The more challenging his studies became, the more he enjoyed them. Being the avid reader that he was, he easily covered the demanding reading assignments of his courses. But still that was not enough to satisfy his thirst for learning. As a result, he became engrossed in a significant amount of extracurricular reading of books, magazines, and journals to such an extent that his knowledge base became second to none. It was in consolidating all of this learning that he particularly found his deep discussions and open exchange of ideas with Christina most helpful. They further expanded his thoughts and solidified his understanding.

The schedule that he had arranged with his father not only was working to his father's satisfaction, but it also ended up working quite well for him. It meant for the most part that he was seldom there when Sean was. With Sean spending so little time at home, Aden rarely ever saw him, and when he did, it was only in passing.

Chapter 30

T he events and tests of life have the potential and power to change people. They can bring out the best, or the worst, in them. In the case of Sean, they brought out the worst. He no longer was the kind and caring man that Christina married. Now with Vicky in his life, his attitude toward Christina over the months steadily had become more abusive and hurtful. Vicky wanted Christina out of Sean's life, but that was not enough. She wanted it all; the house, the money, everything. To minimize Sean's financial losses, her plan was to make Christina leave, by making it unbearable for her to stay. Sean, wrapped up in his materialistic world of passions, corrupt desires, and ambitions, went along without any feelings of guilt or remorse.

Christina being committed and devoted to her marriage endured it all patiently no matter how difficult it became. She was too refined to ever complain or say anything bad about Sean or anybody else. She buried her feelings deep down, always appearing cheerful and pleasant. No one who saw her, not even her children, could tell the hurt she felt inside.

That is no one except Aden. His experiences had brought out the best in him and had enhanced his spiritual awareness, resulting in his heightened sense of perception and insight. It was something that had been developing within him ever since he met Christina; something he had taken for granted. It was as if at times he had the ability to read thoughts and feel emotions of others. Especially around Christina, there were times that he sensed she was in pain.

The mere thought of her sadness evoked intense feelings of compassion, similar to what he had experienced the night that he had met Sean. Even though it had been more than six months, he still had difficulty dealing with these emotions. The fact that he had lived his life without love or emotions until the time that he met Christina attributed to his inability to handle the emotional conflicts revolving around his love for her. With his love growing stronger and deeper with each passing day, he had reached the level of being prepared to forfeit his life for her. Since she never openly showed her sadness, he did not have any certainty that what he sensed was actually right. He only had an ever-growing longing desire for her happiness and hoped that his sense of her sadness was wrong.

Vicky had different hopes and ideas. Her goal was to get Sean to spend more time with her and make life more difficult for Christina. It was not enough that he had been spending evenings with her, she wanted more; she wanted him to spend weekends with her. When spring came, she suggested for them to spend a weekend in the country together. It was the time of the year that the South Australian countryside was particularly well known for its untouched beauty. The wildflowers would be in full bloom and would cover the fields and the hills in patches of vibrant colors like a handwoven Persian carpet.

At first Sean was reluctant, but with Vicky's insistence he agreed. He told Christina that he had to attend a conference over the long weekend in October. That weekend, however, was in the middle of the children's spring school holidays. They had missed not seeing their father and were looking forward to spending time and doing fun things with him during the long weekend. When Natalie and Timothy found out, they were quite disappointed. As always, it was Christina that had to mend their broken hearts and make them understand that it was important for them to be supportive of their father's career.

Without much concern, when October came, Sean was off on his romantic weekend with Vicky. He had spared no expense. They stayed at a secluded bed and breakfast, The Old English Cottage, known for its elegance and service, where he pampered and showered her with flowers and gifts all weekend long. Vicky was in her element. This was exactly what she wanted to have; all of Sean's love and attention. With having had everything according to her wishes, on Sunday morning, over breakfast, she decided to make her move. She told Sean that he was being too soft, and he needed to do more to make Christina leave.

Sean, however, did not agree. It was not that he was concerned about Christina, he was too cold hearted for that. It was that he was happy with the way things were. He had the best of both worlds. He simply told Vicky that it was a question of when and not what more to do. Vicky became quite indignant with his answer. When he tried to comfort her, she turned her back toward him and made no reply. There was no appeasing her unless she got exactly what she wanted. As a further display of her displeasure, she grabbed her phone and started to look at the latest stories as she continued to ignore him. There on the lead story was a picture of Aden. He was surrounded with quite a few girls at an extravagant 21st birthday party he had attended on that Saturday night.

Aden had not been out much because of his feelings for Christina and all the studying he had to do. He had agreed to go to this party since it was during the university break and for one of his closest friends who had really wanted Aden to be there. Making one of his rare appearances, he had in his usual style captured the attention of everyone, especially all the girls and, naturally, the media.

Vicky of course knew of Aden from having seen his picture in the media and had always wished she knew him personally. That morning when she saw his picture in the article, she started to think how lucky those girls were. All caught up in her thoughts and Aden's picture, and not knowing that Sean knew Aden, she had to say something. She stopped her silent treatment of Sean, and hoping to make him jealous said, "Here's a man who has everything; looks, money and all the girls he wants."

That aroused Sean's curiosity. He took a casual look at her phone as Vicky continued. "I should have been there to capture his attention, instead of being here wasting my time on a relationship that isn't going anywhere."

"Even if you had been there, he wouldn't have paid any attention to you, no more than he was to any of those girls in the picture," said Sean. "Why should he? Like you said, he's someone who has everything. He would never be the way I am, so caring, loving, and giving towards you. He would never be interested in you, a beautiful princess or heiress maybe, and certainly none of those girls, they're only there to do his bidding."

"How can you say such a thing?" asked Vicky who was not quite convinced.

"I can because I know the type. Besides, he lives next door to me. He had this huge house built as his 'bachelor pad' that he only stays in sometimes instead of his family's mansion, I guess for his more…personal needs and pleasures." Sean could not be more wrong as he continued with a chuckle, "I've got to hand it to him. He's even got Christina to do his bidding, by tutoring him."

That piqued Vicky's interest, "Why would Christina tutor him? What does she have to get out of it?"

"Nothing!" replied Sean disapprovingly. "She's one of those people that believes we must help others, not because we stand to gain something from it, but purely for being kind and helpful. She lives for that sort of thing. It's exactly for this reason that it's going to take some time before your plan can work. No matter how badly I treat her, she always returns it with kindness. That's why you'll have to be patient."

"I don't understand, why Christina? With all of his money he could have the best of tutors."

"Don't underestimate Christina's ability; she's quite intelligent and knowledgeable. She's probably the best tutor he could have. She graduated at the top of her class from Stanford University."

Vicky, having always been sensitive about her intelligence, became furious to hear that, and more determined to make life miserable for Christina. Sean had just given her new ammunition to use. Her diabolical mind had already started to work, trying to figure out ways to make it happen. Suddenly, she was feeling better; she was seeing new possibilities to achieve her ultimate goal.

Chapter 31

Soon it was November and the end of an important year was fast approaching. After two years of dedicated study, Aden was about to receive his first university degree, Bachelor of Business. The following year he would then graduate from Law. With only one week to go before his final exams, he was spending all his time studying. He was intent on getting all high distinctions to fulfill the challenge he had set for himself a year ago. But more importantly, he wanted to do this as a demonstration of his gratitude to Christina for her invaluable help.

During this week, a new and unexpected business opportunity had arisen for the Bradcliffe Corporation. This involved the potential acquisition of a prestigious chain of department stores headquartered in Sydney which had run into financial difficulty. It was not that John did not have enough on his plate; it was just too good to pass up. Also, having been anxious to get Aden involved with the family business, he saw this as a good introduction to its business dealings. Aden welcomed the idea but told his father that his involvement would have to be after the completion of his exams. That suited John just fine. He had his staff carry out the preliminary investigations and negotiations with the final decisions to be made when he was able to go to Sydney with Aden. To minimize the interruption of his normal work schedule in Adelaide, the meetings were set for the first weekend in December. Aden and John, accompanied by Bill Dutton, his CFO, would leave for Sydney on the Friday evening.

Jane's marriage, after going through many rough patches, had finally ended in a painful separation. Feeling quite depressed over it, she turned to the one person she could rely on, Randall, her long time and trusted friend. To help her through this difficult phase, he offered to take her away from Adelaide. This was exactly what she needed. He then explained the situation to Aden and asked if he could have a few days off. Aden was very supportive of his efforts to help Jane through this difficult time. With he and his father traveling to Sydney during the first weekend in December, he told Randall that he could leave on the Friday and take as many days off as he needed. Randall appreciated that and told Aden that he would lay out his suitcase before he departed. It was midmorning Friday when Randall and Jane left on their trip.

By early Friday evening Aden was packed and ready to leave. While waiting for his father to arrive, he decided to check the internet one last time. He wanted to see if his marks had been posted on the university website, and they were. He quickly checked them and found out that he had gotten a high distinction for every one of his subjects. He quickly printed them. With the results in his hand, he was feeling thrilled.

Thinking back to where he had started from, he had done the impossible, and he owed it all to Christina. She was the one person who made him realize his inherent abilities and strengths and encouraged him to reach his potential. She was the one person who believed in him and selflessly stood by him encouraging and helping him all along. She was the one person who agreed to support his goal of achieving all high distinctions.

Aden was too excited to remain seated. He got up from behind his desk, walked over to the window, and looked out toward the beautiful expanse of the ocean. The exhilarating feeling that he was experiencing was only matched by this magnificent view before him. The copper-colored sun was reflecting off the waves, causing the sky and the ocean to appear in brilliant shades of red and orange. The only wish, the only thought that was going through his mind was a longing desire to see Christina, to talk with her, and to show her his results.

At that moment, his father arrived with Edmund right behind him to take Aden's luggage to the limousine. Aden asked Edmund to wait. He told his father that first there was something that he wanted him to see. He then took him to the study and showed him his results. John was beaming with pride and joy. As he nodded his head approvingly, he said, "This is great." Then, filled with love and admiration for Aden, he embraced him. "And they said it couldn't be done," he said with a smile. "You certainly proved them wrong."

"Thanks Dad." Pleased to see his father happy, he humored him and said, "Was there ever any doubt?"

John chuckled and quickly said, "Of course not." There was nothing that could have made him happier than having Aden in his life.

It was then time for them to go to the airport. But consumed with a desire to see Christina, Aden found himself wishing that he could spend the weekend in Adelaide. He wanted to show his results to Christina, and for the first time in a long time, just to have the simple fun of celebrating with Brian and his other friends. He tactfully asked his father if he could stay and instead, fly to Sydney on Monday. The way that John was feeling he would have given Aden anything that he wanted, let alone acquiesce to such a simple request. Even though he would have much preferred to have Aden with him the entire time, he agreed to have him come on Monday. He told Aden that he would call him to keep him informed of the outcome of the negotiations. In that way he would be apprised of the status of the talks when he would join him on Monday.

After his father left Aden decided to go out on his front terrace. He was feeling on top of the world. The only thing that could have made him happier was a glimpse of Christina. In the hopes of seeing her, he stepped out. With thoughts of her on his mind he found himself wishing with all his heart that he could bring her all the happiness in the world. If he could, he would capture the moon and the stars and give them to her. He would do all this and more as a token of his love and appreciation.

It was a perfect summer night. The cool ocean breeze was softly blowing. The temperature was just right, warm but not too hot with no need for air-conditioning, just an open window or door was sufficient. The sun had now set, and it was quiet and peaceful. There was no one on the beach and all that could be heard was the calming, distant sound of waves gently rolling onto the shore.

As Aden was standing on the terrace admiring the glorious night, he heard voices coming from the direction of Christina's house. It seemed that his prayers had been answered. He was going to see Christina. With a sense of excitement, he quickly went down the three steps to the terrace below. He walked through the gardens on his right, and along the pathway running beside the base of the two-foot-high retaining wall, towards her house. The closer he got, the slower and heavier his steps became as he began to hear what sounded like an argument in progress. Sean and Christina were talking quite loudly, and Christina was obviously upset. Suddenly, his heart sank, his hopes shattered, and every trace of joy and excitement drained from him. While he could not discern what they were saying, filled with concern for Christina, he found himself drawn to the brick wall in between the two properties.

Masterminded by Vicky, Sean was delivering his dirtiest and lowest cruel blows to Christina. Blinded by his lustful desires, his intention was to hurt Christina, and he did not care that there was no trace of truth in the words that he leveled at her. After the children had gone to sleep, Sean, as planned, had started an argument with Christina and skillfully escalated it to the point that Aden had begun hearing it. Sean was intentionally being hurtful, explosive, and angry towards Christina.

"You're nothing but an overage tramp throwing yourself at Aden."

"I have done no such thing," said Christina defensively. "How can you say that?" The mere suggestion of it was upsetting to her, "I have only tried to help him…He is the one who asked for my help."

"Why in the world would he ask you to do that? Everybody knows that he is a genius. You should be ashamed of yourself, lying and being deceitful," said Sean shamelessly imputing to Christina what he himself was guilty of. "You are a mother of two. So, act accordingly and stop cheating on me."

Christina was in a state of shock at what she was hearing. She could not believe how Sean had taken her pure motives and turned them into mud. She felt hurt and was on the verge of tears. She could not take it anymore, "Stop it, Sean."

Sean was not about to stop. He grabbed her by the arms, squeezing them hard, "No, you're the one who needs to stop it. I've had enough!"

Aden now standing by the wall was close enough to hear Christina cry out and say, "You're hurting me."

"Blame Aden for that. It's all his fault," said Sean angrily, pretending to be enraged.

Seeing Christina in tears, his dirty work was done. It was time to go see Vicky. To finish it, he heartlessly pushed Christina down onto the floor, walked out of the room, got into his car, and drove away.

As Christina fell, she hit her face on their coffee table before hitting the floor. Physically she was injured, but more painfully she was emotionally hurt. Lonely in a world of anguish she broke down. Not having cried for all those years, she now wept uncontrollably. It was as if her dam of strength had been broken, and with no one to turn to, she was drowning in a sea of sorrows.

Although unable to see what had happened, with the windows open Aden had painfully heard everything that happened over the last few minutes of Sean's quarrel with Christina. The sound of Christina crying along with her voice echoing, "I will not cry…I will not cry…," in the back of his mind broke his heart and crushed his spirit.

Aden was confounded. *This can't be happening*, he thought to himself, *not to Christina*. Suddenly he was overcome with feelings of compassion for Christina and anger towards Sean. *How could he do such a thing?* Aden wondered, unaware of Sean's sinister plans, and filled with rage, thought of going after him. He stopped. It hit him. He could not confront Sean, when he was the one being blamed. That would only appear to confirm the accusation.

Tragically, it did not matter that Sean's words were untrue and unjustified. What mattered was the fact that Christina was crying, and that he was the reason for it. This was not like the times before when he had only felt or sensed her sadness. This was real. She was in pain, she was crying.

This was the night that he wanted to give her all the happiness in the world, not to be the cause of her sadness. The more he thought, the more unbearable it became for him. Caught in this vortex of great emotional conflict, he began to feel physically weak. For support he rested his right arm and head against the brick wall.

He desperately wanted to try to make sense of what was happening and sort out what to do. In this state of compassion and confusion he did not notice that directly below his elbow there was a razor-sharp piece of brick protruding from the wall. It had accidentally broken off during the construction and inadvertently left in between the bricks where it had been bound solid in the mortar.

The sound of Christina still crying became more and more difficult for him to endure. He felt he could no longer stand. As if unable to sustain his own weight, he had to sit down. While still propping himself by leaning his arm against the wall, he quickly slid down. The sharp piece of brick pierced his skin like a knife. It deeply cut him from his elbow to his shoulder and along the side of his face to his temple. He began to bleed profusely.

Aden was so consumed in his thoughts and feelings of guilt that he did not realize he was injured. When he did notice, he just did not care. His concerns and thoughts were focused on Christina. To him his injuries seemed insignificant in comparison to her misery. His heart ached with longing for her to stop crying. Christina could not help it. She was too heartbroken to stop. The blood continued streaming down his face and arm as she continued to cry.

Christina was the only one that he had truly loved. He could not accept being the reason for her sadness. Nor could he look her in the eyes knowing that he caused her to break her longtime promise. His inability to face Christina and to deal with his guilt pushed him over the edge. He lost all hopes. With no resolution to his conflict, Aden became intensely distraught and disheartened. Physically and emotionally his strength drained from him, until at last he lost his will to live.

Soon he passed beyond the threshold of pain, and all he could think about was leaving this physical life behind. As he was slipping closer towards his end goal, there was one last wish lingering in his mind, the desire to see Christina's face one last time. Although feeling quite weak, he managed to make it inside his house, lock the door, and walk upstairs to his room where he had the picture of Christina with the children. By the time he made it to his room, he had lost too much blood to continue. He just collapsed on the floor before reaching the cabinet where he had kept the photo. Unable to look at her face one last time, he fell into a state of unconsciousness ready to meet his destiny.

No words could adequately describe the tragedy that had so needlessly taken place, with Aden languishing on the floor of his bedroom, while a short distance away Christina was lying on the floor of her family room still unable to stop crying. They both had so innocently fallen victim to the selfish desires of Sean and Vicky, two unscrupulous people who simply did not care. It was a night that even the moon and the stars appeared dim with sadness at what had happened.

Chapter 32

Minutes and hours were slipping away, but sadly for Aden it seemed that time had stood still. It was midday Saturday, time for a short lunch break, when John stayed behind in the plush boardroom to call Aden. He wanted to tell him how the talks were progressing. He also wanted to find out how Aden was doing, and what time he was planning to arrive in Sydney on Monday.

When there was no answer on his house phone, John tried Aden's cell phone, and to his surprise there was no answer there either. He tried both numbers again, and this time he let it ring out to no avail. Just then, Bill walked in to let him know that everybody was waiting for him before they started serving lunch. John was too preoccupied to respond.

"What's wrong?" Bill asked. "You seem distracted."

"I can't get hold of Aden," replied John with a frown on his face.

"Did you try his cell phone?"

"Of course, but he didn't answer that either."

"After a night of celebration, he's probably too hung over to answer anything."

"Aden doesn't drink," responded John appearing concerned.

"He doesn't drink. He studies hard. He gets all high distinctions. What is he, some kind of saint?" asked Bill half-jokingly in an attempt to get John's mind off of the worrying. "I hope you know how lucky you are to have a son like that."

"Yes, I know, not only because of the way he is, but also because of what it means to have him in my life."

This was the first time since he had known and worked for John that he found John opening up and sharing his personal thoughts with him. Bill listened with keen interest as John continued.

"As you know the Bradcliffe core business is currently more profitable than ever before. The way these negotiations are going we stand to successfully acquire this chain of department stores and make an obscene amount of money in the process. In addition, the way the computer venture is progressing, it can easily bring us revenues of billions of dollars once completed," said John reflecting on the strengths and current status of his company. "But," he thoughtfully asked, "what does all this wealth and success mean in the overall scheme of life?"

Bill was a little surprised to hear such a question. He made no reply for he had not really thought about it. John obviously had, for after a short pause he continued, "Last night on the flight over, not having Aden with me as planned, I got to thinking and realized that none of my wealth and material success has any value in terms of bringing true happiness. Sure, they bring momentary joy, but never the real feeling of happiness."

After a pensive moment he said, "When you think of it, true happiness is unlike material joy. It is that lasting spiritual feeling of the heart derived from the people in our lives, and our interaction with each other. It's centered around the way we feel when we love and care for others, from those close to us, and to humanity in general. It is this feeling that gives true meaning to our lives."

"I couldn't agree with you more John. Unfortunately, too many of us don't realize it until it's too late in our lives," said Bill as if speaking from experience.

"Too often we seem to live to work, rather than work to live. I know that. I used to be like that. Two years ago, Aden and I had one of our worst fights. I don't know whether that had anything to do with it or not, but after that Aden became a new person. He transformed from being irresponsible, self-absorbed, and on the path of self destruction to become a responsible, goal oriented, and truly caring person." Filled with intense feelings of adoration and admiration for Aden, he continued, "Because of Aden I changed too, and I began to see life in a new light…it is in fact having Aden in my life that gives it real meaning."

Bill had been more than just a financial officer. He had been a strong supporter of John professionally, and a good friend, and did not want to see John needlessly concerned. To help him through he pointed out that it did not do any good to allow himself to get caught up in negative thoughts. After all, it was Aden that they were talking about. He was a responsible person, and if he was not answering, it was because he was too busy having a good time.

"It's hard to stop being a protective father," John chuckled to himself. "I guess you're right. I don't have anything to worry about. Well on that note we'd better not keep our business associates waiting any longer."

Later on that evening, before going to a special dinner organized for them, John tried calling Aden, and again there was no answer. Trying to stay positive, he figured that it was Saturday night and naturally Aden would be out celebrating and probably could not be bothered answering his phone.

On Sunday, John waited until noon to call Aden. He reasoned that this would give him enough time to recover from his night out. When again there was no answer, he became rather worried. He then called Ian to find out what Aden and Brian had been doing. To his surprise Brian answered the phone and sounded happy to hear from him. "How are you Mr B? How are things going with your talks and negotiations?"

"Couldn't be better," replied John. He was then about to ask about Aden, when Brian said, "Am I glad to hear from you. I've been trying to get in touch with Aden. Could you please ask him to answer his phone or give me a call?"

Brian's request made no sense to John. "You do know that I'm still in Sydney?"

"Yes, I know."

"Then I don't understand. I thought that Aden was with you."

"With me?" asked Brian sounding surprised. "I haven't seen or heard from him since Friday."

That was not at all what John wanted to hear. Still trying hard to remain calm he said, "But he stayed in Adelaide to celebrate his results…"

Brian interrupted, "And he snaked me? He's going to get it, boy is he going to hear from me! I'll go over to his house this afternoon and give him a piece of my mind."

"In that case, just get Aden to call me to tell me what time he will be arriving in Sydney tomorrow."

"Alright Mr. B, will do."

The thought of Brian going to see Aden was comforting enough for him to return to his meeting.

It was late in the afternoon. John had just returned to his penthouse suite when he received a call. It was the call for which he had anxiously been waiting. He quickly reached for his phone. Feeling relieved and happy in anticipation of talking with Aden, he answered, only to find that it was Brian. All his hopes were shattered as he listened to him say that there was no answer at

Aden's house and that his neighbor from across the street had told him that she had not seen Aden or anyone else at his house since Friday.

As he hung up, for the first time in his life he was in a state of panic. Fear had overcome him. His hands were trembling, his heart was pounding, and his mouth felt dry as the desert sand. He found himself praying to God, something that he had not done since he had lost his wife. Now with all his heart he was begging, *Please God, make sure my son is alright*. Through it all a calm came over him, and he knew that it was time for decisive action. He had to act quickly. He wanted to return to Adelaide, but all flights were booked for that evening. He made arrangements for the first available private jet to take him back early in the morning. He told Bill that it was a done deal as far as he was concerned and that he was leaving him in charge to finalize the contract details.

He then spent a good deal of the evening locating Randall. It was late at night when John finally got hold of him. He instructed him to return to Adelaide and to meet him at Aden's house at around 8 o'clock in the morning.

John's plan was to be back in Adelaide at 7:30am, but unfortunately due to heavy ground fog which occasionally plagues Sydney airport, it was 8 o'clock when he finally arrived in Adelaide. His chauffer, Edmund, was waiting for him at the airport with his personal limousine. Realizing the urgency of the situation, he quickly ushered John in and drove off, only to get caught up in the morning rush hour traffic.

It was just after 8 o'clock when Randall and Jane, who had been driving since 4 o'clock in the morning, arrived at the house. They had watched Aden grow over the years and loved him dearly, just like he was their own son. Now, naturally they were quite concerned. Feeling rather nervous and apprehensive, they walked up to the house. With the keys in his hand, Randall made a phone call to John, as he was about to unlock the front door and enter the house.

Frustrated at the slow pace of the traffic John was pleased to hear from Randall. He told him to stay on the phone and to tell him everything that he saw.

Randall and Jane both walked in and closed the door behind them. It was quiet inside the house, and everything seemed fine, that is until they saw the blood stains on the floor. At the shock of seeing that, Jane screamed. Randall quickly put his arm around her to calm and quiet her down, so as not to worry John. But it was too late for that. John had passed beyond worry to sheer panic at the sound of Jane's scream and the terrifying mental images that it evoked.

He was demanding to know what they saw. Randall was hesitant to respond, but at John's insistence, he began to tell him everything as they followed the trail of blood stains up the staircase and all the way to Aden's bedroom.

When they entered the bedroom, faced with the heart rendering scene of Aden's blood stained, lifeless body lying face down on the floor, Jane totally lost her composure and uncontrollably began to wail. Randall with tears in his eyes, and choked up, managed to get a few words out and say, "I'm sorry sir, it's Aden…. He is hurt…badly."

As hard as it was to hear Randall against the background of Jane's cries, John heard enough. His heart sank. In a demanding tone of voice he asked, "He is alive, isn't he?"

"I'm not quite sure sir," replied Randall in distress.

"Then what are you waiting for? Check his pulse!"

"Alright sir."

Randall knelt down next to Aden's body, grabbed his left shoulder, and gently turned him on to his back. That made the badly injured right side of his face and body that had been against the carpet, visible. What they saw was too shocking. It was particularly painful to Jane as she gasped for air. Even for Randall, that sight was too overwhelming, but for Aden's sake he knew he had to stay strong. With teary eyes he began to check Aden's pulse. His hands were shaking. He made a desperate cry, "I…I can't feel anything."

Upon hearing that, the phone dropped out of John's hand. It was as if he had suddenly lost feeling in every member of his body. He dropped down to his knees on the floor of his limousine, put his hands together and fervently began to pray like he had never before done in his life. With tears in his eyes, he beseeched God, "Dear Lord, please don't take my son from me. Please, take anything and everything that I have…, but please I beg of you, give me back my son."

The voice of Randall shouting on the phone brought him out of that prayerful state. He picked up the phone off the seat and listened, "Sir, Aden is alive! He's alive!" He was thrilled. He could hardly contain himself. Randall and Jane hugged each other as tears of joy and hope ran down their cheeks.

Those few minutes had seemed like centuries for John. It was if he had aged 10 years, and now he was a new man, more appreciative of life and grateful to God. He was filled with such joy and gratitude that only the words, "Thank you Lord…Thank you Lord," reverberated on his lips. While at the same time he knew that there was no time to waste, and his full attention had to be on Aden's immediate needs. He told Randall that he would immediately contact Dr Forbes and for him to stand by for his instructions.

Without delay, John called Ian and got straight to the point. He said, "Aden is seriously injured. You have to save him. Randall is at his house. He may have lost a lot of blood." Ian arranged for two ambulances, a special unit from the blood bank, and his nurse to meet him at Aden's house.

Ian was the first to arrive. When he saw Aden, he could not believe his eyes. This cannot be the Aden that he had known all his life. Having lost all that blood and having laid there since Friday with no food or water, his color was white, his face drawn, his skin torn, and his flesh exposed on the right side of his face and arm. It seemed that the plush carpet in his room had acted as a bandage, stopping him from bleeding to death. Infection had set in, and even though Aden was still alive, it was only barely. He was in a critical condition.

Only minutes later, John arrived. Ian tried to stop him from going to Aden's room. He wanted to protect him from seeing Aden in that horrific condition, but he could not. There was no stopping him. He had to see his son. As shocked as he was at the sight, with a heavy heart he walked over and held Aden's unconscious and weak body, gently and lovingly in his arms for a couple of minutes before letting go. It brought tears to everyone's eyes in the room. There were many questions, but no answers. John offered to help, but Ian told him that he had all the help that he needed, and that it was best for him to wait downstairs.

As soon as the paramedics and his nurse arrived, they went to work assisting Ian to stabilize Aden's condition. This had to be done before he could attempt to clean and patch up his cuts and wounds. Aden was immediately connected to a life support monitor, as well as various intravenous tubes providing him with blood, antibiotics, and water with nutrients.

A couple of minutes had passed. Aden seemed to be regaining consciousness, and gradually becoming more aware of what was happening around him. This was not what he had wanted. With great difficulty and determination, and with every ounce of energy he was regaining, he tried to disconnect the tubes.

Ian had stepped out for a moment to get the instruments he needed to clean, suture, and dress Aden's wounds. He then heard his nurse and the paramedic urgently calling him. He rushed back and to his amazement found them struggling with Aden and trying to keep the tubes connected. Then

Aden suddenly flat lined. Ian yelled, "Stop!" He was baffled. This should not have happened. He frantically tried to restart his heart using CPR saying, "Come on Aden…Come on Aden! You have to hang in there!" The paramedic rushed down to get the defibrillator from the ambulance.

Chapter 33

Christina was just returning home from dropping off Natalie and Timothy at school. Unaware of what had transpired, she was shocked to see the ambulances and all the other cars on the street. The closer she got the more concerned she became. Her heart sank when she got to her house and found out that those emergency vehicles were parked in front of Aden's house.

She drove into the garage and got out of the car. As she stood by her car, she found herself faced with a strong urge to go over there, but she hesitated. Through her faith in God, she had always been able to get through difficulties in life. In particular, she had always been able to overcome the sadness in her heart brought on by Sean treating her unkindly. This time it had been more difficult for her than ever before. It had taken the weekend for her to put the horrible incident on Friday night behind her and regain her emotional strength. She was now finally at a point where she could once again continue and look at life with passion, love and kindness that was so characteristic of her. Still, she wondered, knowing how Sean felt about Aden, however incorrectly, was she emotionally ready and strong enough to be subjected to his cruelty again?

It only took a second for her to make up her mind. She had to live her life according to her principles. Since caring for and offering a helping hand to others being a very important and integral part of her beliefs, she just had to go over. Then, without any concern for herself, she walked over to Aden's house and rang the doorbell.

Randall unaware of the drama unfolding upstairs concerning Aden's condition answered the door. "Good morning Mrs. Ashton," he said with a somber look on his face, still visibly shaken and upset from the whole ordeal.

Christina's fears grew deeper with seeing Randall at the door and the sad expression on his face. "Good morning Randall. I saw the ambulances and the other cars out in the front, and I became concerned…I came to find out… Is everything alright? Is Aden ok?" Then she said, raising her voice in worried anticipation, "Is he…?"

As she spoke, the melody of her voice reached Aden in the midst of all the efforts going on to try to revive him. His unfulfilled wish of wanting to see Christina's face for one last time seemed to still be his dying wish. For during the few seconds between the time that Ian had stopped CPR and before attempting to use the defibrillator, as if her voice had touched his soul, Aden's heart started again. Once again Ian was baffled, pleasantly so. He was not about to question it.

The purity of his love and nobility of his character, together with Christina's pure heart and kindness, were attracting spiritual forces. These forces were instrumental in preventing him from dying.

Just then, before Randall had a chance to respond, John having heard her questions, came to the foyer. "Sir, this is Mrs. Ashton, our next-door neighbor."

"Mrs. Ashton," said John politely, but rather uninvitingly. "Christina," she interrupted to make it less formal. He gently nodded acknowledging her name as he continued in his typical stately and reserved manner, "I am John, Aden's father. I couldn't help overhearing you ask about Aden." Not knowing anything about her or who she was, under the circumstances his only interest was to have her leave by keeping his responses very short and to the point. "Aden is injured. The doctor is attending him right now. He should be fine soon. I will tell him that you had stopped by." He then courteously walked her out.

Little did John know that by doing what he did, he took away Aden's reason to live. At the sound of hearing the door shut, Aden's vital signs began to drop. "We're losing him again," shouted his nurse and the paramedic in panic. "It's not possible!" said the bewildered Ian who was doing everything within his power to keep Aden alive.

Christina, still concerned and not satisfied with the answer that she had received, stood behind the closed door trying to figure out what to do. She could not leave. She had not had the opportunity to offer her help. With this strong, unexplained feeling within her urging her to go back, she again knocked on the door. Randall answered. "I'm sorry Randall," she said as she stepped inside the door, "I wanted to see if I can be of any assistance." John came to the door again, and a conversation between the two of them ensued.

The sound of her voice again reached Aden and like the breath of life brought him back. His vital signs picked up again. His heart was now beating sporadically, leaving Ian confounded in establishing what was causing it all. He was searching fiercely in his mind for the reason. Suddenly, he had a hunch, *Could it be her voice?* He was desperate and was willing to give even a hunch a try. He told his nurse to administer anesthetic to Aden as he ran downstairs. He had never moved so quickly before in his life. He got there as John was about to say goodbye to Christina, again.

"Wait John! I could use this lady's assistance."

John was surprised to hear that, "I thought that you had all of the help you needed."

"That was then. Now I need one more person, and no, I still want you to stay down here."

John went along and introduced them to each other. Ian then quickly proceeded back up the stairs and asked Christina to go with him.

By the time Ian and Christina got upstairs the nurse was walking out of Aden's room. With the anesthetic having been administered thought Ian, it was time to proceed. But contrary to his presumption, the nurse had not been able to give the anesthetic. Aden still resisting any effort to save him had fought her. In the struggle the syringe had fallen on the floor, and she was then going to get another one. With seeing her leave the room, Ian wanted to proceed as quickly as possible. Following his hunch, he asked Christina to go in and stay with Aden. Once again, he went to get his instruments before tending to him.

As happy as she was to be of some assistance, in no way was she prepared for what she was about to see. She nearly fainted as she walked into the room and saw Aden. The only thing that stopped her was her strong desire to help. *You have to be strong. You are here to help and not to be a burden,* she kept telling herself as she approached the bed.

Aden was lying motionless on his bed in this immaculate, luxurious bedroom loaded with every creature comfort imaginable, none of which could make the slightest difference to him now. His eyes were closed. Suddenly, as if he had sensed Christina's presence, he opened his eyes, but only just. He was too weak, and it was particularly too painful for him to open his right eye with all of the skin and tissue around it cut and badly infected.

In that heart-warming, tender moment as their eyes met, oceans of emotions surged within each one of them. Christina was overcome with sadness and compassion, the way that she would have felt had one of her own children been hurt. Too overwhelmed to say a word, she stood there praying silently with all her heart for him and his recovery. Aden on the other hand was filled with mixed emotions of the joy of seeing Christina and having his wish fulfilled, and remorse for feeling responsible for her pain and sorrow. As he lovingly looked at her, he noticed the bruise on her face, even though not easily discernable through her makeup, and that only made him feel worse.

As weak as he was, he lifted his hand to the extent that he could, pointed to her face, and asked, "Are you ok?"

She felt confused at the question. Although it was very nice of him to ask, what did it matter how she was at a time like this? To pacify him and to be polite she softly said, "Yes." She then quickly turned her attention to him by saying, "The only important thing right now is for you to get better."

To her amazement Aden shook his head, disagreeing with her. She was horrified, even with the suggestion of such a thought. With teary eyes she admonished him saying, "Don't even think that Aden. Of course, you will get better. You must!"

Aden was deeply touched by her compassion. His eyes were locked on Christina. He was so mesmerized by her that he did not even notice the doctor walking in, that is not until Ian began to clean his cuts and wounds.

Without anesthetic, that process was too excruciating to bear. The pain just took his breath away. The emotional state that Aden was in, feeling responsible for what had happened to Christina, he just closed his eyes and resigned himself to the entire painful process.

Christina could not take seeing Aden in pain anymore. Out of her deep sense of caring, she did the only thing that she could. She took his left hand and firmly held it in her hand while gently caressing it in the hope of bringing him some comfort.

Its effect was more than she had hoped for or could have imagined. Suddenly, as if every trace of pain had disappeared, Aden lapsed into a state of apparent calm and comfort. Even Ian noticed the sudden change which he just attributed to the anesthetic taking effect.

As she slowly sat down on the edge of the bed still holding his hand, she felt as if her inner being, her essence was being drawn away. There seemed to be a strong spiritual connection between them. Like in a dream she found herself in a most beautiful surrounding of rolling meadows, covered with velvety green grass, colorful exotic flowers, and tall, majestic trees. It was peaceful and serene. She felt free of all of her concerns and sadness.

As she looked around, she saw Aden walking towards her. She found herself filled with joy to see him. To her surprise, he was well and strong again with no trace of wounds or bruises on him. He seemed happy, and with a warm smile began to talk to her. They strolled along the paths as they talked and laughed, enjoying each other's company surrounded by all that beauty and serenity. Time had lost its meaning, and in that state, she found herself truly happy.

As they continued to walk, they came to a soft flowing stream with sparkling, crystal clear water. To help her cross it Aden like a true gentleman, extended and offered his hand. As she gave him her hand, their eyes met. He was drawn to her and was unable to take his eyes off her. He moved, closer and closer to her, until he was close enough to kiss her. Christina stood there, unable to move. She found herself spellbound by him and his penetrating eyes until he went to kiss her. She became frightened. After all, she was married, and she could not kiss him. She backed away and let go of his hand. Then as suddenly as she had found herself there, she found herself back in Aden's room still sitting by his side, except no longer holding his hand.

Minutes earlier the nurse had come to give Aden the anesthetic and had become horrified to find that the doctor was already working on Aden, cleaning his wounds. When she told the doctor what had happened, he got upset with her, but not for long as to the amazement of both of them, Aden did not seem to be in any pain at all. Ian had no explanation other than him taking note of Christina holding his hand. Without the anesthetic it should have been excruciatingly painful. It was only at that moment, when Christina's reactive response to her experience resulted in her letting go of Aden's hand that he began feeling the pain again.

Ian saw that, but was not about to stop as he was nearly done. He believed that it was in the best interest of Aden for him to continue and finish as quickly as possible. With the aid of the nurse, he picked up his pace even more.

Suddenly, as Christina looked on, wondering what it was that she had experienced, and in the midst of all his pain, Aden opened his eyes. He gazed at Christina with a loving look as if conveying a deep sense of gratitude for having been there for him. Then he was overcome with the intensity of the pain and lost consciousness.

Christina looked at the doctor with great concern and asked, "Is he alright?"

The doctor had just finished and was satisfied that all of Aden's vital signs had become normal and stabilized. He put her mind at ease by telling her that he was going to be fine. He thanked her and then rushed out to give the good news to John. He then instructed the waiting paramedics to transport Aden to the private St. Paul Hospital.

John's feelings of happiness and gratefulness were only bound by his concern for Aden's well being and his desire to get him back to a state of good health. However, not knowing what had happened and what had caused all these injuries to Aden, he opted to have Aden taken to the mansion instead of the hospital where he would be safe and under close care and observation. Further, he wanted if at all possible, to keep the incident under wraps and out of the hands of the media. Considering that Aden was now in a stable condition, Ian agreed and arranged for the best qualified care personnel to look after him around the clock at the Bradcliffe mansion.

Chapter 34

Aden's elegant bedroom at the mansion was quickly transformed to a hospital room. In order to provide him the best care, various equipment including monitoring systems and a drip unit were brought in and set up. Once the room was ready, Aden who was still unconscious was taken from the ambulance to his room. Ian then checked everything to ensure that it was all under control. With his vital signs stable, Ian felt confident that he was no longer in critical condition and could be left under the care of his nurse. He then went to talk with John.

Ian wanted to have a private conversation with him without any interruptions, and what a better place than the beautiful gardens of his vast estate. "I could use some fresh air John, so how about going for a short walk?"

John agreed seeing the serious look on Ian's face. He figured that it had to be about Aden and prepared himself for the worst. "Ok Ian, just give it to me straight," said John as they started down the red brick path to the lower garden area, "but before you say anything, I would like you to know that all of my wealth, everything that I have, is at your disposal to get the best care for Aden."

"That's not it. Aden is going to be fine," replied Ian still deep in thought.

John was enormously relieved. With a sigh of relief he said, "Where are my manners? In the midst of all that was happening I didn't get a chance to thank you for saving Aden," thinking that perhaps this was what was bothering Ian. "I'm sorry. I would like you to know that I really appreciate…"

"You don't need to thank me," interrupted Ian. "I'm not the one that saved him," he said appearing somewhat puzzled.

"Now you've lost me."

"Sure, I did all the mechanical things necessary for taking care of his wounds, his infection, and so on…" He then cautiously said, "But, it was Christina who saved Aden."

"I think that the stress of this entire incident has gotten to all of us because now you're not making any sense at all."

"John, even the best care and the best medicine can't save a patient, if there is no will to live."

"You hold it right there! If there is anyone who has every reason to live and more, that would be Aden," said John adamantly. "Just before I left for Sydney, he had gotten his results and he had received the highest possible marks on all his subjects under the most demanding condition of yet completing another two years of university in one as he had wanted to. He was about to get involved in the Bradcliffe Corporation. And the list goes on." He then continued without any trace of doubt on his face, "The fact is that he has everything going for him."

"As doctors we're never too shy to take credit for what we have done, but in this case, it was somehow Christina who reignited his will to live."

"So, what are you saying? Do you believe that she is a miracle worker, or some kind of healer?"

"No." Ian was silent for a moment. He then with a sense of assurance continued, "I believe that Aden is in love with Christina."

"So, he's having an affair with her. That is not a big deal. He has had affairs with lots of women before," said John in an attempt to dismiss what Ian was saying as inconsequential.

"I didn't say anything or know anything about having an affair. All that I'm telling you is what I saw, which as best as I can explain appeared to be a great bond of love deeper and stronger than any love that I have ever seen or heard."

The look on John's face said it all. That was not what he wanted to hear. "That's absurd! Aden has been the most eligible bachelor for several years running. He is always surrounded and sought after by the most beautiful girls imaginable. He could have anyone he could possibly desire from a princess to the richest heiress in the world, and he is hardly interested in any one of them. Now you say that he is in love with…with her? I say that you are wrong!"

"I know what I saw, and I just wanted you to know because it might have a bearing on his recovery."

"There could be many other explanations for what you saw. As for his recovery I will personally see to it that he is cared for in every possible way until he gets better."

Ian smiled, "I guess that time will tell."

As they started to walk back to the mansion, John retorted "That's what worries me. What concerns me is how this could have happened." With a worried look he continued, "As much as I want to keep this out of the hands of reporters, I may not have any choice but to get the police involved."

"I don't think that will be necessary," Ian cautiously replied, "for Aden is too strong for anyone to have caused the injuries without a struggle, and there are no apparent signs of struggle or foul play."

"Maybe someone pushed him, or caused this to happen," said John searching for answers.

"Yes, there could be many possibilities, and we can continue to speculate. But there's no point in that, for the answer lies with Aden. Speaking as his doctor I can tell you that he's in no condition to talk. And even when he is better, I'm not sure how willing he will be to talk about it."

Having heard Ian's comments, John was now less worried and agreed to go along with his friend's way of thinking. Especially now that Aden was at the mansion, he knew that his son was going to be safe and secure.

After two days had passed, by Wednesday Aden no longer required any monitoring or drip units. He was still on antibiotics, and although the signs were indicating that his body was on the path to recovery, his emotional state was impeding it. He had now accepted that he was going to live. He felt that if it had been meant for him to die, after having gone so close to death and all that he had been through, he would not be alive today.

While Christina having come over had helped him overcome his anguish of facing her, he still felt miserable. For on the one hand, he was sorely missing Christina, but on the other hand he was feeling responsible for what had happened to her. With no resolution to either one, he had no desire to do anything. His hair was uncombed, his wound covered, and swollen face was unshaven. He just stayed in bed with the curtains closed and the lights off, wishing for what could not be, to see and talk with Christina. Unable to sleep or eat, Aden was withering away, despite all the caring efforts shown by everyone around him.

Across the great expanse of the city and down by the ocean there was Christina. While concerned about Aden she was still perplexed by what she had felt after holding Aden's hand on that Monday morning. Was it a dream, imagination, or a real experience? And if she did truly experience it, then could there be some truth in what Sean had said? The only answer that she could come up with was "No," for her intentions had always been pure.

That Wednesday afternoon, Betty from across the street decided to be neighborly and take some of the children from the neighborhood to visit Aden. After the children had returned home from school, she came over and asked if Natalie and Timothy would be allowed to go with her. Christina welcomed the idea and was happy for them to go. After they were gone, once again forgetting about herself, Christina with all her heart, and with sincerity and purity of thought, began to pray for Aden's recovery.

With Aden having been such a popular friend with all the children in the neighborhood, it was no surprise that they all wanted to go and see him. Betty could only take seven of them, for that was the maximum number of passengers that her van could hold. On the way to the mansion, they stopped and got a teddy bear, a box of chocolate, and a get well card that they all signed.

John was in Aden's room watching Ian give him his daily check-up when Randall walked in and announced the visitors. To everyone's surprise Aden did not want to see them. Thinking that the children could cheer him up, Randall persisted, "Master Aden, Natalie and Timothy are among the visitors and are very anxious to see you."

Hearing that only made him feel more frustrated and upset. For as much as he wanted to see them, he could not take the chance fearing that it might have repercussions against Christina. He just lashed out at Randall, "Are you hard of hearing? I said no!"

"Yes sir, as you wish."

The children were very disappointed to find that they could not see him. They left their good wishes and their gifts with Randall. Minutes later he came back and gave Aden what the children had brought. After he read the card, especially the loving note from Natalie and Timothy, he could feel the pangs of pain grow stronger in his heart. Unable to cope with it he asked to be left alone.

Reluctantly, everyone left. John, however, remained outside of Aden's room and began a heart-to-heart conversation with Ian, "Has Aden said anything to you about how all this happened to him yet?"

"Not a word."

"Seeing him wasting away like this is tearing me apart. I want my son back!"

"I know John. I have done all that I can do for him physically, but emotionally there is nothing I can do without knowing what happened. Unless he opens up, our hands are tied." Then with a sigh Ian continued, "Since he is not willing to talk about it, I am afraid his recovery may take some time."

"That is not acceptable! I am not going to stand back and just watch my son wither away," said John with a concerned and yet determined attitude. "I only hope that my plan will work."

"What plan?" asked Ian curiously.

"Yesterday, I called Princess Elexa to let her know what had happened and that we wouldn't be able to make it on our European tour to meet up with them as originally scheduled. As soon as she learned about Aden, she wanted to come and see him. At first, I said no, but she insisted. After I thought about it for a while, I agreed. She immediately cancelled all of her royal commitments and, as we speak, Princess Elexa is en route to Adelaide, along with her aunt, Duchess Alanna, on a hush-hush visit just to be with Aden."

Ian was not quite sure about the idea. "Seeing how Aden reacted to his visitors just a little while ago," he asked, "how do you think he will react to this plan of yours?"

"Favorably," replied John, appearing positive and confident about it. "I believe that seeing Elexa is exactly what Aden needs to get him through the emotional state he is in. It was less than a year ago that they were together. You should have seen how loving they were towards each other." John believed in his heart that a beautiful princess had to be the one for Aden, not someone who was married and did not have the same high social standing. "At the same time my dear friend," John continued, "I'll get to prove you wrong about Christina."

"I want what is best for Aden as much as you do." Ian then chuckled, "Even if it means being proven wrong."

Chapter 35

John and Ian, while still standing outside of Aden's room, continued talking about Princess Elexa's visit. Inside, Aden, in a state of total physical and emotional exhaustion, for the first time since Monday, fell into a deep sleep. He began to dream. It was a vivid dream where he found himself in a beautiful, open garden surrounded by flowers. Among them there was one rosebush with very soft, pink roses, Christina's favorite. He was drawn to it. With warm and loving thoughts of her, he picked one of the roses. As he held it in his hand, he heard someone gently calling his name.

He turned around and found Christina standing there, looking radiant with her dazzling eyes and vibrant smile. It was as if he had been given the world. Filled with ecstasy he offered her the soft pink rose as a token of the joy he felt. She graciously took it, admired its beauty, and as she inhaled its perfume said, "Thank you for this beautiful gift." Then in a kind voice she continued, "Do you know what the most precious, the most beautiful gift of all is?" Aden with his eyes locked on her, made no reply. He just wanted to hear her thoughts.

"It is the gift of life given to us by God out of his love for us. It is the one gift that we must, above and beyond anything else respect, and no matter what difficulties come our way, we must never stop cherishing it." With her warm smile she continued, "Hardships and difficulties don't come to us by accident. They come to us for perfecting our character. Through suffering, our minds and spirits grow and advance to the point where we are able to let go of self and gain inner and spiritual strength. All of this happens so that we can use our inner strength along with our unique, God given talents and capacities to help others and benefit mankind. Aden…to be detached and spiritually strong are the keys to true happiness. Don't let anything sadden you. Instead, use your inner strength and be a helping hand to the needy, a treasury to the poor, a towering strength to the oppressed, and a comfort to the distressed."

Then with a tender smile and a voice resonating with kindness and hope she said, "Aden, great things have been destined for you. Go and live out your high destiny."

No sooner having said these words, she began to disappear. With all his heart he wanted her to stay. He yelled out, "Don't! No!" He tried with all his might but was not able to stop her from disappearing.

His father and Ian were still outside his room talking when they heard Aden. Without a moment's delay they both rushed in to see what was wrong. To their surprise they found him in a state of agitated sleep. They figured that he must be having a bad dream. They immediately proceeded to wake him.

When he came out of his sleep he was breathing heavily and covered in perspiration. His shirt, pillowcase, and sheets were all drenched. Ian dried his face. Then he quickly checked his temperature and pulse rate and felt relieved to find everything to be normal. After Aden's clothes and sheets were replaced with dry ones, he once again asked to be left alone.

This time he was no longer agitated and despondent. He was calm as he lay in his quiet and dark room, thinking about the vivid and amazing dream that he had had.

After some time had passed, the door opened allowing a sheet of light to spread across his bed. It was his father who had come in wanting to share his thoughts with his son in the hope of helping him out of his low emotional state. Filled with much love and compassion for Aden, he stood by his bed, looked at him, and with a tender heart began to talk.

"Things seem to happen in life for a reason. I mean, I look back and see how you have been such a source of pride and happiness for me. But it wasn't until that moment, when I thought I had lost you that I truly appreciated having you in my life."

Such a display of love and affection made Aden's eyes, even in his weakened state, light up as he continued to listen. "Aden," said John with his voice almost cracking, "you've brought back God to my life…love to my life, and I am eternally grateful for that." He wanted Aden to know how he felt. Even though it was not easy for him to emotionally express himself, he continued, "I guess that what I am trying to say is that I am here for you, to do whatever it takes to help you to get better, whether it means staying home from my work or going traveling with you. Whatever you want, I am here for you."

Aden feeling more at peace with himself after his dream, and touched by his father, found himself in a state of renewed mental strength. As feeble as he was feeling physically, he was able to gather enough strength to say in a faint and somewhat raspy voice, "Thanks Dad." Knowing how his father had stood by him during the past three days, "You've already done more than enough for me."

"I don't mean materially."

"I don't either," said Aden, finally smiling again.

That warmed his father's heart. "It can only be said that I have done enough when you are back to your strong and normal self, and…on that note, out of my concern for you I have taken the liberty of inviting someone very special, who very much wanted to see you, to come." John then walked out of the room and seconds later returned with Princess Elexa.

"Elexa!" exclaimed Aden.

Even though the only source of light in the room was from the doorway, it was enough for Elexa to see how Aden's face had thinned and was covered with scabs and bruises, not at all the Aden that she had remembered and had fallen in love with. It broke her heart and brought tears to her eyes.

"Hello Aden," said Elexa as she bent down and gently kissed him on the left side of his face.

The entire staff of the mansion as well as the health care personnel had congregated in the wide marbled floor hallway outside of Aden's room, with John, Ian, and Duchess Alanna standing just inside the doorway. Everyone's hope for Aden's recovery, particularly his father's, was hanging on Elexa's visit. They all stood there, watching with bated breath for Aden's reaction.

"Why the tears, Elexa? I'm going to be fine," replied Aden.

"You'd better be, and I'm not going to leave your side until you are," said Elexa with tears still trickling down her face.

Aden just smiled. It was a smile of approval. But it was also a smile that said it all. It was filled with power and strength and conveyed the message that he was back. He then lifted his hand and gently wiped the tears from her cheeks.

She took his hand and firmly held it. Then with a loving smile she peered into his eyes and said, "Yes, you're going to be fine."

That was a deeply moving sight, bringing tears to the eyes, smiles to the faces, and joy to the hearts of everyone. It was as if it had lifted the dark clouds of doom and despair from the mansion and replaced it with bright rays of hope, especially for Aden's father.

John with a look of relief, turned to Ian and said, "As you can see, Elexa is the one." Ian was not quite convinced, but he could hardly argue seeing the evident change in Aden.

John was right to a certain extent. Elexa's presence and her genuine, deep feelings and emotions for Aden, did bring back a smile to his face and a notable sparkle to his eyes. Little did he or anyone else know what Aden knew deep down, that it was Christina, who like a guiding light, had led him out of his dark pit of despair to the vista of a bright future.

Also, they were unaware that Aden, after having had his near-death experience, and having endured such pain and mental anguish that culminated in that vivifying dream, seemed to have been created anew. He was like the Phoenix rising again. Now within him was a new sense of spiritual strength beyond the powers of this world, the kind that could only be driven from submission to the Will of God.

Prior to this incident Aden had been both physically and mentally strong, but those strengths could not compare with the spiritual inner strength that he now possessed. This new inner strength was the last piece of the puzzle, making him stronger and more powerful than ever before. Not even Aden himself was yet aware of it or its full potential.

Chapter 36

Elexa did exactly as she said she would and did not leave Aden's side. Her bubbly personality and loving attitude towards him were just what he needed.

That night for the first time since last Friday night's incident, Aden had a small meal and finally with relative peace after those sleepless nights was able to fall asleep and sleep through the night. Elexa lovingly and patiently remained by his side. Even after he had fallen asleep, she continued to stay through all hours of the night until Alanna forced her to leave and get some rest by offering to stay there in her place.

The next day, even after getting only a few hours of sleep, Elexa was exuberant. She was standing next to his bed, ready to greet him as he awoke. Aden was pleased to see her. Finally, after nearly a week of physical and emotional agony he was now feeling better. He actually asked for the curtains in his room to be opened, and even in his weakened condition he was determined to get out of his bed. With his father supporting him on one side and Elexa on the other, he walked. Those first few steps felt great. To see his son back on his feet brought tears to John's eyes and joy to his heart. Elexa was also very happy and excited to see Aden getting back to his old self.

Inwardly, Aden's soul was still wading in an ocean of sorrows. For the one he loved was so close, yet so far out of his reach. Outwardly, he was making good progress. His room was changed back to its original plush and elegant setting. He was back to wearing his designer clothes, except now they fit him loosely. His hair was styled perfectly again, by his personal hairstylist. His beard he left unshaven as a reminder of that fateful night.

Even though Aden was improving with each passing day, he still had a long way to go to regain his full physical strength. Emotionally, he was still trying to sort out his thoughts and feelings, and through it all it was wonderful to have Elexa there.

Elexa could not be happier. To be with Aden was all she wanted. She was like a kid in a candy store, playful, full of energy and enthusiasm; always bringing a smile to his face and laughter to his heart. She could not help but shower him with affection. He even started going for walks with her through the beautifully landscaped gardens and park-like grounds of the Bradcliffe estate, cut off from the world, just enjoying the moment.

On Saturday morning, four days after Elexa's arrival, Alanna, Elexa, John and Aden were all enjoying a late morning breakfast on the terrace. It was a beautiful morning, everything was peaceful and calm at the Mansion, as if a storm had passed leaving no trace. It was a pleasant mid-December day. There was a slight summer breeze blowing, softly caressing the trees and the flowers, and diffusing their fragrant perfume in the air. It was the making of a perfect day. Right after breakfast Aden and Elexa decided to go for a walk.

After they had been walking for a short distance, they came to Aden's favorite lookout point, where the view was breathtaking. On a clear day the city skyline could be seen all the way to the distant horizon. Perfectly placed to take advantage of the view was a wooden slat bench with ornate, painted, cast iron armrests and legs. Aden suggested that they sit and enjoy the view.

As he gazed across the city, he found his thoughts drawn to that fateful night. This time he did not stop himself from thinking about it. His newfound inner strength was making it possible for him to face and analyze the events of last week. What stood out in his mind was how these events not only had brought God back to his father's life, but also had made his belief in God stronger. Through it he had learned to place his trust in God, for if it were not for His Will, he would not be sitting there.

These thoughts together with some of the conversations he had had with Christina suddenly made his vision of life as clear to him as the view below. His vivid dream and what Christina had told him in that dream began to make sense. It all gave him a new understanding and a new direction, that he must use his life for the purpose of being of benefit to others without concern for himself. With that realization he felt uplifted and invigorated.

He turned around and looked at Elexa. He wanted to share his thoughts with her. But through her smile, he somehow sensed that something was not right. "What's wrong Elexa?"

Pretending that nothing was wrong, still with a smile on her face, Elexa replied, "How could anything possibly be wrong when I'm with you? I couldn't be happier."

"I know you are happy to be here, but I know you too well to tell that deep down something is bothering you."

"Why do you have to be so perceptive?" said Elexa as her smile slowly disappeared. "I almost got away without telling you."

"Why wouldn't you tell me?"

"Because I had come here for you, not to unload my personal problems."

"That's where you're wrong. I want you to tell me whatever you have on your mind, especially if there is something that's making you unhappy," said Aden in a caring tone of voice. "I'm here to help you."

Touched by Aden's compassion, she gently kissed him on his cheek, "That's very kind of you to want to help me, but I don't see how. You still have a long way to go before you'll be fully recovered."

Aden took Elexa's hand in his hand and said, "Let me be the judge of what I can and can't do."

With a feeling of appreciation and a sense of relief, Elexa opened up. She told Aden how her country had been in an economic slump for some time, and how as a result there had been a steady rise in unemployment. She further told him how distressful this had been for her father, especially since he loves the people and only wants their welfare and prosperity. With a deep sense of sorrow she said, "While he has been trying very hard, he hasn't been able to turn things around. Then a month ago Armando, the son of one of the richest families in Europe approached my father and offered to put up a multibillion-dollar investment in the form of real estate development, manufacturing plants and so on."

"That sounds wonderful," replied Aden cautiously.

"Yes, it does, but there is a catch…he wants me to marry him."

"How do you feel about him, and this marriage?"

"I hate him! I despise him! He gives me the creeps and makes my skin crawl whenever he's near me. But how can I say no when the lives of so many people in my country depend on me marrying him?"

"There are always other alternatives. There must be other corporations and investment groups that, given proper economical incentives, would be willing to establish their offices and factories there."

"How could I convince my father of that? And as if that is not bad enough, he has got my father thinking that he should be my escort at my Debutante Royal Ball. That was going to be my special night, and there was only one person that I wanted to be my escort." Elexa paused for a moment then with sadness in her eyes she continued, "And that was you Aden! Now that I can't ask you, my special night will be ruined, and without you I won't be able to convince my father not to have Armando as my escort."

"And why can't you ask me?"

"Both your father and Dr. Forbes believe that you're physically too weak to travel. They also say that you need to be here for your fitness training to rebuild your strength, and for your plastic surgery." With teary eyes she affirmed, "And nothing matters more to me than to see you strong and well again."

Aden put his arm around her, comforting her while thinking. It only took a minute for him to decide that weak or not, he was going to help her. "Everything is going to be alright Elexa. I'll just do my training and have the surgery done in Europe. That way I'll be there for you."

"What?" Elexa's eyes lit up. "That would be great," said Elexa with a sense of gratitude in her voice, "but aren't you too weak to travel?"

"I'll be fine," said Aden knowing that his inner strength would carry him through.

"Aden that is such a wonderful idea!" Elexa's demeanor had changed, she was thrilled, "I'll personally help you with your training, I'll organize the best plastic surgeons for you, and I'll stay with you every step of the way, whether you like it or not, until you fully recover."

"And I'll talk to your father about the alternative investment sources. With all my father's connections in Europe, we should be able to put together a list of possible investors."

Elexa was beside herself with excitement, as if all her birthdays had come at once, "You don't know what this means to me. I only wish I knew what to do to thank you for it."

"Just stay happy."

Elexa was back to her bubbly personality and could hardly wait. She had to find out the details, "When can we leave for Europe, Aden?"

"Whenever you want," replied Aden appreciating the urgency of the situation.

"What about tomorrow?"

"Tomorrow is fine, provided…" Elexa was too excited to wait for Aden to finish his sentence. She got up from the bench, took Aden's hand and started pulling him.

"Let's go! We have lots of things to do; we have to pack, I have to call my father, and…"

Aden stopped Elexa, "All that will have to wait until I talk to my father and get his agreement."

"Then let's go and do that now."

When they returned to the mansion, Aden's father, Alanna along with Ian who had just come over, were on the terrace having morning tea. Elexa was too anxious to wait, "We have exciting news…Aden will be coming to Europe with me, and we are leaving tomorrow."

John was stunned to hear that, he took the napkin from his lap, placed it on the table, got up from his chair and said, "Aden, could I see you inside please?"

It was not Aden's idea to spring it on his father like that, but now that it had happened, he could only hope for his understanding. "Sure, Dad" said Aden as he followed him inside.

"What is this about you leaving tomorrow? Is that true?"

"Only if you agree, Dad."

"But why?"

"Elexa needs my help; otherwise, she will be forced to marry someone she doesn't love."

"But you're still not strong enough to travel."

"Don't worry about me. I'll be fine."

Going to Europe was something that Aden had to do. For the first time since last Friday he had begun to look beyond his emotions, think rationally, and see things more clearly. He could not help but wonder what could have prompted Sean to accuse him and mistreat Christina. Unaware of Vicky and her cruel scheming, he could not come up with any answers. Short of any clear explanation, he came to the conclusion that by going to Europe, not only would he be helping Elexa, but also Christina. With him away, Sean would have no excuse to mistreat her, and over the summer all would be forgotten. His own feelings and well being did not concern him, what mattered was helping others. Aden had reached that selfless state. He was giving of himself like a candle sacrificing itself and burning away in order to give light for others.

"What about your university, the Royal Ball is not until the end of February?"

"That is perfect, Dad. I'll leave right after the Royal Ball and be back in Adelaide in time for when the university starts in March."

After a long pensive pause, John shared with Aden what really was bothering him, "While I respect your desire not to talk about what happened last weekend until you're ready, you must appreciate how uneasy I feel not knowing what happened, so much so that I don't want to let you out of my sight." Coming from his heart he said, "Aden, I could never bear the thought of anything ever happening to you again."

Aden understood and appreciated what his father was saying. But he knew that there was no need for his father to be concerned. To change his thinking and to put his mind at ease, he decided to share with him the outcome of the internal struggle that he had gone through during the last few days. "Dad, we have to live the life we are destined to live, not with fear, but rather with courage and fortitude, by putting our trust in God, for after all, He is our ultimate protector," Aden stated positively. "And if there was anything I learned from this incident," he continued on with his cuts being a solemn reminder of his mortality, "it was that in this life while we can, while we are still here, we must try to make a difference by being of some benefit to others."

John could not help but admire his son for his noble and selfless intentions, and as hard as it was for him to let go, he agreed.

"Thanks Dad. Anyway, this is a very busy time for you. Now you can focus on your work without any distractions, and then meet me in Europe when you're done, which should be in about ten days."

"I guess that should be alright," said John with a loving attitude towards Aden, while trying to come to terms with the turn of events. As he thought more about it, the more he came to the realization that going to Europe was, perhaps, the best thing for Aden. After all, what could be safer than being in the Royal Palace with Elexa looking after him?

On Sunday, while Randall packed his bags, Aden spent some time writing thank you notes to Betty and the children, with a special letter to Natalie and Timothy, and asked Randall to deliver them personally the next day.

To avoid any media encounter, John asked them to depart late at night when it was all quiet at the airport. During the hours prior to their departure there was an eerie feeling in the mansion; a feeling of uncertainty. Was everything going to work out they way they all had hoped?

Aden was very quiet and pretty much kept to himself that evening. While he did not wonder about the outcome, he had to deal with the cold reality of his decision. He was not going to be able to see the love of his life for another two and a half months.

Finally, it was time to depart for the airport. All the goodbyes had been said, the luggage had been put in John's personal limousine, and Alanna and Elexa had been ushered into the limousine by Edmund. When it was Aden's turn to get in, he hesitated. With his heart feeling heavy with the sadness of separation from Christina, he stopped and looked down at the city below as if searching and looking for her amidst all the distant flickering lights, wondering if she was going to be alright. His thoughts were suddenly broken, when he felt his father's hand on his shoulder, with a firm grip assuring and encouraging him that it was time to move on.

Chapter 37

Two paparazzi after having noticed Elexa's private jet at the airport, had been secretly keeping watch in various disguises outside the Bradcliffe mansion. As a result, that Sunday night, in spite of the precautions taken to avoid publicity, as soon as the limousine drove off, they were there to follow it. At the airport they managed to take some photographs of Aden and Elexa with their arms around each other boarding the plane. Needless to say, by Monday morning these pictures appeared in various news media with the caption, **Aden with his secret love Princess Elexa jetting off to Europe**.

Fortunately, with Aden's beard covering most of his face, and the angle that the pictures were taken from, his cuts and scars could not be seen. At first John was incensed to see the photos, but when there was no mention or trace of Aden's incident, he calmed down and dismissed the articles.

When Vicky saw the pictures, she became quite indignant about it. With Aden gone and the speculations in the article that he would be away in Europe the entire summer, her devious plan of using Aden to get rid of Christina was no longer of any use. Begrudgingly, she had to once again resort to her seemingly less effective, normal, cold hearted, and cruel ways.

Christina on the other hand, could not be happier to see him well and together with Princess Elexa. Knowing what she knew about Aden and his many wonderful attributes, she always not only felt that he deserved, but also wished in her heart the best for him. And what could be better than being in love with a beautiful princess.

Unfortunately, the reaction in Europe was not so subdued, particularly with Armando. When he saw the pictures with the same captions, he became furious. After having spread the rumors about him marrying Princess Elexa, he felt humiliated and disgraced. And when he learned from Elexa that Aden was going to escort her to the Royal Ball, he became outraged. His pride and arrogance were not about to let that happen. The ignoble Armando decided to eliminate Aden. With Aden out of the picture, he could then reclaim what he believed was rightfully his, without a care about Elexa's feelings.

He certainly had the means to achieve what he wanted. He was always surrounded by his five bodyguards who were brutal, ruthless, and renowned for their fierce fighting ability. They were ready to do Armando's bidding and were generously rewarded for their loyalty. With a word out of Armando's mouth, the job was as good as done.

Aden's physical training was going well, and his first surgery was scheduled to be done in eight days, right before his father's arrival. Aden wanted to be out of the hospital and with his father for the holiday season. At the same time, the bandages could then come off just in time for a small palace New Year's Eve party that Elexa was organizing for her friends to meet Aden.

While everything was proceeding well, unbeknown to them, and without the slightest reason to expect anything, an intricate plot to kill Aden was unfolding. Through continuous surveillance and the use of sophisticated and covert electronic devices, Armando's men uncovered the plans and schedule for Aden's surgery. After they discovered where and when, they decided to make their move at the hospital.

The surgery, as anticipated, went well. While still under the effect of the anesthesia, Aden was taken to a special room, primarily used for the royal family which was located on the top floor of the 12-story hospital building. The major part of his face and arm on Aden's right side were bandaged. Once in the room a security guard was posted outside on a 24/7 watch.

Elexa having patiently waited during Aden's operation was now anxious to see him. Along with her two personal minders she was standing outside of Aden's room waiting for his doctor to arrive. The nurse having checked on Aden's condition just walked out.

"How is he?" Elexa quickly enquired.

"Everything seems fine, Princess Elexa. He should be awake shortly," replied the nurse politely.

Aden was still unconscious and was left alone in his room to rest quietly. It was the perfect opportunity for Armando's men to carry out their plan.

As planned, the first one of his men had gone to the 12th floor, carrying a bouquet of flowers, pretending to be a visitor. When the nurse walked out of Aden's room, it was his cue to immediately signal the second one waiting outside of the building. Having received the signal he knew what to do. He quickly and with great agility scaled the building. In a matter of minutes, he had reached Aden's 12th floor window. He then broke the lock, opened the window, and stealthily climbed into the room unnoticed. The danger for Aden was now mounting. Once inside the room he was in the clear with no one to stop him. He unsheathed his knife to finish the job quietly and quickly.

Just then the doctor arrived on the floor, and directly headed towards Princess Elexa and Aden's room. Unknowingly, he seemingly was about to save Aden's life. But any glimmer of such hope quickly disappeared as Armando's man realizing that he needed to buy more time, intercepted the doctor, and asked him for some assistance. Elexa was about to enter Aden's room, but seeing the doctor momentarily detained, she stopped and waited for him to finish his conversation. Little did she know that time was quickly running out for Aden.

Inside the room with knife in hand, Armando's man began walking towards Aden. He had left the window open which was his intended escape route. As he raised his knife to strike his victim, suddenly and mysteriously a strong gust of wind blew into the room through the open window. The curtains were filled with air and brushed over the nightstand knocking over one of the vases of flowers that had been sent to Aden for a speedy recovery. The vase crashed to the tiled floor shattering loudly.

Everyone on the floor of the normally quiet recovery area was startled by the sound. Without a second's delay the security guard, Elexa, and her minders all rushed into Aden's room. That prevented Armando's man from completing his task. He quickly turned before anyone could see his face and jumped through the window, catching his escape rope, and repelling down the face of the building. He then escaped to a waiting car which sped away before the security team could reach him.

Elexa was so shaken up that it took some time before the doctor and nurse were able to calm her. By the time Aden's anesthesia had worn off she had regained her composure. As she stood by him, tenderly holding his hand, she could not be more pleased to see him open his eyes.

The bandages covered the side of Aden's face to the edge of his lips, making it a little difficult for him to either smile or talk. But he still managed to smile as he looked at Elexa and said, "Thanks!"

Elexa was taken aback. "Thanks for what Aden?"

"For saving my life!" It seemed that Aden even in that near conscious state had sensed and had become aware of what had happened. While Elexa was relieved, she felt responsible for what had happened and could not take any credit for saving his life.

Aden was not concerned at all. He added, "And not a minute too soon," in trying to make her feel better by seeing some humor in it.

Elexa could not see any humor or any way out, "After what happened, I don't blame you if you want to go back."

"And miss all of the fun?"

"I'm serious Aden. I can't let you stay here while your life is in danger because of me."

"I am serious too," speaking with slightly more ease and authority. "I have made a promise to a beautiful princess, and nothing is going to make me break that promise."

Words could not describe how overwhelmed and deeply touched she became hearing that. It was her bright face and warm smile that said it all as she stood by him, looking into his eyes, and firmly holding his hand as if to never let go of it.

Aden's father arrived two days later and was not at all understanding about the attempt on his son's life. With most of the bandages off and his face clean shaven, Aden was once again looking more like he used to. As pleased as John was to see that, he was adamant that Aden should return to Australia.

Once again Aden had the difficult task of persuading his father otherwise. "Dad, I appreciate your concern, but the fact is that nothing happened to me, or I wouldn't be standing here talking to you right now."

That did not convince John. He still persisted, "I will not risk losing you and that's why I want you to return home now."

"What kind of person would I be if I let a cowardly act like this scare me away?" Aden asked his father while assuring him that he knew wisdom must be exercised in every aspect of life and that he was not condoning living dangerously. But the reality of the situation was that whether he was in danger or not, he could not leave. As he further explained, "If I were to leave now, the person who tried this would get what he wanted, and I would break my promise to a very dear friend. This I can't do."

Hesitantly and with a concerned look, John said, "We must assume that whoever made an attempt on your life is going to try again."

"That seems to be the consensus around here. As a result, there has been such an increase in security in and around the palace that I couldn't be safer, even if I were in Fort Knox," replied Aden without any concern. "The point is that nothing is going to happen to me between now and the Royal Ball, and we'll be returning home as soon as it's finished. So, you have nothing to worry about."

"Nevertheless, if your decision is to stay, then I'll stay with you until we return home."

"Dad, I can't let you do that. I know you have very important meetings coming up early in February with Digicomp that you just can't miss."

"Nothing is as important as you Aden. That is around the time that you'll be having your second operation, and there is no way that I'll be leaving you then."

Aden thought for a moment, "What about a compromise?" he asked. "Instead of canceling your meetings, just delay them until after my operation. In that way you can make sure that I am fine before you leave, still have your full schedule of meetings with Digicomp, and be back here in time for the Royal Ball."

John, unable to refute Aden's reasoning, agreed to his proposed compromise.

Chapter 38

Aden and his father stayed on as royal guests in the Palace. That was a source of great support and comfort for Elexa. The weeks that followed in January were quite busy and productive. Aden continued to rebuild his strength through rigorous physical training. However, the major focus of his activity was on the development of strategies and the creation of a framework for a major investment plan to help Elexa's father overcome the economic problems which had been plaguing his country. This was being spearheaded by Aden in a collaborative effort with his father, who through his vast business network, involved many of his friends including some of the wealthiest and most influential figures in European financial circles. This effort resulted in a comprehensive and solid multibillion-dollar proposal which addressed the country's needs. It not only met the praise of his father, but also the praise and approval of Elexa's father, King Theodor.

King Theodor was a kind and deeply religious man who demanded foremost, honesty and trustworthiness from everyone who worked for him. He believed that these qualities are the foundation of civilization and progress. He ruled with fairness and justice, and through them he not only gained the loyalty, respect, and love of his people, but he had also achieved a sense of harmony and unity among them. He put the wellbeing of his people before the good of himself and his family. As a result, not knowing how Elexa truly felt, he had agreed to Armando's plan.

When King Theodor saw how Aden's proposal could benefit the people in his small country, and at the same time through Aden, learned about Elexa's feelings and how she had selflessly kept them to herself, he completely abandoned Armando's proposal. That only infuriated Armando more, and he became even more determined to eliminate Aden.

Elexa's father immediately authorized and ordered the formation of a special Royal Investment Commission. At the suggestion of Aden, Elexa became the Royal Ambassador heading the Commission and presenting the plan to the various potential investors.

Aden together with his father put together a list of possible investment groups. The palace staff, as if in a Wall Street company, began setting up meetings and appointments for the Royal Commission to take place after the Royal Ball.

Although there was not a day that went by without Aden thinking of Christina, he was happy to be there with Elexa in the fairytale-like atmosphere. Everyday he would spend several hours with Elexa familiarizing her with the investment proposal, coaching her on how to present it, and teaching her business finance. With hard work, together with fun and laughter, Aden was able to gradually transform Elexa into a business and financial analyst, ready for the challenge ahead.

The time finally arrived for Aden's second operation. Unlike his first operation, this time his surgery was relatively simple, and with increased security fortunately uneventful. As a result, in mid-February John with full assurance of Aden's wellbeing departed for the US.

Allan Kelly, Declan Harris, and two other key engineers from the research and development team joined John for the meetings with Digicomp. These action-focused and result-oriented meetings went on for ten days. Through extensive consultations the structure was set in place for the work that needed to be carried out in the coming year, in preparation for market entry in the following year.

As soon as the meetings were over John returned to Europe. While the meetings had gone well, Aden noticed how his father seemed preoccupied. He asked his father for the reason behind this.

John had intended to discuss it when they got back home. Now that Aden had brought it up, he seemed to change his mind. He thought that perhaps it was best to discuss it now and get it off his chest. "With our successful research and development leading to production of our first working prototype, we will actually be in a position to introduce the first generation of these new computers into the market in about 18 months."

"That sounds great Dad. So, what seems to be the problem?"

"When we started this project, we knew from the beginning that compatible hardware had to be developed at a later stage," said John confidently.

"With all the work having gone successfully, the time has come for us to put the hardware development phase of the project in place, and it must be done within the next six months. Since neither we nor Digicomp have any experience in this area we have to rely on a third-party company. After a worldwide search Digicomp has identified one particular company that they believe to be most suited and qualified to do the job." He appeared perturbed as he continued after a short pause, "That is where the problem lies. The company that they have identified is Adeltec Industries."

Adeltec, the long-time competitor of the Bradcliffe Corporation, was headed by the unscrupulous Conrad Frost. John was painfully aware of the fact that Conrad could not be trusted as a result of what he had done over the years. Now he was suddenly put in the difficult position of having to trust Conrad with his leading technology that he had worked so hard to develop.

Recognizing the gravity of the situation, Aden asked, "So what are you going to do about it?"

"Fortunately, I don't have to decide for another six months, if I push it. Ideally, I wish that I could have done it in-house. I could even try to form a special hardware division, but that would take time and I don't know if I can afford to take such a risk."

"I have no doubt that when the time comes that you will make the right decision."

"Thanks for your vote of confidence."

"For now, you must put it out of your mind and enjoy our last night here."

"You're right. After all, it is the night of the much-anticipated Royal Ball for Princess Elexa and her special escort who has stirred much attention among the Who's Who of the European Community," he said jokingly. Then finally with a hint of a smile, "And here you are escorting her tonight. I couldn't be more proud of you for having stood firm on your convictions and having helped Elexa and her father in ways that are beyond appreciation."

"It's about caring for each other," said Aden down-playing what he had done.

"I know, and not expecting anything in return. That's what makes what you are doing so praiseworthy."

Aden's thoughts momentarily drifted to Christina, who ever since he met her had helped him in more ways than anyone could imagine, while not expecting or accepting as much as a thank you. His focus returned when he saw his father's smile change to a look of concern as he said, "While I was in the US, I couldn't help but worry about you."

"Now you have nothing to worry about. That's all behind us," replied Aden optimistically. "All we have to do is go and enjoy the celebrations before the night is over."

"Yes, you're right. It's time for the multitude of guests to be dazzled by the charm of the Bradcliffe men, a beautiful princess, and a glamorous duchess!"

"And whatever happened to old fashioned modesty?" Aden retorted jokingly.

"I don't know what you mean. I thought that I was being rather modest."

Aden laughed, "It's good to have you back Dad."

Chapter 39

It was the night of the Royal Ball. The air was filled with excitement. Beyond the ornate gates at the end of the long drive lined with ornamental lights, there stood the palace majestically against the moonlit, starry night sky. It was a magical night as if everything had been sprinkled with stardust and transformed to a favorite scene from a book of fairy tales. The palace sparkled like a jewel as spotlights shone brightly on it. The trees and shrubs along the drive and around the palace twinkled with fairy lights. The palace guards in their traditional uniforms stood by the red carpet leading inside. The sound of music permeated the air with melodies of celebration and jubilation.

The guests arrived, one-by-one in a long line of stretch limousines and were awestruck by the sheer graceful elegance and beauty pervading the palace with neither extravagance nor opulence. As they entered the grand ballroom, tastefully decorated throughout in shimmering silver and gold motif with flickering candles, it was as if they were stepping into the clouds amidst twinkling stars.

It did not take long before all the guests had arrived. It was time for Elexa, escorted by Aden, to make her grand entrance. Aden dressed in his bespoke black tuxedo went to Elexa's room. When he entered the room, he looked as stately as a prince and as handsome and dashing as a catwalk model.

Inside the spacious room stood Elexa in her splendid beauty, glamorously dressed in a long elegant strapless silver gown fitting snugly around her waist, flowing down in full elegance and floating right above the floor. Her dress was tastefully complemented with matching diamond inlaid white and yellow gold tiara and jewelry.

"Elexa, you look ravishingly beautiful," said Aden as he softly kissed her on her cheek. "What are you trying to do, stop every man's heart tonight?" he said with a warm smile.

"No, only one man's," replied Elexa as she looked with a deep sense of hope into his eyes.

Aden simply smiled. Then in his gentleman like manner extended his arm and said, "It is time Princess Elexa. Shall we go?"

It was the first time that Aden had called her princess. The smile on her face showed how touched she was by it. Then in her usual, high spirited and exuberant way she took his arm with both of her hands and said, "Oh Aden, I feel so happy tonight. It is such a beautiful night, even more than I had imagined it would be. And it's all because of you."

Her eyes were sparkling with joy. She did not want the night to ever end. To make it last longer she wanted them to spend some time together, even if for only a short while. "Aden, before going out there and becoming surrounded by hundreds of people let's go for a walk, just the two of us."

"It's freezing out there. I would be fine, but it is too cold for you."

"Not outside, I mean inside the palace conservatory," said Elexa with a pleading and yet charming look in her eyes.

Aden could not refuse. "Why not? This is your night. We'll do whatever you wish."

"Then come with me. I'll show you the way," replied a very happy Elexa.

Hand in hand they walked through the indoor passageway to the conservatory.

"When I was growing up, whenever I got tired of the cold, I would go to the conservatory to play and to pretend to be on some far-off, tropical island. Even now I still go there. It is my most favorite place in the palace."

"And yet, you kept it secret from me?"

"That's because I wanted to share it with you on a special night like tonight," said Elexa as they entered the conservatory.

They were immediately immersed in an Eden-like garden. It was enchanting and delightful being indirectly and dimly lit. Brick paved pathways provided easy access as they wound through to all the different sections. There were lush green and tropical trees, flowering shrubs and groundcover, colorful and exotic flowers everywhere. In the center of the conservatory there was a quaint wooden bridge. Under it flowed a crystal-clear stream, creating a sense of tranquility amidst all the beauty. As Elexa had indicated, it was the perfect place for them to spend a few quiet moments.

"Come Aden, let's go to my favorite part." With Elexa leading the way, they walked through a curved path that led to an open area at the end of which was a brightly lit rolling mound of purple orchids.

"Aren't they beautiful?" asked Elexa. Then without even waiting for Aden's answer she took his hand pulling him towards a narrow pathway. "Now you must come and see the single most beautiful orchid in the world!"

Aden stopped her. "Elexa, it's getting rather late. We really should be returning to the palace."

"Only after I show you this one," she said walking away again.

"Wait," said Aden, grabbing her hand firmly to stop her. "What was that sound?" he said, looking anxiously around.

"I didn't hear anything. Come on, let's go." Elexa then proceeded ahead on the narrow pathway with Aden close behind her.

At the end of the pathway there stood a rare and breathtakingly beautiful orchid immersed in rays of light shining down on it.

"Wasn't it worth the wait?" asked Elexa. When there was no response, she turned around only to find that Aden was no where to be seen! She quickly called out his name as she started to walk back toward the pathway. Then suddenly, right before her eyes, her worst nightmare had come true! It was as if every hope, joy, and dream had been stripped away from her.

There was Armando wearing a tuxedo with his hair slicked back, surrounded by three of his bodyguards walking towards her. Directly behind him were the other two carrying and supporting Aden in between them by holding his arms over their shoulders.

Seeing the horrified and questioning look on Elexa's face Armando callously said, "No, your pretty-face boyfriend is not dead…. yet. He is just taking a nap for the moment."

Relieved to hear that she asked, "With all the security how did you get in?"

"Easy," Armando sniggered. "With a few million dollars, take or leave ten or twenty, you can get in anywhere and get anything, like these electronic gadgets," referring to the ones held by his bodyguards, "that simply lets you penetrate any security system."

"Gadgets or not, you aren't going to get away with this!"

"I'm afraid that I already have," said Armando as he moved close to Elexa.

"So, what is it that you want?" said Elexa as she stepped back.

"You know what I want," said Armando as he started to touch her shoulder. She pushed his hand away as hard as she could, "Never!"

Then with that disgusting, sleazy look on his face he said, "Soon you will learn to appreciate me. Very soon." While breathing on her neck, "That is if you want to keep your little boyfriend in one piece."

"He doesn't mean anything to me," hoping that with such a response Aden would be left alone.

Armando then simply motioned to one of his men, who happily pulled out a knife and put it to Aden's face. "Then you wouldn't mind having his face rearranged, would you?"

"Ok…you win. I'll do what you want. Just leave him alone."

"That's more like it Princess…Elexa," he said in his creepy voice. "What I want is quite simple…. I'll escort you to the Royal Ball. Then we'll get married and live happily ever after."

Even though the mere thought of it was revolting, she felt that she had no choice. For Aden's sake she agreed. She would do anything for him. "I'll go along with whatever you want, as long as you let Aden go."

"Oh, how touching…still trying to save your pretty-face boyfriend. I am afraid that I can't do that. He is what you call, my good luck charm, my guarantee." Then he took out a small electronic device from his pocket, "With this simple, little device, I'll be able to make sure that he remains my good luck charm."

Elexa could not believe what Armando's twisted mind had conceived as he continued, "You see, he is going to guarantee that I get what I want. For if I don't, at the touch of this button," which he gently rubbed with his forefinger, "my men will dispose of him. The choice is yours my…dear…princess. As long as you do what I say, he gets to live." Then with his evil smile, "Now you see why I can't let him go."

Just then a security guard came into the conservatory looking and calling out for Princess Elexa. Armando stood partially in front of Elexa facing her as his men hid Aden's unconscious body behind the shrubs. "You get rid of him, or my men will get rid of your boyfriend, permanently."

Elexa knew what to do. She responded to his call when he got to the beginning of the pathway. Upon hearing and seeing the princess he stopped, "Your Highness, your father wanted me to convey to you that it is time, and for me to escort you and Master Aden to the ballroom."

"That's not necessary; just tell my father that we'll be there shortly."

"As you wish Princess Elexa," replied the security guard, and with no reason to suspect anything, he turned around and walked away.

"You did well princess. Shall we go? We mustn't keep the guests waiting."

Elexa did not move, just turned to look for Aden. His men just then emerged from the shrubbery, still supporting him. "Yes princess, take a good look. This is the last time that you'll ever see him," said Armando spitefully as his men, along with Aden quickly disappeared.

This broke her heart and tears began to well up in her eyes.

"Come now princess, it is time to rejoice! I already feel better. Don't you?"

"What kind of monster are you?" replied Elexa in disgust.

"That's not a nice way to talk to your future husband." Armando heartlessly continued, "You need to have a term of endearment for me. Let's see… what could it be? Sweetheart? Honey? No, they don't sound quite right to me. I know from now on you will call me…'my darling Armando'. Now that that's settled, I think it's time to go." He then started off, forcefully taking her with him.

Filled with fear and concern for Aden's safety, with all her heart Elexa prayed to God to protect Aden, give her strength to get through the night, and help her find a way to rescue him. She wished that she had never asked him to be her escort, then none of this would have happened and he would have been alright.

As they left the conservatory and entered the passage connecting to the palace, her every step felt heavier. Elexa knew by the end of the passage there was no turning back. For beyond the final corner were the double doors that opened to a broad marble staircase connecting to the main hallway which led to the Grand Ballroom.

For Aden's sake she knew she had to be strong. Once they reached the final corner, she put all her emotions aside. She gathered enough courage, put on a brave face, and walked towards the double doors beyond which laid her shattered dreams, lost hopes, and vanished desires.

Chapter 40

The palace guards standing by the double doors saluted Princess Elexa and immediately opened the doors for her and Armando to pass through. Once on the other side of the double door, still feeling distraught, Elexa at first did not even notice someone talking to them. Then in a state of despair she looked up. Both Elexa and Armando were stunned by what they saw.

To their absolute amazement it was Aden. He was standing on the third step up from the ground, leaning against a tall column that extended high to the ceiling. He was unharmed, in complete control of the situation, and full of confidence as he asked again, "Are you going somewhere Armando?"

Armando looked around as if looking for his bodyguards. With no trace of them and in a state of disbelief, still firmly holding Elexa's hand, he said, "It can't be you! That's impossible! No one can get away from my bodyguards!"

"Since I am standing here, I would say that it is quite possible."

With power and presence exuding from him, Aden took a few steps away from the column, and moved closer to where Elexa and Armando were standing. He then looked directly at him and said, "But there are certain things that are impossible in life, and one of them is you escorting Princess Elexa tonight, or ever." Still very much in control, Aden extended his hand to Elexa, "Come, my dear."

Elexa, looking at Aden, was still in a state of shock and astonishment. There he was, her knight in shining armor, rescuing her from the clutches of evil Armando. It was as if she had been given wings to fly. Once again, her vibrant smile returned to her face and the sparkle of life to her eyes as she reached out to take Aden's hand.

Armando was not about to give up. He quickly pulled her back towards himself as he pulled out a gun from inside his tuxedo jacket.

Aden having anticipated such a desperate move by Armando was not at all alarmed by it. Knowing that Armando would not hesitate using it, he had to be quick. With agility and accuracy that he had mastered after all those years of self-defense training, he kicked the gun out of his hand. Aden was so quick that Armando literally did not know what hit him. All that he could see was his gun tumbling through the air. As he helplessly watched it land some distance away, Aden reached, took Elexa's hand, and brought her to his side. Before Armando could react, Elexa was standing beside Aden with his arm around her.

The impact of the gun hitting the floor caused a shot to be fired which echoed upstairs in the main hallway. Consequently, it was heard by both King Theodor and John who were anxiously waiting outside the ballroom for Elexa and Aden to arrive. Having heard the shot, they rushed to the staircase behind the royal bodyguards. As they got near the top of the staircase, they could hear Aden talking. Since it seemed that there was no immediate danger King Theodor in his wisdom, stopped his guards from intervening and allowed Aden to finish speaking. They waited near the staircase where they could hear the conversation below with the intent of providing protection should it be required.

At the same time, the security guard in the main control room watching the events on the monitor, began to broadcast Aden's conversation into the ballroom. This he did in accordance to Aden's instructions. Aden wanted everyone to hear what Armando was all about.

"I don't need a gun," Armando could be heard saying. "I could take you on myself."

"Armando, even you aren't foolish enough to make such a futile attempt." Aden could easily have taken him apart, but that was not his intention. He really wanted to expose Armando for what he was.

Armando, knowing the strength and skill of his bodyguards who had obviously been neutralized by Aden, backed away. Suddenly, there was fear in his heart.

Aden continued in a commanding voice, "But, I'll tell you what you really are, a lowlife and a coward."

Armando was furious. "No one has ever called me such things," he said with distain.

"But that's what you are. Who else but a coward hides behind his bodyguards while they do his dirty work, and who else but a lowlife terrorizes innocent people to get what he wants?…Isn't that how you tried to have me killed and force Elexa to marry you?"

Armando sensing the power in Aden's voice did not dare say a word, while Aden with unyielding authority continued on, "At first I couldn't work out why you would do such unthinkable things. Now I know. It's your greed for wealth and power. Your family's wealth wasn't enough. So, you deviously planned to marry Princess Elexa. Then you joined forces with the biggest drug lords in the world with the intention of turning this beautiful and untouched country into a dumping ground for drug trafficking and money laundering, in exchange for essentially unlimited return of wealth and power." He wanted to have a country to rule.

"How dare you make such outrageously false accusations?"

"Outrageous, yes. False, no. How else could you explain the meetings and financial transactions you have had with two of the biggest drug lords since the 11th of December, exactly the day after King Theodor's acceptance of your proposal?"

"That's absurd," said Armando suddenly unable to maintain his poker face. "You have no proof."

"But I do," said a man in a raspy voice stepping forward from behind the security guards. Dressed in a tuxedo he appeared to be one of the guests, but his cold, merciless eyes and his harsh and grim face said otherwise.

With great satisfaction Aden introduced him, "Meet Agent McArthy of the US Drug and Enforcement Agency." Sam McArthy had been collaborating and working closely with some of the key European agencies over the past several months. During that time, he had been able to uncover enough evidence to tie Armando to the drug lords.

There was now real fear in Armando's eyes now as he still tried to deny everything, "You have nothing on me."

"On the contrary. Now by adding kidnapping and attempted murder, he has more than enough to put you away for a very long time, which is what you really deserve." Aden was angry for what Armando had done and was planning to do. "For your selfish desires you were ready to destroy the innocence of this country, and without a care, ruin the lives of so many children and young people with your drugs. And all for what? To be buried under the same dust as a poor person?" Then he continued in a calmer voice, "I wonder what King Theodor would do, if he knew truly what you are on about?"

No sooner than having said that, King Theodor's voice could be heard thundering down the staircase, "He would do what he should have done a long time ago." As he walked down the stairs, "I would like to apologize to you, my dear sweet Elexa, for putting you through all this." He warmly embraced her. "And now have the trash thrown out!"

The security guards quickly converged on Armando. "I'll be happy to take the trash out for you, Your Majesty," said Agent McArthy.

Just then the palace guards, who had been alerted by Aden as to the whereabouts of Armando's five bodyguards brought them in. Armando's arrogance gave way to his fury, "You're all fired!"

King Theodor was not about to allow anything to ruin Elexa's special night. With Armando and his men taken away, he was anxious to get the celebrations started, "Shall we go my dear Elexa? Everybody is waiting."

"Not yet father, I would like to have a few minutes alone with Aden, please."

"All right my dear. We'll wait for the two of you by the ballroom entrance."

By this time, the transmission to the ballroom had ceased. The sound of music could be heard, helping the guests put the unexpected interruption and the unthinkable exposé about Armando behind them. Shortly the air was filled with joy and excitement, again.

Once Elexa and Aden were by themselves, she gave him a very loving and affectionate hug. "This truly is a miracle. When they took you away, I died inside. I couldn't bear the thought of not seeing you ever again. And now, here you are....You don't know how happy it makes me to see you and have you standing right before me."

"You should have never doubted that you would see me again."

"But it seemed impossible...How did you do it? How did you get away?"

"As I regained consciousness and found myself surrounded by Armando's men, the only thought in my mind was, 'Where is Elexa? Is she alright?' When I didn't see you there, I knew I had to come and rescue you. There was no other choice," said Aden matter-of-factly. His years of self defense training had come in handy in taking care of Armando's men.

"That was the most beautiful and courageous thing anyone has ever done for me, and I'll never forget it," said Elexa feeling deeply indebted. "Just like I'll never forget tonight."

Then the two of them proceeded upstairs. King Theodor and John were pleased to see them. It was time to start the celebrations. All the guests stood up when King Theodor entered the ballroom, followed by Duchess Alana accompanied by John.

The special moment had finally arrived. Then Princess Elexa, together with Aden with her hand graciously resting on his arm, made their grand entrance. At the sight of Elexa's sparkling beauty and Aden's regal and handsome presence, sighs of admiration and awe filled the ballroom. This was no ordinary ball. The reaction of the guests was overwhelming as they spontaneously applauded and cheered their arrival. It was as if Cinderella and her Prince Charming had stepped out of the pages of the famous fairytale, dazzling everyone with their splendor.

Touched by the emotional reception, Elexa turned to Aden and said, "This is truly more magical than I could have ever imagined, and it is all because of you.…How can I ever thank you?"

"Simple, just keep smiling."

The clapping continued on for several minutes as they walked to their table on the special cream-colored carpet lined on both sides with flowers and flickering gold and silver candles.

The high point of the night was when Elexa and Aden had their first dance. When the music began, glittering fairy dust was released from above the dance floor, adding to the enchanting feeling of the night. With all eyes locked on them, they walked to the dance floor. As they stepped onto it, the twinkling lights imbedded in the dance floor became illumined. As they walked toward the center, hundreds of fairy lights located all along the perimeter of the dance floor began to sparkle, creating the illusion that they were dancing among the stars.

"Aden, this is so beautiful. I wish that this night would never end. I wish this perfect time that we have had together could continue." Minutes later, still not wanting Aden to leave, Elexa said, "I wish that you could stay with me and together we could make the presentations to the investment groups."

"Elexa, you know I can't. My university started last week, and as it is I will only have one day to prepare for my classes on Monday. But I want you to know that I have no doubt that you will do a great job with the presentations. After all, you did have a great teacher," Aden said with a chuckle.

Elexa laughed.

Aden then continued, "Just remember I'll always be there for you, and I'm only a phone call away."

Finding Aden's response comforting, she simply leaned forward and gently kissed Aden on his cheek. Her loving gesture evoked emotional cheers from the guests.

Just then the music changed. Amidst the cheers they stepped back and began the formal and traditional national dance.

As the celebrations drew to a close, one thing was certain, that this night would be remembered by everyone as one of the most eventful, memorable and magical nights that they had experienced.

Chapter 41

As a gesture of gratitude and respect by King Theodor and Elexa to their special guests, Aden and John, they were flown back to Australia in the royal jet. It was in the style to which they were accustomed with impeccable service all the way. As pleasant as the flight was, what was most striking was their silence.

There certainly was a feeling of contentment. They both had enjoyed their stay in Europe. But it was apprehension slipping into their thoughts that had brought on the silence. They were leaving this wonderful fairyland behind and returning to reality, a reality that was filled with a host of unknowns and uncertainties that they wished they did not have to face.

Against all odds John finally had his perfect product, ideal joint venture, and a sure pathway for entry into the world of electronics. Yet that did not seem to be enough for him to realize his dream. Without the ability to develop the required hardware in-house, not only might he have to face his archrival, but also work with him. That was a prospect that he wished he did not have to seriously consider.

Aden's reality while no less uncertain, appeared more complicated. His experiences in dealing with Armando, and selflessly helping Elexa and her father, had made him go from strength to strength. He had spiritually grown and now possessed much higher moral convictions and aspirations. As a result he more fully appreciated and adhered to values such as truth and justice.

With his newfound strengths he could not help but wonder about Sean. In his mind nothing could justify Sean's actions. True, during the semester he did take up a lot of Christina's time, but that still was not a sufficient reason for Sean's cruel behavior. As a result, he was not sure how he would react towards Sean.

One thing that had remained unresolved was the question of seeing Christina. Having had the time to think more about that fateful night, he could now begin to see things more clearly. What stood out in his mind was Christina coming over that Monday morning. The more he thought about it, the more amazed and impressed he became with the courage and compassion that she had displayed. She had come at the risk to herself and faced people she did not know just to offer her assistance. That was very reassuring for him and helped him arrive at the conclusion that Sean had no basis to blame him. It also meant that she must have not agreed with Sean. Otherwise, she simply would not have come over. This thinking helped him overcome his feelings of guilt, leaving him with an ever-growing longing desire to see and to be with Christina.

Even though in many respects Aden was a new person, but what had not changed was his heart. It was still beating with the same pure love for Christina.

Having had a wonderful time with Elexa, he wondered if he could ever have anything like that with Christina. Would he ever be able to freely see her, hold her, and share special moments with her? Amidst all these uncertain thoughts he found himself wishing the impossible. He wished that he could reverse time, undo events, change the past, and alter destiny to make Christina his. Short of any of that, all he could do was face the reality of the life that he had left behind. Now after nearly three months he was returning home. While he did not know what to expect, he was ready for anything that life had to offer.

When the royal jet landed in Adelaide it was early in the morning on the last Sunday in February. The temperature was pleasant although the forecast was for a hot day. It was typical summer weather.

The Bradcliffe Rolls Royce was already waiting for them on the tarmac. As soon as John and Aden disembarked from the plane they were warmly greeted by Edmund. They waited by the car enjoying the early morning breeze for a few minutes while their luggage was being put into the trunk. When that was finished the royal crew courteously said farewell. Edmund then ushered them inside the Rolls and drove them back to the mansion.

They were enthusiastically welcomed by the mansion staff, who were pleased to have them back and glad to find them both well. For John and Aden, it also felt good to be back. As enjoyable as it had been living in the palace, it was not home. No sooner had they walked in the door their cell phones and all the house lines began to ring. Aden's friends were particularly anxious to see and hear from him. It had been such a long time since they had all gotten together. So, Aden quickly decided to have a barbeque and a swimming party at his house, starting at noon. Everyone was invited.

John would have preferred to have the party at the mansion, but Aden wanted it to be at his house. He wanted things to get back to normal. He had to go back and put the entire painful incident behind him, as if it had never happened. And what better way to achieve this than in a party atmosphere, surrounded by his friends. His father agreed.

Aden and his father arrived at his house a few minutes before noon. Everything had been set up and prepared by Randall and the caterers, and they were ready to receive the guests.

To make sure it was all to his satisfaction, Aden quickly checked on everything inside before anxiously making his way outside to check on things on the terrace and by the pool. All the while he was thinking and hoping that he would see Christina out there. He no longer believed or accepted that he had to be away to protect her.

As he walked out, he saw Christina on the beach with Timothy and Natalie. Suddenly, his interest in checking on things was completely lost. He was being pulled towards her like a moth to a flame. He could feel his heart pounding. He became filled with an overwhelming sense of joy and gladness. He forgot about everything else around him and just walked out onto the beach.

They were all playing and having fun. The children were trying to see how far they could throw pebbles into the ocean. They were laughing together because neither of them could throw very far at all.

"Try holding the pebbles between your thumb and forefinger like this, and then throw it with a quick wrist action," said a voice from behind them. It was a voice that they had not heard for three months, and they could not be any happier or more excited to hear it now.

It was like they had just seen Santa Claus. Filled with such excitement, Natalie and Timothy ran to Aden giving him the biggest hug that they could. "We missed you so much Aden," said Natalie with a giggle. "We're so happy that you're back," said Timothy appearing pleased.

"It's great to be back." Then he looked at Christina. He could feel the rush of joy through him. "Hello Christina," he said warmly with a smile and a gentle look in his eyes. "How have you been?"

"Hi, Aden. I've been fine." She was happy to see him well again. "Timothy and Natalie managed to keep me very busy over the summer, but we had a lot of fun together," replied Christina with that vibrant smile of hers.

"Can you show us again how to throw the pebbles?" asked Timothy keen to learn.

It was not easy to take his eyes off Christina. But to be responsive to the children, he proceeded to show them how.

"Why don't you and the children join us Mrs. Ashton?" They all turned around, and to their surprise it was Aden's father.

To find out what had brought on such a reaction in Aden, he had followed him to the beach. Because of his intense love for his son, anything to do with him and his life was naturally of great concern to him. Seeing the wonderful time that Aden had had with Elexa, he had come to believe that Ian was wrong about Aden and Christina. Now, seeing Aden's attraction to Christina and her children, he began to wonder. *Could there be any truth to what Ian had said?* By inviting Christina and the children to the party, he was hoping to find out for himself what the attraction was.

"Thank you for asking Mr. Bradcliffe, but I don't think I can. I have a few things to take care of."

"It's too nice of a day to be inside taking care of things. They can wait," said John in his persuasive style.

Natalie and Timothy wanted to go. "Please Mom, it would be fun," said Timothy eagerly. "Can we go?" pleaded Natalie.

"But if Daddy comes home, he's not going to know where we are," replied Christina out of concern for Sean.

"We can just leave him a note," suggested Timothy.

Even though she had no more excuses, she was still hesitant. She was not sure how Sean would react. He was always so unpredictable. As she was thinking about what to do, Aden said, "I agree. You should come Christina, even if it is just for a short while."

Aden was no longer concerned about Sean. To have her at his party was better than he could have imagined. This way he would not even have to explain anything to his father since he was the one who extended the invitation to Christina in the first place.

She thought to herself that there cannot be anything wrong with going to a party with her children and being surrounded by lots of people. Even Sean could not possibly get upset with her for that. Seeing the eager look on the children's faces Christina accepted the invitation to go.

"Then we'll see you all in a few minutes," said John, anxious to see if there was anything between them.

By the time Christina and the children got there, the party was in full swing with music, plenty of food and drinks, people talking and swimming. Everybody was having a great time. Aden was standing on the terrace which overlooked the gardens and the swimming pool below. There seemed to be an almost continuous stream of his friends coming to the party, all excited to see him. He greeted and talked with them all as they arrived.

Natalie and Timothy headed straight to the pool. Christina stayed by the pool to be near them, while meeting and talking with some of Aden's friends who were around the pool.

Every once in a while, Aden would casually turn in the direction of the pool and look at Christina. He could not be happier seeing her there. For the very first time he was surrounded by the people that he genuinely cared for—his father, friends, Christina, and her children.

At every glance and every look, his heart overflowed with joy at seeing her and her smiling face, until he saw her smile suddenly disappear. He did not have to look any further. He knew that at that moment Sean must have arrived.

Aden was right. Sean had just returned from playing golf and was on his way to meet Vicky. As usual their meeting was kept hidden from Christina, and it was made under the pretence of going to work. Having seen Christina's note, he had decided to stop by Aden's house. It was an opportunity that he did not want to miss.

By the time Aden made his way down to the pool, Sean had already introduced himself to his father, and was talking with Christina and John. Sean could not be any warmer and friendlier towards Aden, a feeling that was not shared by Aden. After a rather cold and almost businesslike greeting, he invited them to come and sit down for some cold drinks at a large circle of chairs near the pool. He then went over and told the caterer to bring a tray of drinks.

There, among Aden's friends and father, Sean was in his element. He was charming and witty, being the center of attention, joking and making everyone laugh. He was quite unlike the Sean that Christina knew at home.

"If it isn't Prince Charming himself?" said Sean as he saw Aden approaching.

Aden in his usual, aloof style, with no reaction or response amidst the extra attention that the statement evoked, went, and sat near Sean.

"It's really good to have you back, Aden," said Sean with a sly smile.

"It's good to be back."

Then, like a predator waiting for the right moment to pounce on its prey, Sean craftily steered the conversation in the direction where he could make his attack. "You haven't been back for more than a few hours and look how you have livened up our boring and quiet neighborhood. You've even brought excitement to my wife's mundane life." With everybody laughing he cunningly turned to Christina and said, "I hope it's not too much excitement for you dear."

To have her own husband put her down like that, hurt her deeply. She was in a state of shock and lost for words. She was also too much of a lady to defend herself or be drawn into an argument in front of all the people there. Instead, she just concealed her pain and said nothing.

Aden, feeling the hurt in Christina was not about to allow Sean to get away with it. "To pursue certain ideals in life requires certain sacrifices, such as giving up glamour and excitement for your family. And those few who do are to be admired."

Having pulled Aden to her defense Sean was on a roll. "What could be more admirable than you graduating with all high distinctions, 'a mark of a genius' was quoted in all the papers here? Congratulations are in order, not only for graduating, but also for not having to put up with my wife anymore." Sean had callously managed to hurt Christina even more deeply, and he was not about to stop.

"What was it that you said some time ago dear?" acting sincerely, "that you had told Aden about some new management theory that you had read in some book," he snickered. "I felt sorry for Aden for having to listen to someone who doesn't know the first thing about managing people."

That piqued John's curiosity, who had been listening with interest. Wondering why Aden would have talked to Christina about management and not him, he immediately asked, "What is this about?"

Aden was incensed at how Sean could take Christina's selfless and invaluable help and support to him and tear it down like that. That was also something private that nobody knew anything about, and he wanted it to stay that way. But Sean was heartless and did not seem to have any intention of stopping.

Aden could easily continue defending her and win every time, but that would be playing into Sean's hands. This he did not want to do, not in front of his friends and especially not in front of his father who was already perplexed at this interchange.

Sean continued, "Let me see if I can remember. It was something absurd…" Just then the caterer approached Sean to offer him a drink.

Aden, sitting one chair away from Sean, with his quick reflexes imperceptibly tripped the caterer. The entire tray of drinks landed on Sean. That stopped Sean, but there was nothing to stop the hurt that Christina was feeling.

The caterer immediately apologized profusely, and to be helpful quickly handed him a towel. It was of no use. Sean was too wet and somewhat sticky. He had to go home and get changed. He slowly got up from his chair and tried hard not to show how incensed he was. He looked at Aden spitefully and said, "Thank you for the drinks."

Aden, with a contented look on his face simply replied, "Anytime."

Sean turned to Christina and said, "Shall we go dear?" Then still trying to be charming said, "I think we have provided enough entertainment for these people."

The way Christina was feeling she had no interest to stay. She welcomed the opportunity to leave, and after a quick goodbye, she departed with Sean.

With that turn of events Aden's father was not able to arrive at any conclusion, except for one. Regardless of how Aden felt about Christina, John was no longer prepared to leave things to chance. Instead, he was determined to do his best to direct and influence Aden's life, either openly or from behind the scene. He was going to do whatever it took to guide his life in the direction that he knew was best for him.

Chapter 42

Monday was another nice summer day with clear blue skies, bright golden sun, and a soft blowing breeze. For Aden it was not just nice, it was a brilliant and exuberant day. This was the day that he had been looking forward to for the past three months. During this time the thought of seeing Christina, and the hope and desire of spending time with her like he used to, were what had kept him going. The fact that yesterday, Christina seemed happy when he saw her on the beach and accepted the invitation to go to his party, had given him the assurance that things would be going back to the way they were. Today was the day to realize it all, to look at Christina's beautiful face, to gaze into her eyes, to spend time with her, to share his thoughts and ideas with her, to talk to her about his university courses, and many other intellectually stimulating topics. These were the things he had missed, and he could hardly wait to be with her again.

Since he did not have any lectures to attend until the afternoon, he went to the university first thing in the morning to purchase all the law books that he needed, and then rushed back to see Christina. He wanted to show her the books, his schedule of classes, and to set up times for Christina to tutor him. He also had a copy of a paper from the Harvard Business Review as further evidence of the soundness of the theory that Christina had discussed with him. He wanted to show her that Sean's assertions were unfounded. On the way all that he could think about was her dazzling eyes, vibrant smile, kind face and cheerful disposition that always brightened his spirit.

When Christina answered the door, for the very first time ever since she had known Aden, she was anything but cheerful. Outwardly, she appeared her normal self, but inwardly she was sad. Aden was too happy and too excited to notice, or even consider it possible. He just started walking to the family room while talking about his courses. Once in the family room he took out his schedule of courses and handed it to Christina.

She did not take it. With a solemn look on her face she said, "I don't need to see that."

"But you do, to work out the times for tutoring me."

"No. There won't be any tutoring," said Christina struggling to hide her inner feelings.

"I don't understand. You have always tutored me," replied Aden in surprise.

"What is there not to understand Aden? You don't need to be tutored." Christina then very softly murmured, "And especially not by me."

Sean's continual verbal abuse had taken its toll on Christina, gradually eroding her self esteem. Yesterday he had finally managed to shamelessly destroy any remnant of her self-confidence and self-worth. What he had said had made her doubt her ability to tutor him. Also, the way he humiliated her by cutting her down in front of so many people had taken away her sense of self respect and dignity. As a result, she was hurt. Feeling the way that she did, it was not easy to face Aden, let alone to even consider tutoring him. Having lost her self-value, it was as if she had lost her conviction to help others.

He desperately wanted to change her mind. "But your tutoring has helped me in more ways than you know," asserted Aden sincerely.

But she was hurting too much to see things differently. "You don't need to be polite about it."

"Christina, you know I don't say something unless I mean it."

It was no use. After a short pause she said, "Now, if you'll excuse me, I have to take care of a few mundane things. I won't walk you to the door as you already know the way out."

"But Christina…"

"Goodbye Aden," she interrupted firmly. Then on the verge of tears she quickly turned around and walked away.

There was so much that he wanted to tell her to make her feel better, but he had no choice. He had to leave. But before leaving, he took out the paper he had copied from the Harvard Business Review and left it on the table for her to see.

At last Sean had broken her spirit, and tragically, once again Christina and Aden fell victims to his cold-hearted scheme. That was not at all like her. She had never before refused to help or had been so abrupt and brash towards anyone, let alone someone for whom she had such high regard, like Aden. It went against everything in which she believed. Because of the way she was feeling she had failed to hold on to her convictions, and that hurt her even more.

The one thing that could have possibly helped her to look at things differently was the paper that Aden had left for her, but she did not see it. As fate had it, later when Sean came home, he came across it before she did. He took it to his office and left it there.

After leaving Christina, instead of returning to the university, Aden went back to his house. He was feeling angry with Sean, frustrated, and helpless to do anything to change the situation. He simply told Randall that he was retiring to his room and did not wish to be disturbed by him, visitors, or any phone calls. He was in no mood to see or talk to anyone.

He walked into his room, threw his books on the floor, sat in his swivel leather chair, turned on his wide screen satellite TV, and for the very first time began flicking through the hundred odd channels available. He just aimlessly watched the images without the sound.

The cold reality that was facing him was that none of his wealth, genius, or skills could help him get what he wanted. The one thing he wanted more than anything else in life was to be with Christina. As he stared at the TV for several hours with these thoughts going through his mind, his anger and frustration began to give way to apathy.

As important as his studies were to him in providing him with a higher education, they were equally important as a means for him to be with Christina. He looked forward to the times he got to spend with her which were the most enjoyable part of his days. The thought of being unable to see or be with her left him feeling hopeless and despondent, as though he was lost in a desert being consumed away by a thirst that only the oasis of her presence could quench. With no pathway leading him to Christina, he found himself no longer caring about anything anymore. The high ideals that he had so confidently come to believe about education and helping others were now fading away.

It is easy to hold on to beliefs and convictions when things go as expected and desired. But the true sign of faith and personal growth is firmly holding on to them when faced with difficulties and temptations. Drowning himself in his emotions was preventing him from seeing the significance of what he was experiencing. He, like Christina, was going through a test of life. It was something that he needed for his personal spiritual development.

Late in the afternoon there was a knock at the door. It was Randall.

"I thought I told you not to disturb me!" blasted Aden.

"I do apologize, sir, but your father is on the phone and would like to know what time you will be having dinner with him."

"Tell my father that I won't be able to tonight."

"Very well, sir. Then will you be dining out tonight?"

"No."

"Shall I prepare dinner for you here?"

"No! What is it with all these questions?" said Aden taking out his frustrations on Randall.

"Master Aden, I simply wanted to make sure that you are provided for," replied Randall out of concern for him.

"I don't need anything. All that I want is not to be disturbed."

"Yes sir, as you wish," said Randall kindly.

Aden's Dad did not think much about it. Being his first day back he was extremely busy, and it suited him fine to skip dinner. He figured that in this way he would be able to get more of his work done, and he would be able to spend more time with Aden the following evening.

Hours had passed; day had turned to night and night to dawn. Aden still had no interest in doing anything, not even eating or sleeping. In the morning he went to the kitchen, only had a glass of orange juice, and went back to his room.

Randall could not believe it. For the very first time in his entire life Aden was wearing the same clothes that he had on the day before. They were wrinkled. He was unshaven, and his hair was uncombed. Not wanting to upset him, Randall did not ask any questions.

Aden spent the entire morning in his room. He had no intention of going anywhere. He had no reason to go out anymore for he had done it all, and he knew that he could do and achieve anything. He had attended the university and completed his first degree in record time. He had taken care of Armando and rescued Elexa, and he had even handled Sean. What he could not do was handle not seeing Christina, and without her consent there was nothing he could do.

To continue his studies here in Adelaide or away in another country would be too painful. It would just remind him too much of her. While he did enjoy his university experience, the real joy for him was sharing it with Christina. He also thought about going back to Europe to be with Elexa, but that was not the life that he wanted. What he wanted, he could not have.

The more that he thought about his life, the more his apathy grew, and the more he found himself wanting to get away from it all, even if only for a short time, hoping this would give him a chance to work things out. His heart went out to his father, and he did not want to disappoint him. But, he felt he could no longer continue on and stay there. He then recalled a poem by Rumi that he had read once a long time ago which so aptly expressed his feelings:

> *The tale is still unfinished, and I have no heart for it,*
> *Then pray forgive me.*

He just hoped that his father would accept and forgive him.

When it was passed noon and Aden had still not come down Randall decided to let his father know.

John was in the middle of a very important meeting when Randall phoned. He was meeting with all his executives, Declan Harris, and two others of the senior research staff to discuss the outcome of his meetings with Digicomp, and to initiate the process of hardware development.

As important as this meeting was to John, when Tracy, his personal assistant, told him that Randall wanted to speak with him, he immediately left the meeting and took the call in his office.

Not knowing when Aden's classes were actually starting and to avoid jumping to any conclusions as to why he had not been going to university, John called his friend, Sandra Klossen. Since she was not in the office, he left a message for her to return his call as soon as she got back. He also asked Tracy to put the call through to him immediately.

It was late afternoon when his meeting finished. An important and satisfactory conclusion had been reached. A task force was to be formed to carry out some initial research to determine the feasibility of the hardware development in-house. The task force was then to report back on their findings within two months.

As John was leaving the boardroom, he received the return call from Sandra. She was happy to find out that John and Aden were back. "So, where is my star pupil? He has already missed a few classes since yesterday."

"Perhaps he's jet lagged," replied John in Aden's defense.

"In our university days, we never got jet lagged. I guess that kids today are just not as tough as we were," laughed Sandra. "Just tell Aden that I expect to see him tomorrow."

That conversation with Sandra was enough for him to know that, as suspected by Randall, something was wrong. He cancelled everything and immediately left the office to see Aden.

When John arrived at Aden's house, he was still in his room, sitting on his swivel chair, and staring at his soundless TV screen.

"Hello Aden," said John as he walked into the room.

"Hi Dad. Shouldn't you be at work?" replied Aden with his eyes still fixed on the TV.

"I finished early to come to see you."

"Well, I've got another 50 channels or so to go through. You're welcome to join me."

"I was thinking more along the lines of us going out to dinner. So, how about it Aden?"

"No thanks, I'm not hungry."

"Then perhaps we can talk, and…, without that television being on."

After a minute Aden turned off the television, turned around in his swivel chair, and finally facing his father said, "We both know what you want to talk about. Go ahead, ask me and get it over with so that I can get back to my TV."

Aden's father was taken aback with Aden's appearance, but he did not want to bring it up. He had more important things to talk about, "Alright, for starters, why haven't you been going to the university and attending your classes?"

"Why should I? I don't see any reason for it."

John's heart sank right to the floor. He had a shocked look on his face. That was not what he wanted to hear. "To complete your education and to get your second degree," he replied matter-of-factly.

"I have already done that, and one degree is enough."

"That one is in business. You also need to complete your law degree."

"Why? All I have to do is to pick any of these books," referring to the ones thrown on the floor, "and by the next day I could recall and recite every single line of it for you."

"As commendable as that is, earning your degree is much more than that. It's about gaining insight and understanding and expanding your knowledge through interaction with others."

"For what purpose?" said Aden, challenging his father.

"For your future."

"I am a Bradcliffe. My future is already set. I can have any job that I want, even without a degree."

"A job should be earned based on your qualifications, not your name."

"I think that by now you know that I can do anything, if I want to."

"That's my point. Why don't you want to?"

"Because I have lost interest." Aden then out of frustration said the first thing that came to his mind, "I have decided to become a beach bum, to explore all of these endless beaches that we have." He did not really intend to become a beach bum. He just thought that as a way for him to get away.

John's face went pale. His eyes were protruding with worry and concern. He felt ill and distraught to hear that, yet not wanting to stop Aden from talking, he maintained his composure as he painfully and quietly listened.

"There were times today," said Aden with a far away look on his face and a sense of apathy, "when I felt tempted to walk out that front door and to keep on walking."

With a heavy heart John calmly asked, "Why didn't you? What stopped you?"

"I hadn't said goodbye to you."

"Aden, why would you want to do that and throw away everything that you've worked for and achieved? Your life is here," said John desperately trying to stop him.

"That may be, but there is nothing more for me to do here."

"But there…"

Aden interrupted his father. "No use Dad," he said finding it too painful to continue to stay there and not be able to see Christina. "I've already made up my mind and there's nothing that you can say to change it. I am leaving tomorrow."

"If that's what you want, then you leave me no choice. I'll go with you and become a beach bum like you," he said with a slight hint of a smile conveying his sense of commitment that he would do anything for his son.

"What?!" Aden was shocked. "This is something that I want to do. It's not for you. You have your corporation, your project. You have too much at stake to leave, even if it is just for a short while. You can't leave any of that behind."

"Aden, without you there is no life for me here, and none of the things that you mentioned have any meaning," he expressed sincerely.

"Dad, your reverse psychology and putting the guilt on me for leaving your life will not change my mind. I am still leaving tomorrow."

"That was not my intention at all. Aden, while I respect your wishes, I only ask that you wait for one more day to think through your decision."

"I have already given it enough thought."

"Then one more day won't make any difference. The beaches are not going anywhere. If by tomorrow night you still feel the same about your decision, we'll leave Thursday morning, and go anywhere you want."

Aden reluctantly agreed to wait one more day.

That same afternoon, while John was talking to Aden, Christina stumbled on the paper that he had left behind. She had come upon it while Sean was out. She had gone to put his mail in his office. Its title caught her attention. She picked it up and read it with interest. It helped her to see things in a more positive light. She began to regain her self-respect and to once again, after two days, feel good about herself. For not only did it show that she was right, but also naturally assuming that it was from Sean, it was his way of apologizing to her.

Surrounded by glass-covered shelves of books, some classics and many business and management books, it was this paper that brought back traces of a smile to her face. As she looked through the paper again, it suddenly hit her that it was wrong of her to have been so abrupt with Aden. Although she still thought that he was in no need of her tutoring, she felt bad about the way that she had responded to him. At that moment she realized that sadly she had been too wrapped up in herself. Instead, she should have never allowed the hurt she felt to prevent her from holding on to her beliefs and convictions of being of help to others. Now she only wished that some how she could make it up to Aden.

With Aden's life taking on a new direction, it did not seem likely that she would be able to make it up to him.

Chapter 43

That night John could not sleep. He paced up and down his room. Thoughts of Aden and leaving the Bradcliffe Corporation and estate behind were racing in his mind. Although he prided himself on being an ideas man, always able to sort out ways to address issues relating to the running of his corporation, he could not come up with any ideas to stop Aden from throwing his life away.

It was early in the morning, and he was feeling too tired to continue. He laid down on his bed to rest for a few minutes. While in that state of being half awake and half asleep, an idea came to him. He quickly sat up, and suddenly felt rejuvenated. He saw a way forward, and it did not matter that he had not gotten any sleep the night before. He was ready to go to work.

After he arrived at his office, the first thing he did was to draft a letter leaving explicit instructions on how all matters were to be handled in the event of his absence. He wanted to be prepared, even though he felt rather hopeful and confident that his solution would succeed and that the letter would not be needed.

With everything riding on his idea, shortly after 9 o'clock he anxiously picked up the phone and made a call. "Good morning Mrs. Ashton. This is John Bradcliffe calling."

Christina was the only person that he thought could help him. It did not matter that he did not agree with Ian's appraisal of Aden's feelings towards her. What mattered was what she had done for Aden. He felt that if indeed she was the one who had saved his life, then she would be the only person who could influence Aden's thinking.

After the initial greetings he got right to the point. He gave her a brief account of what had transpired. Christina was saddened by what she heard. What could be more tragic she thought, than wasting such a great mind, especially at a time when Aden had achieved so much? Deep down she could not help but wonder, while not seemingly obvious, if she was somehow responsible for his decision. Responsible or not, something had to be done about it. With bated breath she quietly waited to hear what John was planning to do to set things straight.

She was both touched and overwhelmed when John asked her for help. She had not anticipated that at all. "What can I possibly do to help?" asked Christina. She was still full of self doubt because of what Sean had said and done.

"You can talk to him. He values your opinion," pleaded John. Even though she was not sure about herself or Sean's reaction to any of this, she could not say no. This was not about her. It was about helping, and not just anyone. It was about helping Aden, whom she held in such high regard. Once again, her desire to help won over her personal concerns. Knowing that this was not an easy task, especially since she was not to let on that she knew anything about it, she accepted.

As the phone call ended the race against time began. Christina had to figure out what to do and do it quickly. She had to come up with a plan, not just any plan, but a foolproof one as there was not going to be a second chance. With her children at school, she only had until 3 o'clock when she had to pick them up, to do what needed to be done.

She knew better than anyone else what a brilliant mind Aden had. Therefore, not only was it important for her to get him to change his mind, but also to have him become fully committed to his ideals and to fulfilling his high destiny.

She needed to come up with an excuse or a reason to go over to Aden's house. She dropped what she was doing and quickly drove to the mall. She stopped at the first bookstore she came to and started looking for a business-related book. The specific topic itself did not matter. With Aden being such an avid reader, it had to be a new book, hot off the press that hopefully he had not yet read. Fortunately, she did come across such a book which she purchased and then rushed home.

She quickly changed from her casual clothes and shoes into a nicely fitted suit and high heels, an outfit that she had worn to a couple of Sean's company functions. After she fixed her hair, she grabbed the book and walked over to Aden's house. With every step she got more nervous as if she were about to take an important final exam.

As she stood by the front door of his house, she took a deep breath, prayed earnestly to God for assistance, and then knocked.

Randall was not home, and Aden as before was in his room. He still was wearing the same clothes that he had worn on Monday, except now they were more wrinkled, and his shirt was completely unbuttoned. His hair was now disheveled, and he was unshaven. He ignored the knock and continued to watch TV.

Christina knocked again and again. Finally, Aden could not ignore the persistent knock. He thought that perhaps Randall had locked himself out and needed to get his keys. He had done that before. Feeling indignant about having to answer the door, he opened it only to be absolutely floored by what he saw.

There was Christina with her dazzling eyes, vibrant smile, dressed very nicely, and looking absolutely beautiful. He was instantly transported with joy to the heights of ecstasy. Lost in her presence, he completely forgot about his appearance, his thoughts, and even his manners to greet and invite her inside. All that he said was, "Christina?" in amazement.

Christina had expected that kind of reaction. This was the first time ever that she had gone over to his house unannounced and uninvited.

Then with a smile on her face she said, "Hello Aden. It's good that you are home." She continued as she walked in, "I came across a rather interesting book, and I thought that you might like to see it."

Once inside the foyer, while still talking she turned around, and when she saw the way that Aden appeared, she momentarily lost her train of thought. "Is that a new fashion trend?"

Aden, still in a daze to see Christina there, suddenly felt embarrassed about his appearance. He said, "No," as he smiled for the first time in more than two days. He then quickly pulled his shirt together and started buttoning it.

"That's good," replied Christina with a warm smile. "Anyway, I was thinking that we could discuss the book over lunch."

"Sure, that sounds like a good idea. I'll have Randall prepare lunch as soon as he gets back."

"I was thinking more along the lines of going to a restaurant."

"A restaurant?" asked Aden with raised eyebrows. Still not over his initial shock, he was even more surprised.

"Can't two friends have lunch together in a restaurant?" replied Christina with a gentle smile.

"Of course, they can." He was not about to argue over a good thing. "Just give me 10-15 minutes to get changed. Then we can go."

"Take all the time you need," she said earnestly.

"I get the message, but it isn't necessary," said Aden with a smile as he went up to his room.

Christina chuckled at his response. She had only intended to give herself more time to look at the book so that she would know what it was about. She did not intend her remark to be interpreted as needing more time to get ready because of his particularly unkempt appearance.

Before long he was ready, stylishly dressed and looking as handsome as ever. "Is there any particular restaurant you would like to go to?" asked Aden accommodatingly.

Christina quickly stopped reading the book and said, "As a matter of fact there is, the Heritage on Mount Lofty. I love its old English style and character. The gardens are beautiful and it's a lovely drive." Since it was a 20-minute drive from the city, she thought that it would give them more time to talk.

At first thought Aden was hesitant to go to the Heritage. That was where he used to take a lot of his dates. Christina was too special to him, and he did not want to chance having anyone look at her in the same way. But he would do anything for her, and to please her outweighed any concerns he had. Since that was where she wanted to go, he agreed.

He then escorted her to the garage where all his seven sports cars were kept. "Wow! This is more impressive than an exclusive showroom at a prestige car dealer," said Christina pleasantly, amazed at what she saw.

"Which one would you like me to drive today?"

"I like them all. I can't decide. You choose."

Aden chose his top-of-the-line Mercedes supercar which had been customized for him and had the right touch of class and elegance for Christina.

Once inside the car Aden simply started the engine with the touch of a button.

"No need for keys?"

"Its onboard computer recognizes my fingerprint and allows me to start the engine without the need for a key."

"That's the coolest thing I have ever seen in a car," said Christina enthusiastically.

"Here, Christina, put your finger on this screen." And as she did, Aden typed in a few commands to the computer and then turned off the engine. "Now you start the engine," he said to Christina.

"But how?"

"Go ahead, try," said Aden as he relaxed in his seat and waited for her reaction.

Christina did and the engine started. The spark in her eyes appeared even brighter as she looked at him with a big smile and said, "I really like this. I wish I had it in my car."

Aden was pleased to have been able to impress her. That was something he had not much opportunity to do with their focus always having been on his studies. "I programmed your fingerprint into the computer," he said with a content look on his face, "and now you are the only person besides me who can start this car without a key."

That got them started on talking about cars as they drove off. After they had been driving and talking for a while, Christina heard a song on the radio that she liked very much.

"I love this song," said Christina excitedly. I heard it the other day when I was driving Natalie and Timothy to school, and I hadn't heard it since then."

For the first time ever since Aden had known her, Christina was openly showing her emotions and freely expressing her feelings. And he was enjoying every moment of it, treasuring every new thing he was learning about her.

"Too bad that it's over," said Christina sounding a little disappointed.

"Would you like to hear it again?"

"Sure, I would. It has such a happy beat. But I don't even know the name of it. I'll just have to wait until they play it again."

Aden simply pressed a button on the sound system and the song began playing.

That was totally unexpected, but she was happy to hear her song again. She could not stop smiling as she asked, "How did you do that?"

"I had the computer save it," said Aden delighted to have been able to make her happy once again.

"I love this car! Don't tell me, next you are going to push another button and lunch will be served."

Aden laughed, "Not quite, but if you like I can arrange for it next time."

"No, that's alright, everything is perfect as it is." And it was. With all his personalized additions, all his cars were unique and one of a kind. "I've always liked sports cars." Christina continued, "But I hadn't seen anything like this before, and I have seen quite a few, especially during my second summer at Stanford."

"Why, what happened then?" asked Aden curiously.

"My boyfriend…" hearing the word 'boyfriend' piqued Aden's interest even more.

"He wanted to buy a sports car that just had to have everything. To find his perfect car he test drove every kind of sports car that you could imagine. Almost everyday he would come and take me with him. He would test drive the cars, and then we'd go out to dinner. Sometimes we'd go dancing or to a movie afterwards. We had fun together that summer."

"Was that Sean?"

"No that was Eric. Finally, after a month or so he bought his dream car. But none of the cars that he looked at or bought could compare to this one."

"So, what happened to Eric?" asked Aden interested to know.

"Eric was a fun-loving guy, and even though we had a great time together, gradually we drifted apart as he became more interested in money and all the things that money could bring, like power and status. At the end of that summer, I met Sean and did not see Eric after that."

"What about Sean, was he fun loving, too?"

"Sean was different. He was the sweetest, kindest, and most caring guy I had ever met, and that was how he won my heart."

Aden was surprised to hear Sean described that way. He never associated such qualities with him, especially not after the way he had seen him treat Christina last Sunday. He wondered if he was wrong about Sean. While he did not want to put Christina on the spot, he had to know what Sean was really like. To find out he asked, "Is he still like that, I mean sweet, kind, and caring?"

Christina lost her smile and became very quiet. After a moment's pause, as if searching for the right thing to say without being negative towards him, she replied, "In life we are often faced with temptations, challenges, and trials that test our convictions. Sadly, under pressure and stress, some people change and lose the wonderful qualities and convictions that they possess."

Even though her response did not directly answer his question, it was enough to confirm his thoughts about Sean. Just at that time they arrived at the restaurant. Christina was still quiet and seemed to be lost in her thoughts. All that he wanted was to see her happy and smiling again.

After he parked the car and turned off the engine, he turned, looked at Christina, and told her, what Confucius once said, "Beautiful green gardens mean red hot fire inside, and when there is red hot fire, good fortune awaits you."

Christina listened and thought carefully for a moment about what Aden had just said, then broke out laughing, "Confucius did not say that!"

"That's because he didn't think of it. Otherwise, he would have."

Christina was once again her cheerful self. At her suggestion they stayed out and walked through the gardens. It was such a gorgeous day, and everything seemed so vibrant. In a short while they came across a wooden bench under an arbor of climbing roses that overlooked a picturesque valley of green fields covered with native plants and shrubs.

It was just the perfect spot for sitting and talking. Christina while enjoying the view, turned to Aden and said, "You know, nature is so amazing. It's ever growing with its beauty and majesty, and still ever remaining changeless. Even the tests and trials of the winter are powerless to prevent it from returning to its beauty in spring. I wonder why people can't be more like that?"

"Because it's never easy."

"And yet, not only is it so important to hold on to our values and principles, but also necessary for our personal growth. When I think about what you have achieved, I see how admirably this point has been demonstrated over the past two years." Aden just listened, enjoying the compliments he was receiving.

Christina continued, "I guess I would say that it's not a question of it being difficult, but rather our sense of commitment and ideals." The stage was now set for her to ask what she needed to, "Promise me Aden…" said Christina with an ardent longing, "that you will never change and will never let go of your goals and beliefs."

Aden was caught off guard with such an unexpected request. He had to think about it before attempting to answer it. He got up and took a few steps away from the bench. Considering that he had already let go of his goals, he turned towards Christina and gave the only answer that he could, "No, I don't think that I can make such a promise."

That was not the answer that she had hoped to hear, but she was not about to give up. "Since no one is ever tested beyond their limits or capacity," said Christina based on her personal convictions, "I believe that you can."

"Even if I could, why should I want to?" said Aden not quite convinced.

"Because it is important to hold on to our aspirations and convictions, otherwise what good are they if we falter every time things get hard or don't go exactly the way that we want them to go?"

"Still, as valid as that may be, why should it matter if I make such a promise?"

"It matters because…you have too much to offer to allow chances and changes of life to alter your convictions and goals, take away your determination, or in any way diminish your high character. And that is why you need to make a commitment that no matter what the circumstances may be in life, you won't let go of your high ideals in which you so firmly believe."

Aden was touched. He went back and sat on the bench again, looked into her eyes, and said, "All that sounds quite nice, but that is not what I'm asking. I want to know why this is so important to you."

After a short pause and with genuine sincerity Christina gently said, "Because I thought you were different. You had restored my faith in people, in human character…"

Those few, simple words were all that Aden wanted to hear, "No need to say anymore. You have my promise."

Her face lit up. Christina was truly happy to hear that, for both Aden and his father. She knew that to have his son back on the right path would please John. And once again Aden would be able to continue to fulfill his high destiny. She looked at Aden and said, "You don't know how happy this makes me."

"Happy enough to have lunch now?" he said jokingly.

"Yes, definitely," said Christina with a contented smile.

Inside the restaurant, naturally, everybody knew Aden. The manager warmly welcomed them personally, "Would you like your usual table, Mr. Bradcliffe?"

Normally he would not have minded the personal attention given him, but seeing the surprised reaction on Christina's face, he did. In trying to downplay it, he simply said, "A table by the window would be fine."

"As you wish," replied the manager as he took them to their table which overlooked the beautiful gardens outside.

"So, you come here often?" asked Christina casually as she opened the menu.

"I used to, but I don't have time anymore." Not wanting to talk about that part of his life which to him seemed like a long time ago, he quickly steered away from it by asking Christina what she would like to have.

After Christina glanced at the menu, she noticed that Aden was not looking at his. "You decided very quickly," she said in surprise.

"Yes, I did."

"And I still don't know what to get. So, what are you having?"

"I'm having the same thing that you are," said Aden looking quite dignified, sitting comfortably back in his chair.

"But you don't know what I'm having," said Christina with a chuckle. "I don't even know what I'm having."

"It doesn't matter."

"What if I decided to have a crispy salad of creeping crawlers, a main course of an eight-legged creature, and…, and for desert a sugar coated lizard tongue. Then what would you do?"

"Have the same thing…with a side order of antacid," replied Aden confidently, with a slight smile.

"That's crazy, you wouldn't do that."

"Yes, I would."

Just then their waitress was walking by. Aden motioned for her to stop. "We're ready to order." He then ordered two of everything that Christina had just said. Christina broke out laughing. The waitress stood there, not knowing what to do. "You'd better write this down." So, while also laughing, she did. "And to drink, we'll have two tall glasses of octopus juice."

Eventually, they ordered from the menu. Christina was still feeling concerned about his future. She knew for him to remain fully committed to his goals he needed to be mentally challenged and intellectually stimulated beyond the scope of his studies. While waiting for their lunch to be served, an idea came to her, and she decided to run it by him.

She asked him about his courses. After he talked to her about them, she said, "While your courses sound interesting, no doubt they will offer no particular challenge." Aden smiled, acknowledging it. Christina continued, "I was thinking now that you're going to have more time and having completed your business degree, it would be good for you to do something extra such as give lectures in the Business School and talks at corporate functions and organizations."

"I don't know if I am qualified enough to do that."

"Who could be more qualified than you? No one could equal you in your breadth of knowledge. Combine that with your depth of understanding, which I know is quite good, and I say that you would make an excellent lecturer."

It was not something that Aden had considered. After thinking about it for a minute, he liked it. "That is a pretty good idea. I'll talk to Professor Klossen about it."

Then in a soft and gentle tone of voice Christina said, "When the time comes, if you should need an audience to practice your talks on, I'll be happy to listen to them."

Aden was pleasantly amazed to hear that. Now he could get to see her again. It was something that he had longed for and had lost all hope that it would ever happen again. He was over the moon, even though he did not show it. "A good audience would be willing to listen to a range of topics, from business to law cases, and to interject ideas, give suggestions, and enter into discussions on important points," said Aden attempting to have her involved with his studies again.

Christina smiled at his clever answer, and this time she agreed, "Then you've got yourself the best audience possible."

"I couldn't agree more."

"I was kidding, not about being your audience, but about being the best."

"I wasn't," said Aden with a penetrating look conveying his deep love for her, a look that was interrupted by the serving of lunch.

After the waitress had finished and left their table, Aden asked, "Is something on your mind?"

"Not really," Christina replied hesitantly. "Why do you ask?"

"You've held your fork in your hand for a couple of minutes without touching any of the food on your plate."

Aden was right. Christina was still thinking about Aden's future. While she was happy about his commitment towards his studies and his willingness to give talks and lectures, she believed that it was not enough. She felt very much like his father, that to further ensure his happiness he needed to be more outwardly involved. But she was having difficulty with John's approach, and in trying to work it into her conversation. Aden's question gave her the opening that she was looking for. "Very observant of you," she said. Then candidly she continued, "I was just a bit concerned that you think that life is all about work and no play."

This was another unexpected comment. Aden wondered what point she was trying to make, as he said, "That's something I never thought I'd hear from you."

"I mean, it is good to work hard," she said in her defense, "but you have to have some fun, too. When I was at Stanford, I used to study hard during the week, but I always went out on Saturday nights." It could be seen on her face how talking about it brought back pleasant memories of those days, as she continued, "Eric knew how much I loved to dance. Very often he would take me dancing."

"And Sean didn't because he didn't like to dance."

"How did you know that?"

"Just a wild guess," although it was an obvious deduction for Aden from what he knew about Sean.

"Anyway, Eric and I used to have a lot of fun dancing."

Aden was beginning to develop a dislike for Eric.

Christina continued, "We used to laugh a lot too because I would learn the new dances quickly, usually after only seeing it once. Eric on the other hand couldn't do this, and it always took him a while."

"That's pretty good. I don't know many people who can learn a new dance step after seeing it only once."

"That is, other than yourself, you mean," replied Christina referring to his photographic memory.

Aden just smiled and made no reply. "Then," Christina continued, "it must be a lot of fun for you too, to go dancing."

"Actually, I don't go clubbing anymore." He had not had any interest since he had met Christina. "I've been more focused on my studies, not to mention that I don't care for the atmosphere there."

While Christina agreed with Aden, she had to support John. Going clubbing was his idea. He wanted Aden to meet some new girls and start dating again in the hopes of him finding the right girl, settling down, and getting married. He thought that in this way he would never have to worry about losing his son again.

As she thought about it she wondered if something good could come of it, and there was. "I know what you mean," she replied. "Unfortunately, so many young people, especially teenagers, think that they need to smoke or swear to be 'cool', or drink and do drugs in order to have fun. The problem is that they don't have good role models. They need to have a role model like you whom they idolize."

She felt relieved as Aden did not dismiss the idea. "It would be good if you went," Christina continued, "that is, only for a short while, for them to see you and for you to have fun and be with your friends or meet new people."

Aden, spellbound by Christina, could not help but appreciate her sweet and caring attitude towards him and his life. While he had not told her before, he said, "I want you to know that I always value your thoughts and ideas."

"If you think that flattery is going to get you out of eating crispy crawlers salad, you'd better think again," said Christina jokingly.

"I have to stop being so obvious," said Aden facetiously.

They both laughed, a laughter that continued throughout their lunch, echoing the sounds of the joy of one friend helping another, of sharing special innocent moments in a whirlwind of colliding destinies.

Chapter 44

The effect of Christina's talk was better than John had hoped or considered possible. By that evening he was ecstatic to learn that Christina had been able to reorient Aden's thinking.

Aden was once again set on pursuing his high goals. First thing the next morning, with a new sense of commitment and attitude towards life, he went to see Professor Klossen. After all, he had a promise to keep.

Professor Klossen's response to Aden's suggestion was more than favorable. In fact, to Professor Klossen this was heaven sent. She had just been approached to do some leading-edge consulting work, which was to start in six weeks. As much as she wanted to take on this work, she was faced with the problem of finding a suitable replacement to handle her lectures. With Aden walking in and offering to give some lectures, her problem was immediately solved. Fully aware of Aden's brilliant mind she was quite confident that he would work out better than any other professor she could have gotten.

Soon, Aden found himself in the midst of not only completing the final two years of law in one, but also preparing and putting together the lectures he was to be giving. For the first time he found there was not enough time in a day to do all the things he had to do, and he liked that. The best part of it all was that he got to see Christina everyday, except on weekends when he would spend time with his father at the mansion.

John was very happy that Aden was going to be lecturing at the university and felt even more proud of him. Unfortunately for him things were not going that smoothly at work. The task force completed their study and concluded that it was not feasible to do hardware development in house given the time constraint. They further concurred with Digicomp that Adeltec Industries was the best choice for the job.

That was not what John wanted to hear. He did not want to have anything to do with Conrad Frost. Contrary to the findings of the task force, he made a unilateral decision to initiate a hardware research and development program immediately. His intention was to carry the hardware development through August, and possibly September before making a final decision. He was not about to give up without a fight.

To ensure its success, John decided to be personally involved with the development process. This added to his already heavy workload and kept him practically living at work. At the same time Aden was also very busy making the final preparations for his lectures. While they were both happy doing what they wanted, they hardly got to see each other, and when they did it was only for a few minutes.

To avoid drawing unnecessary attention to Aden, Professor Klossen only mentioned to her students that she would be on leave of absence for the next term and that another lecturer would be handling her courses.

On the first day of the term, not knowing who to expect, the students were completely surprised to see Aden walk in confidently with his usual handsome look and stately gait. He was dressed well in a bespoke suit and shirt, handmade Italian shoes, and not a hair out of place. While they knew who he was from having seen his pictures in the media, they did not know why he was there.

Aden walked behind the podium of the 400-seat capacity lecture hall. As he briefly looked at the 300 odd students sitting there, he quickly cleared the air. He introduced himself and said that he was taking over Professor Klossen's lectures for the term.

One of the students was quick to raise his hand and ask, "Aden, I can call you Aden, right?"

Aden moved to the front of the podium and said, "No Josh. You may call me Professor Aden Bradcliffe, or for short, Professor Bradcliffe." Josh was taken back, not by Aden asserting his position and title, but by Aden knowing his name, so much so that he forgot what he was going to ask.

Another student raised his hand, "Yes, Steven" replied Aden.

Steven was also surprised that Aden knew his name, but went ahead with his question, "How old are you? Aren't you a bit too young to be a lecturer?"

"As for my age, obviously, you haven't been keeping up with all the media, why don't you ask Jema sitting on your right, I bet she'd know."

Once Jema got over her excitement that Aden Bradcliffe knew her name, she told Steven that Aden was 22.

"The answer to the second part of your question," Aden continued, "is that acquisition of knowledge has no limits or boundaries. That is something I want you all to remember, that when it comes to education and learning, there is nothing that you can't achieve or that is beyond your reach if you put your effort, mind and heart into it."

Another question was raised. "Professor Bradcliffe, my name is Roger, and I was wondering how you know everyone's names?"

"Simple Paul, I memorized them," which he had done easily by looking at the enrolment list with class photos a few minutes prior to the lecture. "By the way you might want to check with the real Roger sitting behind you before using his name next time." Everyone laughed.

By this time, they all had begun to look at Aden with a new perspective, and in a new light. That he was not just a rich, spoiled bachelor, but rather someone to respect. That was further confirmed as Aden continued, "The Lecture notes with reading assignments will be made available on the internet prior to each lecture. Make sure you come prepared, as the lectures are interactive, and you will be called on to answer questions. Yes, it will count toward your final grade, together with the assignments you turn in to your tutors and two exams; one mid term and one final exam."

After a short pause, with an even firmer and more serious tone of voice Aden said, "If you're here to work hard, learn and have fun, then this class is for you, but if you're not ready to work hard, then I suggest you choose another class, because by the end of this term you're going to know this subject inside out. We will look at old principles, explore current theories and their practical applications, and create new ones as we go along." He then stopped and with a demanding look asked, "Is that clear?" They all nodded their heads indicating that it was quite clear.

"Now, if there are no more questions, we can begin." Aden then, with his immense knowledge and flawless memory, without referring to any books, or notes, proceeded to give his first lecture. He only used limited but creative visual aids, as well as occasional anecdotes to help the students with their understanding.

What came across loud and clear was that he is a powerful, articulate, and charismatic speaker. He had captured everyone's attention. With all eyes locked on him, he delivered a most stimulating, thought provoking and entertaining lecture. Having spent the past two years with Christina delving into every question, topic, and subject, it was not at all surprising for him to give such a lively talk.

By the end of the week news of Aden being the lecturer for the term and of his first lecture had spread like wildfire. On the campus and at all the cafes at and around the university, Aden and what he had done and said, were the hot topics of conversations.

At the end of the second week, all his lectures were filled to maximum capacity, even after moving some of them to larger halls. Every single student sat there, lecture after lecture in awe of Aden's brilliant mind, eloquent speech, and down to earth attitude. And lecture after lecture, he continued to inspire and evoke an unprecedented desire and determination in them to learn and do their best.

None of them had worked so hard and enjoyed it so much. What added further to their fun was talking to their friends about Aden, and the friends looking forward to hearing about him.

Jema and her best friend Abby, who was still in high school, were like that. Everyday, they could not wait to call each other and talk about Aden. "So, what was he wearing today?" Abby would ask, and Jenna would answer her in detail. Then Jema would tell her about the things he had said and done during the lecture.

"Jema, I can't take it anymore! I have to come to one of your lectures to see him."

"How can you? You have school everyday."

"I don't care. I'll cut classes, I'll skip school," replied Abby eagerly.

"Even then it won't work; there are no empty seats in any of his lectures."

"Jema, you're my best friend, you'll have to find a way for me to come."

"Ok, I'll see what I can do," agreed Jema to make Abby happy.

The next day Jema talked to Aden about it. Aden, now being a firm believer of encouraging and supporting high school students, told her to leave it with him to work out a way.

By the end of the following week, Aden had gotten the department to organize an open day. On that day students from various high schools could come and learn about the department and what was taught there. As part of that they would get to see Aden's lecture projected on a wide screen in another hall.

Abby was thrilled to hear that. Even though on the day she did not get to see Aden up close in person, she enjoyed seeing his lecture. When Jema came over to her house, she could not stop talking about him.

"Oh, Jema, I can't eat, I can't even breathe when I think about him. I am in love with him, with Aden Bradcliffe. I want to marry him and have him all to myself forever."

"Sure, you and a million other girls."

"But those million other girls all put together don't have what I have, they can't compare with me," said Abby arrogantly.

She had every reason to say that. She was a 17-year-old spoiled teenager who was just beginning to come on the young scene and as a result was little known in the social circles. Among those who had seen her she was known for her voluptuous and ravishing beauty. Her long flowing blonde hair, her alluring big blue eyes with sweeping long lashes, her full lips, and her shapely figure all coming together and creating an intoxicating beauty. A beauty that could easily captivate any man's heart. Abby did not want just any man, she wanted Aden. She knew too well that he was not just an ordinary man, but she was too conceited to let that stop her from trying to put him under her spell.

Students were not the only ones talking about Aden; soon the other faculty members were also talking about him. They knew him as a brilliant student, now they had come to know of him as an equally brilliant lecturer.

Professor Klossen told John about Aden's abilities as a speaker, and once again he could not be more proud. He was so pleased to hear that he thought of having Aden give a talk at his Executive Club, the most exclusive club in Adelaide. The club had a long-standing tradition that once a month they would have a special high profile guest speaker, and all the 'Who's Who' in wealth and power would attend this high-ticket event.

John, being the influential man that he was, and the Bradcliffe family being a founding member of the club, wielded a lot of power. As such he could dictate the time and the speaker of his choice for the event.

"How about being the guest speaker at the Executive Club, Aden?" John asked while they were having dinner together.

"Do you think your conservative fossil colleagues are ready to hear me?" he said jokingly.

"It doesn't matter if they are or not. I want to hear you give a talk, and I want them to hear what a good speaker my son is," said John proudly.

Aden smiled. As he would do anything to please his father he agreed. "What about the topic? What do you want me to talk about?"

"It can be anything you want, for example, you could talk about the future of business. Everybody always likes to know where to make the next million or two."

"Alright, I'll have a think about it."

"Is sometime in July ok?" asked John anxious to fix the date.

"Dad, have you forgotten that I'll be in Europe then? That is when I have my semester break and I promised Elexa that I would help her finalize the best investment plan and initiate the economic reform programs for her country."

"Yes, I had forgotten it. I have too much on my mind," said John sounding slightly distressed.

"Perhaps that is what you need, to come to Europe and have a break."

"If it weren't for my project, I would have dearly loved to come. It's at such a critical stage that I really must be here for it."

"I understand, Dad."

"Then, what about August?"

"The end of August is good."

"Then the end of August it is."

Chapter 45

It was early August and Aden had just returned from Europe. He was feeling quite good about the outcome of his trip. He had been able to see the fruits of his efforts. For the last six months, Elexa had been diligently following through the development and investment plan that Aden, in consultation with his father, had creatively and thoughtfully put in place in January. She had been meeting and talking with all the possible investors. Now, with Aden's help the selection process had been completed, and contracts had been finalized and signed. As a result, the infusion of investment and the implementation of the various reform programs had already begun. King Theodor and Elexa could not be happier, for Aden had done in a few months what the Minister of Industry & Development and his staff had not been able to achieve in years.

Aden's feelings, however, stemmed from his altruistic beliefs of having done something philanthropic, just like Christina had done for him so caringly and selflessly over the past two and a half years. Now he had been of benefit to Elexa and her country without gaining anything in return and that felt good.

As usual, shortly after his return, Brian and his other friends had come over to see Aden to catch up and hear about his trip. They also wanted to tell him about a new club called The Electric. The opening night was by invitation only, and they had all been invited. If past experience was any indication, they did not have much hope that he would accept to accompany them. But they really wanted him to go. Brian tried his best to convince him. To their surprise, Aden, feeling upbeat, remembering Christina's suggestion, and learning that The Electric promoted and supported clean energy, agreed to go.

The Electric was quite unique and innovative in using the latest computer automated technologies to minimize sound and air pollution and provide an environmentally friendly atmosphere. All the speakers were focused on the dance floor, leaving the rest of the club with relatively lower noise levels.

The design and décor of The Electric was also quite original, dazzling everyone with its warm and vibrant ambiance. As they passed through solid double doors, they were enveloped by its indirect dim lighting, its sophisticated look with wooden framed oil paintings showcasing various rainforests and national parks, and its trendy open layout with sleek contemporary furniture. Standing on the landing there was a panoramic view of three different sized interconnected wooden dance floors with softly lit perimeters, surrounded by a color scheme of burgundy, cherry, and ruby with touches of aqua against a background of kaki. All the seats and chairs were circular in shape, complimenting the round tables with blue frosted glass tops.

On the opening night, Aden had Edmund drive him and his friends to The Electric in the Bradcliffe limousine. The place was buzzing with excitement. With all eyes on him, Aden in his typical aloof style, walked in. In a matter of minutes everybody was on their mobile phones telling their friends about the club and seeing Aden there after nearly two and a half years absence from the 'scene'.

The mere fact of Aden's presence made it **the place to be**. Surrounded by his friends he walked to the bar and ordered mineral water.

Among the crowd he heard someone calling him, "Professor Bradcliffe." He turned around. It was Jema. "Hello, Professor Bradcliffe."

"Hello Jema. You can call me Aden here."

"My friends would die to hear that," said Jema in her bubbly and enthusiastic way, "only if they believed me. The problem is that they don't believe I know you. I mean they believe I know you, but they don't believe that you know me. And…I was wondering if you could wave to them so that they would believe me."

"Waving is so impersonal," said Aden casually. "Why not give them something more convincing?"

"Like what?" wondered Jema with a puzzled, but excited look.

"Like dancing."

"Dancing with me? I think I'm going to faint."

"Just hold off 'til after the dance."

As they began to dance all heads turned towards them, especially her friends, who were all beginning to feel jealous of her. After the dance Aden introduced Jema to Brian and his other friends.

A very thrilled Jema then returned to her circle of friends. In the midst of all the excitement and screaming, thinking how she could not wait to tell all her other friends, Abby came to her mind. Suddenly, she stopped, "Abby is going to kill me!" And she was not too far from reality.

Abby became furious when she found out. She was fuming with envy, "I thought you were my best friend."

"But I am," replied Jema innocently.

"Then, how could you do this to me?" said Abby feeling hurt and angry.

"I didn't do anything. I only danced with him."

"That's it. I'm going to The Electric this Saturday, and you will introduce me to Aden."

"What if he isn't there?"

"Then we'll continue to go every Saturday until he does come."

"But Abby, you're only 17. How are you going to get in?"

"I will just have to find a way."

The following Saturday they went to The Electric. While they were lining up to get in, the Bradcliffe limousine arrived. Aden and his friends got out. With Aden's name naturally being on the VIP list, they walked in straight away.

Abby's heart began pounding heavily just at the glance of him, "He's sooo…hot," she said with a dreamy look on her face. "I can't wait to go inside and see him." As it was such a long line she became frustrated and impatiently said, "How slow is this line? Can't it move any faster?"

With so many people there, the line did not move faster at all. As a result, it took a while before they were able to get to the front near the door. "Do you have your fake I.D.?" whispered Jema.

Abby took a look at her and said, "Abby Frost doesn't use a fake I.D."

"But you won't be able to get in without it," said Jema nervously.

"Just watch and learn."

"Your I.D.?" asked the muscle-bound bouncer standing at the entrance of the club. His inflexibility to let anyone in without a proper I.D., and his angry rough looks had earned him the name Furious Al. No one dared to go near him, no one that is except Abby.

Looking at him with those enticing, big blue eyes, she moved closer to him, opened her purse, showing him a couple of thousand dollars, and then said, "Here is my I.D." Everything was a game to Abby Frost, a game of manipulating people with her beauty and wealth.

Taken by her beauty, he hated to say no, but he had no choice. "If I let you in without an I.D., I could get into a lot of trouble. I could lose my job."

She moved still closer to him, kissed him on the lips, "Then I will hire you as my personal bodyguard."

He was captured by her and could not pass on such a prospect. He then removed the rope and let Abby and Jema enter.

"Didn't you forget something?" asked Abby referring to the money she had offered him.

"No, this one is on me," replied Furious Al, who was quite taken by her.

Once inside, like a kid in a candy store, Abby was excited and anxious to find Aden. "Come on Jema. We have to go and find him now."

"Can't we sit down for a minute? My feet are killing me after all that standing and waiting out there."

"After you introduce me to him, you can sit all you want."

A few minutes later they saw Aden at a distance in the far corner of the club surrounded by quite a few girls. Abby hurried and pushed her way to him, only to find to her dismay that he was leaving.

Aden had no interest in the girls who were coming-on to him. He had enough and wanted to leave. The longer he stayed, the more he was reminded of Christina, and how he could not be with the one he loved. That made him feel restless and frustrated inside. He would just as soon be at home reading and finalizing his talk that he was going to give next week at the Executive Club. Quickly, he excused himself, said goodbye and left before Jema had a chance to introduce Abby to him.

Abby was about to lose it, but Jema was able to calm her down by introducing her to Brian and his other friends. To Abby, knowing them meant being a step closer to Aden. With her outgoing personality and her alluring beauty, she quickly became the center of attention.

While she enjoyed all of the attention, the only thought on her mind was Aden, and how to get to him. She came up with a plan to hold a party. And, to ensure that Aden would attend, she turned her charm to Brian.

"I'm having a party at my house next Saturday." Jema looked at her with a puzzled look, wondering what party she was talking about. Abby continued, "And I would like all of you to come, especially you Brian."

Brian was extremely attracted to her and, with pleasure, accepted to go.

"Do you know what would make Jema and my other guests happy?…to see Aden there," she said to Brian. Then with an innocent look on her face she said, "And to see my guests happy, would make me happy…and terribly indebted."

To be on her good side, Brian, without any hesitation promised to go to her party with Aden.

Chapter 46

The large banquet hall of the Executive Club was filled to maximum capacity on this Friday evening. Among the guests were the usual mix of community leaders from all sectors of society, heads of corporations, industry, and financial institutions.

There was an air of haughtiness and inflated arrogance that could not be masked with all of the pretentious smiles and superficial friendliness. There were those with raised eyebrows wondering about Aden. After all, he was not a former US president or Nobel Prize winner, like some of the previous speakers. Nevertheless, he was known for his brilliant mind. Having based his talk around his father's suggested topic, 'The Future of Business', none of them were about to miss the opportunity of finding out how to increase their wealth and fortune.

This audience was different from the wide-eyed university students. It consisted of the achievers, leaders and intellectuals of the society, and Aden was very aware of this. However, undaunted and unaffected by their success and prominence, Aden with confidence and in his usual stately manner took to the podium and powerfully delivered his talk. It was a brilliant oration in that it was simple, yet deeply profound.

"**Distinguished guests, ladies and gentlemen, the Executive Board,**" he paused briefly to scan the sea of faces looking at him, then without wasting any time on social niceties, he got right into the heart of his talk.

"**Success...will not and should not be measured by money or material gains, but rather, by service delivered to humanity.**"

Aden's provocative opening statement grabbed everyone's attention, even those who had been only mildly interested and partially listening. It caused an initial whispering wave of, "What did he say? Money isn't important?" which quickly died down giving way to complete silence. Everyone, even the waiters and the busboys wanted to hear what Aden had to say.

"Fortune, fame, and power are what man has sought throughout the ages. He has based his success on them. He has killed, plundered, and betrayed for them. He has done all of that for one underlying reason, and that is to gain happiness, that illusive goal. We see that all his material possessions and achievements have only brought him happiness that is short-lived, one hour, one day, or perhaps a month. This begs the question - Why is it that all of mankind's success and glory have not been able to bring that lasting joy?"

After a short pause and having captured their full focus, he continued, "The reason is profoundly simple and it lies in our failure to recognize our true nature, that man is a spiritual being living in a material world. This failure has deprived him of attaining sustained happiness, the spiritual happiness that comes from living a morally just and spiritual life. Fortunately, humanity is now at the outer fringes of the threshold of reaching that level of maturity, to acknowledge and live according to its higher nature.

As we survey the history of man, we see that he has progressed through the agricultural revolution, the industrial revolution, the electronics revolution, followed by the information explosion. While at each stage man has made considerable material strides, spiritually he has lagged further and further behind. Lost in the wilderness of materialism, humanity has become like a body without a soul. All of this is signalizing the dawn of yet a new revolution; one that he needs in order to survive and achieve what he has been searching for, that lasting happiness and tranquility."

Aden's voice resonated through the banquet hall, "And that is the spiritual revolution, the consummation of all previous revolutions, one that will bring into balance material progress and spiritual progress, one that will bring about consciousness of the oneness of mankind, his inescapable destiny, where humanity, through the living of a spiritual life will be caring for humanity."

His tone of voice was calmer as he continued, "Your duty, as leaders of the community, captains of industry, and members of society is the undeniable challenge to affect changes in concert with the spiritual revolution in the thinking and working of humanity and its institutions. This will require the taking into account spiritual indicators along side the existing economic indicators in the decision-making process of investments and also in the measures of success of any organization. The kind of spiritual indicators that need to be considered and formulated are those that not only monitor, but also will ensure that human dignity, morality, and quality of life are maintained and improved.

Yours is also the unparalleled responsibility to institute philanthropic programs to meet and provide all the basic needs of humanity, such as education, health and a clean environment, just to mention a few. These needs must be met not for just a select few, a select group, a select race, or a select nation, but for every member of the human family, our family. This must be done to achieve a quality of life that is equitable and just.

For without justice, there can be no unity or harmony. Without unity, there can be no peace and tranquility. And without peace and tranquility, there can be no lasting happiness in this world."

Then in a softer tone of voice he delivered his concluding remarks. "**Have you ever wondered what has become of the pomp and glory of those before you? As we look at the dust laden pages of our fragmented history, we see that it has all disappeared without a trace. So, if fame and fortune do not remain, then what does? The answer is simple, selfless acts of service to humanity. For what you take with you is what you give away, and what benefits you is what you do for others.**" Then with a look of confidence and satisfaction for having been able to reach his audience he said, "**Thank you.**" As they sat awestruck, he stepped down from the podium.

The silence that had set in shortly after he had started his talk, still permeated the large hall. The audience remained in their seats with shell shocked looks on their faces, wondering if that was an ultimatum, reprimand, or a sermon. In fact, it was none of these. It was a wakeup call that only a progressive thinker like Aden, the son of John Bradcliffe, known for his brilliance, could with full courage and self assurance, credibly deliver.

The waiters and the busboys that had been absorbed by his talk and had completely stopped serving during Aden's talk were among the first to applaud. As soon as the audience was able to internalize his words, they joined in and continued to clap for a few minutes.

This was not what they had anticipated. He did not tell them how to make more money, but instead he had told them what a weighty responsibility they had toward all humanity for the betterment of the world. While most found Aden's talk thought provoking and moving, there were some who readily dismissed it as too idealistic, and a few who failed to see the value of his talk at all.

Conrad Frost was one of those few. He saw this as a perfect opportunity for his insulting digs. He was upset and venomous. He had just learned that all his attempts and efforts to work with Digicomp had been blocked by John and wanted at least in some small way to get even. He walked up to John, who at this point was standing near Aden, and said, "Hey John, what an amusing talk. Did it come out of a box of fortune cookies? I just can't wait for you to incorporate all of those ridiculous spiritual indicators." His tone of ridicule then changed to that of despise in his voice, "because that will be the day that I'll have you and your precious Bradcliffe Corporation in my back pocket."

Aden could not believe the shallowness of his comment, and he took it upon himself to respond. "At the outset of each of those revolutions there were usually two types of people, those that were visionary in their beliefs and outlooks, and in their commitment to furthering prosperity for mankind embraced the change. And there were those that were shortsighted and rejected the change, only to find themselves surpassed by the revolutionary process bringing about an ever advancing civilization. Therefore, when the time is propitious the Bradcliffe Corporation will begin to institute such measures, and when it does you can rest assured that it will advance so rapidly and quickly leaving behind only dust for you to put into your pocket."

Conrad Frost was lost for words. He had suddenly realized that it was a losing prospect to get into a battle of minds with Aden. He pretended that he had to talk to someone and departed quickly without saying another word.

"Who was that?" asked Aden.

"That was the infamous Conrad Frost."

"I can see why you're reluctant to work with him," said Aden. Then wanting to know what his father thought about his talk, he asked, "What did you think? I hope that I didn't disappoint you."

John smiled, "I don't believe that there will ever come a day that you will cease to amaze or impress me."

"Even though I didn't talk about how they can increase their fortunes?"

"I would have been disappointed if you had."

"Then, how come you didn't say anything beforehand?"

"Because I didn't want to influence your thinking. I wanted to hear your thoughts and ideas," said John with a proud look. "I couldn't have been more pleased. What I heard was most impressive, and I don't know of anyone else who could have given such a talk, especially to this audience."

By this time, they were surrounded by quite a few people who wanted to personally thank Aden and to talk with him. Before turning his attention to them, he smiled at his father showing him his appreciation.

John stood besides Aden, shaking hands with people and thanking them for their praise of Aden. He felt content and proud. This was a welcomed high point for him after having had such a difficult week. He was being pressured by Digicomp to make his decision regarding hardware development.

This was a decision that he still was not prepared to make. He wished that he had another six months, but the time had run out. Digicomp was heavily invested in this project and did not want to lose their competitive edge by delaying the market entry. While John, more than anyone, appreciated that point, he still was not willing to work with Adeltec Industries. Conrad Frost's antagonistic encounter and attitude towards him and Aden did not help matters either.

Nevertheless, a decision had to be made now. John had finally agreed earlier that day during his last conversation with Mark Thomson to make his decision and inform Digicomp by Monday morning. Until then, he was not about to let anything spoil the way that he was feeling this evening. He put all those thoughts out of his mind. With a smile on his face and a look of admiration for Aden he continued to talk with everyone.

Chapter 47

It was Saturday night and Brian was looking for the right moment to tell Aden about Abby's party. He had not told him earlier, because he figured the closer to the time of the party the less time Aden would have to think about it. More likely, he would agree to go.

"Let me get this straight," said Aden in disbelief. "You want us to go to some girl's party that you just met last Saturday night at The Electric, whom you haven't seen since then, and don't know anything about other than her first name? Yeah, I don't think so."

"That's not true. I also know that she's the most beautiful girl I've ever seen."

"Brian, you think everyone is beautiful."

"I can't help that I'm a lover of beauty."

"Just because you think someone is beautiful, is not a reason to go to a party."

"But I promised Abby, that's her name by the way, that you and I would go," said Brian trying his hardest to convince Aden. "Aren't you the one who is always telling me how important it is to be trustworthy? How can I become trustworthy if you make me break my promise?"

Aden chuckled at Brian's reasoning, "Who am I to stand in the path of your quest for a virtuous life? Next time, try to be more sincere about it." Seeing how this meant so much to him, Aden agreed. "Under one condition," Aden added, "that we'll leave if it's not good."

"Let's agree to stay for at least half an hour," said Brian wanting to spend some time with Abby. "Otherwise, how are we going to know if it's good or not?"

"In that case, I'll drive."

"I was counting on that. Nothing makes a better statement than arriving in one of your cars with AB license plate." Brian was right. All of Aden's cars had customized license plates with his initials, AB, followed by a space, and then a number identifying one of his seven cars. They always announced his arrival everywhere he went. That night was no exception. When he drove onto the grounds, the security guard at the gate immediately informed Abby of his arrival.

Contrary to their expectations, it was a huge estate. "Are you sure this doesn't belong to one of your relatives? It has all the hall marks of a Bradcliffe residence."

"Yes, I'm sure."

"If it weren't for the fact that it's modern and more massive, I could've sworn I was at your mansion!"

"Here is an idea, next time you accept to go to a party, find out the person's full name."

"At least I got us invited. Looking at all the cars here, it appears to be quite a party and we would've missed it if it weren't for me." Little did Brian know that Aden was the sole reason for this big party.

The main house was a palatial mansion, opulent and elegant, with two small annex buildings, one for guests and one for the servants and staff. The Frosts had spared no expense in having it built for them. Marble columns, granite floors, exorbitant paintings and sculptures, and extravagantly expensive furniture throughout the mansion were but a few icons displaying their excessive wealth. Weekend shopping trips to London, Paris, or even as far away as New York were not too uncommon. Their motto was, 'If it's not expensive, it's not worth having'. The source of Conrad Frost's wealth was his father-in-law who had made his fortune in real estate and in the cell phone industry. They were the 'new rich', unlike the Bradcliffes who had been wealthy and among the upper class for several generations.

The news of Aden's arrival threw Abby's world into commotion. She was finally about to meet the man of her dreams, of whom she had spent her every waking moment thinking and fantasizing. As excited as she was to see him, she became so nervous that she could not go and meet him. Instead, she sent Jema to welcome him, to give herself time to compose her nerves, and to make sure that her hair, makeup, and dress all looked perfect.

Aden and Brian were shown in by the hostess. While they were slowly making their way in, Jema caught up with them. "Hey, you guys!"

Aden was surprised to see her there, "Well, at least one familiar face, so how'd you get invited to this party?"

Jema laughed, "This is my best friend's party, you know, the one I spoke to you about."

"I'm not sure who you are talking about… remind me again."

"The one from high school…remember?"

"Yes, now I remember."

"Good, now if you'll excuse me," said Jema anxious to get back to Abby, "I'll go and get her to come say hello."

"Great Brian, you've brought me to a high school party."

"Maybe not, I see some people from the Med school. Let's go and talk to them."

With Jema's help, Abby was feeling better and calmer and was able to go and greet her guests.

In the meantime, Brian had decided to get a drink. On his way to the bar, he saw Abby. His heart skipped a beat. He was so taken by her beauty that he completely forgot where he was going.

After a few minutes of small talk Abby said, "Aren't you going to introduce your friend to me?"

"My friend?" wondered Brian, mesmerized by her beauty.

"You know, Aden."

"Oh, that's right," Brain reluctantly remembered. "He's just over there. You wait here. I'll go and get him."

He then took Aden away from the group, "I want to show you something, just look behind me and tell me what you see."

"Something unbelievable!" was Aden's response as Brian had expected, except Aden was not talking about Abby. In fact, he had not even noticed her. What had caught his attention were some people directly behind her. They were their high school geek club.

"I haven't seen these guys since high school," said Aden in surprise as he walked directly past Abby to go talk to them.

Brian, amazed at what had happened, quickly apologized to Abby, and kept her company while waiting for Aden to finish.

The old Aden would not have talked to them, but he was different from what he was like in high school. He now cared about people. He was curious about what they had been doing and wanted to make sure that there were no hard feelings after all that he had done to them. "Hello, guys, it's been a long time since last I saw you."

"Isn't it amazing that Aden Bradcliffe is talking to us?" said Henry.

"It's even more amazing that he recognizes us without us being stuffed in our lockers," said Melvin.

"What's even better is that there are no lockers around," said Josh.

Aden laughed. He liked their sense of humor. "So what are you all doing now? As I recall, Josh, you and Henry were quite good at math and computers. Did you do anything along those lines?"

"Well Henry did. He's a computer scientist, your typical mad scientist!" laughed Josh. "Melvin is a Micro-Biologist, and I'm an accountant working for the second largest accounting firm in the world."

"Not bad, ambitious, successful, and you don't even look…"

Josh finished Aden's sentence "Geeky anymore. And we owe it all to you and thousands of dollars."

"To me? This ought to be interesting to hear."

"At first, things were well defined," said Josh. "I mean, you had the looks and the muscles, and we had the brains. Then we read in the papers what a genius you are. Suddenly, the rules had changed, you had the brains too. That's when we had to do something to bring back the balance. So, we changed our looks."

"I'm glad things have worked out for you guys." After a short pause Aden said, "What I'm trying to say…." While it was not easy for him to say, he believed that it was the right thing to do, "is that I'm sorry for the way I treated you guys. That was wrong. I mean, no one should bully another person." Feeling a bit more comfortable having said it, he continued, "I hope that there are no hard feelings."

This was something that they had never expected, nor anticipated to hear from Aden, and for a moment, looking surprised, they did not know what to say. As they got over their shock and began thinking about it, there seemed to be no point in holding a grudge. Seeing how it was all a long time ago, they accepted his apology.

"Nah, we've all moved beyond it," replied Josh, the more outgoing and secure one of the three.

Henry decided to join in, "Besides, you brought excitement and adventure to our otherwise boring lives in high school."

"And how did I do that?"

"Well, we had this bet going on to see which one of us could guess the right number. Each one of us had come up with an elaborate mathematical formula to make the most accurate prediction. Every day we looked forward to updating and seeing how our predictions were going."

"Dare I ask what you were trying to predict?" said Aden who was getting a kick out of all of this.

"You name it, we tried it. For example, how many times you'd disrupt the class, which, by the way, I won," said Henry.

"How many times you'd get called into the principal's office, or how many different girls you went out with, and I'm proud to say that I got both of those right," said Josh.

From hearing all the talking and laughing, it became obvious that Aden was not about to finish any time soon. Abby was too anxious to wait any longer, so she suggested that Brian and she should join them. Even though Brian would have preferred talking to Abby, to please her, he agreed.

Aden right away noticed Brian standing beside him. He moved back to include him in the group. "You all remember Brian?" he asked, and they all did. But once again, not knowing who Abby was, Aden did not take any notice of her. He just continued on with his conversation.

Since Abby could not join in the conversation, to catch his attention, she asked if he would like a drink. Aden thinking that she was a waitress, without even looking at her said, "Nothing for me, what about you guys?"

Unlike Aden, they all knew Abby and were surprised with his cold response. Then again, they figured that was Aden. Each one of them, like the rest of the guys at the party, had a huge crush on her and would not dream of asking her to get them drinks. They all said they were fine.

Aden, barely turning toward her, very politely said, "No thank you miss." Then he turned back to his friends and continued with his conversation.

Ignoring her like that, as stunning as she looked, and calling her a 'miss', were what pushed her over the edge. She felt as if her entire world had come crashing down around her. Being used to always getting her way, this was too unbearable. She could no longer stay at the party. She very quickly went to the upstairs sitting room, where her parents, Conrad and Gloria, and her eleven-year-old sister, Molly were. She walked in and broke down in tears.

Gloria Frost was the personification of glamour, elegance, and beauty. At the age of 39, with the best beauty treatments that money could buy, she had the skin, face, and body of a 29-year-old. Having been raised in the lap of luxury, she wanted her children to have everything. Since Abby looked very much like her mother, she was her favorite. She always got preferential treatment and she was to have anything she ever desired. Molly, having taken more after her father, did not get the same special treatment, and she was alright with it. She had attributed it to being younger, thinking that once she was older, she would get to have everything like Abby.

The protective mother that she was, she could not bare to see Abby in tears. She quickly rushed to her and put her arms around her comforting her. She was desperately trying to find out what had made her feel so sad. "Tell me darling, what's wrong?"

"My life is over, that's what's wrong." Abby could not stop sobbing, "He doesn't care about me."

"That's not possible. There's no one that wouldn't give his right arm just to be with you."

"Not him!"

"Who darling?" Abby's mother asked in disbelief.

"The love of my life, the man of my dreams, the one that I want to marry."

"Marry?" wondered her family in surprise.

"That's why I had this party, so he could get to know me and fall in love with me. But what's the use, he doesn't even know I'm alive."

"That's only because he hasn't met you. Tell me, who is he?"

"Someone you don't know."

"Then come darling, show him to me, and I'll take care of everything."

Abby reluctantly walked out with her mother. Her father and Molly followed right behind them, to the landing area at the top of the stairs. "There he is, the tall handsome one walking toward the door."

"Aden Bradcliffe?!" said her father in absolute shock.

"So, you know him?" asked Gloria.

"Not really, only in passing," replied Conrad as he thought to himself, *If insulting him can be considered knowing him.*

Just then as Abby watched in horror, Aden walked out and shortly after that, Brian followed. They got into Aden's car and drove off. That totally crushed Abby, "My life is ruined. I'm going to my room and never coming out!" said Abby in tears as she ran to her room.

Gloria was almost in tears to see Abby like that. She asked Molly to go to her room, so she could have a private conversation with Conrad.

"What do you intend to do about this?" asked Gloria in a demanding tone of voice. "It breaks my heart to see my beautiful Abby sad like that."

"Nothing. She's a teenager. She'll get over him soon," said Conrad attempting to change Gloria's mind. "You know how teenagers are. They're always going through phases. Each week they're in love with someone new."

"How can you say that? You obviously don't love our daughter," said Gloria sounding unhappy with Conrad, "otherwise you could see this isn't anything like that. I've never seen her so upset or serious about anyone like this before."

"Of course I love her, but what can I do?"

"For starters, you can get them together."

"This is Aden Bradcliffe we are talking about, not your ordinary starry-eyed, run of the mill kind of guy. He's a genius and very popular…"

"Yes, I know," Gloria impatiently interrupted, "I've seen articles about him in the media. That makes it even better. Finally, there's someone who is good enough for our Abby."

"But Gloria, you don't understand," Conrad painfully admitted. "His father John and I have been fierce competitors for years, ever since I can remember."

"Then, it is time you put away your childish rivalry and invite them over for dinner."

"It's not that simple, John hates my guts. What am I supposed to do? Just walk up to him and say, "Remember me, your number one archrival who has stabbed you in the back and always caused you problems? Why don't we forget all about that? My daughter is in love with your son and wants to marry him?!" Is that what you're asking me to do?"

"Yes, that is exactly what I want you to do," said Gloria quite seriously.

Conrad just shook his head in despair, "I can't do that. John wouldn't see me, let alone talk to me."

"Then I suggest you begin groveling, that's what you are best at. Isn't that how you won me?" said Gloria sternly. She was now upset and brutal. "Abby gets what Abby wants! From now until you deliver Aden, you'll be staying in the guest house. If you fail, I'll put you in the doghouse, and I mean it, literally. And if that's not enough, I'll take the company away from you!"

Gloria had made her position quite clear, leaving Conrad in a difficult and frustrating situation. He loved both of his daughters, and very much like Gloria, wanted to give them everything. But how was he to face John and make what seemed to be the impossible happen?

Chapter 48

It was Monday morning and the mood was intensely solemn in John's office. There were only a few minutes left before the phone call from Digicomp. He was speaking with Allan Kelly, still desperately trying to find a way to carry on the entire project in-house.

"I'm sorry John," said Allan regretfully, "maybe if we had another nine months. Yes, we've made amazing progress, but it's nowhere near where it needs to be to take on such an important project."

"Then, I'll ask for a nine month extension."

"John, we both know that it's too risky. Most likely Digicomp will cancel the project."

"I'd rather take that chance than to work with someone whom I can't trust, someone whose name I can't even bring myself to say…" Just then Tracy's voice could be heard over the intercom announcing, "Conrad Frost is here to see you."

"What?" John looked at Allan in astonishment. They were both flabbergasted, wondering if they heard correctly. They did not need to wonder long as the door opened momentarily and in walked Conrad Frost with Tracy, running after him saying, "Sir, you can't just go in…"

"Good morning, John."

"You have a lot of nerve intruding like that. I ought to call security."

"There will be no need for that. I'm not staying long." Conrad's usual hostility had given way to courtesy as he continued, "I'm deeply sorry for that. I didn't think that you would see me otherwise. I've something very important to say, and it will only take a few minutes."

"Why should I want to listen to anything that you have to say?" asked John rightfully.

"I know you're expecting a phone call from Digicomp in a few minutes, and if you give me a chance, I guarantee to make it worth your while."

John thought about it for a moment and decided to hear him out. "That'll be all Tracy." As Tracy walked out, Allan excused himself and walked out, too.

"This had better be good."

"I know that we haven't exactly seen eye-to-eye, and I'm treading on new ground here," given the urgency of the situation and the shortness of time Conrad had no choice, but to get right to the point. "It's one thing for us to compete here in Australia and once in a while lose market share to each other, but it's another thing for us both to lose a global opportunity because of our senseless rivalry. That will render us subservient to companies like Digicomp that are growing more and more powerful and dominant in the world." He concluded by wanting them to throw away the past, to join hands, and together become a dominant force in the world market. Desperately appealing to John's sense of love for Aden, he said, "I'm not asking this for us, but for our children. I want both of us to be able to leave behind a formidable legacy for them."

With nothing more important to John than Aden and his future, it was the mention of legacy that caught his attention. While what Conrad had said made good sense, he still could not bring himself to trust him.

"All of this from a man whose words are not worth the paper that they are written on, who has no regard for others, and says anything to get what he wants." John was quite candid as he continued, "Now you suddenly barge into my office and expect me to trust you and make my decision based on your words? What do you take me for?"

"A man of integrity, who is fair-minded," Conrad was quick to reply. Then with an almost pleading tone of voice he said, "Who I hope can see it in his heart that this time it's different. As a token of my sincerity, I would like to invite you and Aden over to my house this Saturday to have dinner with me and my family. This is something I rarely do, mix business with my family life." All he was asking was for John to give him a chance to prove that he can be trusted, "You and Aden come and be the judge of that. You can always reject working with me next week, as easily as you can now." After a short pause, "Will you and Aden honor me and have dinner with us?"

While still thinking, Tracy informed John that Mark Thomson was on the phone. Without responding to Conrad's invitation, John politely asked him to wait outside his office until he was finished. As he walked out, John took the call. After the initial exchange of pleasantries, they talked for a while about the various aspects of the project. Then it was time to respond to the unavoidable question regarding the hardware development. With his thoughts centered on Aden's future John said, "I'm entering into negotiations with Conrad Frost, and I expect to have my response by this time next week."

That was all that Mark wanted to hear and agreed to wait until next Monday.

John then asked Conrad back to his office and told him of his decision. For Conrad this was an unbelievable achievement. While outwardly he was cool and collected, inwardly he was ecstatic. He got up from his chair, extended his arm and firmly shook John's hand, "Thank you. I truly appreciate this and look forward to seeing you and Aden this Saturday."

Later in the evening Aden was a little surprised to learn that they were to dine with the Frost family, especially after their recent interaction with Conrad. But, he was happy to go along and support his father in any way that he could.

Aden was a lot more surprised when they arrived at the Frost residence. "What are the chances of that? I was here for a party last Saturday night."

"And you didn't tell me?" asked John sounding unhappy about it.

"That's because I didn't know whose house it was until just now," replied Aden. He then explained the whole thing to his father, and how Brian had to see this girl of ravishing beauty and that he did not want to break his promise of attending the party. "Now I can tell Brian that her family name is Frost."

"Is she?" wondered John.

"Is she what?"

"Ravishingly beautiful?"

Aden chuckled, "That's funny. I didn't get to meet her. So, I can't answer you."

Just then, they were personally met by Conrad, who could not have been more pleasant and gracious. He warmly welcomed them in and introduced his wife Gloria, Molly, and then Abby as she made her grand entrance, walking down the elegant staircase while everyone watched.

John, taken by her beauty, whispered to Aden, "She really is." But Aden made no response.

It was a pleasant evening, and everything went smoothly. The two families hit it off quite well. Throughout the evening there were exchanges of humorous stories, anecdotes, and interesting conversations covering a wide range of topics. But, there was no talk of their impending business association.

John almost immediately took a liking to Abby, who came across as someone very sweet and charming. He made a special effort to include her in their conversation that was otherwise dominated by Aden and Conrad.

Since Aden was not responding to Abby's attempts to allure and attract him, Gloria suggested that Abby give him a tour of the mansion, so that the two of them could be alone. He treated her very nicely, but he was not romantically interested in her.

At the end of the evening, after they had said their good-byes, Conrad walked them to their limousine. "John, if it's alright by you, I will stop by your office first thing Monday morning for us to discuss how we may proceed from here."

"That will be fine," replied John, while thanking him for their warm hospitality.

"It was our pleasure to have you and Aden here, and I look forward to our discussions."

Inside the mansion the mood was quite jubilant. "Isn't he a dream? Isn't he everything I said he is, and more?" Abby excitedly asked her mom.

"Yes darling, he's even more handsome in person than in his pictures," said Gloria, thinking how perfectly suitable he was for their beautiful daughter.

"When I was near him, I couldn't breathe," said Abby as if walking on air, "I just can't wait 'til I'm Mrs. Aden Bradcliffe!"

Just then Conrad walked in and was glad to see everybody in a happy mood. After the girls went up to their rooms, Gloria began to talk to Conrad. In an approving tone of voice she said, "You did very well."

"I aim to please," said Conrad proudly.

For Gloria, this was not enough, "I will be pleased when these two are married."

"You wanted me to invite them over for dinner, and I did," said Conrad taken aback by Gloria's response. "They came, and we had an enjoyable evening together." Having accomplished such an impossible task he asked, "Isn't that enough? Shouldn't we let things take their natural course?"

"That's the problem with you. You always think too small," said Gloria, feeling displeased with his answer. For in her mind whatever would make Abby happy just had to be done.

"But they just met. How can we even be thinking about marriage? It's not like having someone over for dinner. It's a huge thing," replied Conrad overwhelmed at the enormity of her request.

Unaffected by his response Gloria simply said, "That's why we have to start working on it right away." Having made up her mind she assertively said, "We have to get them going out together and dating, so that he can propose to her." A smile came over her face as she excitedly continued, "I have my heart set on a December wedding, when the weather is warm, but not too hot. As you can see, there isn't a lot of time left, less than three months." Then firmly she said, "You have to move now to make things happen quickly."

Once again, the ball was in his court to do something that did not seem readily possible.

By Monday morning, he was as prepared as one could be. He had rehearsed in his mind what to say to convince John for them to work together.

John, on the other hand, also having gone over and over this matter, could not see clearly how he could trust Conrad.

Early Monday morning before the start of the working day, with primarily security staff in the building, the two men met in John's office.

John spearheaded the discussions. "Over the years, I've come to know that when things don't seem to make sense that means that nine times out of ten something isn't right, and I shouldn't pursue that path. Now I find myself in such a situation." And he was right. From his point of view, Conrad's sudden and dramatic change of attitude and behavior did not make sense. While he appreciated the warm and gracious hospitality of Saturday night, he could not bring himself to change his decision.

Just before he was about to say that, Conrad quickly realized it. Suddenly, all his rehearsed speeches were of no use to him. He had to do something drastic, something that he had rarely done in his business negotiations, and that was to tell the truth.

The intensity of the situation impelled him to the edge of his seat as he blurted out, "Abby is in love with Aden." He paused, and with a sigh of relief he continued, "And what do you know, it feels good to tell the truth and get that off of my chest." He dropped back in his seat, as he was now able to relax. Smiling like a man released from prison he said, "I ought to do this more often."

John wondered if it was another one of his tricks, but it was not. This time, it was different. There was a sense of sincerity and desperation in his voice as he continued.

"Just recently I came to find out that my daughter has been madly and deeply in love with your son for some time now, so much so that she hasn't been able to eat or sleep. Saturday night was the first night that she hasn't cried herself to sleep, and yesterday was the first day that she has eaten an entire meal in a long while. That spark of life is once again back in her eyes, and I want to keep it there."

John was beginning to see that this was no trick as he listened to Conrad bare his soul to him, "I'm afraid the only way that she's going to be happy is to marry Aden."

John got up from behind his desk, pacing up and down his office, thinking. Could this be the answer to his prayers? Ever since last December, when he almost lost Aden, he had been worrying about him and his future. Being married would provide that safe and secure life that he wished for Aden to have, especially to someone so beautiful and so wealthy.

With those thoughts on his mind, John began to soften his attitude. Seeing that Conrad proceeded to tell him what he had in mind, "I'm proposing the marriage of Abby and Aden, followed by a merger of our two corporations at a generous 2:1 ratio in favor of and under the name of Bradcliffe Corporation." He no longer had any great attachment to Adeltec Industries. He was tired of being pushed around.

With wealth and power remaining in the family, he was happy to step aside and let John run the new corporation, until Aden was ready to take over what was to become one of the largest corporations in the world.

"Finally, a task worthy of Aden's brilliant mind," John added, and Conrad agreed.

"You and I have worked very hard and long, dedicated our lives to it," said an almost dispirited Conrad. "The time has come to pass the torch. I find myself ready to retire, to go and play golf, tennis, or sail around the world."

"Don't go and start planning your retirement." John had to tell him, "It isn't that simple. Aden is a very strong-minded person. I can't just tell him who to marry."

"John, you're forgetting one very important fact. We are two of the best deal brokers in the world. I believe that if we work together, and with Gloria's help, we can make anything happen."

"But still," wondered John, "what happens if they don't get married?"

"We just finish the project, and obviously there won't be a merger."

John could not see a better outcome than that. As the two shook hands, affirming their commitment to work together, a heavy weight was lifted form his shoulders.

As a result, when minutes later, the call came through from Digicomp, the three men were in complete agreement. There was not even a need to draw up a new contract. It was decided for Digicomp to forward an addendum to the main contract for John's signature, specifying that Adeltec Industries would work as subcontractor providing the required hardware to the Bradcliffe Corporation by March. That would then give the Bradcliffe Corporation six months to integrate their firmware with the hardware and have the first working and operational prototype ready by September of the coming year.

The winds of destiny were blowing hard once again, rendering those in its path powerless to resist its force. However unlikely, it had brought together the major players, averting the disastrous end of a project that was destined to bring untold benefits for the advancement of society. It was a thrilling prospect of achievements for the three executives.

Chapter 49

In the evening over the course of dinner, John told Aden about the agreement with Adeltec Industries, and how pleased he was to have his project back on track.

He further added that since he would be working closely with Conrad Frost over the next few months, he thought that it would also be nice for the two families to become closer. As a first step toward that he told Aden to take Abby out to dinner next Saturday to get to know her better.

"What is there to get to know, Dad? She has the intellect of a doorknob, and the high point of the evening will be an in-depth discussion of something relevant like Ken and Barbie's social calendar," said Aden sounding irritated with his father's suggestion.

"But Abby is such a sweet girl who I think likes you very much."

"No kidding Dad. What gave it away? It couldn't have been that she never left my side, or that she laughed at everything I said?"

"Sarcasm, Aden?"

Aden got up from the dining table, "I am just a bit frustrated with things now."

Hearing that gave John the additional confirmation that he had made the right decision. For once Aden is married, he thought, there would not be any cause for that. "Do you want to talk about it?"

"There's nothing to talk about," said Aden while walking away.

"So, you'll do this for me?" asked John wanting to confirm Aden's agreement. "I mean take Abby out on Saturday night?"

"Why not?" replied Aden as he walked out of the dining room, thinking that his life was not going anywhere anyway.

The source of Aden's frustrations was his upcoming graduation in a couple of months towards the end of November. To go to university, complete his courses in an unprecedented time, graduate and go to work were all the things that he wanted. Except now, with each passing day as he got closer to achieving his goals, he was also getting closer to losing what he treasured the most in his life, talking and spending time with Christina.

The stark reality that he faced was that once he graduated, he would hardly be able to see or spend time with her. That was something that he did not want, nor was he prepared to accept. His father asking him to take Abby out, while he could not be with Christina, was adding fuel to the fire of his frustrations.

The next morning, the engineers from Adeltec Industries met with the R&D team of the Bradcliffe Corporation. Thus began a productive and valuable process of collaboration. Together they mapped out what needed to be done, and by the end of their meeting, they were ready for the challenge, and confident that the work could be completed within the required timeframe.

As the week went by, Aden's frustrations and restlessness grew. Finally, he decided to share his thoughts with Christina. And, when he did, to his surprise she was supportive of his father.

"Parents, because of their selfless love," she said, "only want what's best for their children and only desire what makes them happy. For that reason, they wouldn't ask of their children anything that they didn't believe was in their best interests."

She further continued by saying how highly meritorious it is to honor and respect one's parents and to be the cause of their joy and gladness. It only added to his surprise when she told him how impressed she was by him agreeing to what his father had asked him, even though it was not something that he wanted to do.

Her response, while not lessening his frustrations, took away the sting from what he had to do. As a result, he no longer felt defiant toward taking Abby to dinner.

To help matters, John had tactfully conveyed to Conrad Aden's comments about Abby's intellect. As a result, during the week Abby was extensively coached on various topics ranging from world events to current affairs.

On Saturday night, as he had agreed, he took Abby out to dinner. With his new attitude and her newfound knowledge, however limited, the evening was not as bad as he thought it would be. He actually ended up enjoying himself, but on a different level. It was as if he was having dinner with his younger cousin, sweet and innocent whose simple way of thinking he found amusing.

With the paparazzi always on the lookout on Saturday nights to capture pictures of celebrities, Aden was usually one of their prime targets. That night was no different. Aden being out with Abby was not to be missed. Several photos of them were taken while entering, dining, and then leaving the restaurant.

When he returned home that evening, his father was still up, anxious to find out how things had gone. He was quite pleased and relieved to hear that they had a good time. John then tried to find out more about the evening.

"There's not much more to say," was Aden's reply. "I picked her up, took her to dinner, and then took her home."

While Aden did not have much to say about the evening, the press had plenty. On Sunday morning, a long article with accompanying photographs appeared in various news media, with the main caption reading, **A budding romance between reformed bad boy Aden Bradcliffe and billionaire heiress Abby Frost.**

When Abby's mom showed her the article, she became so thrilled that she screamed. She was ecstatic. "Oh Mom, these pictures are awesome," she said with delight. "I can't wait for my friends to see them. They're just going to die with envy."

Abby's happiness made Gloria feel good and created a sense of excitement throughout the mansion, a sense of excitement that was strikingly lacking in the Bradcliffe mansion.

When John asked Aden if he had seen his photos with Abby, he casually replied, "Just in passing."

"What did you think of the article, talking about your sizzling hot, romantic date?"

"I didn't read the article, no point. They print whatever they wish to sell newspapers."

"I just got off the phone with Gloria Frost a few minutes ago. She invited us to the charity concert next Saturday, and I took the liberty of accepting her invitation for the both of us."

"I don't understand. We were planning to attend anyway."

"Yes, we were, but now we will be joining them in their patron box. That's o.k. with you, isn't it?"

"If that's what you want Dad, then it's o.k. with me."

"Good. One more thing, since we will be together with the Frosts, then it's only appropriate for you to escort Abby."

That would not have been Aden's choice. But seeing how this relationship with the Frosts meant so much to his father, and last night with Abby was not so disastrous after all, he thought that it would be best to accept her as a friend. With this new way of thinking it became easier for him to go along with what his father wanted. He agreed to escort Abby. Also, later that evening when Abby called and invited him to a play at her school, he accepted to go, much to John's surprise.

Up to that point, unlike Conrad Frost who had been pressing for the marriage of Aden and Abby ever since their second meeting, John had not seriously entertained the idea or considered it likely. But now seeing that Aden was unaffected by the pictures in the media and did not resist taking Abby to her school play and the charity concert, the possibility of it was no longer seemingly out of the question. He began to think that perhaps Aden had actually come to like Abby, and with this new, agreeable attitude he could be receptive to the idea of marriage.

Before broaching the topic with Aden, John decided to run the idea past his friend Ian to get his feelings on the subject. Nothing was more important to him than Aden's future and happiness. He wanted to be sure in his heart that what he was doing was the right thing for Aden. He therefore made immediate plans to have dinner with Ian on Sunday, the day after the charity concert.

The concert, being one of the biggest charity events of the year, was quite a media circus. Outside the concert hall on both sides of the red carpet, there was a sea of cameras ready and waiting to capture all the important guests. When Aden and Abby arrived, the media was in a frenzy. They had good reason to be. Aden looked handsome and distinguished as always. He was wearing his signature style, bespoke tuxedo accentuating his tall stature and broad shoulders. His shirt studs and cufflinks were made of platinum with his monogram AB engraved on them. And there was not a single hair out of place.

Abby looked drop-dead gorgeous wearing an emerald-green satin, long dress that had been exclusively designed for her. She had picked it up during her last shopping trip to Paris with her mom a couple of weeks ago. It would be weeks before anything like it could be seen on the catwalks. It was a strapless dress, snuggly fitted and gathered on one side at the waistline. Over the gathers diverging out and down were placed green, blue, and gold colored crystals. Her jewelry set had been designed to match her dress, incorporating five carat, square-cut emeralds surrounded by blue sapphires set in 24 carat yellow gold. Her necklace and bracelet each consisted of seven interconnecting emeralds and her ring had a single emerald. These color combinations made her hair and eyes stand out even more brilliantly than usual, with her eyes appearing a beautiful deep blue color.

She was so thrilled to have Aden with her that all she wanted to do was show him off to her friends instead of talking and getting to know him. Having accepted her as a friend, he was no longer bothered by her shallowness. He found it amusing and went along with it.

With the concert being the second time that Aden and Abby appeared in public together in less than a week, throughout the evening speculations were rife about their relationship. By Sunday morning, all the speculation had been put to rest in print with statements appearing in the latest articles along with their photos asserting that they were soon to be married. Some of this gossip had been leaked to the media by the Frosts, who wanted to push things further ahead in that direction.

That Sunday evening, when John met with Ian, his first remark was that he was very surprised to read in the press of Aden's impending marriage.

"I'm sorry. I should have mentioned it on the phone, but since we were meeting, I thought that it was best to talk to you about it in person."

"I understand, but that isn't what I meant. I am surprised that he is getting married at all."

"Why should that surprise you? Abby is stunningly beautiful, refreshingly sweet and innocent, and madly in love with Aden, everything you could want in a woman and more."

"But is he…is Aden in love with her?"

John hesitated for a moment, "He will be, in time."

"That's what I thought. He's not in love with Abby because he's in love with Christina."

Ian's statement hit a nerve with John. He lost his temper and in an uncharacteristically harsh manner said, "You are the only one who has ever said that! As far as I can tell it's nothing but a figment of your imagination, some wild fantasy, and I'm not going to base my son's future on that." Then he continued more calmly, "You're a father. You know what that's like. Ever since December I have not stopped worrying about Aden. He has so much to offer to the world and deserves to be happy and have a good life. He can have that with Abby. Once they're married, in addition to having a beautiful wife to go home to and with our two corporations merging, he will have an empire to run, exactly what he needs for that genius mind of his."

"All that sounds fine my friend, except that he won't be truly happy without the one he loves." Ian continued pensively, "I know. I have been there. Even though I have a good life now, anytime that I look back, I still feel the pain of losing her."

"But you're forgetting that she's married. He can never marry her. He can never have her…can he now?"

There was silence. Ian was thinking about what John had posed. But before he had a chance to respond, his phone began to ring. It was the hospital calling and he had to take the call. He excused himself and went to the lobby where it was quieter and easier to talk.

John was left by himself, deep in thought. He started to look around the room. Suddenly, he saw what he could not believe. Could this be that ray of hope that he was looking for, he wondered to himself?

It was Sean at a table far off in the corner, with his arm around Vicky, kissing her. He immediately called the waiter and had him take a drink to her and ask Sean to come and see him.

Sean reluctantly came over, and rather meekly said, "Ok, you caught me. I guess there's no point denying it, is there?"

"I'm afraid not."

Sean took a deep breath as he sat down and sighed with relief. "I can't say that I'm sorry. Frankly, I'm glad you did. I'm tired of all of this sneaking around." Then very arrogantly he said, "You can save your breath lecturing me on how to save my marriage. There's no saving it. Go ahead, tell Christina. I want to get on with the divorce and get this over with."

Sean had chosen the wrong person with whom to become arrogant. No one tells John Bradcliffe what to do. It is he who dictates how things should go, and he was quick to set things straight. "It's not your marriage that needs saving. It's your job."

"What does my job have to do with anything?"

"I will put it in simple enough terms that even you can understand."

"I don't have to sit here and take this."

As he was about to get up and leave, John very brashly said, "I could make it so that you won't work for another day in this city, or in fact, anywhere in Australia." Hearing that, Sean could not bring himself to walk away. "Perhaps you might be Ok with that," John continued, "I wonder how your little hussy would be with it?"

Sean sat back down. "So, what is it that you want?"

"It's quite simple, stay married for another three months, until after Aden's wedding."

"But why?"

"Let's say that I want to provide him with additional encouragement to get married."

"With the bombshell that he's marrying, who needs encouragement?" replied Sean having seen their picture in the news.

"Still, if he sees everybody around him getting divorced, he might decide not to get married."

"This marriage obviously means a lot to you. So, throw in a promotion and you've got yourself a deal."

John thought about it for a minute and agreed. "Starting tomorrow," he demanded, "you will have to step out of character and become a loving husband, and a caring father. If you want the promotion, you forget about your girlfriend. If Christina finds out, and this marriage doesn't take place, you will be standing in the unemployment line."

Sean understood well. The two of them shook hands on it, and he left. Just then Ian returned and saw Sean walking from the table. "Who was that?" he asked.

"Just an acquaintance," replied John without divulging who he was, or what he had asked him to do.

"I'm very sorry for the interruption. Unfortunately, an emergency has come up and I must go to the hospital. But before I go, I would like to say that you are right. I thought about it, and the sooner Aden gets married, the sooner he can forget Christina and get on with his life."

"That is, if he indeed needs to forget her," added John for he believed that although Aden had great respect for Christina, he was not in love with her.

After Ian was gone, John called Christina. Knowing that Sean would not be going home anytime soon, he asked if he could see her immediately to discuss a rather urgent matter concerning Aden. While that was an unexpected request, she figured that it must be very important, for otherwise he would have talked about it over the phone. Always happy to help and seeing that the children were about to go to sleep, she agreed.

John spoke from the heart as he talked to Christina about Aden's wedding and why it was important for it to take place and for him to have her support.

While Christina understood his point of view, she had difficulty accepting or supporting it. "I have always believed," she said openly, "that a marriage should be based on love."

"So, they end up hating and hurting each other, getting divorced, and making a few lawyers rich? Because that's what I see love brings when I look around."

Even though based on her own marriage she could not disagree, Christina still was an idealist at heart, believing in true love and in living happily ever after, "But, it doesn't have to be that way."

"Yes, you're right and I am trying to make sure that it isn't like that for Aden," said John caringly, "and it won't be like that, if he marries Abby who loves him dearly, enough for the both of them. In addition, he will have a secure future running what is to become one of the largest corporations in the world."

Seeing that Christina was still not quite convinced, John appealed to her sense of mothering. "As parents we don't run a popularity contest. We make the hard decisions that we know are best for our children. We make them take the medicine when they don't want to, study when they would rather play, go to school when they would prefer being at home. And we do all that because we love them." Speaking from the heart he said, "It's still painful for me to think that I almost lost Aden last December, and I'll go to any length to protect him and to make sure that it never happens again."

With sincerity John asked, "Would you do any less for your children?" to which she replied, "No."

He again asked, "Would you have me do any less for my son?"

Still remembering the pains of that episode, she gently said, "No."

Then in an emotional plea he asked Christina, "Will you help me do what I must do for Aden?"

After a thoughtful moment and with a deep sense of compassion, Christina replied, "Yes, I will help you."

Chapter 50

John felt relieved to have been able to secure Christina's support. On his return to the mansion, he found himself amazed with the unexpected turn of events that evening. He had never done anything like that before. He had always been a man of integrity and had conducted both his personal and professional affairs with uprightness and honesty. Now, haunted by the loss of his wife and terrified of losing Aden he was driven to do whatever it took, as any loving father would, to safeguard Aden's future. Deep down he acknowledged that he was not being completely honest and forthcoming, but he honestly believed that this was in Aden's best interests. He felt confident that a year from now when Aden would be happily married and living a successful life, none of this would matter.

With such convictions and having relentlessly put in place all the key elements needed for the implementation of his plan, John was now ready to proceed with it. All that was left was to talk with Aden. He patiently waited for Aden to come home. When he arrived, he had him join him in the library where they would sometimes go at the end of the day to read and talk with each other before retiring for the night.

John conveniently happened to be reading the Sunday news stories on his tablet, when Aden walked in. He could not have been more pleased to see him. After a brief talk about his day, he casually brought up the articles, suggesting that he and Abby were to be married soon.

"That's a laugh," replied Aden.

"Why Aden? It's not such a crazy idea that the son and daughter of the two wealthiest and most prominent families in Australia should get married. Just imagine the possibilities and opportunities that such a marriage could entail, not to mention what incredibly beautiful children you two would have."

"I don't believe it! You're actually serious about this?"

John in his most persuasive manner was quick to respond in a positive way. He then went on explaining at length why he believed it to be such a good idea, and how it would make him happy to see Aden marry Abby.

Aden was already having a difficult time dealing with his feelings of frustration. Now, hearing all this talk only exacerbated the situation. He lost his temper with his father for the first time in nearly three years.

"There's no pleasing you Dad, is there?" said Aden angrily. "It doesn't matter what I do. It's never good enough for you. I've done everything you have wanted. I'm about to graduate and join you in the company. I've even taken Abby out, and you're still not happy." As he got up to leave, he said, "It doesn't seem that I'll ever be able to make you happy."

That was not at all true. To stop him, John imploringly said, "You can't leave now. We're not finished talking." He wanted a chance to explain. He was in fact very proud of his son and wanted to tell him that he had deep love and admiration for him. He wanted only what was best for him.

Aden was too upset to listen. "Yes, we are. This is insane!" said Aden and stormed out of the room.

Having gotten angry with his father did not help matters at all. It only made Aden feel more frustrated and agitated. He did not sleep well that night and the next day at the university, he could hardly focus. He left early to see and to talk with Christina, the one person whom he knew would understand him.

It broke her heart to see the lifeless look on Aden's face. She knew immediately what it was about and that it was not going to be easy for her to do what John had asked of her.

"I had my first argument with my father in nearly three years," he said dejectedly. "What he's asking is too infuriating."

"Your father loves you Aden," replied Christina kindly. "You have to remember, whatever he asks comes from his heart, from wanting the best for you."

"He wants me to marry Abby. How could that be the best for me?"

"I'm sure that he must have his reasons."

"But I don't love her," said Aden impatiently. "Aren't you the one who told me that marriage should be based on love, and that love is the foundation of everything?"

Yes, she had told him this, and deep down she still believed it to be true. But she had a promise to fulfill, a promise that was going to bring Aden the kind of life and happiness that he truly deserved.

With that in mind, she went beyond her own personal feelings and said, "What's important is to have a loving marriage, and not how it begins," Christina said gently. Then carefully choosing her words she continued, "So many people, who begin their marriage in love, end up drifting apart to the point of hurting and hating each other. On the other hand, there are those who after they get to know each other come to respect and love each other. It's therefore quite possible that after some time you can grow to love her."

Christina's response blew him away. The one person who brought love to his life in the loveless world in which he lived, who always understood him, who was going to bring some sense to all this madness, could not see his point. "I don't believe this," said Aden with a feeling of betrayal. "You're actually siding with my father?"

"Aden," she said in a caring voice, "it's not about taking sides…it's about what is best for you."

Nothing made sense. His world was closing in on him. There was nothing more to be said. To clear his mind, he left and went for an extra long and hard run along the beach. He ran until he could no longer continue. After catching his breath, he started to run back. He still could not make any sense of anything.

When he got near his house, he heard someone calling him. He was too consumed by his thoughts to make out who it was. He heard his name again. He slowed down, looked, and to his surprise it was Sean.

What's he up to? wondered Aden. He had never seen him home that early since he had moved into his house.

Sean, pretending to be going for a jog, came up to Aden. He was very friendly towards him. He greeted him as if he was his long-lost friend. Aden was in no mood for that. He just responded in a cold and unfriendly manner and proceeded to return to his home.

Sean stopped him and warmly congratulated him on his upcoming marriage. He then laid it on thick about how wonderful marriage is. The two things that he wanted most in life, Vicky and his promotion were now within his reach, and he was going to do all that he could to get them.

He invited Aden over for a drink and did not take no for an answer, until he agreed. He then went and quickly got Christina to come and join them on the terrace. He was as sweet as honey, which even caught her by surprise. He was very loving and kind to her. He insisted that she sit down and talk with Aden while he went to get the drinks. He then told Aden how lucky he was to be married and that Aden would have so much to look forward to when he marries.

Aden only stayed for a short while, just long enough to finish his drink. He had to go and sort out all those thoughts he had on his mind. After he returned to his house he began to think. He was desperately trying to make sense of things. He wondered about Christina's response and Sean's uncharacteristic behavior. Both were unexpected, but what could have been the reason for such behavior? Unaware of what had transpired behind the scenes he was not able to understand things. It was as if he was lost on a foggy sea without anything to guide him to shore.

In such a despondent emotional state, the only conclusion he could arrive at that made any sense was that Christina wanted him to get married to save her own marriage. With such a realization the path forward became clear.

To make his father happy and to bring happiness to Christina, his true love, there was only one thing to do and that was to marry Abby. That was a small price to pay. After all, self sacrifice was the essence of true love.

Later that evening when he was having dinner with his father, he told him that he had decided to go through with the wedding. John was amazed that his plan had worked, and certainly much better and quicker than he had hoped. He was thrilled, but seeing how difficult this decision was for Aden, he restrained himself from overly showing his excitement.

Aden had only one request from his father, and that was to keep everything simple. John had no problem with that, except he said, "No doubt the Frosts are going to want a big wedding."

"As long as you keep me out of it and allow me to do my studies and prepare for my exams, you and the Frosts can have any kind of a wedding that you want," replied Aden, who simply did not care.

The next day, which was Tuesday, John in trying to accommodate Aden's wishes of simplicity, invited Abby to the mansion for dinner with them. Abby gladly accepted. He also arranged for the purchase of a seven-carat flawless solitaire diamond engagement ring from the most exclusive jewelry store in Sydney and arranged for it to be delivered to the mansion in time for the evening dinner.

During dinner Aden was rather quiet, while John and Abby did most of the talking. After dinner, Aden took Abby out on the terrace and proposed to her without getting on his knee, or showing any feelings or emotions, let alone romance. Abby was much too excited to notice and too self absorbed to care. The only thing that she saw was the ring, and that was all that mattered to her.

Later that night, as Aden sat alone in his room, having done what he had to do, he was faced with a realization of finality. Up to that time, he had lived, however dim, in a state of hope. Now, no matter how painful and undesirable, he had to resign himself that he was never to have his true love, the one person, who had inspired him, transformed him, and touched him with love at the innermost depth of his soul. Wondering if the stars of destiny had made a mistake, he submitted himself and his life to the Will of God.

Chapter 51

There were jubilations at the Frost mansion. Abby was so happy that she could hardly contain herself. She was walking on air, with her hand extended, showing off her diamond ring.

Naturally, Gloria could not have been more pleased, especially with her husband Conrad for having accomplished such a feat in such a short time. This, of course, meant that she could have the December wedding that she wanted. This left very little time for planning and preparations. However, that did not concern her, for there was nothing that money could not overcome.

The wedding date was set for Saturday, 30th of December. Within a span of 24 hours the best of the best wedding planners, chefs, decorators, florists, and designers were flown in from all over the world to immediately start planning and organizing the wedding. The only requirement that the Frosts had was that it had to be daring, expensive, and preferably never before tried. The media hailed it 'The Royal Wedding of Australia'.

John and Gloria came to an agreement to limit the number of guests to 500 in order to keep the wedding an exclusive event. They booked the entire first two floors of the Excelsior, the most exclusive hotel with the most elegant ballroom in Adelaide, for the wedding. This was to ensure that none of the restaurants and coffee shops would be open that night, thereby limiting the flow in and out of the hotel primarily to the wedding guests.

Since Aden wanted everything else to be kept simple, in contrast to the wedding, the engagement was a small dinner party with only 20 guests. There was no spark of life in Aden. Emotionless, he went through the motions of getting engaged with neither a smile on his face nor joy in his heart.

What made matters more difficult for Aden was knowing that he could never stop loving Christina and wanting to see and be with her. With that realization he decided not to let his graduating and getting married stop him from seeing her and the children, whom he also loved very much.

After the engagement, in a daring move, he told his father and Gloria, who were discussing the bridal party, that he wanted Timothy to be the ring bearer and Natalie to be a flower girl. That immediately raised a few eyebrows, but he did not care. Seeing that it was not negotiable, they reluctantly went along with his request.

Next, he wanted everyone to get to know the Ashtons as one of the close family friends, so that after he was married, they would be included in future social functions.

To start it off, he decided to have a party at his house after the completion of his exams, on the second Saturday in December. He invited about a hundred of his close friends and relatives. With only two weeks left to the wedding, and having already had such a small engagement party, it was an event for everyone to get to know Abby. However, in reality it was Christina and the children that he wanted everyone to meet.

As it turned out Sean was going to be out of town on a business trip that weekend. At first, Christina barely knowing anyone at the party, felt uneasy attending it. But when Aden insisted, and considering that the children were in the bridal party, she agreed to go.

In typical Bradcliffe style, everything for the party had been prepared with that perfect mix of class, elegance, and attention to detail. The exotic flower arrangements and candles throughout the entertainment areas, together with gold plated serving platters and cutlery, and the finest crystal and china dinnerware provided the right touch of style to the party.

Prior to the start of the party, John was the first one to arrive. He was quite pleased to find how beautifully everything had been set up. Then shortly after him came the Frosts. The intent was for Abby to be there alongside Aden to greet and welcome the guests.

Abby as usual, looked stunningly beautiful. She was wearing a long soft blue color dress made of chiffon. It was low cut and had two diamanté straps that crisscrossed in back and matched her diamond necklace and long drop earrings. She felt so happy to be there next to Aden that she was almost giddy. Aden was wearing a perfectly fitted dark charcoal, bespoke suit. In contrast to Abby, he was aloof with no expression or trace of emotion on his face.

Christina, after helping Natalie and Timothy get ready for the party, ended up running late. By the time she got ready, and they made it to Aden's house, all the guests had moved into the large lounge area where they were talking and having pre-dinner drinks and hors-d'oeuvres. Randall answered the door and walked them to the wide landing area five steps above the lounge.

Christina had her hair and makeup done and was wearing a long flowing scoop neck and sleeveless evening gown. It was a stylish black stretch satin dress with see-through mesh over the shoulders, silver and shimmering black beads along the neckline, and clusters of shimmering black beads scattered all over the dress which complemented the sparkle of her vibrant eyes. It was nicely fitted, showing off her slender waistline and slim, but shapely tall figure.

Aden was standing toward the back of the room talking to a few of his friends. He was in the middle of his conversation as he casually looked toward the landing when Christina appeared. She walked towards the edge of the landing with poise and grace. With every step her long hair gently brushed over her shoulders, and her long dress elegantly floating above the floor swayed from side to side. Her beauty dazzled him.

True that Abby's voluptuous and physical beauty was unsurpassed, but what set Christina apart, particularly in the eyes of Aden was her inner beauty. Her kindness that shone brightly through her vibrant eyes, her loving and caring attitude that was gently reflected on her face, in addition to her physical beauty, were what made her so distinctly attractive. She always had that almost magical effect on him of lifting up his spirit and brightening his heart. That night she even had a greater effect on him, as it was the first time that he had seen her dressed up and glamorous. She was looking more beautiful and radiant than ever before.

His emotionless and expressionless face suddenly lit up. Spellbound, he was unable to complete his sentence in response to his friend's simple question, "Which law courses have you just completed?"

"Law courses...?" was all Aden said, having lost his focus.

"Yes. Which ones?" his friend asked again.

Mesmerized by Christina and without replying, he walked towards her to greet her. His friend wondering what had so completely captured Aden's attention, immediately turned around to see where he was going. In a domino effect, in a matter of seconds everybody was looking at Christina and her children, who were still standing on the landing.

The sudden attention made Christina feel self conscious. Turning to Randall, she very softly asked, "Why is everybody looking?"

"Because they've never seen such rare beauty," replied Randall without hesitation.

Christina smiled, "Randall, you always have the perfect answer."

Randall however, actually meant it.

Aunt Nellie, who was standing near the landing, was the first to approach and welcome them. "Come my dear. Come and join us."

As Christina walked down the steps, she extended her hand, shook Christina's hand, and said, "I am Aunt Nellie, and you are?"

"Christina," replied Aden, who had just made his way to the steps.

Christina was happy and relieved to see Aden, finally one familiar face.

"And these are her children, Natalie and Timothy," continued Aden as he looked at Christina with a smile and warmly welcomed her.

"What lovely children. It's obvious where they get their good looks from," replied Aunt Nellie. "My dear, you look too young to have children. You should say that they are your younger brother and sister," she said in her usual style of speaking her mind. "Believe me, half the women here would kill to have your figure."

Christina laughed, "Aunt Nellie, you are just too kind."

"Beautiful and modest, what a rare combination. Tell me Christina, how do you know Aden?"

"We're neighbors."

"Where are you originally from?" asked Aunt Nellie, who was curious to learn more about Christina.

"California, near San Francisco."

"That's one of my favorite cities. I love its charm and character," admitted Aunt Nellie pleasantly.

"It might also interest you to know that Christina," said Aden and then placing a bit of emphasis to indicate a sense of pride and accomplishment as to endear her more to Aunt Nellie, "is a Stanford graduate."

"That's wonderful," replied a very excited Aunt Nellie. "When I was young, I wanted to go to Stanford, but my father was old fashioned and sent me to Oxford instead. Now, come and tell me all about Stanford."

Things were working out better than Aden had hoped. With Aunt Nellie having taken such a liking to Christina, Aden did not need to do anything after that. He went about attending to his guests, as Aunt Nellie took it upon herself to introduce Christina and her children to everyone, which made them feel welcomed and accepted immediately.

Soon, dinner was served, and to make it easier on Christina, Aden had arranged for Jane to take care of Natalie and Timothy. With so many people around the long dinner tables, Christina decided to go on the terrace for a while on this warm, beautiful night. The view was absolutely enchanting, the stars were shining brightly above, the garden lights were softly illuminating the rose bushes and flowering shrubs, and in the distance the waves were gently rolling onto the shore, glistening as they broke on the sand.

Aden, looking for Christina, was quite pleased to find her on the terrace, "There you are."

As if feeling a bit nervous about being there, Christina replied, "I've always admired your gardens from afar. I just wanted to see them close-up."

Aden made no reply but smiled warmly. He was delighted to be with her.

Christina continued, "They really are beautiful." Then she turned, looked at him, and said, "And Abby is such a lovely girl."

As though not hearing her comment Aden responded, "You look very beautiful tonight."

"Aden, have you even heard a word I have said?"

"Yes, yes…yes, and shall we?"

"What?" said Christina with a confused smile on her face.

"Yes, I have. Yes, the gardens are beautiful. Yes, she is lovely. And shall we go for your personal tour of the gardens?" asked Aden confidently.

"No, I couldn't…I mean, I can't take you away from your guests."

"As long as there is food, they won't notice that I'm not there, and there's plenty of food to keep them going for a while. So, shall we go?"

"In that case…Alright," agreed Christina with a brilliant smile.

"These are no ordinary gardens. They are second only to the Hanging Gardens of Babylon. The only difference is that the walls are not as tall," said Aden, who could with his instant recall of any fact, say such things and getaway with it. That was how they started their tour of the gardens, with humor and laughter.

It seemed that the winds of destiny had stopped blowing just long enough to allow them to enjoy each other's company for those brief moments. As they stepped onto the garden path, it was as if they had entered a world of their own. Forgetful of the hundred or so people in the dining room, together they walked, talked, and laughed.

When they got to the lowest level, very gentlemanly like, he stepped aside and invited Christina to sit on the bench facing the ocean as he stood leaning against the railing across from her. For the first time, without talking or thinking about his university courses or his future, they shared funny stories with each other. Christina talked about the time that they had just arrived from America, and Aden related some incidents from his high school days.

Wrapped in a sphere of their own, without any thought of the party, Aden continued talking with Christina. He was having such an enjoyable and wonderful time that he had not noticed the passing of time. Suddenly, it all ended by Abby's insistent calling to him from the terrace above.

Hearing that, Christina knew that it was time for him to return to his guests and for her to go and check on the children. "Thank you for the tour, Aden," she said as she walked back towards the house.

Aden then walked up to Abby and said, "Don't ever interrupt me when I'm talking to my guests."

"But I was bored."

"What?" said Aden in disgust and disbelief. "You called me for that?"

"Well, my friends and I got tired of having nothing to do," said Abby pouting. "We want to get the dancing started."

Even though Aden could not believe it, he still maintained his composure. Seeing Brian standing nearby, he called him over and asked him to look after Abby and her little friends. Brian liked Abby and was only too glad to oblige, which freed Aden from dealing with her childish behavior.

It was not long before music could be heard. The ballroom was equipped with a sound and light system and a dance floor as good as, if not better than, those in the best clubs in town. Aden also had hired two of the hottest DJs to play all the latest music.

Christina had barely finished her dinner when Natalie and Timothy came up to her and dragged her to the ballroom. They had learned the latest dance craze called 'sync-un-sync', a style of dancing that was suited to all the new music and wanted to show it to their mother.

"Look, Mom!" said a very excited Natalie. "First we both do the same steps together, then he does the steps and I follow, then I do it and he follows, then we do the steps together again." The two of them went on to the dance floor and started to show their mom how it was done.

They looked so cute and happy together. It did not matter that they made a few mistakes. They all laughed about it. She felt so proud of them that when they finished, she started clapping for them. As she was applauding, she heard

Aden, whom she had not noticed standing right behind her, say, "Now you've seen it once, let's see how well you've learned it."

Christina knew that he was referring to the statement she had made earlier that year when talking about her university days. That was then, and now things were different. She did not know what to do when he extended his hand to take her to the dance floor. She bashfully stepped back, "I really wasn't paying attention."

"Come on Mom! You can do it! It's a lot of fun!" said the children encouragingly.

She was still hesitating. "That's what I thought," said Aden, "it wasn't true."

"Of course it was!"

"Then what are you waiting for?"

Caught up in the moment, she agreed. She took his hand, and together they went on the dance floor. For the first time in a long time, with Sean not being there to put her down or make her feel bad with his slighting comments, she was able to let down her guard. Once again, she was feeling free spirited, like her university days.

As soon as the DJs saw Aden coming toward the dance floor, they put the spotlight on them. In a matter of seconds everybody stepped back and cleared the dance floor for them.

With her eyes locked on him for fear of making a mistake, and his on her for the joy of being with her, they began to dance. What was immediately striking to everyone was how incredibly good they looked together, as if they were made for each other. This was further supported by how well they danced together. Even though there was no close contact, they moved as if they were one, ever so gracefully, like poetry in motion.

It was truly a pleasure to watch for everyone, except for Abby, who was watching from behind the lines of people gathered around the dance floor. Although she was with Brian and her own entourage of starry-eyed teenage boys, she became insanely jealous. She left her friends and ran to her mom, complaining that Aden was dancing with someone else and was not paying enough attention to her.

Gloria comforted her by saying that she did not have anything to be jealous about, for after all Aden was well known as a playboy and for his womanizing ways. She told her that she could not expect him not to dance or talk with anyone. What mattered was that he had chosen her to marry, and she better not mess it up by worrying about little things like that. She further told her that if she did not want him dancing with someone else, then she should go and get him to dance with her. Abby, feeling better, took her mother's advice and went back.

Aden and Christina had just finished their dance. "That was quite impressive. You're not only a quick learner, but also a graceful dancer," remarked Aden.

Christina, having felt a bit tense up to that point, was relieved to hear that. "Coming from you, it's quite a compliment," acknowledging openly, however indirectly, how highly she thought of him.

Before he had a chance to say anything, the music had started and Abby had wrapped her arms around him, pulling him away to dance with her. Christina smiled, thinking that this was how it should be, Aden dancing with his beautiful fiancé. She left the dance floor and went back to the lounge area.

Unlike dancing with Christina, Aden's heart was not in it at all, and he could not wait for the dance to finish. As soon as the music stopped, he left Abby with her friends and went to see where Christina was.

To his dismay he found her surrounded by a few of his father's friends, all of whom were joking and having fun with her. Although it was all in good spirit, he did not like it at all.

One of them could be heard saying, "Just say the word and I'll leave my wife. Just don't tell her that I said that." Another one replied, saying, "Forget about him. Come with me. I have no wife, but I do have a most expensive luxury yacht. Together we can sail into the sunset and…"

Aden tried to indirectly stop them by stirring things up, "What a line. Sounds like something from a soap opera."

"Ouch! He got you there," said the first one.

"With my billions, I don't need a line."

"What billions? Don't you mean millions?" said a third friend.

"With Christina by my side, I will turn millions into billions in no time."

"Why wait when she can have a billionaire now? And I promise, unlike your husband, not to ever leave you on a business trip. I will stay by your side at all times," said the third friend.

"That isn't a promise. That's a threat! Who would want to look at your face all day long?" replied the second one.

All the kidding and laughter caught the attention of some of the other guests, who came and joined in. With it becoming a larger group, to Aden's liking, the conversation shifted to other topics. Even Abby's parents joined in for some of the time. But Abby, having no interest in talking, avoided that area and stayed with her friends in the ballroom the whole night.

Even though it was getting late, Natalie and Timothy did not want to leave. They were having fun playing all of the arcade games that Aden had hired for them. Seeing that they had no school the following day, Christina did not mind and let them stay for as long as they wanted.

When they got too tired to play anymore, they came to where Christina, Aden, and some of the other guests were sitting. Natalie went to her mom, and Timothy went and sat beside Aden. After a few minutes Natalie also went and sat on the other side of Aden.

After an evening of food, socialization, and laughter, all that remained on this unforgettable night of nights was the pure and beautiful emotions that Aden felt. As he held the children in his arms and looked at Christina sitting across from him, his heart overflowed with intense feelings of love and happiness. He thought to himself that there was nothing he would not do to make Christina happy. As Christina looked across and saw Aden with the children at his side, she was touched by the love he felt for them, and they for him. She felt overwhelmed by the kindness and consideration he had shown them. She found herself thinking what a remarkable person Aden was and how more than anyone, he deserved to be happy.

With most of the guests gone and the children getting sleepy, it was time to go. Even though Christina did not want to take Aden away from his guests, he would not have it any other way. In his usual, dignified manner he walked her and the children back to their house.

When Aden returned a few minutes later, Aunt Nellie and her family, having already said goodbye to the Frosts and John, were waiting by the front door for him.

"You know that I always hate to see you go Aunt Nellie," said Aden, offering his arm for her to hold onto as he walked her to the limousine.

"I couldn't be happier with the choice you have made for your wife Aden," said Aunt Nellie as she warmly and gently clasped his arm.

Aden was a little surprised with her enthusiastic and high opinion of Abby. She had always had a similar way of thinking as him. For that reason, he could not understand how she liked Abby so much, when under a different set of circumstances, he would never have considered marrying her. Nevertheless, he thought that she was sweet for being supportive of him.

"Even if I had tried, I couldn't have found anyone more perfect," said Aunt Nellie. Then turning to James, "You could get a few pointers from Aden in this regard," which he just hated to hear. She continued, "I mean, what more can you ask? She's beautiful, extremely intelligent, and a Stanford graduate!"

Aden smiled. Now it all made sense.

"I don't need any pointers from Aden," James was quick to respond. "I had quite a long intellectual and stimulating conversation with her. I think that we hit it off well. She has that rare combination of beauty and intelligence. If she were available, I would marry her myself seeing that Aden is marrying Abby."

"Who's Abby?" asked Aunt Nellie.

"Aden's fiancé, the gorgeous blonde we met at the beginning," said Trudy. She then turned to Aden, "Mom forgets everything nowadays."

Aunt Nellie then pulled Aden close to her before getting into the limousine and whispered, "You get to know everyone better when you pretend to be senile. Take it from me, dump the blonde and marry Christina."

If Aden could, he would in less than a heartbeat. He just smiled, kissed her on the cheek, and said, "It's always a great pleasure seeing you."

The Frosts and John were the last ones to leave. Once they were gone Randall, Jane and the caterers started to clean and tidy up the place.

Aden was feeling spiritually quite high from the wonderful night that he had had. He walked on the terrace, took off his jacket and tie, played the song that he and Christina had danced to, made himself comfortable on a lounge chair, and relived every magical moment of the night that he had spent with Christina.

In the background while working, Jane said to Randall, "It is wonderful to see Master Aden so happy. He has finally found the right girl to marry." When to her surprise Randall made no reply, she asked, "Don't you think so?"

"It really isn't my place to say," said Randall as if hiding his true feelings.

"But you have been like a second father to him."

"Let's just pray to God," replied Randall, "that Master Aden will find the happiness that he so deserves."

Chapter 52

Aden was still on a high on Monday evening when he received a disconcerting phone call from Duchess Alanna.

He had tried several times during the past few weeks to get in touch with Elexa. He wanted to personally talk to her and explain why he was getting married. Since he had not been successful in reaching her, he had asked his father to hold off on sending her a wedding invitation until after he had spoken with her. John then had passed on his request to Gloria who was arranging for the invitations to be sent out.

Knowing that his father had taken care of his request, Alanna's call was totally unexpected. She told Aden that she and Elexa had just returned from a four-week diplomatic tour. Among the pile of correspondence waiting for Elexa, had been Aden's wedding invitation. It became clear that Gloria had intentionally ignored Aden's wishes.

Seeing the invitation had made Elexa feel betrayed. Because of their special friendship she thought that this was something he should have told her personally. She believed that by not talking to her about it, he had not kept his promise. That saddened her. Deep down she had always harbored the hope that someday they would end up together. Now with that hope gone she felt quite upset. As a result of all these feelings, when Aden asked to talk to her to remedy the situation, she refused. Alanna explained to Aden that she was too hurt and upset to accept. In the heat of the moment, she told her aunt that she never wanted to talk to him again.

Incidents such as this made Aden face, sooner than he would have liked, the cold reality of his life. This was something that should have, and could have, been easily avoided. Instead, it was causing him to lose such a special and close friend, with whom he had shared a very unique friendship. Even John, in his persuasive manner, while able to convince Alanna to come, could not get Elexa to change her mind.

For Aden, the winds of destiny seemed to have gathered momentum. They were now blowing hard from every direction, eroding even the slightest sense of control that he had for his life. Having put his trust in God, he had felt that somehow things would work out. But now he was beginning to doubt that his life would ever be to his desire. The ray of hope that he had had, however faint and distant, only seemed even further away when he saw Christina the next day.

Christina too, had been feeling good and happy since Saturday night. With Aden having treated her and the children so kindly and everybody having been nice, it was no wonder that she had felt that way. Her Cinderella feelings, however, all disappeared when Sean returned on Monday.

Sean quickly had learned from the children about Saturday night and how Christina had danced with Aden. Thinking how that could have jeopardized his chances of getting his promotion, made him furious. There was no stopping him. He, more than ever before, made her feel bad and guilty about herself and Saturday night. Even though she had done nothing wrong, she took it all quietly, burying her hurt feelings inside.

When Aden dropped by on Tuesday, while her words did not say it, he could see it in her eyes. He knew immediately that it would have been caused by Sean. Feeling somewhat responsible for it he wished with all his heart that he could take away her hurt. Instead, he had to content himself with the thought that things would get better after he got married in ten days. And prior to that, he would be able to make her feel better with what he was planning to say at his graduation next Tuesday.

This was not the official university graduation ceremony, but a private one at the Bradcliffe mansion that John wanted to have. He had it especially organized in recognition of Aden's enormous accomplishments of completing his university degrees in half the time with the highest possible marks, something that had not been done before. He felt proud and wanted to celebrate it with all their friends and relatives.

At first, Aden was not in favor of it, but seeing how much it meant to his father, and how it was an opportunity to express his appreciation to Christina, he went along with it.

On Friday he stopped by to give Christina directions to the mansion. She thanked him, but told him that was not necessary, for most probably she would not be able to go.

Aden could not accept that for she had already agreed to go. "Why not?" he asked.

"I just don't think I should," she simply replied without any display of emotion.

"But I would like you to come and hear my talk," replied Aden adamantly.

"Sean thinks it would be inappropriate for me to go," said Christina, painfully admitting the real reason behind her not going.

He was about to lose it. She was the main reason for him having agreed to have the graduation and wanting to give his talk. But he maintained his cool and decided not to argue against what Sean had said, even as absurd as it was. Instead, he quickly and decisively said, "Alright Christina, you have it your way. You don't have to come if you don't want to."

"I don't?" asked Christina with a surprised look on her face.

"No. That just changes where I give my talk. If you're not there I'll just leave and come here."

"You can't do that!"

"Yes, I can, and I will."

Christina panicked. She knew he would. "What about your father, all the guests and the news reporters?" she asked with a worried look on her face.

"They'll just miss out," said Aden very casually. "So, I'll either see you at the mansion at a quarter to eleven or here at a quarter past eleven."

Early Sunday morning preparations for this purely high society graduation party had begun at the beautiful grounds of the mansion and continued through Tuesday morning.

One large white marquee was put up for the ceremony with a stage at one end and rows of theater style chairs through it. Another one was set up quite elegantly adjacent to it for the sit-down lunch. All the tables and chairs were covered with white linen tablecloths and covers. There were beautiful flower arrangements on the tables, on the stage and everywhere throughout both marquees. This was a proud day for John, and everything was exquisitely arranged to perfection.

The reporters setup their equipment earlier that Tuesday morning and were there when the guests began to arrive at around 10:30am. Among the guests were quite a number of prominent people, as well as Professor Klossen and a few other university professors.

By 10:40am most guests had arrived, and John was anxious to get things started. He called Aden to the stage, where all the speakers were to be seated, for some photographs before they began.

Since Christina had not arrived yet Aden figured that he would have to be leaving shortly. He thought this way his father would at least have some pictures of him. After the pictures were taken Aden looked at his watch, it was 10:45. With still no sign of Christina he started to walk off the stage. He was not about to celebrate his graduation without her.

He wanted Christina to hear what he had to say. If it were not for her he would have been somewhere, drunk or hung over, lost to the world, living an unsatisfying and aimless life. Instead, because of Christina's help and support, he had accomplished the impossible and become the remarkable man that he was.

"Where are you going, Aden?" asked John with a concerned look on his face.

"To take care of something."

John became horrified, "Aden, we are about to start, whatever it is can wait."

Aden turned around to tell his father that it could not wait, when he saw Christina walking in and being shown to her seat. "Yes, you're right Dad. It can wait."

Aden walked back on stage, and within a few minutes the ceremony began. There were several talks of praise mixed with the right touch of humor by Professor Klossen and the other professors, followed by a very touching and complimentary talk by John.

Then it was time for Aden to say a few words. He, in his usual capable style gave a rather moving talk. His speech was mainly meant for Christina, but he had to indirectly express his appreciation of her. As a result, his father, Professor Klossen, and even Brian took it as if it were, if not fully at least partly, intended for them. They were all touched by it. It was not that he did not value the contribution of each one of them, especially his father whom he held in high esteem. It was that Christina had done for him what was unique and beyond compare.

"In life, there are many crossroads," was how he opened his talk, "finishing high school, going to university, graduating from the university, and entering the work force, just to mention a few. While each one presents us with an opportunity to celebrate or commemorate our achievements, more importantly, each provides us with a challenge and a cause to ponder and reflect. Who are we? What is our purpose in life? And how should we live and spend the quickly passing days of our life?"

Having set the stage and quickly captured everyone's attention with his opening statement, he thus continued, "This inherent need and desire within us for self understanding and search for meaning, which is vital for achievements and progress in life, sometimes gets obscured and lost in our daily lives and dealings. To create a sense of purpose we fill our lives with meaningless pursuits and activities, which only take us further away from the truth about ourselves and our lives. As we wonder lost through the desert of life, if we are lucky enough, we find a special person, a parent, a teacher, a friend, a mentor, who points us in the right direction, helps us find the true meaning of life, and guides us to realize the undiscovered greatness within us."

He paused, lovingly looked at Christina sitting toward the back of the marquee, and he then continued, "I myself was fortunate to have such a special person in my life, who helped me see that there is a dual purpose in life. One of personal growth and transformation closely interconnected with that of transforming society. We are here not only to improve ourselves intellectually, materially, and spiritually, but also to help build a better world for everyone to live in.

Education alone is what can help us achieve our purpose in life. For education is the key that can unlock the unlimited potential and capacities that lie hidden within us. It can cause each person to develop and become a moral and virtuous human being, capable of soaring to new heights never imagined nor reached before."

Aden then went on and explained how his university studies have had such a profound effect on his life. "Now that I have completed my university studies," he openly expressed, "I find myself awestruck and overwhelmed with the selfless guidance and support shown to me during my studies. Without it, I would not be standing here today."

Christina was truly impressed by his high and noble character. There he was, on his special day, instead of accepting the achievement that was rightfully his, through his hard and dedicated work, he was acknowledging the support she had given him. Something she did not expect at all.

With Sean always belittling and putting her down, to actually have someone appreciate what she had done, meant a lot to her. She was so deeply touched by it, that tears welled up in her eyes. She quietly took out a handkerchief from her purse and gently wiped the tears.

"I'm with you honey," said the friendly lady sitting next to her. "I always cry at graduations and weddings," she said wiping her eyes with her handkerchief.

When Aden saw that, as if having lost his train of thought, he stopped and paused for a moment. What he had said was coming from his heart, and he was glad that it had also touched Christina's. Feeling content, he gathered his thoughts and continued in his usual, eloquent manner.

"As we go through life we seldom look back or take the time to thank those who made it possible for us to achieve our goals, those who brought us to this world, those who taught us, and those who inspired and guided us. An occasion such as a graduation then becomes a perfect time for expressing thanks and gratitude, rather than receiving praise. While to say thank you is thoughtful, it is quite evanescent and inadequate. For, it is what we do that matters, not what we say. True expression of gratitude comes from the way we live our lives and the extent which we are of benefit to society and humanity."

It is said that humility is a sign of greatness, and Aden amply demonstrated that as he concluded his talk. Without taking any personal credit for having achieved the impossible, with proven brilliance of mind, nobility of character, purity of motives and even extraordinary powers at times, he simply said, "As I pass through this unique crossroad set before me, my highest hope and aspiration is service to humanity. So, in the years to come, I hope that through my service I may prove worthy of having received all the unconditional kindness and support over the last three years. Thank you."

His talk brought the cheers and applause of everyone. As it was from his heart, not only had it touched Christina, but many others.

John while clapping walked to the podium. He stood next to Aden, turned to the audience and said, "A couple of weeks ago I asked Aden what he would like to have for his graduation gift. Perhaps a yacht, a villa, or another sports car, I suggested. He said to me, I need these like the ocean needs water. He simply told me that he really didn't need anything. That certainly was a humbling response for me," John added with his dry sense of humor. "As I stood bewildered, I wondered for a moment which one of us was the father." Everyone laughed. He continued, "Upon my insistence Aden told me that what he really wanted was in some way to contribute towards further expansion and progress in education and research." He then turned to Aden with a deep sense of pride and said, "It is my pleasure to present you the Aden Bradcliffe Scholarship Fund, an international fund established to provide funds for higher education and research."

As he embraced his son, everyone applauded. Aden's face was beaming with delight. He could not have been more pleased with his father's choice of graduation gift for him.

It truly was a moving moment bringing tears of joy to Christina's eyes. She could not have been happier for him and more proud to know him than she was at that moment. What a contrast between the lost, self-centered, egotistical boy she had met three years ago, desperately seeking his father's approval, and the powerful, selfless man he had become, enjoying his father's undying love and admiration, and commanding everyone's respect and praise. There stood a true hero. Aden did not have superpowers, a cape, or a magical weapon. He had something more special; a love for humanity and a desire to help build a better world.

With Aden graduating and getting married in less than a week, Christina's work was done.

The father and son quickly became surrounded by a multitude of guests coming to congratulate Aden. While appreciating it all, he was only thinking of going and talking to Christina. With so many people around him he could not even see where she was. It was not until most of them, after congratulating him had gone to get seated that he could begin to look for her. But to his dismay, she was no where to be found.

For Christina, the smile on Aden's face had said it all. To see him happy and surrounded by all his family and friends was all that mattered. To not overstep the bounds of propriety, she had left.

With Christina gone, no smile was left on Aden's face. He was disillusioned and looked disappointed. This prompted his father to ask him what was wrong.

"What could possibly be wrong?" replied Aden, concealing his true feelings.

Just then Abby walked up to them, very cheerfully took Aden's arm and said "Let's go! It's time for lunch, and everyone is waiting for you and your dad. They can't start until you come."

Aden just contented himself with having had Christina there for his talk and went along with Abby and his father.

Chapter 53

As soon as lunch was over Aden excused himself, told his father that he had something to take care of, and left. Regardless of the fact that some of the guests were still there, including Abby and her parents, John was too happy to argue about it.

He was anxious to see Christina, talk to her, and find out what she thought about what he had said. But to his surprise she was not home. He thought that she might have gone to pick up the children from their friend's house. He waited for her to come back, but she did not return until late afternoon, after Sean had come home from spending the day with Vicky.

Aden had no choice but to wait until the next day to talk with her. First thing Wednesday morning he went over to Christina's house, only to find that she was not home. He tried a few times to see her during the day, but again she was not home. She did not come back until that evening at about the same time as Sean.

Late that night when alone in his room, not having been able to see or talk with Christina for the past couple of days, it felt as if he was going to lose his mind. He could not take it anymore, nor could he handle it if this were how things were going to be.

Then under the stress of the situation, with his judgment clouded, he decided to do something that for the fear of losing her, he had not done in the past three years. He was going to tell Christina how he felt about her.

Determined to see her, the next day on that Thursday morning with only two days to go before his wedding, he left the house at the same time as Christina did to take her children to their school holiday activities. Driving at a distance behind her, he was hoping to find the opportunity to talk with her. She dropped off the children and went for a drive along the ocean. After a while, she stopped, parked the car, and went down for a walk on the beach.

With the wedding so close, Sean could taste the victory of getting the promotion that he wanted. He no longer saw the need to pretend to be nice to Christina as he had been told by John. He reverted back to his harsh and abusive ways towards her and did not care how hurtful he was. Once again, she was put in that tenuous position to deal with his offensive behavior. This time it was more difficult. She was finding it hard to stay positive and strong and not to let Sean crush her spirit. Unlike before, she was failing to see that there was wisdom behind things that happen in life. As a result, her faith and beliefs were being severely tested. She kept wondering what she had done to deserve this. She had only been a loving and supportive wife and mother, dedicating her life to her family. Was not that enough? That none of it seemed to matter to Sean, was hurting her inside and eroding her self worth and confidence.

What made it worse was that she was already beginning to miss not having Aden there as before. To have been able to help and support him, had in fact been a positive and bright spot in her life, overshadowing all the negative. Now all of that was about to change, and she did not quite know how to deal with it. With no one to turn to, going to the beach was her way of getting away, searching for answers in the hope of finding a way to cope with it all.

After walking for a little while on this gloomy and overcast day, she stopped. She then walked back and sat on the retaining wall in front of the sand dunes, just below the car park where Aden had also parked.

She was so lost in her thoughts that she neither saw nor heard Aden walking towards her. Filled with joy to have found her, Aden approached her and said hello.

With seas of sadness surging in her eyes, she looked up and saw Aden. She was surprised. He was the last person that she had expected to see there. Aden explained how he had been trying to see and talk with her for the past two days, but she had not been home.

"That's true," was all Christina said in a lifeless voice.

"When I saw your car here…I stopped and came to see if everything was ok, and if there was anything that I could do for you."

"Only if you could reverse time, undo the past…" replied Christina, venting her emotions. Catching herself being so self-absorbed, she stopped. Then with a little more life in her voice she said, "I'm sorry…what is it that you wanted to talk to me about?"

After a moment's pause, he came right out and said, "I'm thinking of not going through with the wedding."

But before he had a chance to explain why, Christina instantly, forgetting about her own problems, and only focusing on his life, in a very strong and adamant voice said, "You can't do that." Her heart was so pure that she could not let her personal feelings interfere with what was best for him.

"Why not?" asked Aden not anticipating such a response from her.

Thinking about his future life and happiness, like his father, and the promise that she had made to him, she said, "Because your future lies on this path and so does the future of thousands whose quality of life will depend on you, as the head of the conglomerate."

Christina turned toward the ocean and motioning towards a large cruise ship out in the distance she said, "You are like that big luxury ocean liner carrying thousands of people to many exciting ports of call. Without it none of those prospects will be possible or attainable." She then looked at him and gently said, "A high destiny awaits you Aden, and this marriage will help you achieve that."

He was impressed by her opinion of him, especially since she had not expressed these thoughts before. Yet, he was more interested to know how she saw herself in that context. So, he asked, "And how do you see yourself?"

"Like that small sailboat," Christina replied without hesitation, "aimlessly floating away hoping someday to reach the shore." Then in a soft tone of voice she said, "We come from two different worlds. In an unlikely turn of events our paths crossed for a brief moment, before diverging in different directions."

"I don't agree with that," said Aden defiantly.

"It isn't ours to agree. No one can alter or turn back the pages of destiny."

Even though he still did not agree with her, he was not there to argue. As he looked into her eyes, with his heart overflowing with his deep love for her, all he wanted to do was to tell her how he felt about her. He hesitated, and just at that moment his cell phone began ringing. It was Abby calling. He rejected the call. The phone rang again. He then put it on silent. It began vibrating. This time, he turned it off completely. Seconds later, his car phone began to ring. Having left the window down it could be heard loud and clear.

"Someone wants to reach you badly."

"It can wait."

But it continued to ring. "It must be important," said Christina. It was not important to Aden. He knew that it was about the last fitting for his tuxedo. He was supposed to have been at his personal tailor's salon 20 minutes ago. He would just as soon ignore it.

But she was too concerned for him. She stood up and said, "I think that you ought to answer that. And I must go now."

He did not want her to go, but they could not talk as long as the phone was ringing. To stop it he had to answer it. There was nothing else that he could do about it. He asked her not to go, but she did not stay. She did not want to keep him from what he had to do. When he went to his car, she did too. As he answered the phone she got into her car, waved goodbye, and drove off.

He ended the call as quickly as he could to try to stop her, but by the time he got out of his car, it was too late. He became so frustrated that he hit the car phone on the roof of his latest Ferrari as hard as he could, leaving a dent. But he did not care.

All he had wanted was to see and talk with her. Now she was gone, leaving him feeling empty inside. Thinking about the sadness in her and how strongly she wanted him to get married, once again led him to believe that for her happiness, he had to go through with the wedding. To pursue and tell her now about his true feelings, he began to see, was too risky. It was a chance he was not willing to take if it meant losing her and her friendship. Instead, he had to resign himself to be satisfied with seeing her in the evenings and at social gatherings.

After that brief encounter, with Aden being busy and Christina making herself scarce, he did not see her anymore, not even on Friday. He tried a few times during the day, but Christina was not at home.

Early Friday evening, about an hour before his bachelor party was to begin, his father dropped by unexpectedly. Aden was surprised to see him since they had agreed that he would drive there himself. But there was a special reason behind his father's visit.

John, beaming with excitement and happiness, hugged Aden and told him that he could not wait until the bachelor party. He wanted to give him his gift now. Aden had neither anticipated nor expected any gift from his father. Naturally, he was quite surprised to hear that, but nowhere near as surprised or as shocked as he was when he found out what it was.

With a big smile John handed him a letter. The more he read it, the more his heart sank. Although on its own it was all good, he was not ready for its consequences.

Through John's and Professor Klossen's efforts, and mainly based on Aden's outstanding performance and remarkable records, Aden had been accepted to Stanford University's MBA program. He was to start early January. That meant, following his honeymoon, instead of returning to Australia, he and Abby would fly directly to San Francisco and on to Stanford. There they would start their new life together and live in a mansion in Los Altos Hills that John would be purchasing for them as a wedding gift.

As wonderful as it was, it had clear implications, which Aden was not ready to accept. He could not even force a smile or pretend to be excited about it, whereas under a different set of circumstances he would have been.

John by his own design knew that this was all too sudden for Aden, and he would need time to appreciate it. Believing that it was in Aden's best interests, he was not concerned about his lack of enthusiasm. He felt that before long he would see the value of it all.

After they talked for a while John left for the party. Aden was to follow shortly, but instead he went to see Christina. Sean answered the door. He had just gotten home. Without any small talk he just asked to see Christina. Sean got her and then went to be with the children.

Aden handed her the acceptance letter to read. Halfway through it she stopped, looked at him, and said, "This means that I won't see…" she then caught herself and did not complete her sentence. This was not about her. It was about his future.

"I am thinking of not accepting it," said Aden.

"Don't you dare do that," Christina responded admonishingly. This was the second time in a span of two days that she had spoken to him in this manner, but only because of her deep concern for him and his future.

"Why should I accept it?"

"Because it is too good of an opportunity to pass up," said Christina more calmly and with a caring tone.

"But all I want, and need is here."

Remembering the happy and carefree times that she had experienced at Stanford and wishing how she could go back there, she said, "Aden, what you have here will still be here when you return, but what you will gain by going there will be invaluable. And…I can't think of anywhere more suited to your intellectual needs than Stanford. Nor can I think of anywhere more romantic and charming than the San Francisco Bay area for a newly married couple to start their life together."

There was not much more that he could say without divulging his true feelings, which he could not do. Given that, although contrary to his wishes, the path forward had become quite clear. He had to go to Stanford to maintain her respect.

With Aden already running late for his bachelor party, he did not stay much longer. He simply thanked Christina and left.

At that moment Sean walked in, "What was that all about?" he asked curiously.

"Aden has been accepted to the Stanford University MBA program."

"He's the luckiest guy in the world. He's got everything that every man dreams of having," said Sean enviously. He did not even for one moment appreciate what he had, nor considered that he, in fact, was the luckiest man, for he had the only thing that Aden truly wanted.

At his bachelor party Aden seemed distant, which everybody attributed to pre-wedding jitters. As the evening went on he became even more preoccupied with thoughts of Saturday being his last day in Adelaide, so much so that he did not stay until the end. He excused himself and left.

After Aden was gone Ian pulled John aside to have a talk with him. "I've got to hand it to you John. I didn't think you could do it, but you did. You've got Aden to get married, and to the girl of your choice."

"I know that he isn't now, but a year from now he will be thanking me for it," said John firmly believing that he had done the right thing for Aden.

"What about going to Stanford, whose idea was that?"

"That was mine," John openly admitted.

"That's what I thought," said Ian disapprovingly.

"What is that supposed to mean?"

"That perhaps it wasn't such a good idea," Ian responded frankly.

"Don't tell me that you are still on about that wild fantasy of yours about Aden being in love. Even if that was the case, which it isn't, then cold turkey is the best thing for him," said John adamantly, "just one clean break to get him started on his new life. In either case I believe that going to Stanford is in his best interests. It was a great opportunity for him to study and enjoy his life for at least a couple of years before getting involved in the demands and stresses of running a big corporation."

"Let's hope you're right. It's not easy to leave the one you truly love behind."

Ian was right. It was the hardest thing that Aden had ever been faced with. After he got home, the reality of it being his last night there started to hit him. Just as he had begun to accept his new life and have a sense of control over it, it had spun away, out of control, from him.

He had never imagined that on the eve of his third anniversary of meeting Christina and falling deeply in love with her, that he would be saying farewell, not knowing how soon he would be able to see her again. Nor had he, or could he, imagine his life without seeing her. She had given meaning and purpose to his life and had been there for him every step of the way from the darkest to the brightest hours of his life. She had inspired, encouraged, and supported him. Her cheerful and caring personality had always brightened up his life. Now the thought of not having her in his life was tearing him apart.

Unable to focus on anything, amidst feeling sad, Aden was drawn to the window. As he looked out, he saw Christina standing on the terrace in front of her house.

She had come out for a few minutes to get some fresh air, searching for fresh hope, a fresh outlook to help her cope with the difficulties she was faced with in her life there. At the same time Aden stood there in his room, unable to cope with life without her.

The winds of destiny had turned to gales, leaving behind fragments of broken hearts. There stood the one he loved, so close, yet so far away. He had so much to tell her, yet nothing could be said.

While it was heartening to see her, even if it were only for those few brief minutes from afar, it made him realize even more how things would be without her. In a state of despair and anguish he spent a sleepless night at his house.

By the morning, as the sun's rays began to shine, he had arrived at a state of complete self-surrender and reliance on the will of God. In that state Aden found himself with a new sense of courage to go through with what he had to do, and strength to conceal his emotions and feelings for the respect and happiness of Christina.

When his father arrived a few hours later for the big day, Aden was ready for it.

Chapter 54

The eagerly awaited wedding day filled with jubilation and wonder had finally arrived, surrounded by all the media hype that it deserved. After nearly three months of essentially nonstop, around the clock planning, designing, building, and organizing, under a shroud of secrecy, it had all come together splendidly.

The much talked about wedding lived up to all expectations. It truly could be said that it was a royal wedding. It was elegant, extravagant, and exclusive. Except, this wedding, where possible, had gone beyond most traditional boundaries and established new standards, which were both unique and daring. From the onset the stage was set for what had been billed as the wedding of the century.

The weather could not have been more perfect on this late December day. It was a brilliant, sunny day with a pleasant temperature of 82oF. With excitement in the air the 500 guests in all their glitter and glamour began to arrive and were immediately engulfed in luxury and awe. As they emerged from their limousines, it was as if they were entering a garden, for they immediately stepped onto a plush green carpet covering the sidewalk and steps and walked under a grand 9-foot-high and 6-foot-wide arbor with interconnected arches leading to the cathedral's main doors. The arches were covered with green foliage, white gardenias, other rare flowers such as light blue and lavender colored roses, and hanging wisterias. Each flower had been especially selected for its color and fragrance. The same flower combinations were also used extensively inside to decorate the entire front of the cathedral, all the walls, and along the isle, creating a unique illusion of a redolent garden setting within the cathedral.

Shortly after all the guests had been seated Aden arrived in the Bradcliffe limousine with his best man, Brian, followed by his three groomsmen. As usual, Aden looked stately and handsomely distinguished. As he stood in front of the cathedral waiting for his bride to arrive, there was no trace of smile on his face, or in his heart. He felt empty and heartbroken.

Minutes later the bridal party arrived. Abby's maid of honor was Jema. She and the three bridesmaids were dressed in pale blue satin gowns, and the four flower girls were wearing pale lavender organza dresses. Their arrival, together with the groomsmen, and Timothy as the ring bearer, set the stage for the much anticipated arrival of the bride.

Abby and her father arrived in the Frost's metallic midnight blue stretch limousine. She was wearing a magnificent, white silk dress, especially designed for her. It fitted perfectly around the chest and waist. It gradually flared out to a full flowing gown with a 20-foot-long detachable train.

There were more gems on her and her dress than in a jewelry store. Her tiara, necklace, earrings, and bracelet were all elegantly made of three tiers of the highest quality, dark blue sapphire, light blue sapphire, and brilliant white diamonds. The dark and light blue colors were chosen specifically to accentuate her deep blue eyes. The same color gems, not rhinestones or zirconium, were used around her waistline and the edge of her off-the-shoulder short sleeves. Her veil was made of French lace, hand embroidered along the edge in a scalloped pattern. In the center of each of the semicircles of the scalloped pattern of the veil were placed the same three-color gems in the shape of a three-leaf clover.

The bells began to chime. Abby alongside her father entered the cathedral and dazzled everyone. She looked stunningly beautiful and radiant. Overjoyed and happy she walked down the isle to the man of her dreams. She was the envy of every girl, to be the one to marry the unattainable Aden Bradcliffe.

Abby's thrill and excitement began to mount when Aden in his stately manner walked up to her and offered his arm for her to hold onto, and piqued when she was asked, "Abby, do you take Aden to be your lawfully wedded husband?" It was an out of this world experience for her as she, with great eagerness said, "I do."

The minister then turned to Aden and said, "Aden, do you take Abby to be your lawfully wedded wife?" He made no reply. Total silence overtook the cathedral. The minister asked him again. Before making any reply, he turned around looking for Christina among the guests. He was hoping to have a last glance of her. But he could not find her in the sea of faces looking at him, wondering why he was not answering.

What he did see was his father's worried face, urging him to say, "I do." Those short few seconds seemed like centuries. They kept everyone tense and on edge, until he turned back and finally said, "I do."

At that moment he proved beyond any doubt the depth of his devotion and the purity of his love for Christina, for he had made the ultimate sacrifice—himself, for the one he truly loved.

Following the ceremony they had their photos taken at the Frost Estate. After a short rest it was time for the much awaited and speculated reception. No one could have imagined the treat that they were in for, an unforgettable and memorable night.

While the guests were arriving and being seated, the banquet hall was dimly lit, creating a soft and pleasant atmosphere. It was elegantly set up. Each table had a three-tiered flower arrangement made from deep blue, light blue, and white roses, tastefully mixed with some native Australian wattle and other greenery. At first glance it seemed just like another rich wedding reception without anything out of the ordinary. That was until everyone had been seated, and it was time for the bride and groom to arrive.

Their arrival unveiled the stupendous setting that had been so carefully designed for their wedding. The orchestra began to play, and a soft color spotlight illumined the entrance as Abby and Aden entered the banquet hall. The MC announced, "Ladies and gentlemen, please welcome Mr. and Mrs. Aden Bradcliffe." All the guests arose and applauded them. He looked regal and she looked glamorous with all her jewels sparkling under the light.

All the guests were requested to be seated as the bride and groom proceeded down the pathway with light blue carpet being rolled out before them to the head table. Then synchronized with their steps, the dimly lit banquet hall was transformed to a delightful garden of water and lights. Behind them, with every step that they took, the centerpiece of each table became a lighted water feature and the plain walls, a lighted waterfall. The guests were awestruck. With so much happening around them they did not know which way to turn so as not to miss any of the wonder unfolding around them.

The dinner had been exquisitely made to perfection. Each course had been prepared by a different, internationally renowned chef, and presented like a work of art.

The wedding cake was seven layers and stood two meters tall. Each layer appeared to be suspended in air on a lighted glass plate.

For their first dance, a special dance floor had been prepared, consisting of a glass covered, softly lit pond with white and blue water lilies. It created the illusion that they were dancing on the floating flowers.

The entire evening continued at that high standard of exclusiveness, with one amazing effect after another. It was no wonder that the finale was no less impressive than the rest of the wedding event. A line of limousines waited outside this six-star hotel to take the bride and groom, their immediate families, and close friends to the airport, where a chartered luxury plane awaited to fly them all to Hawaii for another night and day of celebrations, before returning and leaving Abby and Aden to enjoy their honeymoon.

None of the glitter and glamour of the night could put a smile on Aden's face. Throughout the evening he kept looking for Christina. Even though he could see Sean and the children, she was nowhere to be seen. As the evening drew closer to the end, he became more anxious. He wanted to see her one last time. But, time was running out and he had no recourse nor anyway to find her.

Then one of the hotel staff walked up to him and handed him an envelope. The message inside put the first smile of the day on his face. After reading it, he quickly excused himself and walked out of the banquet hall.

There stood, in her usual vibrancy and elegance, Princess Elexa. Having learned from her Aunt Alanna what had actually happened, she felt bad for the way she had acted. She had come to apologize and patch things up with Aden.

He was certainly happy to see her. He gave her a hug and began to say, "I'm sorry for…"

Elexa interrupted, "No Aden, I'm the one who should be apologizing. That is why I've come, to ask for your forgiveness. You were there for me when I needed you most. You put yourself on the line for me, and instead of me being there for you, I abandoned you. I'm ashamed of that and I hope that you can forgive me."

"Of course I forgive you," Aden smiled, "I'm just glad to have you back."

Elexa was ecstatic to hear that. "I promise that I'll never let you down again." Very eagerly she continued, "To prove that to you, before I go just tell me if there is anything that I can do for you, and I'll do it."

While listening Aden noticed Natalie and Timothy walking from the courtyard. His face lit up. He became overjoyed. He had found Christina. He simply said, "You have already done more than enough by coming here." For if it were not for her being there, he would never have found Christina.

"Just call me first, next time you decide to marry someone you don't love!"

Aden chuckled, "I will." They hugged each other and Elexa left.

He had to go and see Christina, but there was no time left. The MC could be heard making closing remarks, and his friends were hurrying him to go back inside. Once inside the hall, he walked up to Abby's dad and said a few words to him. John who was standing nearby talking to Ian became concerned, wondering what that was about. Whatever it was, Conrad seemed to be agreeing with it.

Seconds later, the MC announced that it was time for the last dance and the bridle party's departure to the airport. As soon as that announcement was made, Conrad accompanied Abby to the dance floor, and Aden started to discretely walk away. It became clear what Aden had said to Conrad. With so many things having been done in such original and unique ways in this wedding, it was no wonder that Conrad liked Aden's idea and willingly agreed to have the last dance with Abby.

Chapter 55

With everyone's attention directed towards the dance floor, they did not take notice of Aden walking away. But John did, and he was not happy about it. Together with Ian, he went after him. Before he could catch up with him, Aden had walked into the courtyard.

The courtyard was softly lit and had a warm and quaint atmosphere about it. There were four flowerbeds covered with blooming flowers, separated by four paths, each leading to a beautifully ornate fountain in the center of the courtyard which was surrounded by shrubs and flowers.

There was Christina sitting on a bench in front of the fountain. She looked beautiful, wearing a nicely fitted light gray organza gown. The color of her gown reflected the way she was feeling. She was in a world of her own, drowning in a sea of ambivalent feelings, trying to cope with all that was going on in her life until the call of the last dance caught her attention. She then knew that the end was near. Feeling troubled, she looked up and to her utmost surprise, she saw Aden walking into the courtyard.

John was dismayed. "I have to go and stop him," he said forcefully.

"No, I can't let you do that John," said Ian, adamant to prevent him from going after Aden. "Haven't you already done enough?" he asked passionately. "You've had him get married. You've arranged for him to go away. Now, you want to deny him these few minutes to say goodbye?"

John reluctantly stopped, thought for a moment and said, "I guess not. I suppose that I can let him go. It's going to be all over anyway."

It was such a bittersweet moment for Aden to see Christina. As overjoyed as he was to see her, he was equally saddened, knowing as she did that this was goodbye. She was puzzled to see him there and did not know what to say.

For Aden, it was all clear. He knew what he wanted and exactly what to say. Standing in his stately manner, he asked, "May I have this dance?"

Still sitting on the bench, she gently shook her head indicating, "No," thinking that he should not be there.

"Can't two friends have a last dance?" She could not say no to that. With the sound of music softly filling the air in the courtyard, she gracefully took his hand and arose from the bench. With their eyes momentarily locked together, they began to dance.

There were no words to be said, no thoughts to be expressed. The tenderness and the sweetness of those moments were beyond the reach of any syllables and words. As it neared the end of the song, they stopped. While still looking down, she took a step back. She did not have the strength to look at him.

But he wanted to see her dazzling eyes for one last time before leaving. He softly touched her chin, gently lifting up her face. No longer capable of holding back her emotions or hiding her sadness, she looked up at him with tearful eyes.

Those tears, like a sharp knife cutting through his heart, plunged him into an abyss of sorrow. If it could have made a difference, he at that moment would have gladly given up everything he had, not to leave. But that was not to be.

John and Ian, waiting on the other side of the courtyard glass doors, could see this heart wrenching scene. "What did you mean," Ian asked, "when you said it will be all over anyway? Seeing how deep and strong his love is, what is there to stop him from getting on a plane in a week or two, and returning home?"

John made no reply.

"Suddenly, you don't seem concerned. Why is that?" wondered Ian. "What are you up to John?"

"All right. I might as well tell you. But no one knows about this, and I would like to keep it that way."

"That's fine."

"On Tuesday Sean will be getting his dream job promotion as the head of the Australasia operation of a large electronics company, located in Singapore. Along with that he will be given four first class tickets for him and his family to travel there by the following day to urgently start his new position."

"How do you know this?"

"Sean had asked me, and I arranged it for him."

"How could you do this John?"

"Why not? This is what is best for everyone. Upon their arrival they'll be chauffeured to their mansion where they will live a life of luxury. Their furniture will be packed and shipped to them the day after their departure. By the end of the week, they will be starting their new life in a new country with new cell phones, email addresses, and so on."

Ian listened in amazement, "They can still contact Aden."

"Not after tonight. I have arranged for him to have new phone numbers and email addresses, too." Feeling quite content John continued, "A clean cut is what he needs. You said so yourself."

"So, what you're saying is that this is the last time he'll ever see her? And he doesn't even know it?" Ian felt horrified at the thought of it, "I can't bear to watch it. I've seen many heartbreaking things in my life, but this tops them all!"

"This is no time to get emotional. Pull yourself together. We've to go and stop him."

"Stop him from what?"

"From doing anything foolish."

As Aden looked into Christina's eyes for those final few moments, he could not say a word. Neither could she. Feelings of sadness and emptiness filled the air. The music had stopped, and it was time to go. Christina through her teary eyes could see John and Ian walking toward them. She took another step back, gracefully turned around, and walked towards the side door.

Aden wanted to go after her, and it took the full force of John's and Ian's might to stop him. When she walked through the door and disappeared, it felt as if all his strength had been taken from him, and he was about to collapse. But Ian helped him through it. Then they quickly whisked him away to the limousine waiting outside for him and his bride.

Soon, an overjoyed Abby with her father and the rest of the family emerged through the crowd waiting outside. Behind them came the other guests who were leaving with the bridal party, each going to their own limousine. Abby was escorted inside the limousine. As Aden was about to go in, he heard someone calling his name.

He turned around and saw that it was Timothy who was calling him. He had come together with Natalie to say goodbye. Aden talked to them very lovingly. Natalie then took off her favorite flower ring that her mom had bought for her in San Francisco and gave it to Aden. Timothy followed suit and gave him his favorite key ring.

"We want you to have these," they both said.

Aden was very touched, but said, "I can't take these, they are your favorites."

"But we love you," said Natalie with teary eyes. "And we want you to take them so that you won't forget us," said Timothy with a sad face.

Aden hugged them, accepted their gifts and said, "I…I'll never forget either of you. As soon as I get to California I'll call you, and I'll send you emails every day," so he thought.

While he had tried to prepare himself for leaving Adelaide, he was not quite prepared for these final moments and the teary goodbyes. It tore him apart, and it showed. Having had very little sleep during the week and no sleep the night before did not help matters at all. John and Ian who were waiting by the limousine could tell. John suggested for Ian to stay with Aden. At first, Abby was surprised to see him in their limousine, but when she learned that Aden was not well, she welcomed the idea.

As soon as they got to the plane, Ian took Aden to the front first class lounge section. He explained to Abby that it was best for Aden to be alone. She understood and did not think twice about it. She quickly got involved with her friends and began talking about the wedding. Ian also told the flight attendants not to let anyone through as per doctor's orders, with the exception of John.

Minutes later, John arrived and went directly to the front. Since it was near takeoff, Ian left them together and went back to take his seat. Soon the plane, in the midst of continued jubilation and celebration, took off.

In contrast there was no feeling of rejoicing or excitement in the front. With no one there to interrupt, they were finally presented with an opportunity to have a heart to heart, father and son talk that was long overdue.

Aden benumbed with what he had been through sat quietly without any expression on his face. John, wanting to cheer him and make him feel better, started to talk about the wedding and how wonderful everything was. "All night everyone was thanking me for inviting them to this wedding and telling me how impressed they were with everything and what a great time they had. They couldn't praise it enough." With still no reaction from Aden he continued, "They also thought that you are a lucky man, who has everything; a gorgeous heiress for your wife, wealth, power, unmatched intelligence, and a guaranteed bright future."

"Then I'm a prisoner of my good fortune," replied Aden somberly.

John was taken aback, "How can you say such a thing, when you have everything that any man can dream of having?"

"I gladly would give it all up, to have the one thing that I want."

"I don't understand. What could you possibly want that you don't already have?"

After thinking for a minute, Aden said, "The woman that I love."

Hearing that, John could no longer maintain his composure. With his seatbelt still on he sat up straight and leaned as far forward as possible, "Who would that be?" he asked, finally faced with what he had long dismissed, hoping for it not to be true.

"Christina," replied Aden with such fervor and feelings of love that it could be palpably felt by his father.

John sank back in his seat. This was not something he wanted to hear.

"Surely you mean that you love her as a mother figure."

"No. I love her as a friend, teacher, mentor…but most of all as my soul mate."

"Does she share your love?"

"No," Aden sighed. "She doesn't even know that I love her."

"Why is that?"

"Because I was afraid. I could not bring myself to tell her." Aden said in a low-spirited voice, "I didn't want to lose her."

"You did the right thing not to tell her. After all, she is married and has a family that she needs to care for. Now you need to forget her and get on with your life."

"I can't. I can't stop thinking about her, nor could I ever stop loving her. Every fiber of my being longs to be with her."

"Then why did you agree to get married?"

"I did it for you…and…"

"And?"

"For Christina."

John appeared puzzled, "How do you mean for Christina?"

"When I saw how strongly she wanted me to get married, I figured that it had to do with her marriage." After a short pause, "I don't expect you to understand this, but to make her happy, I agreed to marry Abby." With a heavy heart and sadness in his eyes and voice, "I never imagined that it would mean being apart from her."

John more than understood, for he knew that he was the reason behind Christina's response. But he was not about to tell Aden that, nor about seeing Sean with Vicky, nor about having arranged for Sean and the entire family to be moved from Adelaide, for he still believed that what he had done was in Aden's best interests.

Instead, he decided to share with Aden the reason behind what he had done. "Your mother was also from America," John opened up with a sense of remorse for the way that things had turned out, "of unsurpassing beauty and intelligence. I met her at Oxford University. She was studying there on a Fulbright Scholarship."

"After 23 years, you are telling me this now?" Aden was amazed. "You've avoided talking to me about her all this time. Why now?"

"Because I want you to know why I did what I did, why I wanted you to get married." Then as if seeking Aden's forgiveness, he meekly said, "I only wanted you to be happy. I never intended for you to feel this way."

Aden made no reply. He just listened as John continued, "Your mother and I fell madly in love with each other and got married shortly after we both finished our studies. It was a beautiful marriage, and we had two glorious years of indescribable happiness together. Then your mother became pregnant with you, and we were elated and excited about it, until... that tragic moment."

The smile on his face gave way to sadness, "Due to some unforeseen complications, she gave her life bringing you into this world...At that moment, I died inside. The pain and anguish of losing her was too much to bear. Then, I did the unthinkable, blamed you for it, pushed you out of my life, and drowned myself in my work."

John then related to Aden, as he had never done before, the next tragic event in his life. "The untimely death of my father didn't help matters much," he continued on, "I felt I had the weight of the world on my shoulders. I had to fight hard and long to turn things around and make the Bradcliffe Corporation a success. My work became my life, and I pushed you even further away."

While it was not easy for him to say, he told Aden that he was truly sorry for what he had done. Aden appreciated his father's openness and learning about his mother, but nothing short of seeing Christina could ease his pain.

John could tell, and in the hope of making him feel better he went on, "About three years ago when things changed between us, I began to see some of your mother's wonderful qualities and strengths in you. I was overjoyed with the man that you had become, one that would make any father very proud."

Then with a deep sense of love towards Aden he said, "That was when I realized how much I wanted you to be part of my life." He then explained how after the events of last December, fearful of losing him, he had decided to secure his future.

"Not just any future," John said eagerly, "I wanted you to have a better life than I, without all of the heartaches and hard work. That is why I was in favor of this marriage. It secures your future without the struggle to be successful, and most importantly, without the agony of losing the one that you love as I did."

Aden, feeling distraught, looked at his father and said, "It seems that neither one of us got what we wanted." Much to his dismay, John could not disagree. This was a cold realization that only exacerbated the way that they were feeling.

Ian who was waiting nearby, like the true friend that he was, could tell that it was time to come forward to help them through this difficult moment. He brought each one of them a glass of juice.

Aden at first refused, but Ian insisted, "This is a long flight, and I will not have you become dehydrated."

Aden eventually took it and drank it. He had barely put down the empty glass when he fell asleep.

John looked at Ian in surprise, "What was in that drink?"

"A couple of strong sleeping tablets. With the way that he's feeling, it's the best thing for him."

"I couldn't agree more with you. I feel so bad and responsible for what he's going through and…" Before he could finish his sentence, he also fell asleep.

"This is the best thing for you too, my friend." As he covered each of them with a blanket, he said, "Things will look brighter in the morning."

Chapter 56

Having crossed the international dateline, it was early Saturday evening when they arrived in Hawaii. The sweet perfume of hibiscus and orchids wafted in the air as they checked into their Oceanside six-star hotel. The entire top two floors, including the bridal suite had been reserved for them. A magnificent banquet of superb food and entertainment had been organized for them with an 8:30pm start, which was followed by music and dancing under the stars, a perfect setting for a romantic evening.

Romance was the last thing on Aden's mind. After the dinner and entertainment had finished, he joined his father and Abby's father who were enjoying a cup of coffee over a conversation about the only thing that drove these two men—business.

Having joined forces together, now the future possibilities seemed endless. In addition, having access to Aden's brilliant mind opened new prospects which were quite thrilling, especially for Conrad. He was so enthused that several times when Abby tried to take Aden away to dance with her, Conrad stopped her. He told her that after he and John left, she could have him all to herself, but for now, she would have to wait. That suited Aden fine. The way that he was feeling he had no interest in dancing with her anyway.

After a while a few of their friends, each successful in their own respective areas of business, joined the conversation. An interesting and intellectual discussion, with many humorous anecdotes ensued, lasting right through to the middle of the night. Abby became too tired to wait any longer. She said goodbye and went up to their suite.

It was around 4 o'clock in the morning when Aden finally went up to their suite. Abby was fast asleep. Without waking her he also went to sleep. He had only slept about two hours when vivid dreams of Christina roused him from his sleep.

He was shaken up by seeing Christina appear so very sad. He sat up. He did not know what to make of his dreams. Christina should have been happy, not sad. He could not go back to sleep thinking about it. He got up and got dressed. To clear his mind, he went for a run along the beach, while Abby was still sleeping.

After he got back it was time for breakfast and a full day of activities for everyone. These included swimming, snorkeling, water skiing, and beach volleyball, followed by a magnificent Hawaiian Luau for lunch. Afterwards a shopping spree was planned. By the end of that Sunday afternoon, it was time for all the guests to say goodbye and return to Adelaide, leaving Abby and Aden to begin their honeymoon and their new life together.

That was a big ask for Aden, to start off a new life with someone he was neither interested in, nor attracted to, nor had anything in common with. But he had made this commitment, and now he had to somehow get through it. He tried very hard and was able to conceal the emptiness and sadness that he felt inside.

That night after a quiet dinner, they went up to their suite. It was their first time alone since the wedding. Even though his heart was not in it, he sat beside Abby on the bed, put his arm around her, and began kissing her. As he closed his eyes, thoughts and faint images of Christina appeared. He tried to stop it, but the images only became clearer and stronger.

Feeling frustrated, agitated, and almost short of breath, as if having an anxiety attack, he got up from the bed. This was not how he had imagined his wedding night to be. After all those years of being with so many girls that he hardly knew or cared about, he wanted this special night to be with the one that he loved. He could not bring himself to be with someone he did not love.

He went into the bathroom. To calm himself down he splashed some water on his face, but that did not help. Still feeling frustrated with his life, he threw the towel that he had dried his face with at the mirror, knocking down the water glass that was on the counter, spilling water all over it. He had to get out. He went back into the bedroom and got dressed. As Abby watched with a shocked look on her face, he simply said, "I'm sorry. I can't do this," and walked out.

He went to the beach, the only place that he thought he might find peace and comfort. He sat on one of the lounge chairs there, thinking, trying to make sense of things. But nothing seemed right.

He thought that with him getting married, Christina's marriage should have improved, and she should be happy. *But, why the dream? Why is she appearing so sad?* He also thought that he should have been able to go through with this marriage. After all, Abby is a beautiful woman. *Why then is it that I can't?* he wondered to himself. Emotionally, he was not able to handle being married to someone who lacked the qualities he had come to expect and regard important such as sincerity, selflessness, high-ideals, and a sense of friendship and harmony. It seemed that there was a greater force at work, the power of true love.

However, he had chosen this path, and there was no turning back. He had to try to make it work. After spending the rest of the night on the beach, he went back to the suite. It was now early Monday morning. Feeling compassionate towards Abby, he was nice to her, but not overly warm or friendly. He still could not understand why she had insisted so much on marrying him, knowing that he did not love her.

They spent the morning sightseeing and then returned to the hotel for lunch. While they were having lunch the hotel manager, Jean Pierre, who knew both of their families quite well, came over to personally ensure that everything was to their satisfaction. After a few minutes of small talk, he offered to arrange a romantic dinner for them that evening. Abby quickly welcomed the idea. To appease her, Aden accepted his offer, and in his aloof manner thanked him.

Jean Pierre in his warm, charming style complimented Abby on her beauty and told Aden that he was a lucky man to have her as his wife. Seeing how friendly Jean Pierre was, Abby in her immature way decided to use him to show Aden how desirable she is to other men, to make him want her more.

To encourage him on, Abby responded very warmly toward him. Jean Pierre, captivated by her beauty, seeming to have lost his mind and against his better judgment, continued to act very friendly towards her.

Little did she realize that her behavior actually had the opposite effect on Aden, and only made him less interested in her. Christina by having been the essence of refinement and gracefulness had set the bar high. Being used to such a high standard, Abby's antics were unacceptable to him. But since he was trying to make this marriage work, he overlooked it and tried not to think about it.

By this time which was Tuesday in Adelaide, Aden's father, Abby's family, and the remainder of the party arrived back. Although tired, Conrad was still on a high from the wedding and the trip, and he was anxious to get the agreement between the two corporations signed and sealed. John had not been eager to do that, for up until the wedding he had not been certain that Aden would go through with it. Now with the wedding out of the way, he agreed to meet that evening and finalize things over dinner. This in his mind was the first step to ensuring a bright future for Aden.

Following dinner, they had their corporate lawyers join them, and in their presence they both signed the agreement. Thus, a new era began, with the merger of the two corporations to be completed in several stages over the next three years. The new corporation was to maintain the name "Bradcliffe" and to be headed by Aden upon his return to Australia. Both men felt quite content, especially since the current product development was progressing as planned and on schedule. Now there was nothing to stop them from becoming a major global corporation.

As the evening in Adelaide drew to a close with the two fathers satisfactorily having further solidified the tie between the two families, Aden and Abby's romantic evening with so much hinging on it was beginning to unfold.

Abby and Aden were personally greeted and warmly received by Jean Pierre at the front of the restaurant. He had arranged for one of his staff to present Abby with a beautiful bouquet of fragrant Hawaiian orchids which she just loved. Then they were taken to the best table in the restaurant which had been specially set up and decorated for them with flowers, heart shaped candles, and glitter. A roving violinist played romantic music for them as they were seated. While they were looking at the menu, Roderer Cristal Rose 1996, one of the best and most expensive bottles of champagne, selected by Jean Pierre was brought to their table.

Since Aden did not drink, he asked for it to be taken away. "But honey," said Abby, "can't I have a little taste of it, please?" Once again to appease her, he agreed. He asked the waiter to leave the champagne and to bring him a bottle of mineral water.

Aden had done so much in his life that nothing about the evening could impress him. Abby on the other hand was thrilled and excited by everything. She was especially enjoying her champagne and did not want to stop after her initial 'little' taste. She continued and had a few more glasses of it while they were waiting for their dinner to be served.

Aden suggested that she should stop and not have any more, at least until she had eaten her dinner. But she did not want to wait, "Honey, I want to have fun," she said, "After all it is our honeymoon, and I should be able to drink as much as I want."

He was not happy with her response, but he overlooked it. Starved for intellectual conversation and wanting to take Abby's mind away from drinking, he tried to have a meaningful conversation with her. That did not get very far. He could have had a more intellectual conversation with a lamp post. She had no interest in anything that he was saying. All she wanted to do was to drink and talk about people, what they were wearing and doing.

All of this made him miss Christina even more, her vibrant personality, her proper and ladylike mannerisms, her elegance, her intelligence. He had to keep reminding himself that was all in the past, and regardless of how much he wished that things were different, this was his life now.

After they were finished with their main course, Jean Pierre stopped by to make sure that everything was to their liking. Abby was feeling drunk and happy. She acted very warm and friendly towards him and without any hesitation said that everything was great. To make Aden jealous she insisted that he join them for coffee. When he did, she openly flirted with him. Little did she know, you cannot make Aden Bradcliffe jealous.

His world was closing in on him. Feeling disgusted, he got up from the table and said that he was going outside for some fresh air. He then asked Jean Pierre to escort Abby back to their suite, which he was pleased to do.

In seeking strength and courage to go on, he found himself at the beach again. The sound of the crashing waves took him back to times past, to his house in Adelaide where so many great memories were made. Having gotten so little rest this entire time, feeling relaxed by the gentle sea breeze, he fell asleep on one of the beach chairs.

Abby was too self absorbed and self centered to be bothered that Aden had left. In fact, it was the opposite. She was pleased with herself thinking how successful she was in making him jealous. Without any concern or care she just continued drinking and flirting with Jean Pierre.

After a little while, Jean Pierre, thinking that Abby had had enough to drink, suggested that it was time for him to escort her back to her suite. He did not stop at the door. He went inside to make certain that she was alright. He made her some coffee to help her sober up and stayed with her until she finished it. He then got up to leave, but she asked him to stay a while longer, or at least until Aden got back.

He could not refuse her. He was too enraptured by her beauty and her inviting helplessness. He called his assistant at the front desk, asked him to let him know when he saw Aden coming, and stayed.

Abby got whatever Abby wanted. She already had Aden, and now at that moment she wanted Jean Pierre. That was all that mattered. Without any concern about the moral implication of being married, or whether it was right or not, after being married for only three nights, she began to kiss him. Weak with desire, he gave in to her seductive advances and passionately kissed her back.

Aden, emotionally and physically drained and exhausted, was still asleep on the beach, while this was going on up in his bridal suite. He had been asleep for some time when he started to dream of Christina again. At first it was blurred, but soon it became clear. It was no longer those last teary images of her from the wedding. Now they were vivid images of her sobbing and weeping. The intensity of her sadness awoke him.

He got up from the beach chair. With so many thoughts flooding his mind, he started to walk back and forth along the beach. He knew in his heart that he could no longer dismiss and brush his dreams aside, nor could he stand back and not help Christina. But could he base his thoughts and actions on a dream, he wondered. Seeing that his dreams and insights had not let him down in the past, and had in fact served to guide him in the right direction, he felt confident that he could.

Unaware of what had transpired between Abby and Jean Pierre, he made his decision. He became filled with power and strength, as if the shackles that had weighed him and his spirit down were broken. At last, feeling free, he took out his cell phone and called his father.

Happy to hear from Aden, he excitedly answered the phone, but his excitement soon subsided. Aden felt that the best way was to just come right out and say what he had on his mind. "I have decided," he told his father, "to have my marriage annulled and return to Adelaide."

There was dead silence on the phone. His father's heart sank, thinking about the agreement he had signed, and the severe penalties associated with breach of contract that he had put in to protect the Bradcliffe Corporation from Conrad.

"Why, Aden?" asked John anxiously trying to gather his thoughts. "Is this because of Christina? You should know by now that you can never have her."

"I have tried, but I can't go through with it. Even if I can't have the one I love," he told his father, "I should at least marry someone that I like and with whom I have things in common."

"Like who?"

"Well, like Elexa."

"After not being interested in her all of this time, now you suddenly like her?"

"I have always liked her, but that's not the point." Then very adamantly Aden continued, "The point is that under normal circumstances I would never have married Abby, even if she was the last woman alive."

"But under this set of circumstances, you willingly married her because of Christina. Isn't that what you said?"

"Yes, I did," Aden painfully admitted, "but…that reason no longer exists."

"How do you mean?"

"No time to explain. I will tell you all about it when I see you in Adelaide. I am catching the first flight back."

"No Aden! Don't do that. Don't throw your life away," said John in a desperate attempt to stop Aden from leaving.

"I already have thrown my life away. I am returning to get it back."

"Wait Aden, there is no point in coming back. She won't…," but he did not get to finish saying, "She won't be here."

Aden interrupted him, "I have made up my mind. I'll see you soon." With a sense of urgency, he ended the call, immediately called the airline, and made reservations on the first available flight that was departing in three hours.

The moment of truth had arrived. Now, he had to tell Abby. While he felt compassionate towards her, there was no other way. To end it was the right thing to do, and certainly better for her than being married to someone who did not love her and could not stand to be with her.

With his mind made up, it was time to go and talk with her. As he walked through the lobby, Jean Pierre's assistant saw him. He immediately called Jean Pierre to let him know that Aden was on his way to the suite.

After he got out of the elevator, he reached into his pocket and took out the key to his suite. Inadvertently, Natalie's flower ring that he had put on Timothy's key chain fell out of his pocket and rolled behind a large planter with a tall and wide, leafy tropical plant that was positioned in the hallway. As he bent over to pick them up, the door to the suite opened, and Jean Pierre walked out with jacket and tie on his arm and his shirt still unbuttoned.

While Aden could not be seen from the doorway, especially by someone who was in a hurry to leave, he could see quite well through the leaves, and he saw plenty. Directly behind Jean Pierre was Abby. When he found no one in the hallway, he turned back. With their arms around each other, the two kissed before he quickly dashed off and disappeared into the stairwell. She then went back inside and shut the door.

As he stepped out from behind the planter, Aden looked up and softly said, "Thank you, God." It was the confirmation that he was seeking. Now he knew that he had made the right decision and that those dreams of Christina had been to save him from the biggest mistake of his life. Guilt free, he opened the door and walked into the room.

Anticipating his return, Abby was sitting on the bed, pretending to have been waiting for him. "Hi honey," she said in her alluring way, trying to entice him. "I missed you so much. I was lonely without you." Without any concern that she was not telling him the truth, she continued with her lies, "I've been waiting for you. Now, I'm so happy you're here." She walked up to him and tried to put her arms around him and kiss him.

Aden stopped her, "No use pretending Abby," he said firmly. "I'm going to have the marriage annulled."

She was shocked to hear that, "You can't do this to me!"

"There can be no marriage when there's no love," said Aden as he got his suitcases and started to put the few things that he had unpacked back into them.

"But I love you enough for the both of us. I love you so much that it hurts."

With a distinct look of disbelief Aden looked at her. But he was too much of a gentleman to bring up what he had seen earlier. Without saying anything he continued with his packing.

Abby began to wonder, *Is it possible that he knows?* To cover her tracks she said, "If this is because of Jean Pierre, I want you to know that he doesn't mean anything to me. You are the only one that I love, the only one that I want."

Her words had no effect on Aden, and he continued with his packing. She could not believe this was happening. She always got what she wanted. She became upset, "You can't leave. You're mine!"

Just then Aden finished packing, and as he closed his suitcases, he looked at her and said, "Love is not about possessing someone. It's about giving and sacrificing."

Abby was desperate to get what she wanted, "I can give and sacrifice," she said.

"What does it mean to give and to sacrifice?"

Abby did not quite know what to say. She had never thought about it.

"It's over Abby," said Aden firmly.

She became emotional, but he remained calm. He could have easily torn her apart for lying and cheating, but he was quite civil about it and did not mention it. As he walked towards the door, he told her that he will have a porter pick up his suitcases.

She became furious and spiteful. As he was about to open the door, she yelled out, "Yes, I did kiss Jean Pierre, and I enjoyed every minute of it! And just so you know, I have been with many others." Still trying to be hurtful, thinking that somehow this was going to change his mind, she continued, "No, I hadn't saved myself for you, and I'm glad I didn't."

Her temper tantrum and childish mind games had no effect on him. He simply stopped, turned around, took off his wedding ring, put it on the table and said aloofly, "Here's a gift for your next lover." He opened the door and walked out as she screamed with anger.

Chapter 57

When Aden arrived back in Adelaide Randall was waiting at the airport on explicit instructions from John Bradcliffe. He was discernibly very happy to see Aden and unable to maintain his usual reserved composure. "Good to have you back, Master Aden," he said excitedly.

"You don't know how good it is to be back."

"I brought your Mercedes as you asked." This was the car that brought back those special memories of Christina, sitting by his side, driving to the hills. "However," Randall reluctantly continued, "Your father has instructed me to take you straight to the mansion."

"You've done well Randall. Just take my luggage and tell my father that I'll be there shortly." Then with a hopeful and eager look he said, "I have to take care of something first."

"Might I suggest a shower and shave before you go?"

"No time for that." Aden was too anxious to see Christina that he could not wait or delay seeing her, not even for a minute. He had to go and find out how she was and what was making her sad. He wanted to help her. No matter what it took, he was ready for it, even if it meant confronting Sean.

"Very well, Sir. I will see you at the mansion soon." Then with a big smile, "Please give my best regards to Mrs. Ashton." Randall knew and was happy about it.

Aden quickly got in his car and drove off. Without stopping at his house, he parked in front of Christina's house and went directly to see her. With his heart pounding hard at the thought of seeing her again, and at the same time being apprehensive of what he may find, he knocked on the door.

Seconds passed. There was no answer. He knocked again. This time seeing the silhouette of a person approaching the door, put his worries to rest. Finally, he was about to see Christina. With such joy and enthusiasm, he waited for the door to open.

When the door opened, it was as if an icy cold wind had blown over him, stripping away the warmth of joy and excitement he felt in his heart. He stood perplexed and puzzled at what he saw. It was a strange woman that he had never seen before. He quickly overcame his surprise and courteously asked to see Mrs. Ashton.

She was no stranger. It was Vicky, house sitting. While he did not know who she was, she knew very well who Aden was, and tried to be cunning, "I'm Mrs. Ashton," she replied.

Thinking that she must be a relative, he clarified his request, "I mean Mrs. Sean Ashton."

"Yes, that's me. What can I do for you?" asked Vicky with a sly smile.

Feeling frustrated, he clarified once again, "I would like to see Christina."

"There is no such person here."

Hearing that, he became impatient, pushed past her, walked into the house calling for Christina, Natalie, and Timothy. When there was no answer, he ran upstairs to their rooms, but there was no trace of them. All their toys, pictures, and clothes were gone.

He went back downstairs and demanded to know, "Who are you? Where is Christina? Where are the children?"

"I told you who I am, and I don't know where they are."

He did not have time or patience for this. He wanted so badly to see her and to know where she was that he lost it. This time imperiously and assertively he commanded, "Stop playing games with me. Tell me the truth!"

"But I am telling the truth. I am Mrs. Ashton."

Hearing that, he became so incensed that he did not hear her say, "Or I will be soon. Sean is divorcing Christina and marrying me."

"I'll take this house apart brick by brick to find her unless you tell me where she..." Suddenly it hit him. He backed off wondering, *Could this be true? Did I hear it right?* The anger disappeared from his face. Then, in a calmer tone of voice he asked, "What did you just say?"

"Sean is divorcing Christina to marry me," she replied proudly.

This was something that he had neither considered nor expected, not in a million years. It felt as if suddenly he was given all the treasures of the world. His dreams, Christina's sadness, and so many other things all began to make sense. Filled with unbounded joy, he again asked where Christina was.

"Honestly, I don't know," said Vicky with a hint of sincerity. "All I know is that she has gone back to America and taken the children with her." Then, having rather liked his rough handling of her and secretly desiring him, she came on to him. She moved close to him and said, "Since Christina is not here…Perhaps I can be of some assistance."

Disgusted with her, he just pushed her away, "You and Sean truly deserve each other." She looked at him and wondered if that was an insult or a compliment.

Aden was still stunned and amazed, not only at what had happened, but also at how quickly it had all taken place, "What, you two met over the weekend," he asked curiously, "and decided to get married?"

"No," Vicky laughed. "We've known each other for a couple of years now. In fact, if it weren't for your father, Sean would have ended his marriage a lot sooner."

"What?! What does my father have to do with that?" he asked with a puzzled look.

"It was your father who told Sean to wait until after you got married."

"That doesn't make any sense. My father wouldn't say such a thing," said Aden not buying what Vicky was saying, "Besides, why would Sean go along with it?"

"Because three months ago your father promised him a great promotion which he got on Monday."

"No, I don't believe it. My father would never do such a thing."

"If you don't believe me, ask your father."

Filled with such intense emotions he left to do exactly that, to see his father and ask him himself. But first he called Debbie, his father's personal assistant at home and asked her to get him to California on the quickest possible flight, no matter the cost, even if it meant chartering a plane for him.

He was overwhelmed with mixed feelings of joy and anger as he got into his car. He drove so fast that he did not know how he got to the mansion. He stormed into his father's office and said, "Tell me you didn't stop Sean from getting divorced."

Aden's father made no reply, for he could not say that it was not true.

"I don't believe this. You actually did stop him," said Aden with a horrified look on his face.

"Someone had to watch out for your future."

"For my future?" said Aden angrily. "Because of you I have been to hell and back! How could you do this to me?"

"How could I not? You are my son. I care deeply about you. I had to do something until you come to your senses."

"Come to my senses for what?"

"For realizing that this is not love. It's just wanting something that you can't have."

"I can't believe you're saying this…," but before he could go on, Debbie walked into the middle of their fiery conversation.

She was very excited and proud of herself. With January being one of the busiest months for travel and all the flights getting booked far in advance, she had done the impossible. Through her contacts and her persuasive charm, she had been able to book a flight for Aden.

In a jovial voice she said, "I've done it. I've been able to get you on the first available flight departing in an hour and a half!" With excitement she continued, "Hurry, you must leave for the airport now in order to make the flight."

"There is no need for that," said John very firmly. "Simply cancel everything now!"

"No! You can't do that!" protested Aden, as Debbie stood there in total amazement.

"Yes, I can, and I am," said John very sternly. "It's now time for you to come to your senses. Abby is on her way back to Adelaide. As soon as she gets here the two of you will sit down and talk things over for as long as it takes, until you get this marriage back on track."

Chapter 58

It was a light and airy room, delightfully decorated in a cream color motif with soft touches of pale and antique pink. A large painting of a small creek running through the green hills and meadows of wildflowers, together with two smaller paintings of bouquets of flowers adorned the walls of this moderately spacious room of this California suburban home. A few carefully placed souvenirs and a couple of cuddly stuffed toys of her teenage years and university days added to the cheery and happy atmosphere of the room.

The mood in the room was anything but cheery and happy for these feelings had long left Christina as she sat quietly in the corner of her room, filled with sadness and sorrow. Tears uncontrollably streamed down her face. Helpless to stop herself from crying, she gently wiped the tears away every so often.

A soft knock on her door took her out of the depth of her sorrows. "Christina, may I come in?"

"Yes Mom," she meekly replied.

The door opened and her mother walked in. She appeared calm but concerned. She had a kind and radiant face, beaming with affection. There was a definite family resemblance. She was shorter than Christina at 5'4" and had a smaller build. On the inside she was a pillar of strength because of her intense faith and love of God.

She bent down and tenderly kissed Christina and lovingly said, "My dear sweet Christina, you've been mostly in your room for the past three days. You've hardly eaten or said a word to anyone. I know it's not easy for you, but you're not alone. Your father and I are here to support you in any way that we can." Then with the full affection of her heart she took Christina's hand into her hands and said, "Will you let us help you?"

"There's nothing that you or anybody can do to help me," replied Christina with teary eyes.

Christina's mom was taken aback by her response, but she maintained her positive attitude and gently said, "While we don't condone divorce, unless you can reconcile your differences, you need to accept it and move on."

"I'm not crying because of my divorce," said Christina with a heavy heart.

"Then why are you crying?" asked her mom with a confounded look.

"I'm crying because I miss him too much," replied Christina sadly.

"Well, that's natural. After all, you were married to him for nearly 10 years," said her mother trying to console her.

"It's not Sean that I miss."

After a moment's thought, Christina's Mom got up, walked to the door, closed it, and with a worried look she asked, "Were you having an affair?"

"Of course not, I would never..."

"Then, who is it that you're missing?"

At first Christina looked down, as if trying to work out what to say. Her mother waited patiently. Then welcoming the opportunity to share what was in her heart, she looked at her Mom and said, "Aden, a most amazing and wonderful person, the dream man of every woman." Suddenly, traces of life and energy appeared in her eyes and voice as she began to talk about him. "He's strong and powerful, dignified and eloquent, principled and a true gentleman. And what is most attractive about him is his unparalleled depth of understanding, knowledge, and intelligence." Then after a short pause and with a far away look, she continued, "Yet, what touched my heart was his gentle mannerism, never harsh nor impatient, and always kind and caring."

Christina's mother agreed that he sounded amazing, almost unreal, but she wondered, "Does he know how you feel about him?"

"No. I didn't even know it myself until after Sean and I split up. I began to think about my life and how things had gone wrong, and if I were to do it over again, what I would do differently. Then it came to me," she said finally with a smile on her face, "that I would want to marry someone like Aden. The more I thought about it, the more I realized how much I loved him."

"And now you are sad because...?"

"Because I'm not going to see him ever again!"

"I don't understand. Why not?"

"Because last Saturday he married Abby, a gorgeous teenage billionaire heiress, and he's now on his honeymoon starting his new life," tears welled up in her eyes. "What makes it more painful is that even if he wasn't married, and I was younger and didn't have any children, he still would never have fallen for me."

"You're being too harsh on yourself."

"No, I'm not. Aden and I come from two different worlds. He's from a world of wealth and riches, dating royalty, always surrounded and sought after by beautiful women, and I come from…from nowhere."

"Christina, how can you say that? You're a very charming, intelligent, beautiful woman. Any man would be lucky to have you."

"Is that why Eric left me to make money? And now Sean left me for Vicky?" retorted Christina feeling discouraged and disheartened by her life.

"My dear daughter," she said with such love and affection, "everything in life happens for a reason. We may not be able to see the wisdom behind it, but God only ordains that which is best for us."

"That certainly is true for the Vickys and Abbys of the world, who have no morals or scruples. But what about me? When is it going to be best for me and people like me, who try to be good and do the right things? Do we even matter?"

"Of course, God cares about everyone."

"I've sacrificed myself and my life for my children and my husband. I gave it all that I had, and even when Sean was so mean to me, I still said nothing. I endured it patiently for the good of the family, and all that it got me was sorrow and pain." Feeling angry and frustrated, Christina continued, "Maybe if I had been more like them and didn't care whether what I did was right, I wouldn't have lost everything."

Her mother could not bear to see Christina so heartbroken. She lovingly tried to comfort her based on the beliefs and understanding she had about life. "Difficulties and hardships are very much part of life," she said to Christina. "That's how we grow stronger, become detached, and draw closer to God. That's how God tests and proves the hearts of his loved ones. And you should be pleased as I am with you, that you did what was right and passed your test, while Sean and others did not."

"What good did that do me?"

"I know that it's hard to see the good in something that is painful. That's because only God knows the end in the beginning. But you must try." She then continued in her gentle voice reminding Christina what she already knew and had only forgotten under the stress of the situation, "While we may not see it, God never leaves us, and He continually showers us with gifts of life. Sometimes these are material, but often contrary to our expectations and wishes His rewards are spiritual and more enduring."

"That may be, but the problem is, I can't eat, I can't sleep, and I can't stop thinking about him." After a short pause she shared with her mom how when she was a teenager, she had made a promise to herself that she would not cry. "Now look at me, I've completely broken my promise."

"My dear daughter, there's nothing wrong with crying. It's natural to cry. It helps us to relieve our emotions and get through the sad moments. But it's not good to cry excessively. We have been created to be happy and joyful." Then very compassionately she said, "Christina, you've cried enough. You need to stop and to let the healing begin."

"I can't. I miss Aden too much. For the past three years he's been such an integral part of my life."

"Not only can you, but you must," her mom asserted kindly. "That's all in the past. That part of your life no longer exists. You need to focus and think about your life now, and your beautiful children. They've lost their father. They can't afford to lose their mother, too. They need you, and you need to be strong for them. God has given you the capacity to love. Now you must turn that love towards Natalie and Timothy."

"How can I do that Mom, when every fiber of my body is in pain?"

"By putting your trust in God and submitting to His will. Only then will you become free, content, and happy." Then very firmly, yet lovingly she said, "But as you know, it's not enough to just put your trust in God, you have to also do your part…, as hard as it may be for you, you must forget Aden, and put every thought of him out of your mind and heart and begin a new life with a fresh start."

Christina did not know what to say. Her mother continued with warmth and tenderness and told her that with her father they would take the children out to the park for the afternoon to give her a chance to shower, put on some makeup and nice clothes, "Once you look better, you'll feel better. Then we'll all go out to dinner to celebrate the start of your new life." She got up, hugged Christina, and said, "You are a very strong and capable person. Don't ever forget that, and don't let Sean or anyone else take that away from you." She very lovingly went on, "I have every confidence in you that you can do this."

Christina seeing no other alternative followed her mother's advice. After she got ready, while waiting for her parents and children to return home, she went outside to the backyard to clear her mind and to prepare herself for her new life.

It was her first time out since she had returned to her parent's home. It was a nice, partly sunny, cool winter day. After a couple of days of rain, everything looked and smelled fresh. The ornamental pear trees surrounding the gazebo were in bloom. Their small white flowers stood out against the rolling green hills, where she had spent many happy times as a teenager, full of hope, looking forward to her future life.

But now on this day, she had no happy thoughts. She stood on the gazebo, distraught and disheartened. She wondered how she was going to cope with everything that had happened in her life. How could she forget Aden, who had been such a source of strength and hope for her, even though she had not realized it at the time.

She had no choice. Feeling helpless, with teary eyes, she turned to God. With all her heart, she implored Him to give her strength and to help her through what she had to do.

Chapter 59

The Hand of Providence had at last restrained the gale force winds of destiny. All that was left behind was broken hearts, shattered dreams, and scattered lives. It seemed that finally after three years a period of relative calm was beginning. But who was there that still had enough courage and strength to go forward?

An ominous silence had filled John Bradcliffe's office as his powerful presence and domineering demand pervaded every cubic inch of that room. From behind his desk exuding a presence of unquestioned authority with his piercing eyes he looked at Debbie. In that look, as she meekly stepped back, he conveyed to her in no uncertain terms that he was done with her and that she had better carry out his instructions to cancel the reservations. He then turned his face towards Aden and with a penetrating look said, "You are staying here. That's what's best for you, and that's all there is to it."

All his power, however, paled to insignificance when it came face-to-face with Aden's power of pure love, the most potent force in the universe. He stood in front of his father's desk, and with unyielding strength said, "There is nothing that can stop me from going to Christina."

Aden was not being defiant or disrespectful towards his father, for he had great respect for him. He just had to make him realize that this was not an ordinary love. "This is not an infatuation, a challenge, or merely physical love." He firmly and calmly continued, "It's deeper and stronger than true love. It's spiritual love." Words could not adequately describe Aden's feeling of love for Christina, or what he becomes when he is with her. "Christina touches me within the depths of my soul," he openly expressed, "and when I'm with her I find myself filled with such strength and ecstasy that it's beyond this world."

This was not what John wanted to hear for he knew what was best for Aden's future, and this was taking him away from that golden future. "You're not being rational about this or your future."

Aden's love was radiating outward as he said, "Dad, I was willing to wait ten lifetimes for her. Now a miracle has happened. Now I have a chance to be with the one I love, a chance for true happiness. What could be more important about my future than that?"

"You don't even know if she is going to return your love and want to be with you."

"That's true. I don't know that. But I know that I have to see her and tell her how I feel."

While it was important for them to have this conversation, time was running out for Aden to make his flight. Just then John noticed that Debbi had not left the office. He was not pleased with that, "That will be all!" he said impatiently.

Aden continued, "Dad, all that I'm asking for is your blessing. I can't do this without it."

Feeling frustrated with how things were going against his wishes, John lashed out at Debbie who was still in his office, "You've been told what to do. Go and cancel the reservations…now!"

Aden thought that it was over. So did all the other staff that were full of hope and excitement, standing right behind Debbie in the hallway.

But Debbie did not leave. She cautiously but determinedly took a few steps forward, took a deep breath and said, "No, Sir." That was very bold of her, for no one, especially his staff, would ever dare go against John's wishes.

"What!?" said John furiously.

"No Sir, I will not cancel the reservations." Everyone was shocked to hear that.

"Do you know who you are talking to?"

"Yes Sir, I do. I also know that you can fire me for that, but I will not stand back and allow Aden's life to be ruined."

It took a lot of courage for Debbie to say that. However, she took such an audacious stand because of the love and affection that she had for Aden. He was like a son to her. She had worked for John for more than 20 years, and during that time she had carried out his wishes to the letter. But, this time she could not do it.

She had seen how unhappy Aden was when he married Abby. "I cried at Aden's wedding," she said passionately, "and they were not tears of joy. It broke my heart to see him marry someone that he didn't love, just to please his father."

"That's enough!" said John incensed at her insubordination.

But Debbie was not quite finished. "Please Sir, Aden finally has a chance to be truly happy and he deserves that."

Just then Randall walked in from the hallway, stood by her, and said, "I agree with Debbie. Master Aden deserves this chance to be happy."

Then Jane walked in and said the same thing. Before long, all the staff walked in one-by-one and supported the sentiments already expressed.

Aden was touched by all their loving support. It was something completely unexpected and unanticipated by John. *In my eagerness to secure Aden's future, could I have been so blind not to have seen what they were expressing?* thought John to himself. Without saying a word, he got up from behind his desk and walked over to the large window overlooking his vast estate, wondering what to do.

If he were to allow this marriage to end now, Conrad Frost would not simply revert back to the conniving competitor that he was. He would become a powerful and ruthless enemy, and with the signed contract in his hands, he would set out to destroy him. He would be putting himself at risk of losing the Bradcliffe estate and corporation. He would be jeopardizing the success of his dream project, his lifelong ambition that he had dedicated and devoted so much time and effort to achieve.

Still looking out of the window with so much at stake he found himself faced with one final question, *With my project, estate, and corporation all riding on this marriage, especially now when after three years of tireless effort success of my electronics venture is within my reach, could I afford to have this marriage end?* The answer was simply, *No*.

He turned around, with all eyes full of hope locked on him, walked to Aden. With every step the apprehension of what he was going to say mounted in the room. Then after those brief seconds that seemed like hours, John stopped in front of Aden, looked at him, embraced him, and with a gentle voice said, "You have my blessing."

The tension in the room suddenly changed to joy. Murmurs of laughter and sighs of relief echoed in John's office. Some of the staff hugged each other out of gladness, while others thanked John and told Aden how happy they were for him and offered him their best wishes.

In the final analysis, it was their family's unity and Aden's love and happiness that was far more important than anything else. For that reason, John did not disclose to Aden any of the adverse consequences that this decision entailed, nor did he tell Aden anything about the contract between the two corporations.

Aden was overwhelmed and grateful. "Dad…I don't know how to thank you for your support."

"Just have a happy life," was all John lovingly said to his son.

Aden smiled, "I probably used up all of my wishes, but if I could have one more wish," he said from his heart, "I wish that you could join me in California."

Debbie cut in with a big smile, "You can call me your fairy godmother. Since I'm going to be fired anyway, it won't matter if I tell you that I already took the liberty of booking two additional seats on another flight leaving tomorrow."

John chuckled, "No, I'm not going to fire you, but why two seats?"

She then explained that she thought that it would be good to have Randall there to look after Aden while he was studying at Stanford.

"I would be honored to go," said Randall caringly and without hesitation.

"It seems that it's all settled," said John indicating his agreement to go. He then turned to Aden and asked, "Do you even know where Christina is?"

As Aden searched for an answer, it came to him. He vividly remembered that beautiful and radiant autumn morning when Christina was sitting on the terrace in front of her house writing to her parents. He recalled their address and told his father.

There was no time left. "I don't know if you can make the flight now," Debbie voiced her concern.

"But I have to!"

"No worries Master Aden." said Edmund, "I know a few shortcuts. We should get there on time."

They, fifteen in total, left for the airport with Edmund leading the way. After they arrived at the terminal Aden rushed to the check-in counter with everyone right behind him. The man behind the counter, without the same sense of urgency took his time checking his computer. He then looked at Aden and said, "I'm sorry. The plane left the gate five minutes ago." Everyone was disappointed to hear that.

Aden's heart sank. "I have to get on that plane," he said adamantly. He was not ready to give up. He quickly asked, "Is it still taxiing on the tarmac? If it hasn't taken off yet, maybe I can still make it."

"That wouldn't be possible. Anyway, I believe that it has already taken off," said the attendant. However, in an attempt to be helpful, he called the gate. After a few minutes of rather excited exchange with the person at the gate, he turned to Aden with everyone anxiously huddled around him and said, "You are not going to believe this. It seems that the plane has returned to the gate due to some minor technical difficulty." He immediately arranged for Aden to board the plane.

Before departing, Aden first said goodbye to all the staff amidst tears of joy and sadness. Then turning to his father, he hugged him firmly and told him how much he appreciated his support.

In contrast his arrival in San Francisco was quiet. There was no fan club to greet him. He was met only by the driver of the limousine that Debbie had booked. He was to take Aden to his hotel and then to Christina's parents' house.

This was such an anxious time for Aden. Seconds and minutes were not moving fast enough. It had been nearly a week since he had seen Christina last. He could hardly wait to see her and talk with her. Those nerve-racking moments finally ended when he arrived at the house. It was just as he had pictured it in his mind, based on the way that she had described it.

As he walked up to the front door, he found himself feeling like a nervous teenaged boy asking a girl out for the first time, not knowing what her response would be. But the rush of seeing Christina came to an end when there was no answer. Disappointed, he returned to the limousine and asked to be taken back to his hotel.

From the front yard Aden could not see that Christina was outside only a short distance away. In the backyard she was immersed in a world of her own while waiting for her parents to come home. She did not hear Aden ringing the doorbell and knocking on the door.

The limousine started off. Feeling disheartened, Aden put his head back against the seat and closed his eyes. Suddenly it hit him as he recalled Christina's words about the rolling foothills behind the house. It was as if he had found her. Overcome with a compelling urge to go and see he yelled out, "Stop!" The driver responded to his demand and screeched to a stop.

Aden did not wait for him to pull to the side of the road, but quickly opened the door and got out. He knew in his heart where she was.

The limousine driver just shook his head. As he closed the door that Aden had left open, he said to himself, *All of these rich people are the same…very eccentric!*

Without any hesitation he walked through the gate and to the back of the house. There as he had seen in his dream, against the serene and beautiful background of rolling green hills, beside the gazebo stood Christina, the object of his love and desire. With his heart pounding with boundless joy, he began walking towards her.

Christina, hearing the sound of footsteps, slowly raised her head. With tears in her eyes, her vision was blurry. As he got closer and her tears dried, she began to see more clearly. To her amazement, it was Aden!

She was absolutely astounded. Caught up in the excitement of seeing him, without questioning how it could be possible for him to be there, she hugged him. Then suddenly she stopped and took a step back. It dawned on her that this could not possibly be happening.

"I must be losing my mind," she exclaimed distressfully. "I'm imaging things."

"No, you aren't," said Aden with a chuckle.

"Then I must be dreaming because you can't be here. You're in Hawaii on your honeymoon."

"There can be no honeymoon when there is no love. I couldn't go through with it."

"I don't understand."

"Christina, you once told me that there is no greater force in the universe than the power of love, that we were created to love, and it's love that fulfills the purpose of our lives," Aden paused. "I've come to fulfill my life."

As he took her hands in his, she felt as if her heart had stopped beating. He lovingly gazed into her dazzling eyes and said, "I love you Christina…I've loved you since the first moment that I saw you."

How could this be happening? How could she have Aden's love? *Am I dreaming?* she wondered to herself. It was too beautiful to be true, too glorious to be real. She could hardly breathe, afraid that with a breath or the blink of an eye, it would all disappear. Even if all her wishes and dreams had come true, it would not have been as beautiful as this dream.

"Even if this is only a dream, I'll cherish every moment of it," she said to Aden in a daze, "for I would gladly give up ten lifetimes to spend one moment with you in a dream."

Hearing that, Aden gently put his arms around her. As the power of their pure love began to shine, time began to slow down, and everything around them; the flowers; the trees; and the hills began to fade.

All that could be seen and heard was the symphony and the splendor of their love as he kissed her, a kiss that captured the essence of their pure and spiritual love for each other, a love that had triumphed over wealth and power.

As they stood embracing each other, in a sea of light, it was as if their souls were soaring in the spiritual heights of sheer rapture and ecstasy.

The End

Acknowledgement

Having written *Beyond Fame and Fortune: Finding a Hero* I am faced with the most formidable task of writing the acknowledgement as I find words inadequate to express my gratitude especially to my husband, Laird, whose continued help, support, and encouragement made it possible for me to follow my dream and write this book.

I am truly appreciative of the insightful input and pertinent editorial comments provided by my daughter, Jenifer, and my son, Jason.

I am deeply grateful to my mother, Mahin, and my father, Ataollah Mavaddat for raising me with faith and high ideals and instilling in me respect and yearning for values and virtues.

I am also thankful to my sister, Taraneh Darabi, and brother, Vafa Mavaddat, for always having been there for me, and my sister-in-law, Geri Kennedy, for reading the manuscript and offering her encouraging word.

Next book in the series:

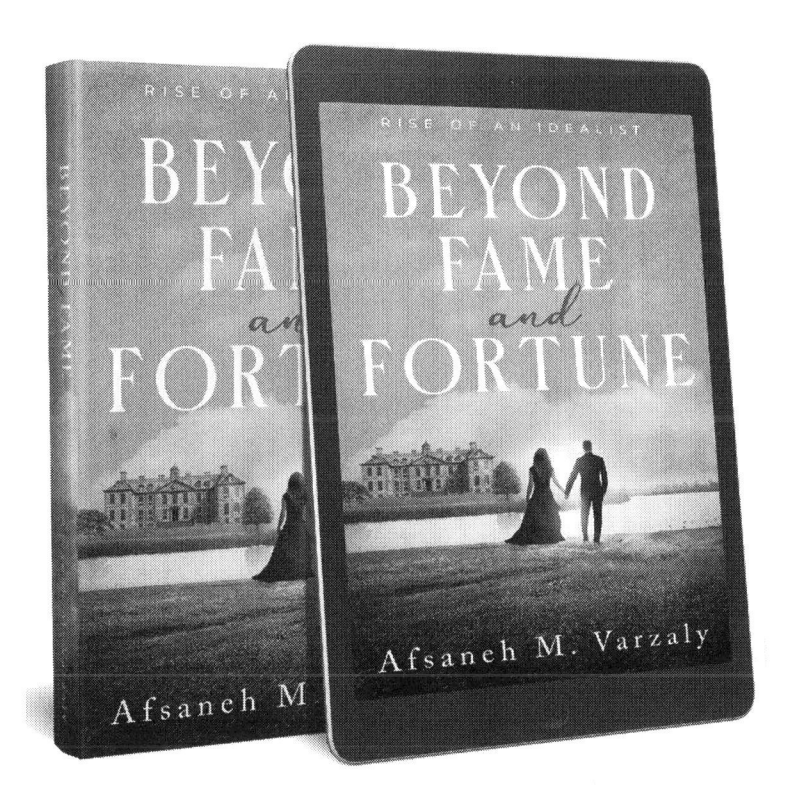

Printed in Great Britain
by Amazon